FIND THE WIND'S EYE

A Novel

Alton Fletcher

ALDEBARAN
PRESS

Aldebaran Press
4196 Merchant Plaza #528
Woodbridge, Virginia 22192

ad Dei gloriam

ISBN-13: 978-1-7361668-0-2 Paperback
ISBN-13: 978-1-7361668-1-9 Kindle ebook

Cover design: Jennifer Quinlan, Historical Fiction Book Covers
Cover art: Revenue Cutter on Patrol, Patrick O'Brien

Library of Congress Control Number: 2021901085
Printed in the United States of America

Dedicated to

Gwendolyn Cheryl Bull
my constant muse

and

In loving memory of
Fletcher Alton Babb

Foreword

A nation divided. Lawlessness and civil strife. Riots in the streets over issues of race and injustice. An unpopular and controversial president, decried by many as incompetent and divisive at best, though praised by others for upholding the rule of law in a time of chaos and conflict. Such were the conditions in the United States of America—not just in recent years, but over a century and-a-half ago.

As shadows lengthened on a sunny afternoon in early June of 1854, fifty thousand Bostonians turned out along the city's waterfront to protest in anger and contempt as a small topsail schooner, a government vessel flying the colors of their own country, departed the harbor. The schooner carried no cargo, except for a single human being, a prisoner whose only crime had been to seek his own freedom.

He was a fugitive slave. His name was Anthony Burns.

The Fugitive Slave Act of 1850 required that Burns must be returned captive to the slavery from which he had escaped not three months earlier. The President of the United States, Franklin Pierce, ordered the Revenue Cutter *Morris* to extradite Burns in accordance with existing federal law, transporting him by government vessel "at all costs" from Boston to Norfolk, Virginia. The people of Boston, outraged at the federal government's infringement on individual freedom, stormed the courthouse and killed a deputy U. S. marshal, trying to prevent the rendition and free Burns. Nevertheless, the *Morris* carried out her assigned mission.

Such an unlikely tale would not be hard to invent, though many might find it hard to believe. However incredible this story might be, it is a true part of American history.

Today, we live in similar circumstances that certainly lend credence to the old adage that history often repeats itself. We find ourselves observing events, perhaps even participating in them ourselves, that seem incredible to us, even as they threaten to tear apart the fabric of our nation, just as they did in 1854.

At such times, the men and women in service to our nation are called upon to keep the public order. They consequently find themselves embroiled in precarious dilemmas, like the one depicted in Alton Fletcher's excellent and timely novel, *Find the Wind's Eye*.

This fictional account of the rendition of Anthony Burns tells the story of a young lieutenant in the Revenue Cutter Service who questions a presidential order to enforce the law. It is an order, though lawful, that he believes to be immoral and unjust.

The questions of conscience, character, and leadership raised in this book pertain every bit as much to the officers and crews in present-day Coast Guard ships and boats as they did 166 years ago in the Revenue Cutter Service.

Military service members, sworn to uphold and defend the Constitution, often are called upon to do things with which they disagree. At times, they may be right to dissent, but at others they might be mistaken, however well-placed their intentions. The question is, what to do about it?

The decision to faithfully execute a lawful, though disagreeable, order is neither easy nor blind—nor does it mitigate a nasty outcome. Sometimes, even doing the right thing turns into an unmitigated disaster. It's easy with the benefit of time, distance, and hindsight to criticize leaders who have made such decisions. Those who would criticize them would do well first to raise their right hands and know what it means to swear before God and country to uphold and defend the laws of the land.

This is a story about a man in service to his country who strives to live by that oath, despite the personal consequences and potential costs. It might be fiction, but it raises important questions and highlights essential truths about what it means to live and act with integrity in an increasingly ambiguous world.

Let me take this opportunity to salute the men and women, throughout our nation's history, whose sworn duty has been to protect and defend our Constitution and way of life—especially those who have served in the Coast Guard and its antecedents. They have ventured forth in the worst conditions, often with limited resources, to willingly put their lives on the line to fight enemies (both foreign and domestic), enforce the laws, and save lives. In all that time, hardly a day has passed when they have not faithfully lived out their core values of Honor, Respect and Devotion to Duty.

James M. Loy, Admiral (Retired)
21st Commandant of the U. S. Coast Guard
Former Deputy Secretary of Homeland Security

*In truth, there is no such thing in man's nature as a settled and full resolve,
either for good or evil, except at the very moment of execution.*

~ Nathaniel Hawthorne

1

—*Boston Federal Courthouse, June 2, 1854.*

Outside the broken window, the crowd's fury rose to a keen howl as unrelenting as a raging storm at sea. The people wanted more blood, no mistake, unless justice should prevail. Nothing else would satisfy. Third Lieutenant Andrew Gunn had never seen the like. Truth be told, he found it hard to blame them, though in part it was his blood they demanded.

A well-aimed brick proved their resolve. It shattered the last unbroken pane in the ground-floor window where Gunn crouched inside the courthouse. He ducked and shielded his face from flying splinters of glass. The brick landed not three feet from him on the floor with a dull thud and broke into scattered pieces. A quick glance through the smashed window verified that, after four hours of slinging rocks, bricks, and epithets at the building, the mob in the courtyard had not tired of threatening to storm the courthouse doors as they had the night before.

In fact, their number in the square had grown by more than half in the last hour, pressing ever closer toward the eastern entrance of the courthouse, which Gunn and his men had barricaded shut against an expected attack. A squad of armed marines outside the entrance presented the first line of defense. Their leveled rifles, bayonets fixed, measured the short gap between them and the menacing mob. Each of the four entrances at either end and on both sides of the long, rectangular building were guarded the same way.

Mid-afternoon shadows cast a partial twilight over the courtyard. Gunn peered over the windowsill at the livid faces in the throng, fearing—among other equally horrid things—that he might spy a neighbor, or even a friend among them.

He shook his head. It was an unlikely prospect for a man with few true friends. Come to think of it, if this current predicament had been, say, a shipwreck at sea, he and all his friends could have abandoned ship in a skiff—with room to spare for a wet cat, no less. Hang it, after today most likely the crazed cat could have the run of the boat.

A shipwreck in some ways might have been preferable to this bind. In the two years since his commissioning in the Revenue Cutter Service, no other situation, however hazardous, had caused him to think so. Even among the shipwrecked there was usually at least some hope of rescue. But there was no ready rescue or escape from his sworn duty as a federal officer.

He again ducked below the sill, as the most reliable man among his band of fifty edged up and knelt beside him.

"Kettle's about to boil over, Mr. Gunn." Boatswain Thomas Nelson took a swig from a canteen, wiped his mouth with the back of his hand, and offered to share. "And where the blazes are the Boston cops, anyhow?"

"I've been wondering the very same thing, Nelson."

"Well, somebody needs to do something. Them people evidently don't take too kindly to sending runaway slaves back to their masters. They ain't likely to just pick up and go home quiet, I reckon."

"You reckon, do you?" Gunn drank deeply from the canteen. The tepid water tasted of their ship's dank scuttlebutt, but it was the only refreshment to pass over his tongue since his morning tea.

Nelson screwed his mouth into a wry smile and shrugged. "Call it a hunch, sir."

"Yes, well, truth be told, I'm not real fond of the idea, myself."

Gunn drank again, too fast. He coughed and passed the canteen back. Part of him, perhaps not the best part, wanted to be out there among the protesters. But there was nothing for it at the moment. His duty was to uphold the law and keep the peace, if at all possible.

"All due respect, I'd wager that's maybe why the cap'n sent you up here this morning, sir. If anybody can keep this powder keg from touching off, you can."

Gunn wished his ship's captain had assigned anyone else the duty to escort the prisoner to their cutter, waiting at anchor in the harbor. Handpicked or not, it was no honor to be chosen—no doubt about it.

"I'd say he's made better calls, all due respect."

Nelson shot him an odd glance. "If you say so, sir. As for me, I surely can think of at least two or three other things I'd be better off doing this afternoon." He pulled at his right ear and winked. "Maybe four, if I ponder it awhile."

Gunn winced from a sharp twinge of pain in his ankle. "We both have our orders, like it or not."

The smile faded from Nelson's lips. "Right, sir. Keep the peace, if any remains to be kept."

"That's right. And get Anthony Burns down to our ship in one piece. That's the main thing." Gunn took another quick peek and ducked under the sill.

"What do ya think, sir?" Nelson jerked his thumb toward the broken window. "Come nightfall, if that mob ever finds the nerve to rush the doors like they did last night, no tellin' what'll happen next, 'cept a lot more folks is likely to get hurt bad, this time."

"We'll be out of here long before then. I expect the militia corps should be here soon."

"I dunno about that, lieutenant. I have my doubts, and they're beginnin' to get the best of me." Nelson smoothed his full black beard, salted with gray. A frown deepened the creases around his sharp eyes and the constant furrow of his sweating brow.

"You worry too much. Let's get back to the rest of the men. Stay down."

Shards of glass crunched underfoot as they crept across the littered floor toward the makeshift barricade to rejoin the other men. Upturned desks and chairs, commandeered from the surrounding offices of the court, jammed the splintered door of the east entrance, hanging ajar on its hinges.

"If you ask me, sir, somebody needs to worry for the both of us," said Nelson, as they reached the safety of the barricade. "I'll wager the march down State Street to the harbor won't be no Independence Day parade. And more'n likely, we'll be the main targets in these here uniforms."

Gunn retrieved his bicorne hat from the floor, where it had lain since he removed it to be less conspicuous at the window while scanning the crowd.

"Like I said, Nelson, you worry too much." Gunn smiled. "But that doesn't mean you're wrong." He replaced his hat and tugged at the starched cravat cinched around his throat.

Nelson was right, as he often was about many things. Their uniforms were conspicuous among this ragged bunch of hired deputies. They both wore the full regalia of the Revenue Cutter Service, often mistaken for naval dress uniforms. His own brass-buttoned cutaway coat, one shoulder replete with a gold epaulette, marked him as an officer. Not only did it make him a likely target, but it set him apart from the fifty or so men assigned to him, many of whom now and then shot wary glances his way.

Hunkered together in a half dozen groups, the men crouched low and away from the windows along the corridor and both sides of the wide staircase leading down to the barricaded entrance. A quick survey of the sullen faces around him revealed flickers of doubt in their eyes as they braced for the expected onslaught. He tried to read them, gauging their intentions, but intimations were hard to come by among this lot.

Gunn was accustomed to leading men more acquainted with shipboard order and discipline. Among the crew of his ship, he had gained a hard-earned reputation for firm, but fair leadership and more than competent seamanship. His years at sea had not prepared him for this task, however. Except for Nelson, these men were not members of his crew. He had no idea how to keep hired guns, deputized by the federal marshal as a show of raw force, both ready and willing.

Most of them were inveterate teamsters and stevedores, wearing the same stained, foul rig in which they worked the harbor docks. Their faces bore the weary glares common to those who wait for others to make up their minds. If they felt any compunction at all about what they had been deputized to do, it was hard to tell. But it was quite evident that their unease about the potential for violence had grown along with the crowd during each passing hour.

As a whole, they somewhat resembled penned livestock, milling about before an approaching thunderstorm. For that matter, so did the stifling air that hung over them, suffused with the rank odor of men who sweated for a living.

One man caught his eye, stood, and approached. He towered over Gunn.

"Lieutenant, is it?"

"That's right. And you are …?"

"Wilkins." The large man rubbed his unshaven face.

"Wilkins, let me offer you a bit of advice."

"And what would that be?"

He nodded toward the broken window. "You're a tall man. Tall men make good targets. If I were you, I'd try to make myself short. The shorter, the better."

Wilkins shifted his weight, then crouched next to him. "It's been four hours since the verdict. How much longer we gonna wait, lieutenant?"

"Until the federal marshal gives us the word to move."

"And, when will that be?"

"When he's good and ready, I expect."

The man stiffened his shoulders. "Me 'nd the boys, we're fed up with waiting." Others gathered around, grumbling, nodding. "Seems like a lot of trouble for one lousy nig—"

"He's a man, same as you."

"Same as you, lieutenant. You sure ain't no better than the rest of us, not even with that fancy uniform."

"True enough, Mr. Wilkins." He thought about reasoning with the man but decided instead to appeal to baser instincts. "He wouldn't like it, you know."

Wilkins wiped his brow on a grimy sleeve. "And who's that?"

"Uncle Sam. He's not that generous, Wilkins. And he can get real cranky. He won't take it kindly if you leave without earning your pay."

The man shifted his weight and snorted. "Ain't been paid, yet."

"And you won't receive a bent cent, if you leave now."

One of the other men crept forward. "We won't get nothing if we're dead, neither."

"Yeah, like what happened last night to Jimmy, the poor mope. And you weren't here to see that, were you, mister?" Wilkins pointed a finger at Gunn's chest. "Jimmy Batchelder was a good friend of mine, ya know. Saw him kilt like a dressed pig, knife to his belly. Ain't gonna happen to us. Right boys?"

"'Sright." The boys nodded.

Gunn brushed away Wilkins' pointed finger. His mouth went dry as hemp. "You've given your word. All of you. You swore under oath to perform the duties of a deputy marshal. You wouldn't like the consequences of refusing to carry them out, one way or the other. Trust me."

"My word's as good as yours or any man's," said Wilkins. "But like the pay, it ain't worth nothin' if I'm dead."

They all ducked as splinters of glass and wood exploded with the latest barrage of bricks and rocks, spraying more debris across the marble floor. One rock bounced against the leg of an upturned chair and ground to rest on the floor at their feet, where Wilkins had stood a moment ago.

"I'm very glad to hear that you're a man of your word, Wilkins." Gunn leaned close to the other man's face. "Because the only thing stopping that mob from busting through this door right now and killing you or another one of your friends is that they believe you'll *keep* it." He drew back and raised his voice a notch. "That goes for every last one of you. Our troubles will only get worse, unless every man Jack holds up his end. Stand fast. It won't be long, now."

It wasn't his best moment. But it had the desired effect.

2

Gunn hoped his own misgivings were not as evident as the disquiet on Wilkins' face. Though the reasons were quite different, the cause of their concern was the same.

After a week-long trial, the judge's verdict earlier that day—all but a forgone conclusion—had ordered a fugitive slave's return to servitude in accordance with the Fugitive Slave Act. The verdict had precipitated this raging tempest, though its fury had been building all week.

Bostonians had seen the same thing happen several times before in the four years since Congress passed the law, forcing Northerners in effect to become slave catchers. Many had determined not to let it happen again, regardless of any consequences, even bloodshed if necessary.

The rising tide of public opinion against what they considered the heavy hand of the federal government finally had breached a long-held protective barrier of civility, lately worn thin. The split now divided families, friends, and neighbors, leaving them stranded as though on opposite sides of a gaping sound, newly formed. No safe harbor was to be found for anyone who found himself in the stormy middle. Not now. Not for the foreseeable future.

Wilkins and the other men sat wary and silent, back in their places at the barricade.

Nelson muttered, "Pleasant bunch. I think you might have won them over, sir."

"Not likely." Gunn slipped his revolver out of its holster and inspected it. His hand shook slightly for a moment, like a sail starting to luff.

"That's the second time in an hour, Mr. Gunn," said Nelson.

"It's nothing."

"I meant, twice now, you've checked your weapon. Don't trust the ship's gunner?" Nelson grinned.

"Much as I trust anybody. Leastwise when he's sober." Gunn managed a smile as he checked the cap-and-ball load in each of the six chambers of the Navy Colt. On his belt hung an ammunition pouch, which contained extra rounds, though time likely would not allow a reload against the onrush of an angry mob. He holstered the revolver, while breathing the desperate wish that he would not need it. Out of habit, he felt for the hilt of the sword at his left side.

"Riders comin'." One of the deputies had ventured to a window. Gunn joined him. Outside near the entrance, a troop of mounted cavalry shouldered their horses through the pressing crowd. One rider dismounted. He held a cocked revolver in one hand and brandished his saber in the other, screaming at the mob to back away. Several drew back to let him pass, railing curses and epithets. The marines guarding the door stood aside, keeping their weapons aimed at the crowd.

"Let him in," Gunn said.

"Make a hole, boys," said Nelson, as he began shoving aside some of the upturned desks and chairs to clear a path to the doorway.

Smeared on the doorpost, a day-old bloody handprint attested to the death of the first casualty and promised more to come. Gunn was resolute not to let that happen.

The cavalry officer shoved open the door and made his way through the gauntlet of furniture. The deputies scraped the door shut as best they could, then hurried to repair the barricade. The officer sheathed his saber, holstered his weapon, and glanced around, landing his gaze on the only two men in uniform. Gunn stood and drew him away from the door, back toward the center of the transverse hallway between the east and west entrances.

"That was a brave thing to do, lieutenant," said Gunn.

The officer regarded him up and down, an eyebrow raised. "You navy?"

Gunn raised himself to his full height. "Third Lieutenant Gunn, Revenue Cutter Service."

"Why the Sam Hill are you here?"

"President Pierce seemed to think it a good idea." Gunn managed a smile.

"You in charge here?"

"Of this entrance, yes, lieutenant."

"*First* Lieutenant Griggs. I have word from General Edmands. The militia is on the way. Marching down Tremont Street from the Common, right now. They're hauling a cannon."

Gunn shook his head in disbelief. "A *cannon*? To guard one man?"

"That's right. It might come in real handy with that mob out there. Where's the marshal?"

"Come with me."

As they departed, Gunn shouted over his shoulder, "Nelson, keep the lid on here, best you can." He led the way across the grand hallway, toward the stairs leading to the basement.

Approaching drums beat a quickstep cadence, and fifes squealed a military march somewhere in the distance, past the north end of the courthouse. A block or so away, the Old Statehouse clock struck twice.

Gunn reached inside his waistcoat pocket and pulled out his watch. Seven minutes slow. He snapped it shut and rubbed the dented silver case between his thumb and forefinger, as he would a prized amulet, which it was, of sorts. Reluctant as he was to admit it, that watch had served him well as a reliable token of order and regularity in his daily life. In his own mind, at least, it kept at bay the chaos that had marked his childhood.

Until now, of course. Today, of all days, the watch-talisman had failed him. For one thing, it had failed to keep proper time. More important, and far more irksome, it had done nothing to ward off the surrounding maelstrom.

By now, an inkling of haplessness, pervasive as the dampness of salt air, had seeped in and settled as a dull ache at the nape of his neck. He probed the pain with his free hand, muttering a curse, while tucking the watch back into his pocket.

As they passed through the transverse hall toward the stairs, the cavalry officer caught Gunn's arm.

"Looks like somebody butchered a hog." Griggs pointed to the floor in front of the stairway that descended into the depths.

A whiff of clabbered gore hung in the warm air, mingled with the faint, but acrid odor of gun smoke. Dozens of blowflies hovered to the hum of death over darkened bloodstains on the floor, daubed with a hasty mop and sprinkled with sand.

"Welcome to our little hell, lieutenant. Watch your step."

He descended the staircase, limping with each step from the pain in his right ankle, a reminder of last night's events. Upon reaching the basement, they passed two marines guarding a jail cell that held Anthony Burns, the fugitive slave. They found Marshal Watson Freeman at the south end of the dimly lit corridor, speaking with his principal deputy, Asa Butman.

"And hurry back, Asa. It won't be long, now, I expect."

Butman turned on his heel and walked past Gunn without a glance. Freeman, on the other hand, greeted him with the mutual respect that had developed through two years of working together on previous occasions.

"You quite all right, Gunn? You seem to be limping. Are you hurt?"

"It's nothing. I'll tell you about it later, marshal." He gestured an open hand toward the cavalry officer. "This is Lieutenant—"

Griggs glowered. "*First* Lieutenant."

"Of course. First Lieutenant Griggs has a message for you from General Edmands."

Freeman waved an impatient palm. "First or last, spill it, Griggs."

"The troops are forming outside the courthouse. Should be ready to march in about ten minutes."

"You can tell the general for me that it's about high time. We've waited long enough for you fellas to finish drilling. That crowd outside means business, and it's growing by the hour."

"Is that all, marshal?"

"Tell him that as soon as he has his column formed in Court Square, we'll join him with the prisoner. Leave room for my men in the middle of the column."

"All right." The officer hesitated. The long ends of his unkempt mustache twitched.

"Well, go on, *first* lieutenant." Freeman shooed him. "Be off with you, my good man. Skedaddle."

Griggs spun about-face, stomped down the corridor and up the stairs.

Freeman shook his head. "Sabbaday soldier. But what're you going to do? We need his help. Guess I shoulda been nicer."

"No joke. We'll need him and a whole battalion of his friends."

"So, tell me, Gunn. What's with the lame hoof?"

"Got caught in that mob last night. The same one that left blood all over the floor upstairs, I expect."

"Wait a minute." Freeman touched a finger to his broad brow. "Were you part of that?"

"No, no. Of course not. They stampeded us as we came out of Faneuil Hall, after the speeches at the Vigilance Committee meeting."

"Who's *us*?"

"I was escorting a young lady. She fell underfoot in the street. I tried to help her up, and some tarnal plug-ugly stepped on my ankle. You should have seen his face. Pure, unadulterated hate. Waving a pistol in the air, mad as a March hare. Must have been a good five hundred more just like him, all headed this way. Nothing anyone could do to stop them."

Freeman nodded. "They killed one of my deputies. Almost killed me. You were at that meeting? Numbskull. What in tarnation for?"

"Like I said. A woman."

The marshal's upper lip ticked and his nose wrinkled as though sampling a foul odor. "Woman? What woman? Who?"

"Her name's Elizabeth Faulkner. She wanted to hear the speeches. I offered to escort her. Never guessed we'd see that kind of trouble."

"Must be quite a woman. What did your captain have to say about it? I would think he'd have warned his crew to stay away from such meetings."

"He did. Doesn't know."

"That so? Better keep it that way." He winked and pointed at Gunn's right leg. "I'm worried about that gimpy pin. Are you up to this?"

"Fit as a topman's fiddle. Slight sprain, is all."

"You sure? You've got an out, if you want to take it."

Gunn hesitated, then shook his head. "Duty calls, sir."

"Good. We're going to need every man we can get."

"I can see that."

"Not quite what you were expecting, is it?" Freeman grinned. "What? You didn't think that you and Nelson were going to just march Burns down to the ship all by yourselves, did you?"

"I wasn't sure what to expect when Captain Whitcomb sent us up here this morning. No matter. We're more than ready, marshal. What's the delay?"

"We're trying to avoid any more trouble. Already lost one man. There's been enough bloodshed."

"I'm worried this mob might boil over if we wait much longer."

"Look, a Boston Police captain resigned this morning. He's protesting the outcome of the case. And about fifty other policemen deserted their posts along the route to the wharf. So, federal troops have been sent to fill the gaps. Besides, we're hoping to wait out the Vigilance Committee. Thought maybe they'd eventually lose their nerve. But we'll move as soon as possible. We've just been waiting for General Edmands to get his troops ready."

"Well, do you think we'll have enough men? That's a big crowd out there."

Freeman nodded. "I think so. Fifty special deputies at each entrance, so that's two hundred. Along with the marines and infantry, we'll have fifteen hundred, all told, I figure."

"Fifteen *hundred?*"

"By order of President Pierce, himself."

A low whistle came from the shadows inside the jail cell. "That's a lot of men, marshal, sure enough. Are you sure you need so many for just one little ol' pris'ner?"

"Shut up, Burns," barked one of the marine guards.

"It's all right. Let him say his piece," said Freeman. "A lot of good it'll do."

"You don't need so many men, marshal. I already give you my word I won't run." A rustle came from inside the cell as the prisoner rose to his feet and stood against the wall, veiled in the shadows. "Done runnin'. Things would jest get worse for me from here on out if I tried. Colonel Suttle hisself said if I don't go back, he'd take it out on my brothers and sisters."

"It's not you I'm worried about, Burns. Other folks ain't quite as sensible as you."

"Not sure how to take that, marshal." Burns pressed his forehead against the bars. "Other folks might say the most sensible thing for a man to do in a situation like this is try to get away."

"I mean you've given me no cause to think that you wouldn't keep your word. So far."

"I'm a truth-teller. Haven't told nary a lie since I was twelve years old. You have my word."

"Let's keep it that way."

Gunn broke in. "Are these fifteen hundred men all armed, marshal?

"Well armed, and authorized to use force, if necessary."

"Why do you need me, then?"

"You've seen my deputies. An unruly bunch. Anything can happen. I'm very glad Captain Whitcomb sent you and Nelson along. I asked for you by name, by the way, in case you're wondering.

"Why is that?"

"I know I can trust you to keep a lid on it." Freeman chuckled. "You should never play poker, Gunn. Don't look so chagrined. Look, you're both sworn federal officers. I expect you to help lead these deputies and get Burns all the way to your ship without a scratch or a stubbed toe. On anybody."

"Easier said than done."

"Now, that ain't no lie," said Burns.

3

Deputy Butman returned, sauntering down the dim corridor toward them. His massive face reminded Gunn of a bulldog that had once gotten the better of him as a boy while he raided a farmer's orchard back home in Concord. Butman had two men with him, the well-known fiery abolitionist, Reverend Theodore Parker, and a black minister whom Gunn didn't know, but had seen in the courtroom during the trial.

"Boss, this man claims he has an urgent message for you," growled Butman, pointing at the black minister.

"What is it?"

"Sir, I have been authorized by a certain group of friends to make a final effort to redeem Tony's freedom," said the breathless minister. "We are prepared to offer a handsome price. Eleven hundred dollars." Pulling out a long handkerchief from the left pocket of his frock coat with one hand, he wiped his tawny face and forehead, removing his spectacles with the other.

"Mr. —"

"Reverend. Reverend Leonard Grimes."

"Well, Reverend Grimes, I'm afraid that ship has sailed," replied the marshal. "Colonel Suttle has refused to sell at any price."

Gunn couldn't believe that he was actually hearing one man barter for another's freedom. Until that minute, the idea of slavery had seemed a remote, archaic evil, having no bearing on his limited world. Now it felt palpable, and it stunned him like a sucker punch to the face.

"But we have the cash, I assure you." Grimes replaced his handkerchief, pulled a wad of bills out of his other pocket, and held it up.

Anthony Burns gripped the bars of his cell. Standing tall and erect, he peered out from the darkness, his eyes dim with faded hope.

"It's no use, Reverend Grimes," Burns said. "We fought the good fight. What's done's done. Colonel Suttle will have his way, no matter what. God bless you for trying. And thank you."

"But eleven hundred dollars," said Grimes.

"You can put away your money, reverend," said Freeman. "The District Attorney said it would not be in Colonel Suttle's best interest to conduct a sale here in town, since it is against the law to buy and sell slaves in Massachusetts."

Grimes' shoulders sank. "This is a sad day for Boston and for our country. What is to be done now, Reverend Parker? The law has won the battle, and we are defeated, I suppose."

"A sad day, indeed," brayed the flush-faced Reverend Parker. Slight in stature, he stood with feet splayed, like a boy trying out his father's shoes. "The law may have won this little skirmish, but the war has just started. As the head of the Boston Vigilance Committee, let me remind you all, there is a higher law in operation to which we all will be called to account." He turned his burning gaze on the marshal. "As for you, Mr. Freeman, let the ruffians, rascals, and scallawags you hired to kidnap this poor man be your advocates when you stand before the final judgment seat."

The marshal frowned down into Parker's face. "Reverend, no thanks to your little speech last night, which caused an attack on this building by an angry mob, I nearly met the good Lord face to face. One of your men with a blade missed me and killed one of my so-called ruffians."

"One less john for the waterfront brothels, I'd say. If one of your thugs was killed, I'm sure he had it—"

Freeman's eyes narrowed. "If I were you, preacher, I would be careful to say no more, unless you don't much value your *own* freedom."

"You would not dare, marshal."

"I'll soon have an empty jail cell, preacher. Thou shalt not tempt me, nor try my wrath. We'd better not have any more trouble like last night, or there will be the devil to pay, reverend. I can promise you that."

"Please, Reverend Parker," said Burns. "I don't want no more trouble or bloodshed on my account."

"There. So be it. Now, I think it is time for you gentlemen to be on your way." Freeman pointed toward Gunn. "This man will see you out."

Grimes interjected with raised palms. "Mr. Freeman, we had hoped to accompany Tony to his embarkation. I am his pastor, after all."

"I'm afraid that will not be possible, preacher." Freeman turned his back to Grimes with a brusque gesture toward the staircase. "Mr. Gunn."

Parker bristled. "Sir, even thieves and murderers have the benefit of counsel and clergy in their hour of need. But Tony has done no crime."

"*Tony* will have plenty of company. I will see to that," said Freeman.

Grimes turned to face Burns. "Goodbye, Tony. You'll be remembered in our prayers every day. God be with you. And I will be in touch. You are not alone. Be of good courage."

Burns nodded.

Moving toward the staircase, Gunn beckoned Parker and Grimes to follow him, leaving no doubt that they should comply.

Grudgingly, they did.

When they reached the ground floor, Gunn started toward the east entrance. Reverend Parker stopped him.

"Sir, our people are at the south entrance. May we go out that way?"

Gunn nodded and turned instead toward the long, high-ceilinged corridor that led to the south entrance. The three men walked wordlessly, their footsteps echoing in the granite hall. When they arrived, the deputies stationed there opened a portal in the barricade for them.

As soon as they exited through the double wrought-iron doors and stepped onto the portico, the din overwhelmed them. The shouting crowd packed the street, shoulder to shoulder, fists and hats raised, between the courthouse and the police station across the way.

A brass field cannon had been drawn up in front of the courthouse steps, aimed toward the displaced crowd. The sergeant drilled his crew in a loud, shrill voice, repeating commands to simulate loading and firing the cannon.

Off to Gunn's left, a small squad of marines kept two people at bay on the steps to the portico. A young woman, dressed in purple, carried a basket dangling from her arm. A straw bonnet shielded her face from view. The man with her was bent over to retrieve his palmetto hat from the steps.

When the woman turned toward him, Gunn was astonished to recognize his younger sister, Marguerite. The man with her stood up. His long, aquiline nose and a full chin-curtain marked his unmistakable features as Henry David Thoreau, his former teacher and their family friend.

Gunn drew in a sharp breath. "Marguerite. What in this world!" He pushed through the cadre of marines and took his sister by the arm.

"Why, Andrew." Marguerite's surprise couldn't have been greater if a genie had summoned Saladin himself out of thin air from the ruins of Askalon.

"What are you *doing* here?" He shouted to be heard over the crowd, trying not to sound angry.

Marguerite pointed an accusatory finger toward the door, her face deepening in color.

"I—we want to help that poor man in there. These men won't let us in." She raised the basket on her arm. "We brought him some food. What are *you* doing here? Why aren't you on your ship?"

"I am on duty, Meg. Special assignment. You must leave, both of you."

"What? How—how can you … are you part of this monstrous act? Would you truly help send a free man back to slavery?" She glared at him, tucking a stray wisp of black hair underneath her bonnet.

Thoreau leaned into him. "I had not pegged you, Andrew, as another fool made conspicuous by a painted coat." His bearded chin wagged toward the marines.

"I am no fool, sir." Gunn set his jaw and turned to address his sister. "Meg—"

"Don't call me that, Andrew." She yanked her elbow out of his grasp.

"Marguerite—"

"Lieutenant," insisted one of the marines, "does this lady belong to you?"

"She's my sister."

"Sister or not, the marshal says she can't come in. If she was my sister, I'd tell her to move back, before there's trouble."

"One moment, corporal."

"Sir, we have orders to use whatever force is necessary—"

"I'm aware of that, corporal," Gunn snapped, over his shoulder. "Marguerite, please go home. It is not safe here. People might get hurt."

"You'd better do as the man says, missy," sneered the marine.

"That's enough, corporal. I'll handle this."

"We'll not be handled, make no mistake." Thoreau's straw hat shook in his hand. "I taught you better than this, Andrew. Show some courage, man. Stand with us. Help the cause of freedom."

"See here, Mr. Thoreau. You take no care of any consequences. That's well enough for you. But, sir, if you would look to the freedom of anyone today, see that my sister leaves here. I'm sorry, Marguerite, but you must go. *Now.*"

"I don't know how you can live with yourself. May God have mercy on you, Andrew," said Marguerite. "On all of us."

"Amen, sister. But these marines certainly will not."

Marguerite and Thoreau descended the steps and receded into the burgeoning crowd. The two ministers were nowhere in sight, now obscured among the two thousand or so people assembled at this end of the courthouse.

Before going back inside, Gunn scanned the crowd, hoping not to find Elizabeth Faulkner or her family among the faces.

There was no telling how this day would end or whose blood might be shed before it was over. Or whether he would be willing to shed any, should it ever come to that.

4

At nearly half-past two, the marshal's men filed out of the courthouse into the square. As planned, the posse of two hundred deputies formed a ragged quadrangle—double ranks on all four sides. Gunn joined the fifty men assigned to him on the right side of the human stockade.

Their lopsided phalanx followed a column of a thousand or so troops, facing north along the square. Major General Benjamin Franklin Edmands led the column on horseback, waiting imperiously at its head with fifty mounted lancers. Another two hundred marines and the horse-drawn cannon brought up the rear.

The din quieted as Freeman, leading the prisoner, emerged from the shadow of the doors into the bright sunlight. Butman followed close, carrying a set of manacles, clanking unchecked at his side. A low groan crescendoed in responsive waves throughout the surrounding crowd.

Anthony Burns was dressed as a grandee in what appeared to be a new suit. Although cheaply made and ill-fitted to his six-foot frame, it was complete with a dark green frock coat, paisley vest, striped trousers, and gaiter boots to match.

No less surprising than his attire, however, was the fact that both hands were free. He shaded his eyes with the left one. He used the right, grotesquely deformed into a claw, to wipe sweat from his brow. Beneath a ragged scar of taut skin, a bony lump protruded an inch from the back of the near-useless hand.

Freeman led his prisoner through the cordon of men and took his place within the formation, at the front. Burns followed him in the center, with Butman trailing both.

Gunn got his first good glimpse of the prisoner up close. On his face, another scar, two inches long, traced the bottom of his right cheekbone. That scar and the mangled hand were the unmistakable flaws that had identified him in court, dooming him to return to the servitude he had fled.

Despite these markings, the man's most prominent feature was an aura of strength that had nothing to do with his physical presence. Rather than the defining stigma of anger, fear, or hatred, as Gunn had expected, something else registered in his face. Peace, but without resignation—maybe best described as forbearance.

"Now, remember what we agreed, Burns," said Freeman. "You gave your word. We'll leave the handcuffs off as you asked. I've done that. But don't you do anything that would force me to put holes in that new suit of clothes the boys bought for you."

"I remember, marshal. Don't you worry. I will never forget what you all done," said Burns, shaking his head. "Never." He licked his dry lips.

"Let's get this over with," Freeman croaked.

General Edmands ordered the troops to shoulder arms. The entire column, except the marshal's posse, obeyed in unison, their weapons rattling and bayonets glinting in the afternoon sunlight. The cavalry drew and shouldered their sabers in one swift, precise movement.

Gunn drew his sword and Freeman ordered the deputies to shoulder their weapons. Most of the men seemed wary, some fitful. Nelson stood opposite him, cutlass in hand, appearing confident as usual.

Edmands gave the order to advance. The drum corps began a

quick, steady beat, which echoed against the buildings around the square, drowning out the growing tumult of the crowd. The column moved forward, stepping to the cadence. The marshal's posse lurched ahead in a haphazard formation, unaccustomed to a regimented march.

The parade executed a right-column movement out of the square into Court Street, then proceeded down State Street past the Old Statehouse. When Gunn made the turn, he started at the sight of Marguerite, standing on the near corner with Thoreau at her side. Thoreau's indignant face blazed scarlet. Nearby stood Bronson Alcott and a small contingent of other prominent citizens of their hometown in Concord, the small, close-knit village of philosophers, writers, and freethinkers where Gunn had grown from boyhood to young man.

A woman pushed through to the front of the crowd and stood next to Marguerite, who took her hand. It was Elizabeth Faulkner, the woman he hoped someday to marry. Marguerite pointed to him. Elizabeth turned her head and looked straight at him, her eyes fiercely burning. As he passed by, she embraced Marguerite, placing her head on his sister's shoulder as her body shook with sobs. Gunn's eyes blurred as he gazed straight ahead, blinking away tears.

He thought of falling out of formation, stopping to join his sister and friends to satisfy his own sense of justice. But doing so would dishonor his commission and violate his oath before God to uphold the law. That thought was too terrible, as terrible as marching on. His feet kept the pace.

Black crepe hung from nearly every window along the street, a suitable raiment for the occasion, given his immediate sense of loss. It was an odd, dissociative sensation, as though he had died and was observing himself participating in his own funeral march. Yet, he wasn't dead, as much as he might have wished to be, and this cortege wasn't about him. Not so much, anyway.

The five-story building that housed the *Commonwealth,* a Freesoil newspaper, was dressed from top to bottom in black cambric. American flags draped from the windows, fluttering in the small breeze that ran through the street. From the roof, a cable stretched from one side of the street to the other, suspending an outsized, makeshift coffin overhead. The coffin was painted black, the word "LIBERTY" emblazoned in white along the side. A doleful church bell tolled in the distance.

The parade path swept before them in a sloping curve along State Street, a third of a mile down to the gleaming dome of the Custom House at the waterfront. Silhouettes filled the shadows of every window and doorway, and onlookers lined the tops of buildings. Thousands thronged the street, cascading in every direction like troubled water spilling through a broken dam. The constant, deafening roar of the crowd mimicked the sound of a rushing river.

A fusillade of bricks, eggs, rotten vegetables, and a cloud of cayenne pepper rained on the cavalcade. The men ducked and dodged in the narrow street to avoid the missiles, though some found their marks. Gunn flinched as a woman's hairbrush hit him on the arm and clattered to the street. He was lucky. One man stumbled and fell, his head gushing blood. Others stopped to help. The crowd surged toward the weakened flank, but the deputies pushed back.

"Steady, boys," called Freeman. "Eyes front. Close ranks. Don't let nobody through."

They marched past the steps and portico to the Merchant's Exchange, which provided an amphitheater of sorts on the right side of the street. Onlookers jostled on the steps for better position to see the spectacle. Overhead, on a rope stretched across the street hung an inverted American flag, its blue field down, a signal of distress.

Burns kept his stoic eyes forward.

A line of militia blocked a side street, standing in front of a wagon parked across the entrance. Lounging nearby, a squad of soldiers passed a bottle, laughing. Several appeared to be drunk. In unison, they warbled the chorus of "Carry Me Back to Ol' Virginny."

A band of hooded men brandishing revolvers rushed from beyond the wagon. They pushed past the drunken militia and headed straight for Burns. Gunfire split the air, followed by panicked screams from the crowd. A bullet ricocheted from a lamppost and whizzed past Gunn's head. The double wall of deputies held fast and fought the marauders back, pistol-whipping, disarming, and unhooding the lot as they tackled them to the street.

Butman forced his way forward, drew his revolver and cocked it, aiming to fire at one of the fallen men closest to him.

"Hold your fire, men," Freeman ordered.

Gunn lunged and grabbed Butman by the arm with his free hand. The revolver fired into the air. Butman spun around, thrusting his elbow back. He struck Gunn a glancing blow across the bridge of his nose. Gunn saw stars. He stepped back, stunned, and stumbled to one knee.

"Butman!" shouted Freeman.

A revolver cocked next to Gunn's left ear. In an instant, he pivoted toward the sound and raised his sword to defend himself, only to find Butman, wild-eyed, holding the muzzle to his forehead.

With a flash of steel, Nelson's cutlass pressed against the big man's throat. Butman froze, awareness tightening his bulldog face. His thumb un-cocked the revolver. He brushed the cutlass aside with his forearm, staring down at Gunn and breathing heavily.

"Apologies, lieutenant," he muttered.

"Never mind, Butman. Forget it." Gunn drew a handkerchief from the pocket inside his cutaway and wiped the blood that trickled down his cheek from a small cut on his nose.

Nelson helped him to his feet, then picked up his fallen hat and handed it to him.

"I know. I worry too much," said Nelson. "But Captain Whitcomb made me promise not to let anything happen to you, sir. Just followin' orders."

Gunn nodded his thanks.

Five deputies fell out of formation to escort the beaten men to three policemen who had rushed over to assist. Others closed the remaining gap in the line.

"Get back to your post, Asa," said Freeman. "All's well, Mr. Gunn?"

"Yes, sir, all's well."

"March on, men."

Gunn daubed the bleeding cut. His nose felt bruised but not broken. He pressed the cocked hat back on his head and resumed his place. Nelson and Butman fell back into formation. The procession began moving again.

A young black woman, maybe eighteen or twenty years old, stood bareheaded on the edge of the sidewalk. She stepped into the street, causing the men to step around her. Grief disfigured her finely sculpted features. She wept, her brow knitted, eyes fixed on Burns, face streaming with tears. Her clenched fists beat against her breast and she cried out, "*Why* you ain't man enough to *kill* yourself, 'stead of being a slave?" Sobbing, she sank to her knees.

Burns turned toward the woman, the first time during the march he had looked anywhere but straight ahead. His shoulders sagged with an invisible burden. Tears streamed down both cheeks. He lifted his face to the clear, blue afternoon sky, then shut his eyes. He stumbled toward Gunn, who stopped his fall.

"Steady, Burns." His mouth was dry, and the words caught in his throat. He had developed a terrible thirst.

Burns grabbed his arm. "Maybe I would be better off dead. Do you think so, sir?" he whispered hoarsely.

Gunn shook his head. He swallowed. Words wouldn't come. "I— I can't answer that."

"Walk on, Tony," said Freeman. "Remember your promise."

"Lord, almighty, give me strength." Burns steadied himself, drew his tall frame upright, and walked on.

They continued the few remaining blocks to the corner of Commercial Street, near the Custom House. There, ranks of infantry and marines lined both sides of the road to the wharf. They kept the crowd at bay, while the remainder of the column passed by.

The bystanders quieted, except the few who wept openly. The drums stopped their cadence, replaced by the steady tread of boots on cobblestone, the rattle of weapons, the trundle of the cannon, and the rhythmic clops of the team of horses.

Gunn consulted his watch. Thirteen minutes had passed from the time the procession left the courthouse. It seemed like an hour, as though time itself ran slow, rather than his watch.

Still cautious, Freeman ordered his posse to keep their formation intact down to the foot of the pier, as they left the column. The marines fell out and formed a rear guard.

The horse-drawn cannon rumbled on. One horse snorted as it labored the last hundred yards. The sergeant in charge stopped the caisson, ordered his men to unhitch the team and prepare to load the cannon onto the bow of the waiting steam tugboat, *John Taylor.*

The paddlewheel steamer sat waiting, port side to the wharf, bow pointed toward the open harbor. Its single stack billowed black smoke. Scores of other ships and several fishing schooners occupied the surrounding wharves. In the distance, the tall masts and broad spars of clipper ships formed great crosses against the sky.

Sailors lined the yardarms of every nearby vessel, like flocks of silent starlings in winter trees. From their perches they watched Burns take his last steps on free soil.

Freeman grabbed Burns by the arm and parted the wall of deputies as he led the way toward the short bridge that crossed to the steamboat pier. He motioned Butman and Gunn to follow. Nelson fell in with them.

"This is where I leave you, Gunn. I'm sending four deputies along. They'll answer to Butman," said Freeman.

"Very well, sir."

Freeman turned to Burns. "Can you swim, Tony?"

"Nossir, I cain't."

"In that case, we'll leave your hands free." Freeman stopped at the bridge. "Now, don't give my deputies any trouble, and everything will be fine. You hear?"

Burns nodded. Butman took him by the arm and started across the bridge.

Freeman offered his hand to Gunn. "Farewell, lieutenant," he said. "My respects to your captain." He leaned closer as they shook hands and spoke into Gunn's ear. "I don't have to tell you to watch your upper story with Butman, do I? Man's got a mean temper. And keep a close eye on that snake, Colonel Suttle, too. He'll spit in your eye with a smile."

5

The first mate met them at the gangway. "Come right aboard, lieutenant. We've been waiting fer ya. Boiler's hot and she's ready to trot."

Gunn walked up the brow of the *John Taylor*. "May I see the captain?"

"Right up that ladder." The mate pointed with his thumb to the upper decks. "You'll find him in the pilothouse, I expect."

He climbed the ladder to the first deck. Not a sail to be found on this vessel. What she lacked in grace, she made up in raw power. Black smoke rolled from the single smokestack, which towered twenty feet above the second deck, abaft the enclosed pilothouse.

Gunn walked forward and bowed his head to allow the peak of his cocked hat to pass unfettered through the open pilothouse door. He never had that problem on the open deck of a schooner. The pilothouse was hot and cramped. Except for the ship's wheel, located abaft the binnacle, it appeared nothing like the open cockpit of his own ship.

The captain stood next to the wheel, eyeing Gunn with one eyebrow raised. "Lordy, lordy. What have we here? Which way is the war? Don't get blood on my deck, if you please. What can I do for you, admiral?"

Gunn withdrew his handkerchief and daubed his nose again. The handkerchief came away with a dark smear of clotted blood. He folded it and tucked it away. "Third Lieutenant Andrew Gunn." He bowed his head, slightly. "At your service, sir."

"Well, well. Cap'n Martin S. Dobbins, and pleased to meet you, I'm sure." He spoke with a nasal tone, as though his nose were pinched nearly shut. "I'm a busy man, admiral. State your business, if you please." Dobbins canted his head to one side and jutted out his chin, his eyes squinted, always peering into a bright horizon.

"Sir, I have orders from Captain Whitcomb of the Revenue Cutter *Morris* to see to the safe transport of a federal prisoner to our ship. She is now anchored in the harbor near the Castle. I believe you—"

Without aiming, Dobbins spat tobacco juice into a spittoon next to the binnacle. He wiped his sleeve across his chin, covered with a tobacco-stained wispy white beard.

"Stunner," he exclaimed. "You have orders, do ya now? Well, I don't take orders, I give 'em, see? You, sir, have kept me waiting long enough, and I will not hesitate to say it. I expected you hours ago." Dobbins spat again, hitting the spittoon with a dull ring. "Stunner," he blurted. "I've burned coal enough to fill a barge, tryin' to keep up a head of steam, see, not to mention my crew standin' idle and burning daylight. I expect full payment for it, too, I can assure you. You'd best get your man aboard and be quick about it."

Gunn followed as Dobbins shuttled his short, squat body through the hatch. They passed into the open air and leaned over the rail. Burns was boarding the steamboat, dragging his feet, upheld by the four deputies, trailed by Butman and Nelson. One deputy, sidearm drawn, remained outside as they ushered him inside the nearby door on the main deck and shut it.

Closing one eye, Dobbins gathered himself, then let loose a jet of tobacco juice, which sailed in a long arc to the water below, landing with a soft smack and a tiny splash.

"Stunner." He called to the mate below. "Jasper, soon as you get that blasted cannon aboard, we'll be off."

Jasper acknowledged. With a quick nod of his white head, Dobbins scurried back inside the pilothouse, like a hermit crab seeking shelter. For the next twenty minutes, he scuttled back and forth between the pilothouse and the rail to check on progress.

The crew hoisted the cannon with the forward boom onto the bow and secured it with tackle and chains. It pointed aimlessly over the water, affording the stubby tugboat an absurdly warlike aspect, like a fat, toothless old man who had been called to arms as a last line of defense.

Gunn watched, smiling at a bit of dark humor in an otherwise mirthless day. These artillery men were not trained to fire a field cannon from the deck of a moving vessel—a grind even for a veteran ship's crew, as Gunn knew from his own experience as the cutter's gunnery officer. They likely would have had difficulty attempting a broadside at point-blank range, though the bellicose appearance might serve as a warning to other vessels to keep their distance, at that. In simple truth, however, the soldiers were returning the gun to their island home at Fort Independence.

The second after the cannon was secured, Dobbins gave the order to cast off. The engine groaned into life, black smoke and embers spewing from the stack. The deck throbbed beneath Gunn's feet.

Dobbins quietly gave commands to the helmsman at the wheel. He sang out the time to no one in particular.

"Twenty-two minutes past three o'clock. Blast it all. A full day gone to waste."

Gunn consulted his watch. Eight minutes slow. He clenched his jaw and squeezed the watch in his palm before tucking it away.

A light offshore breeze had sprung up. The deck crew took in the mooring lines, and the large paddlewheels turned slowly at first, then gaining speed. The water rushed through the paddles as the boat gathered momentum and lumbered away from the wharf, creating a wake as she went.

The whistle sounded one long blast to signal the vessel's departure, and the tug steamed into the harbor, shouldering other boats aside like a bumptious dignitary through a crowd. The mournful whistle nearly drowned out the full-throated roar of the assembled sailors, who waved farewell with their hats. As the boat steamed by, the chorus died away, overcome by the rush of churned water.

The trip to Castle Island was a short two miles, past the piers and shipyards of East Boston out toward the flats and headlands of South Boston—about twelve minutes by steamboat, once up to speed. The tug virtually made her own wind, which soothed Gunn as it washed over him at the rail in front of the pilothouse. His shoulders relaxed for the first time today, but pain nagged his neck, adding to his sore nose and still throbbing ankle. He couldn't wait for this day to end.

He breathed deeply of the fresh air, which carried the scent of open water. It brought a welcome refreshment, but he could not relax entirely. He noticed for the first time the fresh blood on the cuff of his shirt, and more on the lapel of his uniform coat, a ready reminder—as though he needed one—that this was no afternoon pleasure cruise among the harbor islands.

Dead ahead, the familiar silhouette of the *Morris* was easy to spot as she lay at anchor in front of Castle Island. The wooden cutter stood in stark contrast to the granite seawall surrounding the pentagonal fortress known as Fort Independence. Her sails were laid in their gear, ready to be loosed. She'd swung her head around toward land, facing into the freshening breeze, and pulling impatiently at her anchor cable.

In contrast to the pug-nosed, smoke-belching steamboat, the *Morris* evoked admiration of a distinctive sort, redolent of a passing age. Designed and built just six years ago as a gaff-rigged, foretopsail schooner, commonly called a "Baltimore Clipper," she sported sleek, graceful lines. Her two masts raked aft, like tall trees leaning in a full gale. Even without sails set, she appeared yar and ready to run.

Down the length of her black hull ran a broad white stripe, which covered the gun ports, five on each side. Despite having ten ports, she carried only six naval guns, six-pounders, three per side. The bow and stern bore swiveled chase guns.

Though lightly armed compared to her naval sisters, she could put up a fierce fight. Her design was well-suited to her purpose to intercept and stop smugglers, privateers, pirates, slave traders, or anyone else whose intent was to break the customs laws of a nation not yet seven decades old and still struggling to secure its place in the world. The awareness of serving in such a fine ship had always stirred pride in Gunn—until now.

Today she would begin an assignment unprecedented in the sixty-four-year history of the Revenue Cutter Service, called upon to restore one man's reclaimed private property—not a salvaged ship, nor a stolen cargo of gold, jewels, or exotic spices. Rather, the cargo consisted entirely of one human being who had slipped the bonds of slavery to seek his own freedom.

Gunn again kneaded the back of his neck, breaking from his thoughts, and turned to repair below to let Nelson and the others know of their imminent arrival at the cutter. He wanted to make sure they were ready to move.

Out of the corner of his eye, he noticed that a small lug off the starboard bow had changed direction, now headed on a collision course with the bow of the steamboat. All three men in the stubby sailboat were armed with rifles.

"Captain!"

Dobbins hurried outside the wheelhouse, and Gunn pointed to the danger.

"Jasper, stop the engine. Five short blasts on the whistle."

The first mate did as he was told. The tug's whistle split the air. The engine died to a grumble. Black smoke belched from the stack and the paddlewheels slowed to a stop.

"Back her down, Jasper."

Soon, the paddlewheels started turning in reverse. The tug slowed to a crawl.

In less than a minute, the lug passed directly in front of them. The three sailors had laid their weapons in the bottom of the boat. The tillerman stayed put while the other two lifted a bucket. They leaned over the side, nearly tipping the sailboat, getting as close as possible to the bow of the tug. Passing underneath, they heaved the bucket and its contents toward the target. Red paint splattered against the hull. The bucket bounced away into the water and landed upright, spinning and bobbing in the backwash of the tug. The boatmen raised their paint-bloodied fists.

"Live free or rye!" They all guffawed. Two of the men dropped their trousers, aiming their bared buttocks toward the steamboat. The man at the tiller steered them away, jeering and thumbing his nose. The other two toppled into the bottom of the boat, laughing.

"Drunken idjits." Dobbins nodded with satisfaction and shouted over his shoulder. "Let's go, Jasper."

Presently, the paddlewheels stopped, then began turning forward again, and they proceeded on their way.

"I'd guess this trip is a bit unusual for you, Captain Dobbins."

"You'd guess wrong, admiral. Seen it all. I'll haul anything or anybody anywhere, long as the money's good. Don't make no difference to me, see."

"As long as it's legal, you mean."

"You sayin' this trip is legal? Is that so?" Dobbins shrugged. "Like I said, see, long as the money's good."

Before long, the steamer had turned broadside to the *Morris,* standing off about fifty yards, facing into the mounting breeze. A longboat from the cutter closed the distance and came alongside. The deputies took Burns out on deck and waited until the boat secured its painter to the tug's port side.

Butman and his four deputies climbed unsteadily down into the longboat, each clinging anxiously to the rope ladder as it swayed alongside. One by one, they timed a toehold in the boat, as it lurched from underfoot. Then they helped Burns ease into the boat.

"Hold on with both hands, Burns," said Nelson.

"Only got one good one," said Burns, holding up his claw.

Nelson followed, making the leap look as easy as clambering out of a tall bed. Gunn was the last into the boat. He tried to imitate Nelson, but his foot slipped, and he sat hard on the thwart.

A few minutes later, the coxswain steered expertly alongside the *Morris*. A rope ladder dangled down the starboard side at the gangway. The men climbed aboard the cutter, led by Gunn. Burns was lifted aboard without incident, and the others followed.

"Get that longboat stowed," shouted the captain from the quarterdeck. "Prepare to weigh anchor."

First Lieutenant John Prouty, the ship's second in command, welcomed the deputies aboard, but said nothing to Burns. He introduced Gunn to Colonel Charles Suttle and his agent, William Brent. A tall man, his narrow face accentuated by a russet van Dyke beard, Suttle tapped his cane twice on the deck and tipped his panama hat in greeting. Brent touched his top hat and caught Gunn's eye with a sly, unsettling glance, as though he knew him, or something about him.

Gunn saluted Lieutenant Prouty, who returned the salute.

"Mission completed, sir."

"A bit worse for wear, I see, Mr. Gunn." Prouty eyed the bruised cut on his nose, and the bloodstains on his uniform.

"Just a bit, sir."

"Very well, then. Get below and change your uniform. And be lively about it. You have the next watch, Mr. Gunn. No rest for the wicked, mind you."

6

The *Morris* rarely needed a tug to sail in or out of port, except for the most unusual circumstances. Today was one of those. Once the *Morris* weighed anchor, the *John Taylor* took the cutter in tow, not because she was unable to sail under her own power, but to allow a livelier departure, hauling her infamous cargo as quickly as possible away from potential trouble.

So, when Gunn assumed the watch, the two vessels in tandem were already heading east-by-southeast, leaving Castle Island and the city of Boston astern. With the faster tug's assistance, and without dependence on the light wind, the *Morris* pulled handily away from most, if not all, pursuers. As an added measure, the captain had ordered all guns to be placed in battery.

Captain John Whitcomb went below as soon as Gunn began his watch. It was always gratifying whenever the captain exercised such confidence in him as to retire to his cabin, even for a short while, which he was not prone to do with the other officers.

The off-going watch officer lingered on the quarterdeck. Second Lieutenant William Richmond spoke in the condescending tone he had consistently used with his subordinates since reporting aboard two months earlier.

"I expect that'll be quite a shiner there, Mr. Gunn," he said in his

Tennessee drawl. "Whatever happened, may I ask?"

"Let's just call it a misunderstanding, Mr. Richmond. I'll leave it at that."

Richmond clucked his tongue. "Looks to me like the outcome was fairly definitive, no mistake." His sneer caused his mustache to appear more lopsided than usual. "And not in your favor. That's what happens when a boy is sent to do a man's job. I warned Mr. Prouty not to send you. I see I was *right*."

"As you say, sir, *rat* you are." Gunn smiled, mimicking the southerner's drawl.

"I see nothing humorous about the matter. Neither should you, if you're still so anxious for that promotion. Watch yourself, Mr. Gunn, as I certainly will be." He turned on his heel, walked forward to the wardroom companionway, and disappeared below.

Gunn had started his watch right before eight bells. It was the first dogwatch, which meant two things. First, it lasted only two hours, rather than the usual four. Second, soon afterward he could finally sit down to a meal, ending a long day of subsisting on nothing but two hard-boiled eggs, biscuits and tea.

As she approached Spectacle Island, the cutter turned eastward through Middle Harbor and President Roads. Flocks of full-rigged merchant ships, some British, some French, and some American, lay at anchor in the shelter of Deer Island awaiting their turns to enter port.

Most of the boats that had chased the *Morris* from the Inner Harbor gave up pursuit and turned back. The Hingham ferry, a paddlewheel steamer, kept pace astern on the same track.

They passed Long Island Light on the starboard side, entering Broad Sound, when the breeze began to freshen. Captain Whitcomb returned from the cabin. Gunn stood aside, allowing him to mount the steps to the quarterdeck on the windward side, nodding as he wordlessly passed by.

After making the turn, the tug slowed to enter the Narrows, an aptly named sliver of water that passed between the islands that were as familiar as home for Gunn. As boys, he and his younger brother, Thomas, had learned to sail in a small dory among these islands. Over many summers, they had learned to navigate, read the currents, and spot dangerous waters, as well as understand the vagaries of wind and weather. Vivid memories flashed through his mind, as they often did when Gunn sailed these waters, but he focused his attention ahead.

As they cleared the southern tip of Lovell's Island the ferry that had been following veered off to the right, past George's Island, heading to a first stop in Hull, and then on to Hingham, as though nothing out of the ordinary had occurred that day.

The sight of that ferry always made him nostalgic. He had taken it many times over the years with his mother, brother, and sister to reach his uncle's grand house in Hull, built on a hill overlooking the water. There, they often spent a good portion of the summers, at the invitation of his mother's sister.

William Mitchell, who owned the house, was a former sea captain, married to Gunn's Aunt May. Mitchell also owned a shipping company, Glastonbury Enterprises. The Mitchells had no children, so they'd been very generous to the three Gunn children and their mother over the years. Mitchell had amassed quite a fortune, which allowed him to build the large house with a view of the approaches to the harbor, where he could watch his ships come and go from its broad porch. Aunt May, who loved to name things, had dubbed it "Stormcrest."

The prominent white house with the green roof, now visible less than a half-mile away on the hillside above the town of Hull, had been the only place of real solace during many years of turmoil and dismay in his family after the contentious, scandalous divorce of his mother and father. At present, the house was dark and offered no comfort.

His aunt and uncle were staying in Boston, at their brownstone townhouse on Tremont Street. Gunn presumed Marguerite must be staying with them while she was in town, away from their home in Concord. Perhaps she had left the townhouse unnoticed that morning, because he doubted that Aunt May, protective as she was, would ever have permitted her to venture out alone during the tumult over Burns.

But today, it seemed nothing was as it should have been.

7

Fine on the starboard bow, the lightship at Minot's Ledge lay ahead at anchor. With a hull painted bright red, she stood out even at a distance of several miles. Her sole duty was to warn other ships to steer clear of an obscured shelf of rock jutting out from the land. Countless ships had foundered on those rocks in the fog or during storms, despite the lightship's vigil.

Beyond the lightship, about five or six miles to the southeast, a steamboat headed toward the *Morris*, probably the inbound ferry from New Bedford. A full-rigged clipper ship approached from the east, about six or eight miles out. Nothing else in sight.

Gunn sighed in relief at their safe departure. Maybe now things would get back to good order. The captain stood on the quarterdeck, smoking his pipe, seeming to take his leisure. His calm demeanor afforded the distinct impression that everything was as it should be, and nothing could possibly go wrong. Gunn knew better. As always, Whitcomb's watchful eyes, always alert to hazards of any kind and ever mindful of the unexpected, took in every detail of their situation.

Yarrow, the helmsman, stood at the wheel nearby. He broke the silence. "Do you know where we're headed, Mr. Gunn?"

"Norfolk."

"I wonder what Norfolk is like. Have you ever been down south,

Mr. Gunn?"

He nodded. "Sure. The furthest south I've ever been is Savannah. But that was a few years back before I entered the service. I used to sail as a deckhand on one of my uncle's packet ships. I've been to Norfolk several times."

"*You* sailed as a deckhand, Mr. Gunn?" His wide eyes evinced a new-found respect.

"I did. I sailed up and down the coast for two years. Hardest work I've ever done. Got the scars to prove it." He showed a scar on the back of his hand from a sailmaker's awl that had passed through his palm. Yarrow's whistle proclaimed his admiration, entirely undeserved, since the scar resulted from Gunn's own carelessness while mending a sail.

Yarrow reflected a moment. "I haven't ever left New England. How long do you figure this trip will be, Mr. Gunn?"

"About eight or nine days for this leg, I should think. The captain says he expects to be in Norfolk by the tenth or eleventh. Who knows after that?"

A young seaman of about seventeen, Yarrow could hand, reef, and steer as well as most, but carrying a conversation was not his forte. That made two of them. They both grew quiet. At length, Yarrow spoke again.

"Sir, I've heard tell that Yankees are not welcome in the south."

"Well, now, we have Lieutenant Richmond on board. He hails from Tennessee. We'll send him ashore first with a flag of truce. Not to worry."

"That's gold, sir?

"I'm not saying it will work, mind you." Gunn winked. "What else have you heard?"

Yarrow hesitated. "Well, sir … it's just that some of the boys are saying that Li'l Bill is likely to be taken and sold into slavery, once we touch land in the south. Cookie, too."

"Who says so?"

"I'd rather not say, sir."

Captain Whitcomb slowly paced the deck within earshot.

"I am quite certain the captain would never let anything of the sort happen, especially not to his own steward. And certainly not the ship's cook." Gunn smiled.

The captain stopped pacing and took the pipe from his mouth. "I'd sooner let them sell Mr. Gunn, here. But I doubt he'd bring much profit, seeing as how he can read and write." He grinned and resumed pacing. "Mind your helm, now."

Yarrow matched his grin. He tugged on his tarpaulin hat and focused his attention on the compass in the binnacle.

Yarrow was a likable fellow. There was something about the artless, affable seaman that reminded Gunn of his brother, Thomas. A bit too gullible, perhaps, but like his younger brother, few men had a heart more tender or true. Uncle William had once observed that Thomas would have made a fine ship's captain someday, if the crew didn't first steal him blind and sell the ship out from under him, due to his overabundant faith in human nature. Thomas had not lived to hear that quip, which eventually served in part as his eulogy.

Thomas and he had decided to go to sea at about the same time. Rather than pursuing a college degree as his mother insisted, Gunn sought to follow in his uncle's footsteps and asked to serve on one of his ships. Thomas begged to go with him until their mother relented. They served together for two years as deckhands on a coastal packet under the watchful eye and tutelage of one of Mitchell's most trusted captains, at the end of which time Uncle William had offered them positions as third mates. Both of them found the monotony of coastal trade rather boring, however, not to mention witnessing some unsavory practices with respect to forged manifests, which Gunn reported to his uncle. Mitchell put a stop to it and admonished the captain.

Gunn at first accepted the promotion and transfer to another ship, but soon began seeking a commission in the Revenue Cutter Service, with the willing aid and encouragement of his well-connected uncle as well as others. Thomas, eighteen months his junior, chose instead to sign on to a China clipper. He craved the adventure to foreign lands, far from the quiet desperation of home. In less than a year, however, Thomas fell in with bad companions and became addicted to rum and opium. One night during a voyage home, he disappeared and was presumed overboard somewhere in the South China Sea. The weather had been dead calm. Nobody noted his absence until the next morning.

Three years had passed since the death of his brother. Despite the passage of time, an upwelling of grief even now forced Gunn to turn his back to Yarrow to conceal his sorrow and put it away. He went about his duties in silence.

Nelson strode aft through the waist of the cutter and mounted the steps to the quarterdeck. He stayed on the leeward side, affording the weather side to the captain, as custom required. He ducked under the main boom and continued to the cockpit, where he addressed Gunn.

"Mr. Gunn, I request permission to pipe hands to the evening meal."

For some time now, Gunn had been catching whiffs of Cookie's famous fish stew and sourdough bread, wafting aft from the galley stack. Having not eaten since breakfast, he was famished. The captain was looking aloft, however, gauging the wind from the attitude of the commissioning pennant at the truck of the mainmast.

"Boats, I think the captain is getting ready to drop the towline and set sail. I hate to say it, but supper must wait."

"Cookie won't be happy, sir."

"He's been disappointed before."

"Ain't that Bob's own truth. How's the nose, sir?"

"It's not broken, I think." Gunn touched the tender spot. "Lucky that."

"Too bad. It adds character." Nelson pointed with a grin to his own crooked nose. The unspoken code among men of the sea would not allow them to speak more of the close brush with death at the barrel end of a hog-leg revolver.

The captain turned to him. "Mr. Gunn, we have a fair wind, I'd say. Get us unhitched from this hag and make all plain sail."

"Aye, aye, sir." He turned to Nelson. "You heard the man." He picked up the brass speaking trumpet from its cradle, and aimed it forward, shouting, "All hands to halyards and braces. Prepare to make sail."

Nelson answered the call to sail stations with a trill on his boatswain's pipe, as he retraced steps to the forecastle. The men sprang to their stations, joined by the watch below, streaming topsides from the forward companionway.

The tug reduced speed to allow slack in the heavy line, and a few minutes later the *Morris* was set free. Gunn ordered the helm put down to swing the bow into the wind, making it easier to raise the sails.

The *John Taylor* turned aside the opposite way, the towing hawser following in a shrinking arc as it was hauled aboard. The brass field cannon on her main deck glinted in the afternoon sun. Below that, the smear of red paint stretched like a bloody snarl along the bow. The squat figure of Captain Martin S. Dobbins stood outside the pilothouse. He stretched his short neck and leaned over the rail in one final salivary salute to the cutter. The tug headed toward the city, paddlewheels reeling.

If the circumstances hadn't been so serious, Gunn would have laughed aloud. "Stunner," he muttered.

"Sir?" Yarrow was typically attentive to the voice of the watch officer.

"Steady. Steady as you go." Yarrow turned the wheel and the cutter's head steadied up, the wind just off the starboard bow.

The crew was ready at their sail stations. Gunn picked up the speaking trumpet and bellowed. "Set the mainsail. Set the foresail."

Prouty urged them on from his station at the base of the mainmast. "Cheerily, lads."

The commands started a flurry of well-coordinated activity among the experienced crew of twenty, divided into several teams along the length of the ship. The crew sang out in a unified, rhythmic chant, as they hauled together on the halyards, hand-over-hand. The mainsail and the foresail, the two largest sails, went up quickly and smoothly, luffing in the breeze.

"Tend your sheets." Gunn eased the mainsheet himself, since it was close at hand, to keep the mainsail from filling entirely just yet. He gave the order to set the staysail and the two jibs, inner and outer, all the way forward at the bow. Those went up without a hitch.

As the sails started to fill, Gunn told Yarrow to put the helm down, and the cutter's head began to fall off before the wind. Immediately, the little ship settled into a smooth, slow canter, gradually gaining headway.

"Very well, Mr. Gunn. Make your heading sou'east-by-south, nothing to the south'ard of that," ordered the captain. "Trim your sails accordingly. Set the fore topsail and t'gallant. Let me know when we are within a half-mile of Minot's Ledge. Be sure to keep that mark on your starboard side. I'll be in my cabin."

Captain Whitcomb stepped off the quarterdeck, down into the cockpit, on his way to the cabin hatch. Gunn backed out of his way, as he sidled past. The captain stopped short next to him and eyed his wound.

"Mr. Gunn, you've been a busy man, today. Since you have returned whole, though a bit worse for wear, and your charge is safe and sound, I trust all went as planned."

"Aye, sir, for the most part, it did. Petty Officer Nelson was of great service, or things might have turned out quite differently."

"What would we do without Nelson? Well done to both of you. See Cookie about that nose. He likely can help." And that was all. Not a word about their distasteful mission. Nothing to ease his growing concern. The captain vanished down the companionway into the cabin.

"On the foremast. Set the topsail. Hands to the braces for a port haul," called Gunn. The crew worked with alacrity. The quicker they finished, the sooner they would eat. In a little more than a quarter hour, all the sails were set and sheeted home.

The *Morris* steadied up on the course ordered by her captain, her sails trimmed to best advantage on the starboard tack. The ship heeled to leeward, slicing through the water toward the appointed destination and away from home waters.

By the time they stood off Minot's Ledge, the steadfast sun had transited well into the evening sky, casting the cutter's long, wavering shadow over the passing waves. Gunn reached for his watch, noting the time, and rubbed the burnished surface between thumb and forefinger, but there was nothing for it. He snapped the case shut, tucked the amulet back in his pocket, and called for the captain, as ordered.

They had departed the harbor without incident. Though they were passing through a hazardous stretch of water that had brought many good ships to ruin, it was well marked and easily avoided in good weather. Other dangers lay ahead, however—unseen, unmarked shoals of a different sort that weren't named on any chart, but no doubt they could bring a good sailor to ruin, just the same. The luckless unease that earlier had settled in had grown into a sense of foreboding that Gunn could not shake.

It was as though the ship were reaching headlong under full sail into a gathering white squall.

8

G unn awoke in utter darkness, stricken by shock and blind fear as his head and left shoulder slammed against the washstand next to his bunk. He found himself sprawled on the deck. He felt for a handhold as the ship shuddered, lurched, and rolled again to port, her timbers groaning like a wounded animal.

Warning shouts split the night air. The distant, sharp reports of wood cracking and lines parting rang out like gunshots. Heavy thuds and crashes on the deck above followed in quick succession. A voice strung tight with urgency shouted down the open companionway, "All hands on deck."

Struggling to his feet, Gunn brushed open the damask curtain that separated his small stateroom from the wardroom. Lieutenant Richmond's dark form brushed past him, his bare feet treading heavily, carrying his boots as he rushed for the ladder.

Prouty's voice came from the open hatch, calm and deliberate. "Come, gentlemen. Shake a leg."

Gunn wriggled into his undress uniform, shrugged on his worn frock coat, half-laced his boots, and grabbed his cloth cap from its hook on the bulkhead, all to the sound of urgent cries above him.

He had gone to bed right after the evening meal, exhausted from the previous day's events. It was now the middle of the night, sometime before four o'clock, which he knew only because he had not yet been awakened to stand the morning watch.

Gunn moved carefully across the wardroom toward the ladder, bumping into the table in the center of the room. He tripped on a toppled chair. Pain radiated through his right ankle, reminding him he needed to favor that side. It was stiff and hurt more than it had the day before.

Across the way, a head poked from between the curtains of the top berth, opposite his. It was Brent, whose beady eyes shone in the darkness. Gunn was startled, having forgotten for the moment that Brent and Colonel Suttle occupied the stateroom. They had insisted on displacing Miller, the other third lieutenant on the ship, even though Prouty argued it was against regulations. Miller had been forced to move in with Gunn, temporarily inhabiting the bunk above his, although currently he was on watch.

"What is it?" Brent asked, timidly.

"I don't know, Mr. Brent. Best get dressed and be prepared to come up on deck. Be sure to wake Colonel Suttle."

A muted reply came from within the curtained stateroom. "I am fully awake, I assure you, sir."

The boatswain blew the shrill, long-winded notes of his pipe. "Hands to sail stations."

Gunn hurried up the ladder and arrived on deck to a dense fog, through which the tops of the masts, which extended a hundred feet above the deck, were invisible. Mist hid the bow of the ship, obscuring everything but the hazy confusion of activity on the foredeck.

Attempting to recover the headsails, the crew grappled with flailing lines that seemed alive. The topsail yard, its sail still attached by one clew, hung shattered and cockeyed in the rigging, the broken end resting on the deck. Rigging, ropes, and canvas were strewn everywhere. The blows of several axes punctuated the struggle to cut away the damaged rigging up forward. The fore staysail luffed wildly, clapping like close thunder.

"Mr. Miller, keep her head into the wind," shouted the captain.

Whitcomb stood at the forward edge of the quarterdeck, holding to the mainmast and straining to see through the mist. He was fully dressed, though hatless, and looked like he had not slept. Third Lieutenant Sam Miller, the youngest and most junior of the officers, peered squeamishly over the captain's shoulder.

"Mr. Prouty." The captain's bellow rang in the dense fog.

"Aye, sir." Prouty appeared from the foredeck like an apparition, conjured through a wall.

"We have got to get these sails down. Are we free yet?"

"Yes, sir."

"What's the damage?"

"We've lost both the fore topsail and t'gallant yards, captain. Both sails are ripped to shreds. Some of the bowsprit is gone, and we've lost both jibs."

"Well, get that widow-maker of a sail in hand, before she parts or kills somebody."

"Aye, sir."

"Are we free?"

Although Prouty had already answered the question, he responded without pause. "Yes, sir. The other ship is away."

"Away where, sir? Away where?"

"I'd say she's to windward of us, captain."

"You'd say so, would you?" the captain growled, searching off to starboard into the heavy fog. "Well, keep an eye peeled up there. We don't want to tangle with her again."

"Aye, sir." Prouty disappeared back into the mist.

"Get up forward and help them, Mr. Gunn," Captain Whitcomb shouted, pointing to the bow. "Belay that. Put some hands to these sheets and halyards. We need to back the mainsail and strike the foresail if we can. We must heave to right here."

The captain glanced over his shoulder.

"Mr. Miller. Why don't I hear the ship's bell? Answer me that. You should have been ringing it as soon as the fog rolled in. Sound it, man. Every two minutes. Ring it rapidly, as loud as you can, for a count of five. Now, if you please."

"Aye, aye, sir."

"Not you, Mr. Miller. Get somebody else to ring the blasted thing."

Miller pointed to one of the seamen, who did as the captain ordered.

Gunn found Second Lieutenant Richmond, and they each gathered six men. Richmond handled the mainsail. Gunn took the foresail, sending three men aloft to cut away the remaining rigging from the foreyard and ease it down to rest fully on the deck. By the time they had finished, his team had brailed in the foresail, secured it to the mast with gaskets, and started to clear away more of the debris.

The light breeze allowed them to get well under control. Within minutes, the cutter stood hove to. She kept minimal headway on, enough to maintain bare steerage in the fog, while the crew cleared away the wreckage.

And wondered what had happened.

9

Asa Butman poked his head up from the hatch of the main hold, where the deputy marshal and his men lodged. "Anything we can do to help?"

Gunn stood nearby, alongside Lieutenant Richmond, who answered the question before he could respond.

"No, sir. I think we have things well in hand. Thank you very much for your concern." Richmond's southern drawl gave his reply a graciousness beyond his nature.

"What the blazes happened?"

"We collided with another ship. Thankfully, there wasn't much damage."

"What ship?"

"We do not know, Mr. Butman. She did not have the courtesy to leave a calling card."

Butman snorted. "Sounds like every woman I've ever known. Anyone hurt?"

"Apparently not, since you have asked the question. Your men are the only ones not accounted for, I believe. Are they all right?"

"I think so. Yes."

An awkward silence. "And the negro?"

"He is alive and well, sir, and he thanks you for askin', I'm sure."

The ship's bell rang rapidly again.

"What in blazes *is* that?" asked Butman.

"It's a signal letting the other ship know our position, to avoid colliding again," said Gunn.

"Makes sense, I reck'n. How long is he going to keep that up?"

"Most likely until we locate the other ship, or the fog lifts."

Butman mugged his umbrage. "That will make it a long night, I expect." His head disappeared again below the open hatch.

"Delightful fellow." Richmond smoothed and twisted the ends of his long, full mustache, which curled in a rakish fashion—his signature gesture whenever offering critical commentary. The crew had begun to mimic the gesture in the two months since his arrival onboard, behind his back, of course. While previously assigned to the cutter *Andrew Jackson*, William Richmond had worked a mutual exchange with the *Morris*'s former second lieutenant, who had been seeking to return to his native home in Savannah. Apparently, the exchange had worked to Richmond's advantage, too, for undisclosed reasons. It had not worked out so well for Gunn, however, who was in line for promotion. His hopes to fleet up to second lieutenant had gone hard aground.

Rumors of Richmond's irascible character had preceded him and were speedily confirmed upon his arrival. Gunn had learned to give Richmond a wide berth, and so he intended now, as he started toward the quarterdeck. He wanted to find out more about what had happened.

"Mr. Gunn." Richmond stopped him.

"Yes, Mr. Richmond?"

"You were slow to arrive on deck when all hands were called."

"Was I?"

"You were. Next time, you should make every attempt to be the *first* on deck, when called. Best let no man cast a shadow on you in future."

"Of course, sir. I will remember."

"See to it."

Prouty appeared again. "Make way, if you please, gentlemen. Look lively, now. No reason to stand about lollygagging. There's work to be done." He brushed past. "Mr. Richmond, I want you to relieve Miller on watch. He is shaken, I'm sure. It's about two in the morning, I expect." He peered at his watch, although it was too dark to see its face. "I will spell you in an hour. It will ease the captain's mind, I should think, to have someone else at the helm.

"But, sir—"

"I realize that you had the last watch, but Mr. Gunn has the next one. He's our best navigator, and we'll need him bright-eyed when we go through Pollock's Rip later this morning."

The ship's urgent bell rang again, ending further discussion.

"Aye, sir." Richmond bristled as he walked aft.

"Mr. Gunn, see to it our guests are looked after. I'm certain they're alarmed."

"Certainly, sir. Can we continue on?"

"Well, the jib boom is gone, and the martingale, but the bowsprit and bobstays are pretty much intact. We can probably jury-rig a new jib boom. But, the topsail yard—"

"I don't know what all that means, but it sounds fairly ominous." Brent stood on the companionway ladder, only his upper body visible above the coaming, holding fast to the rails on each side.

"It's nothing we can't handle, Mr. Brent," said Gunn. "How is your companion, the colonel?"

"I'm well enough, to be sure." Suttle answered from the darkness below. "Although I am thinking it might have been better to take the train home, no matter the hazards."

"I understand, colonel. We are not in any danger, I assure you."

"Is it possible to have some light down here? Things are somewhat at odds."

"Of course, Mr. Brent."

Brent stepped down the ladder, and Gunn followed. He felt for a match from the well on the bulkhead, struck it, lit the overhead lamp, and adjusted the flame. The brimstone of the matchhead mingled with the usual pungent mixture of whale oil, wood, hemp, and canvas. The lamp glowed, sending to the four corners of the wardroom a warm, diffused light that swayed with the motion of the ship.

Clothing, books, and other personal belongings were strewn about the wardroom. The sideboard, fastened along the aft bulkhead, seemed undisturbed, except for one drawer and a cabinet door, both ajar. The small, unlit coal stove, which inhabited the aft corner on the port side, had its door sprung wide open, beckoning on its hinges. Of the six scattered chairs around the table in the center of the room, one had toppled over.

Gunn quickly policed the wardroom, setting things to rights. Brent and Colonel Suttle recovered their belongings, grumbling about their rude awakening the entire time. They stowed their items more securely than before in the two large drawers, set side-by-side beneath the bottom bunk, which Suttle had summarily claimed for himself.

The housekeeping took longer than it might have, due to the constant bobbing of the cutter, no longer sailing smoothly through the waves. When all was situated, Gunn started up the ladder to the main deck. As he brushed past the two passengers, excusing himself, Brent caught him by the arm.

"Mr. Gunn, would it be all right for us to come up on deck? The air down here is somewhat … stale." In the lamplight, the color of his face would have matched a glass of yellow chartreuse.

"Of course, Mr. Brent. Just try to remain out of the way of the crew. They are still getting things back in order. Best to remain in the waist of the ship, near the companionway."

Beads of sweat covered Brent's brow, despite the coolness of the night air. His eyes lowered to the deck. He wavered on his feet, holding to the bulkhead with both hands.

"To leeward, if you will," said Gunn, noting his condition. "Port side."

"Right. Thanks. Um ..."

"Left side." Gunn pointed.

"Of course."

Back on the main deck, Gunn crossed the few steps to the booby hatch, which covered the main hold. He slid the hatch cover, already halfway open, back to its stops and climbed down the ladder. As he stood on the lower deck, his head brushed the overhead.

A lantern swung from a nail in one of the timbers, casting an eerie glow. The scene resembled the stark realism of a Daumier lithograph, depicting the human condition at its most humble. The dank, fetid odor made it real.

The men lay on straw mattresses in a space cleared among coils of manila rope, spare rigging, and other stores. The four deputies sprawled in various states of undress, their discarded clothing tangled with the wool blankets that partially covered them. They breathed heavily, moaning, their heads lolling in unison with the movement of the ship.

Asa Butman sat apart from the rest, regarding his men with open disgust. It was no wonder he had offered his help on deck. The sour odor of vomit pervaded the cramped space, wafting from two buckets, both nearly half-full of mustard-colored swill, and mingled with the acrid stench of unwashed men. The combination was enough to turn the strongest stomach.

Anthony Burns sat wedged between the ladder and the base of the mainmast, hidden in the shadows of the hold. He still wore his new suit, from what Gunn could tell. His arms embraced the base of the mast, shackled at the wrists. He had been sick on himself. His face pressed against the mast, his eyes clamped shut, though it was evident from his posture that he was not asleep.

"Mr. Butman, why is this man shackled?"

Butman shifted his position. "This here is a fugitive slave, Mr.

Gunn. He's already run off once. I ain't gonna let it happen again."

"And where would he go?"

"You ever seen a rat what's been cornered Mr. Gunn? He'll swim for it, if that's a choice. Even if it means he'll die tryin'."

"Unshackle him, Mr. Butman. He is too sick to go anywhere."

"I will not. I have been told to make sure this fugitive does not escape, and that he lands safely in Norfolk. I intend to do just that." Butman eyed Gunn squarely, eyebrows raised.

"You would all do well to come topsides. Get some fresh air. It will help with the seasickness. Stay out of the way, as best you can."

One of the men lifted his sallow head and tried to get up, then dropped back onto his soiled bedding. Burns did not move.

"I will speak to Colonel Suttle. We'll see what he says about this matter."

"Best not meddle, Gunn. Who d'ya think told me to keep him under lock and key?"

Gunn used his sleeve to wipe the beaded sweat trickling down his brow. It was not a warm night, but the closeness of the air in the hold had gotten to him. He scrambled up the ladder, inhaling the cool, clean air outside. Alighting upon the coaming, he steadied himself.

His mouth began to water, but he fought back the rising queasiness. He searched for a horizon. There was none through the fog, so dense that a wisp of cloud swept over the deck.

With sea smoke swirling about him, he recalled Thoreau once insisting in a school lesson that justice is best served when men become their own law. Given what he had just witnessed, it occurred to him, and not for the first time, that perhaps his former schoolmaster still had a great deal to learn about men, after all.

10

Gunn found the first lieutenant near the mainmast, coiling the outhaul.

"Mr. Prouty, may I have a word with you?"

Gunn drew Prouty as far aft on the quarterdeck as they could manage, until the acute angle of the mainsail blocked their passage.

"Sir, I thought it my duty to inform you that Burns is being held in conditions that are unacceptable, at least to my way of thinking."

"How so?"

"He is bound to the mainmast, both arms shackled around the base." Gunn demonstrated with his own arms held in a semicircle. "He cannot lie down or stand. Further, he has pissed, soiled, and puked all over himself."

"He is in the custody of Mr. Butman, is he not?"

"Sir, Butman says Colonel Suttle has directed him to keep Burns in shackles. It is unnecessary cruelty in my view. Something must be done about it. I thought I should bring it to your attention."

"Very well, Mr. Gunn. I am placing you in charge of the prisoner while he is on board this ship. Talk to the colonel. See that Burns is tended to properly."

"Sir?"

"You heard me. Take charge of the prisoner. You will have the captain's full support to do what is necessary to provide humane treatment. Obviously, the good colonel has forgotten who is in charge."

Brent appeared out of the darkness at Prouty's shoulder.

"I beg your pardon, Mr. Prouty. I could not help but overhear you talking about Burns. It is a small ship, after all. Is there something I can do to assist?"

"As a matter of fact, Mr. Brent, you can. Mr. Gunn tells me that Burns is being kept in deplorable conditions. I thought we had an understanding that he is to be treated as a human being while in this ship."

"What more would you have us do, sir? May I remind you he is a prisoner."

"I am deputizing Mr. Gunn, here, as our master-at-arms. He is now the warden of the prison, if you will. He will oversee the treatment of the prisoner while he remains onboard. What you choose to do later is your affair. You may convey these arrangements to Colonel Suttle and Mr. Butman. Do I make myself clear?"

"Are these the captain's orders?" Brent pressed toward Prouty, his legs unsteady, holding fast to the rail.

"They soon will be," said Prouty, rising to his full height. "You may consider them his."

"I see." Brent's little eyes burned in the darkness, darting, searching for a refuge, and finding none. "Colonel Suttle will not like this very much, Mr. Prouty."

"Then he can take up the matter with the collector of customs, once we reach Norfolk. Until then, he has no appeal. Now, if you will excuse me, I have other duties."

Prouty ducked under the boom, holding onto it with one arm and swinging himself into the cockpit in one swift motion. It was surprising how spry Mr. Prouty could be. Despite many years at sea, he had managed to keep youth in his step. Gunn knew he would waste no time in locating Captain Whitcomb to inform him what he had done in his name.

Brent turned on Gunn. "Colonel Suttle has influence at the highest levels in Washington. Do you realize that fact?"

"Sir, the fact that a United States government vessel is providing transport at no cost to him and his ... company ... leaves no doubt in my mind of his connections."

"Then have no doubt you will regret this, Mr. Gunn. You should learn not to interfere where you are not wanted."

Brent's face was close, his pointed nose an inch from Gunn's. He drew back mainly to escape the man's foul breath, which reeked of vomit and brandy.

"You are one of the sympathizers, are you not, Mr. Gunn?" Brent spoke loudly enough for someone else to hear, if they should have an interest.

"What do you mean?"

"Did I not see you at Faneuil Hall the night of the riot, night before last?" When Gunn didn't answer, Brent continued to press. "Oh, yes, Lieutenant. I was there, too. I was there to find out what the Vigilance Committee was up to, and what we might expect from Reverend Parker and those other lawbreakers."

"Perhaps you are mistaken."

"Come now. I'm sure I saw you. You were there with a beautiful young lady, were you not? I remember, because I recall thinking how lovely she was. What a handsome couple you made."

"If I was there, sir ... it would have been to listen to what was being said. Nothing more."

"Well, we both heard what they said, and we saw what they did, isn't that right? And you, Mr. Gunn, were in with them."

"That is not true."

"Deny it, then, as did everyone else who broke into the courthouse that night and murdered a man. Regardless, I'm certain of the fact."

"I was not party to any such event, Mr. Brent."

"Have it your way. But I wonder if your captain will see it

differently." Brent withdrew his face and put his hand to his mouth, leaning forward at the waist.

"Port side, Mr. Brent. Away from the wind." He heard Brent retching over the side as he left him.

Gunn walked forward, down the steps to the main deck and found Colonel Suttle and Asa Butman standing at the port rail, smoking cigars. The ship's bell rang again.

"Mr. Butman, be so kind as to unshackle the prisoner and bring him up on deck," he ordered.

"Just a moment there, sir." Colonel Suttle said. "What do you mean to do?"

"I mean to bring Burns up on deck to get cleaned up and take some fresh air."

"That slave is my property, sir. I have not authorized this liberty." Colonel Suttle struck the deck with his cane.

"No, Colonel, you have not. But I must insist. Butman?"

"On whose orders?" The darkness could not hide Suttle's indignation.

"On *my* orders." The captain stood near the mainmast, towering above them on the quarterdeck.

"Captain, I must object. Burns is my property, and he must be under my command," insisted Suttle.

"Colonel Suttle, I am the captain of this vessel. What happens aboard is my responsibility and mine alone. Therefore, everyone on this ship is under my command. I thought we had made that clear."

"As you say, sir, but I must register my objection in the strongest terms. Others shall hear of this, you can be sure, *Captain* Whitcomb." Suttle's sardonic emphasis on Whitcomb's title left no doubt as to his view of the captain's authority. He waved his cane at Butman, motioning for him to comply.

Butman flicked his cigar over the side. The glowing embers arced through the air and disappeared into the darkness. He walked to the booby hatch and entered the hold. In a moment, he returned, every sullen movement exaggerated, as he climbed back onto the deck.

Anthony Burns poked his head out of the hatch and peered about him. He held on to the ladder as though his life depended on it, his right elbow crooked around one of the rungs, favoring his deformed hand. Gunn reached to grab his left arm and Butman grabbed the other. The other deputies would be of little use in their present condition.

Gunn yelled over his shoulder to Lieutenant Miller.

"Sam, get some help from the crew."

"Right away. Hang on." Miller hurried forward. Meanwhile, the two men lifted Burns, as he climbed unsteadily out of the hold.

"Steady now, Burns. Try to get your footing. Are you all right?"

"I think so. Bless you, sir."

The putrid stench hit Gunn's nostrils again. He turned his head away, as Burns cleared the coaming and took a cautious step onto the deck.

Two crew members hurried to meet them, and Miller followed. They took Burns by the arms as his knees buckled. Gunn and Butman let go, and the sailors half-carried, half-dragged the large man, his feet treading every other step.

"Take him forward to the head on the leeward side," said Gunn. "Get those clothes off. Strip him down to the skin and douse him with seawater."

"What's to be done with his clothes?" Miller rolled his eyes as the sickening odor reached him.

Burns slouched in his new suit of clothes, now likely so soiled no decent person would want to wear them ever again.

"Do what you can with them. Put them in a cargo net and hang them over the side to rinse them out. Salvage what you can. We'll try to replace everything else."

"Mr. Gunn. A word, if you please." Captain Whitcomb motioned for Gunn to follow him onto the quarterdeck.

"Aye, Captain." Gunn mounted the steps. Whitcomb drew aft and chose a spot near the windward rail, then turned to face him.

"Mr. Prouty has told me that he has given you charge over Burns. I want you to make sure he is cared for properly, as though he were a human being." He paused on that discordant note. "As the person that he … is."

"Of course, sir."

"But hear me, now. Do not antagonize these men. Do you understand?"

"Aye, sir."

"One more thing. Well done." It was as much praise as Whitcomb ever gave.

11

The fog had lifted somewhat, enough to reveal stars shining overhead. The full length of the cutter was visible, but still no horizon. And no other ship yet in sight.

It was unusual to be invited to stand apart with the captain on the quarterdeck. The conversation already had run short, but Gunn was enjoying this privilege. He relished its rarity, like the few times he remembered as a boy being alone with his busy, often preoccupied father.

"Looks like we are going to find our way clear of this soup, sir."

The captain nodded his approval. "Maybe we'll even find the idjit who hit us." He fingered the end of his full silver beard. "It's odd we haven't heard his bell, a gong, some sort of signal. A shout, for Pete's sake. You would think he'd want us to know where he is."

Gunn had his own suspicions about the collision. It was no stretch of the imagination to ask whether those who wished this mission to fail might have had a hand in trying to end it. Having so recently gained the captain's welcome approval, however, he had no desire to squander it with unsolicited speculation. He would keep his mouth shut and wait for the captain to voice any concern.

He tried to think of something else to say. The silence stretched on. Perhaps he had been dismissed and simply didn't realize it. He looked toward the invisible horizon, wanting to allow a little more time. The captain cleared his throat, and the silence resumed. Then Whitcomb spoke.

"Hard business, this. Not pleasant for any of us." He wiped his brow with a handkerchief. His face and hair were damp with the heavy mist.

"Yes, sir. It is not a situation I imagined when I joined the service."

"Nor I." The captain tapped his fingers on the rail. "You have been on board—what?—two years, now?"

"Yes, sir. Nearly so."

"You know, Mr. Prouty told me something very odd the other day. About you. It made me curious."

"About me, sir?"

"About one of the men who sponsored your application for a commission. Nathaniel Hawthorne, the author. Is that right?"

"Yes, sir."

"Imagine that."

Another short silence.

"He's a Bowdoin man, y'know, same as me. Though he's from away, bein' a flatlandah." Whitcomb smiled, emphasizing his down-east dialect, which he usually managed to subdue. "I'm very curious. How are you connected? How did it come about that such a man should recommend you for a commission?"

"Well, sir, my family has known him for many years. We first met at Brook Farm when I was about ten years old. My mother took my brother, sister, and me to live there after my father ... departed. Mr. Hawthorne was living there, too, at the time."

"Your father passed away?"

"No, sir. He simply left us."

Gunn had not intended to mention his father. He rarely talked about him. It had just slipped out. A glance over his shoulder assured him that Richmond, who had moved closer, seemed deeply engaged in his duties and presumably out of earshot. He figured he could trust the captain with the information. He was known as an honorable man, one of few words, not prone to speak ill of others.

The captain diverted his eyes at the mention of a family scandal and changed the subject. "Brook Farm, y'say? That experiment in the new socialism? A failed one, from what I've heard."

Prouty mounted the quarterdeck and approached the captain. Gunn was glad for the distraction.

"Sir, we've got things well in hand forward." Prouty saluted. "But it will be about a half-hour until we can get everything squared away to the point that we can head south again. Still no sign of the other ship. Meanwhile, Burns is being looked after properly, thanks to Mr. Gunn, here."

"Very well, Mr. Prouty. Thank you."

"Captain, I request permission to relieve Mr. Richmond of the watch," said Prouty.

"Granted."

Prouty turned toward Gunn. "I'll expect you to relieve me on time at the morning watch, Mr. Gunn. Get some rest after the prisoner is tended to."

"Aye, aye, sir," Gunn said, turning to go. The captain stopped him.

"Stay for just a moment longer, if you please, Mr. Gunn. I'm still curious about something."

"Certainly, sir."

Prouty nodded and stepped the few yards to the cockpit to conduct the relief of the watch.

"So, how did it happen that Hawthorne took such an interest in your obtaining a commission?" asked the captain.

"Well, he left Brook Farm after about a year and moved back to Concord. We left six months later and moved there, too. By that time, he'd gotten married. As my brother, sister, and I grew up, we saw him from time to time, and he kept a mild interest in our welfare even after his own children were born and he moved away to Salem and then to Lenox. We would still see him whenever he visited friends in Concord. I guess he missed living there and always wished to come back. Two years ago, the Hawthornes returned and bought a house not a half-mile from where we live. We couldn't have been more delighted."

"Is that so?" The captain took his pipe from a pocket and tapped it on the rail.

"Yes, sir. I'd been at odds for a while by then. My mother had always wanted me to be a minister, like my father. God knows why. Maybe to redeem the family name."

"Your father a minister?"

Gunn nodded. "He had a large Unitarian church in Brookline. We lived in the parsonage there. I was nine when he … left."

"I see. Did he just decide—"

"He told my mother that he was leaving to seek his own true heart." Gunn lowered his voice. "Turns out, his own true heart had a name. Alexandra."

"Ah, ha." Whitcomb tamped the pipe's bowl full of tobacco from a leather pouch.

"Yes, a so-called free-thinker, who convinced him that marriage is just another form of slavery."

The hard truth of it was that the lover's name was Alexander. But that fact was too hard to admit. Some truths are too painful to share. They rarely bring real sympathy or understanding.

The captain cleared his throat. "Free thinker. Don't say?" He struck a match, revealing a slight frown as he lit his pipe.

"I've never before told anyone that, sir. I don't know what came over me. My apologies."

"No need. I asked. I'm sorry for your misfortune."

"Well, it's not all bad. My mother's sister and her husband, my uncle William, have always been very kind to us. They helped my mother buy the little house in Concord. My uncle even offered to send me to college, but I wanted to go to sea, instead, and so I sailed as a deckhand in one of his ships. Eventually, the captain promoted me to third mate."

"Stroke of luck there."

"Hard work, more like. But it all came somewhat naturally to me. I've always loved going to sea. Long story short, Mr. Hawthorne knew from the time we lived at Brook Farm that I wanted to be a sea captain. I told him then. He asked me one day when our paths crossed in Concord if that was still what I wanted to do. I said yes, but I didn't want to be away for months and years at a time, so I could be of greater help to my mother and sister. At least for now."

"A sea captain, is it?"

"Someday, yes, sir. Like my grandfather."

The corners of the captain's mouth turned down even more. "Far cry from a minister. Although, I daresay, the sea has a lot to teach about the nature of God and the frailty of men. Not all of it good. Be careful what you wish for."

"Yes, sir. That's what he said, too. His own father was a sea captain. Lost at sea."

"Just so." Whitcomb puffed his pipe. "Hawthorne knew somebody in the cutter service, did he?"

"Well, sir, he had connections at the Custom House in Boston from his days as a measurer. He told me that he'd written to the deputy collector and put my name forward to him. A commission was mine, if I wanted it."

"Who was the deputy collector? Was it Andros?"

"That's right. Others helped as well, including my uncle, but I'm sure Hawthorne's name and his connections made the difference." Gunn smiled. "Besides, he tells a good story."

The captain nodded. "As do you. I'm sorry to hear about your father. How curious. Quite a remarkable childhood. Quite a story, all told."

Gunn shrugged. "I suppose so, sir. I'm sure it seems that way.

"Indeed."

During their conversation, Prouty and Richmond had conducted the change of watch, relaying information about the ship's position and status, weather, course and speed. After Prouty relieved him, Richmond sauntered over to the captain for the customary request to retire below. He saluted.

"Captain, I have been properly relieved by Mr. Prouty. Request permission to lay below."

"First, I'd like you to assess things on the bow, Mr. Richmond. See how things are coming along. Should be just about finished, I expect."

"Aye, aye, sir," said Richmond. As he departed, he glanced at Gunn, smirked and shook his head.

Gunn did not venture to say more, finally managing to shut his mouth. What he might have revealed to the captain, had he not been interrupted, was that he wanted above all to be as different from his father as he possibly could manage, to distance himself in every conceivable manner. He wanted nothing else to do with his father. In fact, more than once he had confided to Hawthorne that he wished his father dead for what he had done to his family. Hawthorne had been quick to admonish him, to strike the thought from his young mind, and told him he must try not to think such things. But those indelible thoughts had remained and persisted until the present moment.

He was fond of the author in more ways than one, and even saw him as a substitute father, having spent many days as a boy in Hawthorne's company, mucking the stables at Brook Farm. Hawthorne wryly called the hill of manure they shoveled daily together "the gold mine." He would tell humorous stories invented on the spot, sometimes to answer Gunn's endless, child-like questions about why things were the way they were. Hawthorne seemed both amused and bewildered by his constant queries, warning that he should take care; if he asked too many questions, someday they might circle around like fairies and carry him away. As a boy, he had taken the advice to heart. Many questions in his life since then had gone unasked and unanswered.

Those hidden things luckily had gone unsaid in a rare, candid moment he had already begun to regret. Gunn cleared his throat and asked the captain's leave to attend to his duties.

Without responding, Whitcomb lifted his head and put his face to the wind, which had veered and freshened noticeably as they had finished talking. In little more than an instant the fog began to lift, the way a bridal veil is raised, revealing at once everything around them, clean and clear.

Cape Cod's Nauset Light stood to the west, its three steady, white lights, commonly called "The Three Sisters," broad on the port bow. They had lost some ground while hove to, no longer sailing southeast. To the north, the fog had receded, leaving a wall of haze but no visible horizon. To the east, the new sky had begun to separate from the dark waters beneath. Elsewhere around them, open water stretched into nothing but darkness.

The captain wheeled about, searching for the other ship. "Well, I'll be jammed. She's gone. Vanished." Under his breath he uttered a quiet, incredulous oath.

They were alone on the sea, sailing under a moonless, starry sky.

12

Gunn used the time remaining before relieving Prouty on the morning watch to make certain Burns received proper care. After Burns had rested for a while in the open air, he stripped off his fouled clothing and the sailors doused him with buckets of seawater. Naked as a shorn sheep but for his wool socks, he wrapped himself in a torn, frayed blanket someone had brought from the forecastle. They sat him down on the foredeck, hunkered against the port bulwark, affording him a chance to steady himself and recover.

"Water. Some water, please," Burns said, shivering.

"Give him some water," said Gunn. "I hate to tell you this, Anthony, but it probably won't stay down. Once the sickness comes, only time will help, but it—"

"Thank you, sir. I've been seasick before. I need to wash this taste out of my mouth."

"Of course."

Burns sipped from the dipper one of the sailors handed him, and then spat the water onto the deck. He tugged the blanket closer around himself.

"Is that blanket enough? Bring him another," said Gunn.

Burns looked up at him. "I can't say as I'll ever be warm again."

"Maybe take those wet socks off. Might make—"

"Don't take my socks. Please leave them be."

"All right, then. One of you men see if you can find some dry clothes in the lucky bag. I'll check on you again soon, Anthony."

"Thank you kindly, sir."

Someone brought another blanket and provided a pail for his use, since he was too weak to stand. He sat with the pail between his feet, his head bowed between bent knees, trembling in the cool air. Every so often, he retched into the pail.

After dragging the soiled clothing in the sea, the crew draped each item in the shrouds and over the rail to dry, though the wool frock coat and trousers would never fully dry in the salt air, even with good weather. The vest had been lost over the side. Someone retrieved a near-rotten pair of trousers and a threadbare cotton shirt from the lucky bag and gave them to Burns to wear while his own clothes dripped dry.

Despite the setbacks of the early morning hours, the cutter made repairs and again headed south, abandoning any attempt to locate the other ship involved in the collision. Gunn relieved Prouty of the watch promptly at three-thirty. Right away, he noted that the crippled ship persisted in trying to head up into the wind and stop, like a lame steed, requiring a good deal of weather helm to hold her steady. He had to keep Bartlett, the new helmsman, on his toes.

At dawn, they passed Chatham light, its two green lanterns shining side by side. The twin towers stood high atop the steep, sandy bluffs of outer Cape Cod. The morning sun, rising from a broken line of lingering clouds on the horizon, painted a coral sheen on the water beneath the eastern sky, a near match for the bright color of the bluffs.

Gunn usually enjoyed the morning watch, even though it typically meant doing with less sleep. The day was new, and he could watch it unfold with the same sense of anticipation one attaches to opening a letter from home, hoping the news will be good.

By six o'clock, the captain was back on deck. He set a westerly course at the Pollock Rip lightship, and then stayed on deck as they passed into the dangerous current and made a dogleg turn into Nantucket Sound. The flood tide carried them into the sound, which was to their advantage for speed over the ground.

As they turned southwest, however, the wind came against them, rising to a moderate breeze. The wind fought them through the narrow channel, causing the cutter to tack back and forth in the choppy water. The men on watch worked continually, rarely stopping to rest as they sheeted the sails, first on the starboard tack and then the port, and back again, snaking their way up the channel, under Gunn's careful hand.

The constant movement of wind-driven waves over a fluctuating, sandy bottom made the passage especially treacherous through Pollock Rip. Many ships had foundered in this stretch of water over the years, and the shallow floor was littered with "dead boats," as Nelson called them. Here and there, an old mast stuck out of the water, marking a shallow grave. The leadsman's incessant chant called out the depth in fathoms, as they probed with caution around the elbow of the cape.

"Captain, ahead there. I see a patch of lighter green in the water and a few small breakers. I'd bet the bottom has shoaled up since we last passed through."

The captain shook his head. "Just the sunlight on the water, more than likely, Mr. Gunn. Steady as she goes. We can't shilly-shally getting through here."

"Over there, sir." Gunn stood next to him and aimed his outstretched, open hand. "A point off the starboard bow. There."

The captain raised his binoculars to his eyes. He nodded. "Well, by gum, steer clear of it, then, just to be safe." The warmth of his voice, if not the words, conveyed approval.

The morning progressed, and the ship traversed safely into Nantucket Sound, settling on a steady course and returning to her normal routine. Even before breakfast, the crew started the daily chores of swabbing the decks, cleaning the brightwork, inspecting and repairing sails and rigging, tarring the shrouds, or painting and repainting anything stationary.

Burns fell asleep on deck, lying on his side, knees to his chest, his blanket clutched around him. He seemed content to stay there rather than returning to the dingy hold. He stirred to the surrounding noises of ship's routine. The new watch was put to holystoning the deck, a typical Saturday morning chore, and they worked around him as best they could.

Even as he finished his watch, Gunn racked his brain to think of a more humane solution to the safety and security of their human cargo. The main hold was not large, measuring only about twenty-five feet long and twenty-two feet at the widest point. The only good alternative was to rearrange some of the crowded cargo to create a separate space for Burns—a kind of brig, for lack of a better term, fashioned out of some of the heavier ship's stores. Burns would be quartered inside and constantly guarded from the adjoining space. That way, he could remain unshackled and have the freedom at least to stand and lie down.

Maybe he should never have opened his mouth. After all, what difference would it make, when all was said and done, whether Burns received temporary comfort? Had he acted on principle in the best interest of Burns, or was he trying to assuage his own conscience? Hawthorne had once told him something about a man's true resolve being evident only in the moment of execution. Hawthorne had written the quote on the flyleaf of a book that he'd given to him. He'd have to read it again later to remind himself.

Seven bells, time again for the change of watch. Lieutenant Richmond came topside, preparing for the relief by touring the weather deck, inspecting the sails and rigging with a critical eye, as though expecting to find something amiss. He stopped, folding his hands behind his back, when he came to the bundled form of Burns, still lying on the deck, nestled against one of the ship's guns. Richmond tweaked his long mustache and continued his inspection.

Nelson ambled aft to the quarterdeck and saluted.

"Good morning, Mr. Gunn. And a fine one it is."

"It's a much better one, now that we're through the Rip."

Nelson grinned. "And you say I worry too much."

"I'm supposed to worry about this ship not ending up on the bottom, one of those dead boats, as you call them."

"That's one thing I never worry about with you on watch, sir."

Richmond walked up behind Nelson. "Don't you have duties to attend to, bos'n?"

"As a matter of fact, I do, Mr. Richmond."

"Well, then, quit your lollygagging and turn to."

"Aye, aye, sir." Nelson saluted and made his way forward.

"Mr. Gunn, what is the reason for that filth on the forward deck?"

"Filth, sir?"

Richmond referred with his chin to Burns' blanketed hulk. "That heap of steaming mule dung. Why is it still there?"

"I don't see any such thing, Mr. Richmond. Perhaps you're mistaken."

Richmond spat on the deck. "Look again."

"Burns was too sick to move this morning, so we left him there to get some rest, if that's what you mean. As soon as he wakes up, we'll take him below."

"Well, get him moved. He's in the way and likely to get hurt where he is. I don't want that on my hands."

"Of course. I will take care of it as soon as you relieve me."

"*Sir.*" Richmond fussed with the cap on his head.

"As soon as you relieve me, sir."

"That's better. See to it. By the way, you ought to know that Colonel Suttle is beside himself this morning." A twisted smile formed beneath Richmond's mustache. "He is, ah, gunning for you, Mr. Gunn. I must say, I don't blame him one bit."

"Thanks for the warning ... sir."

"Don't thank me, you dimwit. I'm not warning you. Just stating fact. Now, where are we headed?"

"Generally west through the sound toward Martha's Vineyard." Gunn pointed to port, about two points off the bow. "That's Great Point Light on Nantucket—"

"I know perfectly well what that is, Gunn. I don't need you to tell me. You're not the only officer on this ship who can navigate."

"Of course, sir."

Richmond relieved him, ignoring his salute.

13

Prouty arrived on deck to gauge the weather and the ship's position. Gunn needed his approval before moving cargo around in the hold, especially at sea. Now that Prouty was up, Gunn could request permission out of the hearing of Suttle and Brent, avoiding confrontation. The captain had said not to antagonize them.

The first lieutenant stood at the starboard rail, eyeing the set of the sails. Gunn explained his idea for the brig. As expected, Prouty readily recognized the difficulty of the situation.

"Well, I doubt there is room in the hold to do what you suggest, Mr. Gunn. We took on extra stores before leaving Boston, due to the length of this trip. I suppose some of the items could be stowed on deck temporarily—some of the water, or the spare canvas, or maybe other gear that will not suffer from exposure." He rubbed his chin, clean shaven between long side whiskers. "Well, now, what about the shot locker? Have you thought of that? The bin has a lock on it."

Gunn was taken aback. "Sir, there is no room at all to stand or lie down in there. Besides, it's half-full of shot. Unless, you would propose storing that elsewhere."

"Just a thought. Well, there may be some room yet in the lazarette.

You could move some things back there. But take the advice of the Bos'n. If he thinks it can be managed safely, then you have my approval to do whatever can be done."

Gunn found Nelson on the foredeck, overseeing the rigging of a temporary jib boom. He explained what he had in mind, and the two of them went aft and climbed down into the hold to assess the possibilities. In the dim light, it took a moment for their eyes to adjust.

The deputies were still largely incapacitated from the effects of *mal de mer*. The smell of vomit, mixed with tar and hemp, lingered in the dank air. Butman seemed to be the only one not affected. As soon as the other two men entered the hold, he got up to leave without speaking. Gunn stopped him.

"Mr. Butman, we intend to move some of the cargo, if we can, to make a sort of brig down here in the hold. Our aim is to guard Burns without having to shackle him to the mast."

"You might as well do as you please, Gunn. What do any of us have to say about it? Just be sure to understand this. If anything happens to Burns, it will be on your head, not mine."

"I understand."

"Understand one more thing."

"What would that be?"

"If he gets loose, I'll shoot him. Simple as that. Suttle can send you the bill."

"I am sure such measures will not be necessary. Besides, the law might look rather unkindly on such a thing, don't you think?"

"Where we're going, my young friend, the law won't give a whit, as long as he don't get loose." Butman's short laugh was laden with scorn. "Same as shootin' a stray dog." He exited through the open hatch.

"Well, sir, at least he called you his friend," Nelson said. "That's an improvement, anyway."

"As my father used to say, 'A friend to all is a friend to none.'"

"Smart man, your dad. Did he make that up?"

"I doubt it. He was never so clever."

"Was? Is he gone?"

"All but forgotten. It's a long story. Let's get busy."

Beyond the perimeter of the small area housing Butman and his men, stores were stacked to the overhead beams on either side of a narrow aisle. At hand were casks of water and crates of rations. Further on, spare lumber, canvas, coils of rope of various diameters, and lengths of chain. On the other hand, several kegs of gunpowder, a locked bin containing shot for the guns, another containing a half ton of coal. In the sail bins, an entire spare set of sails, as well as tools, unused blocks and tackle, and other sundry items of chandlery. All lashed down with ropes and netting, secured for sea. Nelson shook his head.

"We can move some of the casks of water up on deck, and there is some room back aft in the lazarette, but I am not at all sure we can get you what you want, Mr. Gunn. We'll give it a try, though, sir."

"Well, Boats, if you can think of a better solution, I am all ears."

Nelson thought for a moment. "No, sir. She's a small ship. Not too many choices inside a hundred-and-ten feet, unless you count the wardroom. There's the cabin, of course."

"Be serious."

"Well, we can't put him in the fo'c'sle. No room up there. And the men would never stand for it, anyhow. You'd have a mutiny on your hands. I don't see no choice, other than trailing Burns behind us in the dinghy."

"You're still joking, right?"

"You asked, sir. Like I said, ain't a whole lot of options here. We'll make it work."

For the better part of an hour, a gang labored to shift the stores. It was like working a three-dimensional puzzle. Eventually, they managed to clear a space about five feet square against the starboard side, stacked high with crates and heavy equipment. They left a narrow entryway, which could be secured with a cargo net fastened over the opening.

The cramped cell had no bedding. Prouty had borrowed six mattresses from the Naval Yard at Charlestown to accommodate their passengers. One was for the prisoner, but it had gone missing, somehow. Their workaround was to use an old sail to serve as bedding. It was a squalid residence, but at least Burns would no longer be chained to the base of the mast.

After satisfying himself that the plan would work, Gunn arrived back on deck to find Colonel Suttle querying Burns. Brent was not with him, most likely still confined to bed. With an air of indifference, Suttle leaned on his cane, while keeping a firm grip on the ship's rail.

"What is the trouble, Tony? Are you ill?" A weary physician might have inquired the same way about a known hypochondriac.

"Just a little, Mas'r Charles." Burns glanced up, squinting into the morning sun.

"Well, I am sure it will soon pass. Once we get you back on solid ground in Virginia, boy, you'll be right as rain again."

Burns lurched toward the bucket at his side and retched into it.

"There, there, Tony. Try to think of pleasant things ... things to remind you of home, perhaps ... ah, like your favorite, dumplings and greasy fried chicken."

Again, Burns reached for the bucket of swill.

"Colonel Suttle, perhaps it would be better not to ... antagonize," Gunn interjected.

"Antagonize? No, sir. Not I. Certainly not. Far be it from me to antagonize anyone. Besides, how is it anybody, man or beast, could possibly be antagonized by someone who has only the best of intentions? It simply is not possible. Isn't that so, *Mister* Burns?"

"Nossir. I ... I mean, yessir, Mas'r Charles."

"No, sir. Of course, he cannot be antagonized. Certainly not by someone who has shown so many kindnesses over the years.

Wouldn't you say, Tony? Far more so, I daresay, than any kindnesses a stranger might ever hope to provide on such a *fugitive* basis." Suttle eyed Gunn with a raised eyebrow. "So, now, Mr. Gunn. What do you propose? I expect you to provide the finest of accommodations for our friend, here, since you have taken such a generous interest in his well-being and have so little time in which to show it."

"We have made arrangements for him, colonel," said Gunn.

"A fine feather bed, I suppose? In the best part of the ship? Plenty of good light and fresh air?" He stretched the last word to a second syllable.

Gunn held his tongue, in deference to the captain's admonition.

"Well, then. I am certain you will do the best you possibly can for him, Mr. Gunn. It is all in your hands, after all. Tony, you be sure to thank Mr. Gunn for his kindness and hospitality to you, now, you hear?"

"Yessir, Mas'r Charles."

"Of course, you will." Suttle tipped his hat. "Please excuse me, won't you? We will soon have a chance to catch up, Tony. You must be sure to tell me all about your recent travels. *Gentlemen.*" He nodded his head, then turned about and walked away slowly and deliberately, tapping his cane. "Now, I must go and pay my respects to the captain," he called over his shoulder.

Gunn closed his eyes. Small, bright discs danced inside his eyelids, until he opened them again.

Nelson stood before him. "Mr. Gunn, the brig is ready."

"Tony, as soon as you are able to stand, we must get you back down below decks."

"Yessir, Mas'r Gunn."

"Don't call me 'master.' You may call me Mister Gunn, or lieutenant. I am not your master." Burns' shirt fell from the rigging above and draped over his shoulder, its sleeves spread in a kind of empty embrace. Gunn picked it up. "Your clothing is still wet, except for your shirt, which is only a little damp. But I'm afraid the salt water will keep the dampness until it can be cleaned properly. You may put it back on, if you like." He held the shirt out for Burns to take.

Burns looked down at the too-tight borrowed shirt, clinging to his chest. "Yessir. I should not keep what is only borrowed."

"Tony, you needn't worry. The one you're wearing came from the lucky bag. It doesn't have an owner."

Burns gave a waxen smile. "I guess it'd be free, then."

14

Since Thursday evening, Gunn hadn't sat at a table to eat without being rushed. He was hungry. Earlier, he'd snatched a few strips of cold bacon sandwiched between the halves of a biscuit from the galley for breakfast. Cookie had grumbled, of course, though he allowed the petty theft, but he wouldn't grant leniency twice in one day.

Even so, Gunn debated going to the table for the noon meal, likely an uncomfortable setting, given Colonel Suttle's presence. Hunger won out, so he climbed down the ladder into the wardroom, removed his cap and hung it on a hook.

Prompt, as usual, Prouty stood at his customary seat as the president of the wardroom mess, facing forward at the table's head. He waited for the others to join him. Suttle waited with him.

"Won't the captain be joining us?" asked Suttle.

"It's customary for the captain to dine alone in the cabin, unless he invites others to join him."

"I see," Suttle said.

"Sir, may I join you at table?" asked Gunn.

"Very well," responded Prouty. "I was hoping you would join us, Mr. Gunn. Breakfast was a bit lonely this morning, with everyone so ill-disposed."

"It's true," agreed Suttle. "This is the first that I've felt like eating anything since we departed."

They waited, expecting Miller to join them, but the ship's bell rang out seven times, so Prouty ordered, "Seats, gentlemen."

As soon as they sat, Miller slid down the ladder.

"I am sorry to be late, sir. Nature called. May I join you?" asked Miller, breathless, as he swiped the cap from his head and hung it next to his stateroom.

Prouty peered at him over the steaming bowl of beef stew that Dwyer, the wardroom mess steward, had placed in front of him. He nodded his head, and Miller sat down opposite Gunn.

Asa Butman tramped down the ladder.

"My men are still puking their guts out. Mind if I eat with you?"

Prouty regarded him for a moment, as though trying to think of anything he might say to dissuade the man.

"By all means, Mr. Butman. Dwyer will set another place for you."

Butman pulled out the chair at the foot of the table and sat, tossing his hat on the table at his elbow. Dwyer placed a dish in front of him. Prouty stared at the hat, not moving until Butman got up to hang it on a hook.

Prouty passed a basket of cornbread to Suttle, and the meal began.

"We had quite a wild ride last night," remarked Suttle.

Butman snorted. "You don't know the half of it, colonel."

"I do apologize for the rude awakening, colonel," said Miller. "Were you injured? I certainly hope not."

"No, Mr. Miller. No injury to speak of, other than to have shattered any romantic notions I ever held about traveling by ship." He sipped his tea and then smiled. "I must say, I find it hard to imagine how two ships can so readily find each other, purely by chance, surrounded by so much water."

"It does happen from time to time," said Prouty. "More often than you might think."

"That so? Do tell."

"Especially in the shipping lanes. Most ships take roughly the same track to get from port to port in the least amount of distance and time," said Prouty. "Time is money, as Mr. Franklin advises."

"Why, I suppose it only makes sense, doesn't it?" Suttle took another spoonful of stew and wiped his goatee with a napkin. "Still, don't you think it odd, quite astonishing, really, that a ship should come out of nowhere, hit us, and not even bother to stop and try to make contact or seek to make amends? Someone could have been seriously hurt or killed. Why, one or both ships could have sunk to the bottom. Isn't that so?"

Gunn searched Prouty's face, looking for a hint of agreement.

"I hardly think either ship was in danger of sinking, colonel," said Prouty. "But I do agree the prudent thing would have been to stop to assess the damage and offer assistance."

"Well, of course," said Miller.

"So, are we agreed it seems odd?" asked Suttle.

"Well, I'm not sure what you are getting at, colonel. Are you suggesting something nefarious? That the collision might have been intentional, perhaps? Hardly likely."

"Seemed pretty obvious to me," said Butman.

Gunn put down his spoon, less interested in the stew. "Well, sir, such things have been known to happen," he said.

"Precisely, Mr. Gunn. Let us put it to someone impartial, here." Suttle turned to Seaman Dwyer and grabbed him by the arm. "Boy, what do you think? Speak up. Tell us whether you think somebody might have wanted to do us harm last night."

Denis Dwyer stopped in his tracks. A boy of only fifteen, he was the second youngest member of the crew and had been aboard less than six weeks. He had drawn the unenviable tasks that came with serving the officers their food and keeping the wardroom clean and orderly. Offering opinions was not usually among his duties.

"Well, sir. I don't know. S-some of the crew say it was a …"

"A what, Dwyer?" asked Prouty. "Speak up."

"A ghost ship, sir."

Suttle guffawed, and the rest joined in, Dwyer last of all.

"A ghost ship. How perfect. What a truly romantic notion, to be sure." The colonel peered over his shoulder at Gunn with a sly smile plying the corners of his mouth. "And, what do you say, Mr. Gunn? Surely you have an opinion on this matter. You have an opinion about so many things, it would seem."

"Well, colonel, I must admit, it has occurred to me that maybe what happened to us last night was no accident." He voiced the thought lurking in the corners of his mind, ever since the collision. Something about it continued to bother him. Until now, he had been reluctant to say anything.

"Are you serious, Andrew?" A glimmer of redemptive hope flashed in Miller's eyes.

"There. You see?" exclaimed Suttle. "My thoughts exactly."

"Pure fancy, Mr. Gunn," said Prouty. "Not unlike Dwyer's ghost ship."

"Perhaps, sir." Gunn hated the fact that he and Suttle found themselves on the same side of an argument. With such an ally, maybe he should abandon the field. "But with all due respect, Mr. Prouty, I will never forget the anger in the eyes of those people in the city yesterday. You would have thought we were an invading army. Some of them were thirsty for blood, which is no exaggeration and no mere fancy."

"Aw, it wadn't so bad," said Butman. "I seen worse."

Gunn described what he had seen during the march down State Street, omitting the incident with Butman.

"Even so, who would be foolish enough to attempt such a thing?" asked Miller.

"They do not necessarily have to be fools, Sam. There are plenty of men out there who hearken back to the days of privateers and still think of themselves that way. They keep their knives sharpened. I've met some of them on my uncle's ships. I would bet you've met some, too."

"The days of privateers are gone, Mr. Gunn." Prouty's main argument was a dismissive wave of his hand. "You've been reading too many novels. America today is not the America of fifty years ago. We are a nation of laws. No one is above the law, which is the whole point of our creed as Americans. By the way, that's the whole point of this trip, is it not?"

Miller interrupted. "Sir, with your permission, may I be excused? I'd like to stay and listen to the end of this, but I must go relieve the watch."

"By all means, Mr. Miller," replied Prouty. "Watch out for privateers. And ghost ships," he laughed. "In all sincerity, be sure to speak with the captain before you relieve the watch. He has some words of wisdom for you, after last night."

"Aye, sir," said Miller, crestfallen.

"Be of good cheer, Mr. Miller. Get back on the horse that tossed you."

"Aye, sir." Miller recovered his cap and left.

"Gentlemen, I hear what you are saying," Prouty continued. "But let's not succumb to flights of fancy. There are any number of explanations for what occurred last night. Ships collide. Accidents happen. People panic and run."

"Certainly true, sir," agreed Gunn. A wise man would concede the board. Gunn checked his watch. "With your permission, Mr. Prouty, if I may be excused, I have some duties to attend."

"Aw, now, it was just gettin' interesting, Gunn," said Butman.

"Certainly, Mr. Gunn." Prouty glanced at his own pocket watch. "Duty calls."

Gunn rose from his place and nodded to Suttle. "Colonel," he acknowledged.

"A pleasure, sir, I'm sure," came the syrupy reply.

Gunn turned to go.

"Oh, by the way, Mr. Gunn. I almost forgot," Prouty called after him. "Tomorrow is Sunday, and the captain has invited you and the colonel to dine in the cabin for supper. Weather and operations permitting. Mr. Brent, as well, if he is up to it."

"Thank you, sir," said Gunn. "It would be an honor."

"An honor, indeed," agreed Suttle. "What do you say, Brent? Are you awake?"

"I suppose so," said Brent, his answer muffled by the stateroom curtain.

"If Brent don't feel good, I'll go." said Butman. "I clean up pretty good, ya know."

"Another time, perhaps," said Prouty.

"We shall look forward to it, sir," said Suttle. Perhaps we will find another point of agreement, Mr. Gunn. We may have much in common."

"Nothing would give me more pleasure, sir," said Gunn, as politely as he could muster. It was a lie, of course, and far worse in his mind than the one he had told Brett earlier.

15

From the shelf above his bunk, Gunn retrieved two items to read, a book and a letter. He grabbed his leather-visored cloth cap and headed for the ladder. At that moment, Richmond appeared in the companionway and started down the ladder. Gunn stood aside, allowing the second lieutenant to step down into the wardroom. They each nodded a greeting. Gunn climbed to the main deck and was soon in the open air.

A little privacy and quiet would help to clear his head. Those two luxuries were hard to come by on this ship. There was one place he enjoyed more than any other. As with most other activities on the cutter, getting there required the permission of the watch officer, which might have been a problem, had Richmond still been on watch.

The captain was not on deck, most likely still enjoying his own lunch. Gunn found Sam Miller in the cockpit, giving an order to the helmsman.

"Sam, I'd like to go aloft on the foremast."

"Fine, Andrew. Let me know when you come down, if you would. And you'll need to stay clear of the repair work."

He made his way to the foremast shrouds on the port side. Tucking the letter inside the book, and the book into the belt of his trousers, he leapt up onto the rail, and into the forechains. His ankle still hurt as he climbed, but he ignored it. At least his neck was starting to feel better.

He stepped nimbly up the ratlines like a spider on its web, until he reached the futtock shrouds. Then, swinging underneath, he climbed to the foretop and pulled himself onto the narrow platform. He wedged into a comfortable place, letting his legs dangle over what remained of the foreyard gear. His precarious perch hung about eighty feet above the main deck and another ten from the water. With the ship heeling in the wind, he sat directly over the water rushing beneath him.

From this vantage point, he could survey the entire world around him. In the distance to his right were the low, rolling hills of Cape Cod. Ahead on the left, the bluffs of Martha's Vineyard rose out of the cobalt water to meet a quicksilver sky.

The only sound was the wind rushing over his ears, making him feel as though he were one of the shearwaters flying nearby. He could have watched them for hours, freewheeling in the open sky on their long, black-tipped wings, yet always with a purpose, the way life ought to be.

One of the sea birds suddenly dove straight down, veering upward just before hitting the water. Hovering for an instant above the surface, the bird uttered a low, mewling cry, and then flew back into the sky. It made several curious passes, similar to the first one, before it became obvious what was going on. Just below the surface, a lifeless black-and-white form lolled in the waves, probably a hapless mate, too daring for its own good.

The scene was almost mesmerizing. Gunn shook his head. His lack of sleep had made him drowsy. He reminded himself to take extra care.

"One hand for the ship, and one for the sailor," he muttered.

He took the well-worn book from beneath his belt, a volume of Hawthorne's *Twice Told Tales*, which the author had given him when he joined the service, nearly two years earlier. He shielded the book from the wind with his body and opened it to the flyleaf. There was the written inscription, in the author's own lazy, graceful scrawl. It rang as true to him as the ship's bell:

In truth, there is no such thing in man's nature as a settled and full resolve, either for good or evil, except at the very moment of execution.
—Best intentions, N. Hawthorne.

He had it in mind to relax with one of his favorite stories from the book, but first he took out the letter tucked inside, which he'd already read many times. The paper on which it was written had become so frail that it might shred to pieces in the wind. No matter, since he could easily recall what Elizabeth had written, nearly word for word.

My dearest Andrew—

Kindly forgive my rather poor representation of one of God's most beautiful creations, included herein, but my hope is that you will accept it as a token of my lasting affection.

As for our latest conversation, perhaps it will serve us both well to keep ever mindful of a simple truth: what grows wild and freely still grows best under careful husbandry. We must all seek our Heavenly Father's best for ourselves, and submit to His will for our lives, though His careful pruning seems painful or harsh.

It is good for love to flourish, like a favorite flower, with nurture and care, rather than growing wild and free. I think we agree on that point. Though it remains unspoken between us, I've seen the question lingering in your eyes, just as it does in my own heart. But as for my present situation, the fullness of time has yet to come, for several reasons, which doubtless you know. I think it would be a mistake to hasten it. Though you may disagree, there it is.

Yet, even as I write this, I must confess—the truth, which now flows from my pen—that my love for you, Andrew, grows without bounds each day, from when I rise to when I sleep, and even in my dreams. No gated garden wall will long keep it.

With deepest affection,
Elizabeth

He placed the letter back inside the protective pages of the book and closed his eyes, hoping that she still felt the same way.

***

The sense of free-falling startled him. He awoke to find himself still sitting in the foretop, wedged into the remnants of the rigging. Bolting upright, he searched furtively about, relieved to be safe and sound.

His gaze settled on his empty hands. The book and the letter were gone, nowhere in sight. Apparently, he had dropped them as he dozed, most likely to the water below.

He spun around, straining his upper body. A single sheet of white paper bobbed for a moment in the wake of the cutter. Then, nothing remained but empty, troubled water, and the pangs of loss deep in his gut.

16

For a sailor, it's not hard to believe that the forces of nature patiently conspire at length against him, keen on his eventual demise. Until recently, Gunn had rejected such notions as superstition. Then again, his own amulet-watch had proven unreliable lately, hadn't it? He would get it fixed as soon as possible upon their return to Boston.

By five o'clock that evening, the *Morris* sailed past West Chop lighthouse on the northernmost point of Martha's Vineyard. She was leaving her usual patrol area, sailing into new territory. The Elizabeth Islands stretched out ahead, pointing the way toward Long Island, New York. Soon after, the wind diminished to a light breeze, and the cutter's progress through the water slowed to a crawl as she worked her way through Vineyard Sound against wind and current. It was proving to be a long, tiresome transit south.

After Gunn's next watch, he went down to the makeshift brig to check on Burns. He found Cookie attending to the prisoner, trying to get him to take some liquids.

"How are you feeling, Anthony?"

"Better, Mistah Gunn, better, thank you. But I just don't think I can keep anything down."

"Well, you should quit acting like a orn'ry old mule. Go ahead, drink something," said Cookie. "Otherwise, we goin' to have us a burial at sea. Now, drink this down."

"Better listen to him, Anthony. He's the closest we've got to a sawbones. He hasn't lost a patient yet, which is more than most doctors can claim."

"I want to thank you, Mistah Gunn, for your concern."

"No need to thank me. I consider it my duty."

"Duty or not, I tell you, other than my friends and my church people, nobody has cared a whit for me since this whole mess began, excepting you and Cookie." He thrust his chin at the air. "The lawyers, they just wanted to make a name for their selves." He pointed at the door. "And those fellas out there only give me those new clothes to have fun with me."

"We cleaned them up best we could."

"No, sir. I emptied my bowels more than once in the britches. I mean to tell you, it was messy, too. They ruined, you know, and I'm glad of it. Thank you, though."

Instead of water, Cookie provided his own concoction of peppermint and ginger tea. Burns turned up his nose, but eventually began to sip it, holding the tin cup languidly in both hands.

"That's good."

"Course it is," said Cookie. His coaxing finally convinced Burns to nibble on some hardtack. But he soon pushed it away.

"I'll leave it here, case you get hungry later."

"Much obliged, Cookie. I am feeling better."

"Maybe some fresh air would do you some good," said Gunn.

"Yes, sir. I think it just might."

Gunn exited the cell.

"Mr. Butman, see that he gets topside to get some fresh air."

"Whatever you say, *massah*," sneered Butman.

As soon as twilight fell, Gunn went to his stateroom, intending to get some sleep. It had been another bad day. Not long after he had undressed and stretched full length on his bunk, Miller pulled back the curtain and vaulted into the upper bunk, clothes and all, not bothering to undress. His boots tumbled to the deck. Few words passed between them as Gunn pulled the curtain closed again and lay back upon his pillow, staring into the darkness of their tiny stateroom.

A short while later, Miller spoke in a low voice. "She came out of nowhere. No lights. Not a one."

"What's that?"

"The ghost ship. I saw her once in the distance, headed straight for us, and she was gone. Then the fog rolled in, all of a sudden like. Couldn't see a thing."

"It does that around the cape."

"Andrew, do you truly think the collision might have been intentional?"

"I don't know what to think for certain, Sam. It seems possible, at least to me. People do crazy things, especially when their blood is up. These days, there are riots in the streets at the drop of a hat, it seems. People upset over all kinds of things, not just slavery. Whiskey. Religion. Women's rights. Immigration. Name it, they're willing to shed blood for it. Do you remember hearing about that riot in Manhattan a couple years back over which actor could do the best Shakespeare? It left thirty people dead and four times that injured. Sometimes, I think the whole world is going mad, like it's spinning off its axis. But here we are. So, yeah, I guess I do think it could have been intentional."

"I feel like I'm going mad just thinking about it."

"Don't let it get inside your skull, Sam."

"Easier said, than done. The captain won't forget about it, I'm sure."

"Just try to let go."

"Said the thistle to the dog's ear." Miller was quiet after that. Weariness apparently overcame him, despite his worry. Gunn heard him turn over once, then nothing but a light snore.

His friend's last comment kept him wide awake for a while longer, however. It took him back to a warm afternoon in late summer of the year before, sitting with Elizabeth Faulkner in the stone-walled garden at her home in West Roxbury.

She'd been talking about gardening, which was something she loved to do, sharing a bit of knowledge about each of her favorite plants, especially the roses. Finally, she pointed with special attention to a Scottish thistle, of all things, touching the purple blossom tenderly with her slender hand, careful to avoid pricking her fingers on the gray-green nettled leaves and thorns surrounding it.

"Most people think these are noxious weeds," she'd said, lightly laughing. "My father loves them. He brought the seeds over from Scotland in his pocket and grows them here to remind him of home. They have all sorts of medicinal qualities, you know. And I even use the oil from them mixed with lavender in my hair."

"It's quite lovely," he said. Her shining hair fell in a lithe cascade over her shoulders, highlighted by the afternoon sunshine. "The thistle, I mean. If you like weeds in your garden, that is."

She smiled. "My father claims thistles grow where the soil is best."

"Thistles grow where they will, don't they?" A careless observation, regretted at once.

"That may be so, Mr. Gunn." She turned to face him, her eyes narrowing. "Yet, I can assure you, if it were against my father's will, they would not dare."

He was about to apologize for his offhand remark. Then her eyes teased and smiled again.

"*Wha daur meddle wi' me,*" he replied, mimicking the ditty learned at his grandfather Gunn's knee, long ago. He returned her smile.

"Oh, so you speak the Gaelic? Wait 'til I tell father. He'll talk your ear off."

"No, no. It's just something I picked up. Something my grandfather used to say."

"So, he was someone not to be trifled with?"

"He was a fairly gruff old sea captain. So, yes."

"And he taught you. Are you a man not to be trifled with, then?"

"Only by a pretty woman with long chestnut hair and brown eyes."

"P-sssh." She laughed as though he had claimed the world was flat.

"If I asked you a question that I've pondered awhile, would you dare trifle with me?"

She had answered with a smile and a finger to her lips.

Elizabeth had turned nineteen that day. Like the other occasions when they had been together, it had been in the watchful presence of her parents and her younger brother, Robert. On every occasion, just the sight of her made him catch his breath, even from the first time they met.

It occurred at a time in his life when, after so many years of tragedy, good things finally had begun happening to him—all at once, it seemed. They had met at church, her father's small congregation in Boston, where Gunn had started attending not long after his assignment to the ship. Prouty occasionally attended there and suggested it to him, mainly because it was so close to the waterfront. Not to mention, the preacher's daughter was a sight to behold.

Gunn enjoyed Reverend Faulkner's preaching, staid as it was, because it seemed based on something far more solid and meaty than anything his own father had fed him. He would seek opportunities to visit the Faulkner home to ask questions about the sermons, hoping for invitations on Sunday afternoons, whenever the ship was in port. The Faulkners were a welcoming, open, loving family and had readily accepted him, especially for that purpose.

Elizabeth had warmed quickly to him, often asking to sit with him in the study as Gunn sought her father's wisdom about many things. Soon, the Sunday visits were meant as much to see and spend time with her as to seek answers to his questions. Maybe that was true all along. At other times, he contrived to see her by offering to take her younger brother Robert fishing or hunting around Jamaica Pond, or some other ostensible activity, whenever he had the time.

Over time, the frequency and length of visits increased. He and Elizabeth shared long, thoughtful conversations on wide-ranging topics—whatever came to mind—whenever they had the chance, walking in the small walled garden of the parsonage, sitting on the porch, or playing chess by the hour in the front parlor.

Likewise, Reverend Faulkner's natural concern about their obvious attraction grew more evidently into consternation, as he maintained a father's vigilance over them. He made it quite apparent that he didn't approve, though never voiced his reasons. On occasion, Mrs. Faulkner would distract her husband, calling him away to help her with one chore or another. Though sometimes abbreviated by his distant harrumphs, or his regular orbits through the parlor indicating the late hour, their conversations seemed to flow together unimpeded into a continuous, powerful stream of shared thought and feeling.

They had never had the opportunity to be alone completely. But she had seemed content to leave it that way for the time being, given their circumstances. As affectionate as they had become toward each other, she'd made it quite clear from the beginning that she had no thoughts of marriage before she finished her studies to become a teacher, which was her primary preoccupation. It was the only thing they had ever quarreled about. She hadn't given in. Nevertheless, he hoped someday to change her mind.

Last Christmas, Elizabeth returned a book Gunn had lent her, and inside the leaves of the book were tucked the letter and a small watercolor of a purple-blossomed thistle, to which the letter had referred. The lines of the watercolor were simple and amateurish, but the colors perfectly matched the living flower he had seen in her garden.

The letter and the book were gone, lost forever.

The small watercolor, faded now, and curled at the edges, was pinned securely to the bulkhead above his head, the outlines of it barely visible in the night. At least that remained.

Lying on his back, bound by darkness, Gunn recalled the words of the lost letter, every word seeded in his memory. If he tried, he could even hear Elizabeth's voice reciting it to him. He turned to his side and tried to drift off to sleep.

Recent events had deepened his resolve to marry her, maybe because he had so carelessly lost two of his greatest temporal treasures. He was determined not to lose any more, if he could help it, despite any outside forces that might conspire against him.

One thought kept sleep from him, however. It troubled his mind more now than when it had first come to him—the vivid image of Elizabeth sobbing in bitter disappointment on his sister's shoulder. Her grief was a force of nature against which no mere amulet could provide any remedy.

And time, he knew, would only make things worse.

17

Four strokes on the ship's bell rang out. Prouty called the crew to attention in their best at-sea uniforms. From the relative height of the quarterdeck, the captain read aloud from the worn, leather-bound book known as the Cuttermen's Bible, as he did every Sunday after divine services.

In his baritone voice, made loud by many years of shouting over wind and waves, Whitcomb intoned the Regulations of the U. S. Revenue Cutter Service, one by one, chapter and verse. For the sake of good order and discipline, this ritual reminded each of them, captain, officers and crew, of their respective duties to the nation, to the service, and to each other.

Afterwards, Gunn returned to his stateroom and changed his uniform to prepare for watch. Then, he went to check on Burns.

Butman lounged at the rail on the port side near the main hatch, his favored spot, chewing a wad of tobacco tucked in his cheek. Two of his men stood nearby. They looked better than they had the last time Gunn had seen them. The three chatted among themselves but stopped abruptly as Gunn approached.

"Morning, gents."

"That it is, Mr. Gunn," said Butman.

"How is Burns, this morning?"

"He seems well enough. I'll tell him you were asking for him." He spat over the side.

"Has he eaten anything yet today?"

"Some. Not much. Seems more interested in singing than eating."

"Singing? What's he singing?"

"How should I know? Spiritual songs, or some such. Sits there just singin' and rockin', over and over like a lunatic. We couldn't take it no more. Had to come up on deck just to keep from going insane ourselves."

"Or worse, getting saved," said Riley, one of the deputies.

"Same difference," said Butman. The men laughed.

Gunn could hear a faint tenor voice singing through the half-open hatch. "Well, why don't you bring him up here to enjoy some of this fine weather."

"Yassah, if you say so, Mr. Gunn."

"Yes, well. I do say so, Mr. Butman. Why do I have to keep telling you so?"

Butman spat again without taking his eyes off Gunn's face. "You hear that, boys? Why ain't you takin' better care of the prisoner? Now, go on and bring him up here. At least maybe he'll quit his awful caterwaulin'."

Gunn went aft to relieve Miller for the next watch. The cutter had sailed well into Block Island Sound to a position about four miles southwest of Watch Hill, Rhode Island, approaching the low, rocky coastline of Fisher's Island. Rather than following a direct route over the open sea, the captain gave orders to stay in more protected waters along the coast for the sake of the guests onboard, some of whom were still feeling seasick.

After Gunn relieved the watch, Whitcomb ordered him to turn south, holding the southwest wind broad on the starboard bow. Then he went below to his cabin. Gunn made a course by the wind to reach for Montauk Light on the northern tip of Long Island and sailed on.

A short while later, Butman and his men brought Burns topsides. The prisoner turned his scarred face upwards to the sun, sampling draughts of ocean air through flared nostrils. He started humming a gospel tune.

His new suit of clothes, still hanging in the shrouds, was as dry now as they'd get in the moist sea air. The frock coat, its sleeves tied to the shrouds, alive with wind, billowed like the effigy of a desperate man clinging to a lifeline. The deputies took everything down and piled them in a heap at Burns' feet.

"Well, Tony, looks like your duds is as dry as they're gonna get," said Butman. "It's a crying shame they've gone to ruin. Strip down and put 'em back on. The boys and me paid good money to dress you right."

Burns stood stock still.

"Go on, now. Put 'em on. Don't you want to dress proper?"

"No, sir. I will not. I'll keep the ones I got, thank you."

"You'll do as you're told, boy."

"They ain't mine, sir. I will not."

Butman raised his hand. "I'll learn you not to smart-mouth me, you dirty ni—"

"Butman!" yelled Gunn. He walked forward a few paces on the quarterdeck. "You'll do nothing of the kind. He can keep those clothes, if he wants to."

The big deputy whipped around and glared at him.

"Why don't you just go mind your own damned business for a change, Gunn?"

"Hold on, there. Leave him be, Mr. Butman." Colonel Suttle emerged from the wardroom companionway. He approached the knot of men surrounding Burns near the foredeck.

Gunn reached into the cockpit for the spyglass and sidled as far forward as possible along the windward side, straining to hear Suttle. The captain had gone below for his noon meal, making the whole quarterdeck available to him. He raised the spyglass to his eye, feigning a search for landmarks in the distance off the starboard bow.

The conclave up forward parted as Suttle arrived among them. The motion of the ship made Burns unsteady on his feet, and he sat down hard on the foredeck, nearly falling over onto his side. He struggled to get back to his feet.

"Sit down, Tony. Sit down. Good lord. You needn't get up for my sake." Suttle's words came broken in the breeze.

"Good afternoon, Mas'r Charles," Burns said, peering furtively up into Suttle's face, shielding his eyes.

"Why, good afternoon, Tony. How are we feeling this fine day? Better?"

"I don't rightly know how to feel, Mas'r Charles. Can I ask you something?

"Of course."

"What's to become of all this?

"Whatever do you mean, Tony?"

"I mean, what will you do with me now, Mas'r Charles?"

"Well, we might as well get right to the point. No small talk for us, eh, as old friends? I honestly haven't given it much thought. What do you think I *ought* to do, Tony?"

"I don't know, sir. I 'spect you might sell me away."

"Well, now, Tony, it might prove hard to sell you, at that. We have grown so fond of each other, haven't we? Besides, you have cost me a great expense for this grand adventure of yours. Why, I'm afraid lawyer's fees alone will be well over two hundred dollars. I'm not certain I could recover the cost by selling you, even though the good people of Boston offered a princely sum for your freedom. I won't say how much, because it might fill your head with vain notions and make you even more uppity than you are. Now, then, a man concerned with such matters would want to recover costs and turn a handsome profit, naturally. But we are friends, after all, and I would likely find that a difficult proposition. Unless, of course, I sold you down south. Now, *there's* a thought."

"Land ho!" The lookout on the starboard bow pointed and shouted, so Gunn could not make out Burns' reply, but the fear in his voice was plain. The wind shifted, slightly, which caused some of the words to escape on the freshening breeze.

"—you tell me what ship it was—to Boston—go better with you, Tony," Suttle was saying. The wind caught snatches of his words.

"—just couldn' say, Mas'r Charles." Burns slowly shook his head, as though trying to recall something.

"Couldn't or wouldn't Tony? Tell me now, and I—"

Tony again shook his head.

"— about the captain? —know his name?"

"I surely do not know, Mas'r Charles."

"And I simply do not believe you, Tony," said Suttle, the disdain rising in his voice.

The conversation continued out of Gunn's earshot, due to the wind shift. He ordered the helmsman to adjust his heading. Then, he peered through the spyglass in the direction the lookout had pointed. There was the low, moraine shoreline at the northeastern tip of Long Island, and the lighthouse sitting alone atop the spit of land, exposed to all the forces of nature, on its base of rock and sand.

"A stench in God's nostrils," Gunn muttered to himself.

The phrase sprang to his mind with stark prominence, as though it had suddenly appeared in plain view, like the vivid image of the black-and-white stone beacon now standing before him, magnified several times through the lens of the spyglass. It was a phrase he'd heard Elizabeth's father use the last time they were together.

The previous Thursday night, along with her parents, he and Elizabeth had attended the anti-slavery meeting of the Boston Vigilance Committee. Both her parents were ardent abolitionists, as she was. While he understood their sentiments, Gunn thought forcing the issue of outright abolition might bring on a terrible war between North and South, which should be avoided at all costs. But as crazy as things were getting, maybe that result was inevitable.

What he remembered most about that night was that Elizabeth, with her upswept hair and dark eyes, had looked especially beautiful in blue satin, her finest dress. He didn't remember much else, other than the mood of the crowd, which was incensed. Passion was always dangerous and destructive, especially that kind, at least in his mind. As the meeting ended, he'd heard Reverend Faulkner utter those very words. "Human slavery is a stench in God's nostrils and always will be."

The meeting had ended unexpectedly in the melee outside Faneuil Hall. The crazed mob, excited by Reverend Parker's fiery speech, rushed through the dark streets toward the courthouse. Gunn had helped shield Elizabeth as they were swept along in the swift current. Both Reverend Faulkner and his wife saw what he had done to protect her and expressed their gratitude, acknowledging his act of courage and kindness, as they escorted her to the safety of a carriage.

He thought about the events of that night, running them over in his mind as the watch continued. Somehow, his fortunes increasingly seemed to be bound up and entangled in this present turmoil, well beyond his control. His relationship with Elizabeth had been swept up in it, just as they had been swept away by the crazed mob.

The outcome that night could have been worse, of course, and no doubt his standing had improved in the eyes of Elizabeth's father as a result. It was one thing to behave as a gallant defender, but quite another to be taken seriously as a substantial provider for a future wife and family on third-lieutenant's pay. He had hoped a promotion in rank might further improve his status as a suitor. Of course, Second Lieutenant William Richmond crushed that hope when he had arrived onboard the *Morris* earlier that spring. To make matters worse, Richmond seemed to have it out for him, and the situation with Burns added fuel to the fire, although he was at a loss as to the reason.

As though summoned by the Devil himself, Richmond came rising out of the companionway from the wardroom below, walking the deck to inspect the sails. The watch had passed quickly for Gunn, and it was time for his relief.

The ship stood along the coast, making about five knots. The weather remained clear and pleasant, the late afternoon sun warming Gunn's shoulders. A light breeze blew out of the south-southwest. As the ship's bell struck seven times, the captain emerged from the cabin. Richmond approached him to ask permission to relieve the watch. They exchanged salutes, and Whitcomb nodded toward the shoreline off the starboard beam, where East Hampton light kept prominent vigil.

"Mr. Richmond, make your heading west-by-south. Follow down the coastline in the direction of New York. Stay offshore about a mile, or so. Reduce sail enough to keep the ship on as much of an even keel as possible during the supper hour. Let's make it easy on Cookie for the evening meal."

"Aye, aye, sir."

Captain Whitcomb turned to address Gunn. "I'm looking forward to dining with you and the others this evening, Mr. Gunn. It should prove to be a very lively gathering."

"Aye, sir." He had almost forgotten the invitation to dine in the cabin. He still had enough time to freshen up and get his uniform in order. "I am honored to join you, sir."

Richmond's face turned the color of a man with a fishbone stuck in his throat. Gunn tried to ignore him, as though there were nothing extraordinary about a junior lieutenant joining the captain at his table with guests. No doubt, Richmond would somehow exact payment on someone for such a slight later on.

He always did.

18

Supper in the cabin was served in as formal a manner as circumstances allowed. When all was ready and the hour arrived, the pocket door between the cabin and the wardroom opened long enough for the guests to file in. The captain's steward closed it.

Only on rare occasions had Gunn visited the cabin, which compared in size to a modest sitting room. Most often, a visit to the cabin meant trouble, but not tonight. He could enjoy being there, taking it all in.

The room was handsomely—but sparsely—appointed, paneled in the rich, warm tones of mahogany, accented with brass. William Powers, the captain's steward—Li'l Bill, as he was known by his shipmates—had prepared an elegant table laid with china, glassware, and silver utensils, which the captain reserved for special occasions.

Whitcomb welcomed his guests and invited them to be seated. He took his usual place, facing forward, with Lieutenant Prouty to his right, and Gunn to his left. Colonel Suttle and Brent, still looking a little peaked, faced the captain. More than those few guests would not have fit easily around the table, given the close quarters.

The meal started with pleasant conversation over mock turtle soup. After small talk, at Colonel Suttle's request, the captain regaled his guests with a history of the Revenue Cutter Service, since they confessed knowing little about it. As he spoke, his voice eager, the meal continued through the other courses, served unobtrusively by Powers.

Whitcomb told them about the beginnings of the service in 1790. As the first Secretary of Treasury, Alexander Hamilton convinced Congress that the fledgling nation, their independence newly won, needed a means of increasing revenue. America's coffers were empty, and mountains of debt to allies threatened the nation's solvency.

Smuggling continued rampant after the war. American and foreign privateers, already adept at smuggling goods from Europe and elsewhere, deprived the nation of customs revenues.

Hamilton devised a "system of cutters," as he called it, ten ships to patrol the coastline and the major ports along the eastern seaboard to enforce the customs laws. The cost of each of the ships—schooners like the *Morris*, but smaller—was set initially at one thousand dollars, a great expense in those early days of the republic. Of course, several of them considerably exceeded that amount. However, they paid for themselves within a few years.

"He was a great man, our Mr. Hamilton. Unfortunately for him, he never had the opportunity to witness the full benefit of his creation," said Whitcomb. "As I am sure you know, his life was cut short by an infamous duel with Aaron Burr over a personal dispute, carried on through surrogates. You see, gentlemen, these two men talked about each other, and at each other, and past each other, but not directly *to* each other, even in the final moments when they both had weapons in their hands aimed at each other's hearts." He paused for effect. "I propose to you, gentlemen, the error of misapprehension, whether it be intended or not, has led to more conflict and even bloodshed than the world should ever know. Don't you agree?"

As he finished speaking, Whitcomb leaned back in his chair and peered at each man individually. First Colonel Suttle, then Brent, Prouty, and last, Gunn. His meaning was clear, at least to Gunn. This meal was intended to conciliate them, to ease some of the tension that had come aboard with their guests in Boston.

The steward took advantage of the break in conversation to serve coffee. When finished, Powers, whose complexion matched the coffee he had poured, placed the silver service in the middle of the table, and receded into the shadows.

"I quite agree," said Suttle, breaking the silence. "In fact, captain, I would go even further to say that your observation holds as true for nations as it does for individuals. Why, sir, I have come to fear for the very future of America, given the animosity which has come between the North and the South these last few years. And I would grant you the premise that it all essentially flows from misapprehension, sadly so. Sometimes intended, sometimes not."

"What would you say, colonel, is the misapprehension between North and South?" asked Prouty. "It seems to me we understand each other fairly well. The South wants to continue to enslave the black race, and the North wants to free them. And I think we certainly must agree, politics aside, that slavery is the greatest evil of our time. Isn't that so?"

Suttle cleared his throat. "There you have it, sir. Most northerners see things the way you do, Mr. Prouty. Quite so. But it is simply not entirely the case. At least, not as we southerners see things."

Prouty appeared bemused, his whiskers twitching along with his cheek. "Just how do *you* see it, colonel?"

"Well, sir, there are southerners who want to see slavery abolished. There are northerners who do not, and some of them own slaves themselves. Furthermore, lest you think slavery in this country is an institution peculiar to the white man, believe me or not, I even know of negro men who are slavers. Women, too, mind you. You can visit any number of cities in the south, say, ah, Charleston, Savannah, Norfolk, or Alexandria, where I am from, and you will witness it for yourselves. Oh, yes, these are black slave-*owners*, I tell you, and they are very jealous of their property. You see, the issue is far more complex than you have stated, Mr. Prouty, if I may say so."

Suttle waved his hand, the way a schoolmaster might dismiss a poor student.

"Then it is a greater evil than ever I imagined," said Prouty. "All the more reason to be rid of it, once and for all."

Suttle nodded. "I don't disagree, Mr. Prouty. But it will not happen by one people forcing their will upon another. I submit to you, gentlemen, slavery will go its own way, as it has for thousands of years in many places around the world. It is hardly peculiar to the new world, I'm sure you'll agree. However, the future is upon us, and nowhere more so than these United States. New technologies and machinery are invented all the time, taking the place of manual labor more and more as time goes by. Why, I predict slavery will die of its own accord in this nation before long. Maybe in other parts of the world, as well. Perhaps I will not live to see it, but it will happen, I am convinced of it."

"How can you be so certain, colonel?" Whitcomb asked.

"Well, captain, I've had difficulty finding enough work for my own slaves, which is why I lent the services of my man Burns to Mr. Brent, here."

Brent nodded. "Fact of the matter is, gentlemen, there are more free negroes in Virginia today, right now, than there are in Massachusetts, and nearly as many as there are in all of the northern states combined."

"The real issue, as we southerners see it, is that the north desires to subjugate the south, and they are using the issue of slavery to do it," added Brent.

"Subjugate is a strong word," said Prouty.

"Yes, sir, it is, and we will not have it," Suttle continued. "Plain and simple. The northern states have already begun to push for new laws that would give them great advantages in trade over the South.

They are seeking to undermine us economically and politically, so we will be forced to give up a civilized way of life that has existed in this country from a time before there was a congress or a constitution. They are even willing to disobey the established laws of this nation to do it, as we all witnessed in Boston, only three days ago."

"A way of life that depends on an atrocity, colonel," said Gunn.

"Sir, I beg your pardon?" Suttle raised an eyebrow as he frowned down his nose at Gunn.

"The way of life to which you refer depends for its sustenance on the institution of slavery," Gunn repeated. "And now, the Kansas-Nebraska Act, just signed by President Pierce last week, probably ensures the expansion of that atrocity to even more states. So, it's not going away. It's getting worse. Isn't that so, colonel?"

"Mr. Gunn, that will do," said the captain.

"True, true enough, at least for the time being," said Suttle. "However, slavery is but a means to an end, lieutenant. It is a necessary means to an end, upon which even the North depends for *her* livelihood. Where, do you imagine, does the cotton come from to make the fine shirts you are wearing, or these napkins, or the canvas sails for this ship? Who would pick that cotton, if not the slave? Why, you would have to pay a man more than it is worth to pick the stuff. Then, I would gladly wager, you could not afford to buy that shirt, or sail this vessel, or set this fine table." Suttle wiped his mouth with his napkin and tufted his well-trimmed beard.

"So, the end justifies the means, colonel? Hardly a rationale for the cruel treatment of human beings as slaves, wouldn't you agree?" Gunn pressed.

Whitcomb stirred and leaned forward. "Gentlemen—"

"As for the slaves themselves, I grant you their piteous circumstances as … well, chattel, let's be frank. But they are well cared for in most cases, despite what your now famous Mrs. Stowe might think or imagine in her little story book of fantasies. If she had bothered to venture south of Boston, she would have known as much. It is pure fiction. Mind you, what man would hazard his own property to make a profit? He would not long be successful in business, I can tell you. Only a fool would do such a thing. But, admittedly, there is no shortage of those on either side of the Mason-Dixon line."

Gunn tried to quiet his voice. "If the conditions of your slaves are so good, as you say, then why would Burns decide to flee to Boston to seek his own freedom?"

"Mr. Gunn, that is quite enough." The captain's warning had a sharp, crucial edge to it.

19

There was silence for a moment, a silence that seemed to amplify the clink of a porcelain platter, laden with dried apples, pears, raisins, and cheese, as it struck the other dishes, when Powers placed it in the middle of the table. Brent glared at Gunn, while helping himself to a slice of apple and some cheese. Suttle smiled and returned his attention to the captain.

"Let's address the real issue at hand, shall we?" Suttle offered the captain and Prouty a cigar, which they refused. "Do you mind?"

"Be my guest, colonel."

The colonel lit his cigar and sent a plume of smoke into the air. "I'm sure you all would agree with me that Burns is like any other man in one way, if no other. He is quick to see the greener grass on the other side of the hedgerow," he drawled. "Is it not so? Fair enough. I would venture to say, however—and Tony would tell you, if you asked him—that he was unable to find any work but the most menial labor in Boston. And his wages, such as they were, would not have fed a starving dog for very long. He is not alone in that regard among his brethren up north, sadly."

"Unfortunately, he was not asked his opinion on the matter in his trial."

"How would you know that, Mr. Gunn?" asked Brent.

"I was there, sir, on the last day. In fact, he was not asked a single question about his well-being, past or present, nor any of his preferences on the matter."

Suttle smoked silently, watching Powers take up dishes, and then nodded, as he continued.

"Look around in any northern city, gentlemen, or anywhere, for that matter, and you'll find many common laborers who are forced to work like beasts merely for something to eat, and they depend on others for clothing and shelter. Do they wish to live that way? There are many, many kinds of slavery and servitude, as we all know, sir, I'm sure." His arm swept in a wide arc. "And *all* manner of fealty." He assayed the captain's steward with a smug self-satisfaction in his eyes. "Pour me some more coffee, boy."

Powers did as he was told.

"Is my meaning plain, gentlemen, or should I continue? I would sincerely hate for any misapprehension to occur among us on *my* behalf. But I'd hate to beat a lame horse."

"You have said quite enough, colonel." Whitcomb's face had turned dark. "Now, let me be as clear. And this will be the last word on the matter from anyone. This ship is in the service of the United States of America. We are at *your* service, sir. Every man-Jack here, regardless of color, or race, or position on this ship, is sworn to uphold the noble cause of freedom under the law. That is what we are about. And we have all *chosen* to be here. There is but one man on this ship who is not free to exercise his own will. You *own* him, colonel. And that fact should try the conscience of any man who has one."

The captain paused to catch a breath and pulled at his beard. Gunn had rarely seen him seething, shaking, yet still holding, like a taut towline under heavy strain. His face was flushed, the rising fire visible even under the deep tan of his weathered skin.

"I understand you perfectly, sir. And we are grateful for your service to us and to this great nation. Are we not, Mr. Brent?"

"Of course, we are. We mean no disrespect, captain, to you or any of your officers or crew. Y'all have been most generous and supportive, to a man," said Brent, smiling slyly as Powers refilled his cup. His bead then fixed on Gunn. "We do appreciate your position. May I also say, we are grateful to know that President Pierce and the federal government support us. One can never be too sure how these things will go, or where certain loyalties may lie."

Mr. Prouty tried to ease the strain a bit. "This has been a most difficult mission for all of us, colonel ... Mr. Brent," he said deliberately. "I'm sure you both can comprehend."

"We certainly can, sir," Brent nodded.

"Yet, we are doing our best to see this mission through. Every one of us," said Prouty, holding his cup for Powers to fill. "In this instance, the law is on your side, and we intend to uphold it, regardless what our individual situations might be, or our personal feelings, for that matter. None of us would dare support an intentional violation of the laws of our nation, in any manner or form. As the captain said, it is who we are."

"I see, yes, of course," said Brent, again eyeing Gunn, peering sidelong at him over the lip of his cup. His small, darting eyes missed nothing. He paused to drain his cup. "This has been a very trying week for all of us, hasn't it, Mr. Gunn?"

Gunn suspected that he was up to nothing good. "I would agree, Mr. Brent. Yes, it has."

"We are all on edge. And is it any wonder, what with an angry mob threatening all sorts of violence against us? And then the collision night before last, and all. My word, it still has me wondering whether we might have come under attack by that ship, our first night out. Who knows what might happen next? Trying, indeed." He paused. "But you, Mr. Gunn, you are a rock, sir."

"And why do you say that?"

"You have been there the entire way to protect us and our property, never flinching, never failing. Most commendable. And I thank you for your service."

"I have done what any other officer would do, under the circumstances. Certainly, there is no cause to thank me for doing my duty, Mr. Brent. In fact, I would rather you say nothing more of it."

"As you wish. Well, then, captain, allow me to offer praise to you for sending Mr. Gunn, here, to conduct intelligence during our last night in Boston, when the mob attacked the courthouse—brilliant, sir. Simply brilliant."

"Intelligence?" queried Prouty.

"I was doing the same thing, mind you, but it never occurred to me that any of *your* men would be there," Brent continued.

"Where? What are you talking about, Mr. Brent?" asked the captain.

"Why, at the meeting of the Vigilance Committee at Faneuil Hall, when they were plotting murder and mayhem in the streets. Reverend Parker and his cronies got the mob all riled up. Mr. Gunn was there to witness it. You saw it all, I'm sure, didn't you, Gunn?"

Gunn stared at the knife on his plate, playing the tip of his forefinger against the handle. The steady, interminable tick of the captain's chronometer marked the passing seconds.

"Oh, come now, Gunn. You were there. You were in plain clothes, very sensible, of course, but I'd know those handsome features anywhere. You were with that beautiful girl, the one with the dark hair and eyes to match. Charming, lovely girl. What a brilliant couple you made. What is her name?"

"Mr. Gunn?" asked Prouty. "You were under strict orders not to attend any such event."

"Yes, sir, I know." He picked up his knife and held it for a moment, then placed it beside his plate. "The fact is … well, I regret to say, Mr. Prouty, I did attend the meeting."

"And you were part of that mob afterwards, too. Admit it."

"That's an outright lie, Brent."

"Is it? Perhaps Mr. Gunn here has sympathies that he has not disclosed, in addition to his whereabouts," sneered Brent. "Maybe secretly he would like very much to set Burns free. Who knows? Maybe he knows something about the ship that hit us. He was so unperturbed when it happened. Perhaps—"

Suttle reached over and grasped Brent's arm, as if to keep him from touching a hot poker.

"Gentlemen, it is now time to retire." Whitcomb pushed away from the table and tossed his napkin into his half-empty plate. "This meal is concluded. Before we go, let me say how disappointed I am that you, Colonel Suttle, and you, Mr. Brent, as guests aboard my ship, have seen fit to insult a member of my crew and disparage the character of one of my most trusted officers—both done in my presence and at my table, no less. I cannot and will not abide such behavior.

"Captain, I do apologize for—"

"There is simply too much contention on this ship, colonel, and you have brought that conflict aboard with you. Perhaps we can yet relieve it. We will be approaching the port of New York tomorrow, gentlemen. You leave me no choice. I will expect both of you to depart this ship as soon as we can make suitable arrangements."

"Captain, you can't—"

"You should make ready. Goodnight, gentlemen." He glared at Gunn. "You, sir, will remain here in the cabin. You, too, Mr. Prouty."

20

The captain fumed in his chair, pushed back from the table. Prouty was the first to speak, his voice quiet, but firm.

"You went to this meeting, despite the captain's expressed order not to attend any political meetings, especially meetings that involved Burns. Is that right, Mr. Gunn?"

"Yes, sir. I did."

"Would you care to tell us why? Not that it matters."

"It had nothing to do with Burns, sir."

"Mr. Gunn, to this point, you have always impressed me as an officer with superb skills of reasoning and understanding. I didn't ask you what it had nothing to do with. I asked you, why? A simple question. I hope, for your sake, that you have a simple answer, but a good one. And an honest one."

Gunn hesitated. Even to him, despite his strong feelings for Elizabeth, the reason seemed trivial, now.

"A young lady was attending. I went to be with her for the evening, because I knew she would be there with her family."

"You're joking. You're not serious," Whitcomb interjected.

"Perfectly serious, captain. My main purpose was to meet this young woman for the evening. I had a modest interest in the outcome, I admit, but I certainly had no idea that it would turn violent."

"I see. Was she worth it?"

"Sir, I realize it sounds trivial, but I hope you can understand that this is not just any woman, but the one I hope to marry someday. This was an opportunity to see her, and it was close by."

"That is no excuse, lieutenant."

"I know, sir. And I regret the lapse in judgment, but my motives were quite innocent, I assure you. I am sorry, captain."

"Sorry." The captain slammed his open palm upon the table, scattering the remaining dishes. Prouty scrambled to limit the damage. "I should say, sorry."

The anger in Whitcomb's eyes was mixed with a cast of weary disappointment. After a brief silence, he sat back in his chair and smoothed his beard.

"So, you had no desire or intention to partake in the events at Faneuil Hall, this meeting of the so-called Vigilance Committee? The truth, now, if you are sincere in what you say."

"Sir, the truth is, I do agree wholeheartedly with those who say that slavery is a terrible blight on our nation. It must be abolished and soon, if we are to continue calling ourselves a free people."

"Abolished?"

"Aye, sir. That's what I have come to believe after witnessing the reaction of so many people in Boston on Friday. We have ridden the fence far too long, and cannot pretend to value liberty any longer, while so many negroes, men like Anthony Burns, remain in chains. In this respect, I do not believe President Pierce is wise to aggravate the North and appease the South by enforcing this terrible Fugitive Slave law. Don't you agree?"

"I will ask the questions, lieutenant, if you please. You'd better watch yourself, Mr. Gunn. Your first promotion and indeed your career are on the line," said the captain.

"I will, sir. I hope you will not hold my opinions against me. And I will accept any discipline you think necessary."

"This is not a formal proceeding, which is fortunate for you. The reason it is not has little to do with your behavior, however. It has more to do with mine. You see, it has not escaped my attention, despite what you might think, that it is beyond my authority to issue an order not to attend any legal public gathering. That is a right guaranteed to you by our Constitution. At this juncture, you'd better be glad that it is, lieutenant."

"Yes, sir, I am."

"Let me be clear. My orders were for your benefit, for the benefit of everyone else aboard this ship, and for the sake of our mission. It was well within the scope of foreseeable events that something might happen, something much like that mob, especially if we were to be seen taking sides in this matter. It was my intention that we remain neutral in performing our duties, all of us onboard this ship. That is always best when wielding the heavy hand of authority."

"I understand, sir."

"I am not finished, lieutenant. You blatantly disregarded my expressed will. And you deliberately antagonized those men after I warned you not to. But I am willing to overlook that as an error in judgment, in this case, under the present circumstances."

"Thank you, sir."

"What I will not overlook, however—what I will never overlook—is that you deceived me. If you disobey my orders, whatever the reason, at least admit it like a man. And don't hide in the skirts of a woman, Gunn. If you think I'm wrong, you'd best tell me to my face. I will not, I cannot abide such behavior on my ship. I expect my officers to comport themselves with honor and integrity—with honesty and a high regard for the truth, above all things. You have come up short in that regard. mister. What have you to say for yourself?"

Gunn took a slow, deep breath. "Sir, I cannot begin to tell you how much I regret my behavior. I have no excuse for what I did, regardless of the reason. It will not happen again."

***

Fog set in by noon the next day, and the winds turned light and variable. Nothing visible in the sky or on land marked their progress. By the captain's dead reckoning based on tides, currents, and water depth, at four o'clock on Monday afternoon the cutter had reached no further than a position somewhere near Fire Island.

The crew kept busy during the day repainting the dinghy and the booby hatch, but the work took longer than it should have. Word of what had happened in the cabin the night before spread among the men like flame through a lit fuse.

Gunn kept to himself as much as possible. He avoided breakfast and stood the forenoon watch. Then, he excused himself from the noon meal, claiming he was not feeling well. Sam Miller quietly asked what had happened, but Gunn waved him away, shaking his head.

While the others ate lunch, he wrote to Elizabeth, hoping that a mailbag would be sent ashore with the exiled passengers. The letter related all that had transpired since their last meeting and shared his misgivings about the duties thrust upon him. He also wrote a similar letter to Marguerite, adding an apology for his abrupt treatment of her at the courthouse.

He kept busy otherwise by tending to Burns and taking care of his collateral and administrative duties. That occupied his mind, putting aside thoughts of how far his prospects had fallen in such a short time. Apparently, those thoughts were written on his face. He turned from the task of inspecting the ship's ammunition locker to find Nelson at his shoulder, leaning against the foremast. Not much happened on the ship that escaped Nelson's sharp eye.

"Afternoon, Mr. Gunn." Nelson stood upright and saluted him. Gunn returned his salute. "Boats."

"This fog—enough to weigh a man down."

"That it is."

Silence.

"Is there something troubling you, sir?"

"Do I look troubled?"

Nelson shrugged. "Just that you seem to be carryin' a burden, of sorts."

Gunn frowned and shook his head. "Nothing to mention." He walked to the starboard rail and leaned against it.

"I knew a man once, went hunting for rabbits," said Nelson. "He come walking home after a hard day's hunt with a sack over his shoulder. A friend stops and asks him, 'Hamish, what's that ye have in the sack?' Hamish answers, 'I'll not be sayin'. Mind yer own business, if ye please.'"

Nelson joined him at the rail.

"So, the friend, he says, 'Agh, go'n now, Hamish, tell a mate what ye've got there.' Hamish shrugs and says, 'All right then, it's rabbits, if ye must know.' So, his friend says, 'Would ye be able to spare one for an auld friend?' Hamish thinks a minute and says, 'Tell ye what, auld friend, if ye can guess how many I've got in the sack, I'll give ye the both of 'em.'" Nelson grinned. "'Well, then,' the friend says, 'Is it three?'"

Gunn snorted and laughed, raising his eyes to the luffing sails, shrouded in mist.

"It's good to see you can still laugh, even at a bad joke, sir." Nelson winked. "Care to tell me what's in the sack, then?"

"Nothing you'd want any part of, Nelson."

"They say confession is good for the soul."

"What makes you think I have something to confess?"

"Don't we all?"

"Let's just say I feel responsible for that." Gunn jerked his thumb toward the dinghy, piled half-full of luggage.

"Oh, that. I wouldn't fret so much about them, Mr. Gunn. They had it coming from what I hear."

"What have you heard?"

"Only that they had some hard words for you and L'il Bill. Cap'n didn't much like it."

Gunn lifted the cap from his head, smoothed the unruly waves in his hair, and replaced it.

"Worst of it was, they came at us from the side, not straight on. Never saw it coming."

"Shifty then, like a hound licking a dinner plate."

Gunn chuckled again. "Something like that."

"Well, then." Nelson struck his hand on the rail. "See 'em for what they truly are. Have done with it."

Gunn nodded, examining both his splayed palms, as if trying to read his own fortune.

"Sir, beggin' your pardon. If you don't mind my sayin' so …"

"Speak your mind, Nelson."

"Sir, I hate to say it, but you're all in irons, and your helm's unshipped. Seems to me the best thing for it is to find the wind's eye and sheet home."

21

The evening meal in the wardroom started in reticence. Prouty tried to incite some pleasant conversation, but to little good. Of course, everyone avoided any discussion of the previous evening. Dwyer served the meal as though hoping nobody noticed him placing the steaming bowls of potato soup in front of the five at the table.

"Any more reports of ghost ship sightings, Dwyer?" asked Prouty, lifting an eyebrow.

"None as yet, sir," Dwyer said. He managed a sheepish smile.

Suttle chuckled. "Well now, you be sure to sound the alarm, boy, soon as you see one."

Richmond took up the defense. He seemed to be in a magnanimous mood. "Oh now, stop teasing the poor boy. Pay these gentlemen no mind, Dwyer." He patted Dwyer's arm, his hand lingering too long for comfort. Dwyer recoiled with a furtive glance at Richmond, sloshing soup into his lap.

Richmond gritted his teeth. "You silly swab." He grabbed surrounding napkins to wipe up the spill.

"I'm terribly sorry, sir. I didn't mean to— "

"It's all right, Dwyer," said Gunn. "No harm done. It was an accident."

"Yes, no harm done," said Prouty.

Richmond glared at Gunn, then regained his composure. "Never you mind, Dwyer. Yes, it will be all right. See me after the meal and we'll review proper service."

"Aye, sir," said Dwyer. The look on his face said he didn't welcome the prospect. He continued serving the soup.

"Nothing can spoil my mood today, gentlemen," said Richmond. He announced that the captain had granted him permission to take leave to visit his family in Tennessee immediately upon the ship's arrival in Norfolk. His father had taken ill, and his mother had written to ask him to come home for a visit. Consequently, their conversation dwelt on the anticipated visit. Everyone at the table seemed grateful for the diversion.

"How long has it been since you've seen your family?" asked Prouty.

"Five, six years, give or take."

"What does your father do, Mr. Richmond?" asked Suttle.

"My father—we call him Fa—owns a tobacco farm."

"A farm. In Tennessee. How interesting. How many acres does your family own?"

"About three hundred acres along the Cumberland River, northeast of Nashville."

"And how long has the farm been in your family?"

"My great-grandfather was one of the Overmountain Boys, with Colonel John Sevier."

"Ah, yes, of course," said Brent. "A true hero, if ever there was one."

"Anyway, he settled the farm under a land grant after the war, when it was still part of North Carolina. Our family used to own almost a thousand acres, but most of it's been sold off over the years. The taxes keep rising, and it's hard to compete with the larger plantations. I'm the eldest of five, but since I left home, it's only my father and four brothers raising crops and running the sawmill. The youngest is just eighteen. But it costs too much to hire men on. And Fa being Fa, he refuses to buy——" Richmond cut himself short. "He insists on working the land himself. Says it's good for the soul."

"And you don't agree?" asked Prouty.

"I suppose it is, in some ways, sir. Maybe so. Not much good for the back, though, I can tell you."

"Well, now, Mr. Richmond, being from Tennessee, and a federal officer to boot, how do you see the situation in the South?" asked Suttle. "I'm most curious."

Richmond shot a tentative glance at the first lieutenant.

"Let's not revisit that subject, colonel," cautioned Prouty.

"Sir, I assure you, my intentions are benign. I'm only interested in Mr. Richmond's point of view on the state of our nation, given his being a son of the South."

"Very well. Keep it civil, Mr. Richmond." Prouty helped himself to a platter of corned beef and cabbage and passed it on.

"Since you press me sir, my thoughts are that no man should tell another what to think about anything. Live and let live is my motto."

"I see."

"One thing I learned from my father was to despise the self-righteous do-gooders of this world. Their one true purpose is to make trouble for others." Richmond's eyes shifted to Gunn.

"So, you decided to leave the farm. How did that come about?" Suttle changed the subject but kept it on Richmond. He seemed somewhat enamored with him.

Richmond stabbed at a piece of corned beef. "When I was a boy, I was fascinated by the river. I saw men come and go on it, talking about things I had never seen or imagined. I wanted to see for myself where the river went. I wanted to make something of myself."

"And you have, haven't you?"

"I made the rank of second lieutenant in less than two years. Of course, by the time I joined the service, I'd already spent four years sailing ships out of New Orleans."

"Yes, you should be proud of your rank, sir. No doubt you're destined for great things."

"Two years is quite … remarkable," said Prouty.

"Now, what about your father? What did he think of your leaving?"

Richmond smiled. "Oh, he's still hoping I'll return someday. Like the prodigal son, I guess. Momma is just glad to know I'm not a riverboat gambler." He chuckled.

"Do you think you might? Go back home one day, I mean."

"I doubt it, sir." Richmond put down his knife and fork, leaned back in his chair, and swept a hand with a flourish down his slender, wiry frame. "I didn't make much of a field hand, I must admit. Much to Fa's disappointment, I never did take to it—not like my brothers. I preferred using my head over abusing my back. Truth is, I'd probably make a better riverboat gambler than a farmer."

The others laughed with him.

"Your father, is he pleased with what you do?" asked Suttle.

Richmond picked up his fork and dabbed at the wilted cabbage on his plate. "Let's just say, I doubt he'd be willing to kill the fatted calf for me."

"I believe we have much in common, Mr. Richmond," said Suttle. He wore a lopsided smile. "We should talk later. I might have an interesting proposition for an ambitious man such as yourself."

"How's that, colonel? What exactly do you see that we have in common?" Richmond's slight frown seemed doubtful. He smoothed his long mustache and swept the ends away from his mouth.

"Of course, we are both sons of the South. That is obvious. But it goes beyond such remote kinship. You see, my father didn't much approve of my choices, either. My father and his father before him held the contract to quarry sandstone at Aquia Creek in Stafford County. As a matter of fact, Mr. Brent's family was a prior owner of the quarry, long time ago—before they sold it to the federal government, that is."

"The stone was used to build the president's mansion and the Capitol in Washington City," added Brent.

"But I digress." Suttle continued, settling back in his chair. "Now, the quarry was hard, *hard*, work—back-breaking work, I'm telling you. Not unlike your father's farm, from dawn to dusk. I wanted nothing to do with it. Not that I am afraid of a little hard work, mind you. I simply had other plans for my life. I wanted to build a business on my own, which I set out to do. I asked my father for a portion of my small inheritance—"

"Another prodigal son," said Prouty.

Suttle smiled his lopsided grin. "But a prodigal who made good, Mr. Prouty. I bought a very fine little dry goods store in Alexandria. Later, I won a seat in the state senate. Joined the state militia, too, and made the rank of colonel. Not to mention becoming the county sheriff, I might add—though, not to brag, of course. All in, however, my ambitions never included becoming a slave-owner."

"Are you saying you wanted no part of owning slaves, colonel?" Gunn leaned forward.

"You seem surprised, Mr. Gunn."

"I will admit that I am."

"No, sir, none. I swear it. Now, in spite of my success, or you might say because of it, my father was not happy about losing me to my own devices, and he let me know it every time I saw him. He would start in on me, right after we said our hellos. Like a music box plays the same old tune, every time you wind it up, you know. Said he could have used my help closer to home."

"I know that tune, colonel," said Richmond. "I've danced to it."

They all laughed. The mood around the table began to lighten.

"Did he prevail?" asked Prouty. "I mean—"

"Well, sir, now there's the rub. Mine is a cautionary tale, you might say. And I offer it for your benefit, primarily, Lieutenant Richmond, though you may take it or leave it. As you will, of course."

"By all means, sir, go right ahead." Richmond gave his mustache a tentative swipe, seeming to look past Suttle.

"You see, my father died, and then my mother followed him eighteen months on. Now, to pay off the debt and taxes Father left when he died, my mother sold five of the slaves they'd kept to work the quarry. They owned fifteen at the time. Oh, yes. The quarry was nigger work, to be sure. Not fit for a white man—at least, not *this* one. The rest of them had to be mortgaged after my mother died, to pay off her debts."

"Why not just free them?" asked Gunn.

"Fair question, sir. I would have been happy to. But then my mother's debts would have gone unpaid. Hardly the honorable thing to do, wouldn't you say?"

"Why not sell them off, then, and pay the debts, if you had no interest in owning slaves, as you say?" Gunn pressed.

Prouty cleared his throat and held up his right palm. "Mr. Gunn, I'm sure we have no need to pry into the colonel's personal affairs."

"Quite all right, Mr. Prouty. After all, that's getting to my point. You're a bright young man, Mr. Gunn." Suttle shifted his tall frame in his chair, stretching his legs out from under the corner of the table, like a cat preparing to preen itself. "You see, I did not wish to sell them off and break up an entire family. Enough harm had been done. The remaining ten were mostly Tony's relations, brothers, sisters, cousins and such—nine after his mother died. So, I kept them together as a family. But that meant I had to mortgage them, you see. That's right, Tony's hide is mortgaged from his toes to the wooly black hair on his head. Surely you can see, now, gentlemen, why it was so important to get him back."

All eyes were fixed on Suttle. Nobody spoke.

"Anyway, my point is this. We all know life doesn't always go the way we plan. In fact, it almost never does, now does it? So, you might ask yourself, as I have, Mr. Richmond, what would you do if what you least wanted is what you at last receive?"

"That would indeed be a great tragedy, colonel. And, it happens regularly around here, I'm afraid," said Richmond.

"Is that so?"

"Every Tuesday, when Cookie makes a New England boiled dinner. I don't know how you Yankees can eat this stuff." Richmond wrinkled his nose, frowned, and shook his head.

Another round of laughter, subdued this time.

"Oh, joke if you will, lieutenant." Suttle placed his elbow on the table, pointing his fork in Richmond's direction. "But it is a question well worth asking, wouldn't you agree? In my experience, so often what we most despise in life is the very thing that we become. Is this not the case? But looking at it from a more positive point of view, that farm might come in handy for you someday, I'd say. One never knows, does one? We should talk some more. I have an idea that truly might appeal to you."

"I'm all ears, colonel. But I doubt—"

Suttle waved aside any doubt. "I believe ..." He glanced toward the overhead. "I b'lieve it was Shakespeare who said, 'There's a divinity that shapes our ends, rough-hew them as we will.' Macbeth or Hamlet, I think it was, if memory serves. I think that's true, don't you?"

"My father always used to say, 'Man proposes, God disposes,'" Gunn said.

"Did he now?" Richmond snorted. Gunn was immediately sorry to have opened his mouth, other than to put food in it or ask for the salt.

"Wise man, your father," Suttle's voice carried the timbre of a politician, trying not to leave behind any resentment, if he could help it. "Is he no longer with us?"

"I—his whereabouts are unknown," said Gunn.

"Oh? I'm sorry to hear it. Was he a seafarer like yourself? Or did he come upon some other accident of fate?"

"Neither," blurted Richmond. He folded his napkin and placed it on the table. "His father was a minister, who abandoned his family many years ago. Isn't that right, Mr. Gunn? At least, that's what he told the captain the other night. Now, colonel, surely you wouldn't presume to say that Mr. Gunn might follow fatefully in his daddy's footsteps, despite his own determination not to, would you?"

Gunn tabled his fork. An awkward silence followed as the ship's timbers creaked and the water rushed past the hull. Then, the scraping of flatware against porcelain, as the attention of the other men turned disconcertedly back to their own plates.

"What is it, Mr. Gunn?" Richmond sniffed. "I overheard you tell the captain, so I assumed it was public knowledge." He raised the napkin and wiped his mouth with the tip, careful not to disturb the rakish mustache. "Is that not the case?"

"If you will excuse me, Mr. Prouty, gentlemen." Gunn consulted his watch. "It is time for me to prepare for the next watch, I think." He pushed away from the table.

"Certainly, Mr. Gunn," replied Prouty. "Before you go——." He turned to Richmond. "Your comments were most certainly uncalled for, Mr. Richmond. I believe a sincere apology is in order."

"Sir, I'll do nothing—I meant no harm, sir."

"Mr. Richmond." Prouty insisted.

Richmond hesitated long enough for Prouty to open his lips again to speak. "Very well. I do apologize, Mr. Gunn. Sincerely."

"Accepted." Gunn stood up. "Gentlemen."

He retrieved his cap from its hook on the bulkhead.

"I must say," said Prouty, "we've had no shortage of controversy on this trip, thus far. I suggest, for the sake of good order, we should refrain from any remarks around the table more controversial than the quality of the weather or the wetness of the water."

Gunn climbed the ladder to the main deck. He was glad Richmond would be going on leave as soon as they reached Norfolk. *Maybe something would happen to him on the way home to Tennessee.*

It was the thought most closely resembling a prayer to come to his mind in years.

22

The wind picked up just after five bells, at about six-thirty-five on Monday evening, as Gunn noted in the ship's log. Soon afterward, the sky brightened. Breaking through the dingy fog that had hung like crepe in the spars all day, the sun gilded the face of the water in the direct path of the cutter. As the heavy mist cleared away, Gunn scanned the shoreline, where the treetops and brush of the low-lying, unspoiled land blazed with the light of the setting sun.

Fire Island Light was visible in the distance to the northeast. He called the captain, who came up on deck, snatched the spyglass from Gunn's hand, and raised it to see for himself. In his haste, he had neglected to bring his prized binoculars, a gift from the once grateful citizens of Boston.

"High time," Whitcomb muttered under his breath. "Very well, Mr. Gunn. Head for the Highlands and hail the first ship you see."

Gunn figured they were still more than twenty miles from the lightship at the approaches to New York. The wind continued to freshen, backing to the south-southwest, and soon the cutter heeled well over on the port tack, settling into a favorable point of sail on a close reach. She responded to the wind and to the new trim of her sails with a shudder, as though awakening from a fitful sleep. Soon they were headed directly for the highlands of New Jersey at Sandy Hook with several hours to go before reaching the shipping lanes.

The effect of the wind and sea took his mind away from all concern, lifting the sense of dread that had fallen over him. At least for the moment.

Everyone else seemed to enjoy the bounding ride, too. Little by little, the crew arrived on deck after the evening meal. They rested in groups on the foredeck, smoking their corncob pipes or sitting about in the long shadows, shading their eyes from the setting sun, trading sea stories, and laughing at one another's jibes.

After a while, Suttle and Brent came up on deck, basking in the last of the evening sunlight. Suttle offered Brent a cigar, which he took. Suttle lit their cigars with cupped hands, and the smoke whisked away in the wind.

Across from them on the port side sat three of the special deputies, still looking tepid. Eventually, the fourth one popped his head above the coaming of the booby hatch, put his face to the wind, and clambered out. Butman followed, then Burns, who'd been allowed another brief respite from his lightless hole.

Butman broke away from them and joined Brent and Suttle on the starboard side, where they stood talking quietly together. All three appeared quite serious.

Gunn turned his eye back to the sail trim. He sensed a nearby presence and turned to find Captain Whitcomb standing at his shoulder.

"Ease your mainsheet a foot, Mr. Gunn. It'll take some of the bite out of the rudder."

Gunn immediately gave the order to two of the able seamen on watch, who hurried aft and did as they were told. The tackle groaned as they eased the mainsheet, and then it was as though the ship relaxed into an easy canter.

The captain ambled forward a couple of steps, pulled out his meerschaum pipe from the pocket of his frock coat and cupped his hand around the bowl. He placed the pipe in his mouth, tucking his bearded chin into a shoulder against the wind, and lit it with a match struck handily on the oarlock of the longboat. A few puffs, and the smoke trailed over his hands, dissipating into the wind. It was Gunn's cue to step back down into the cockpit, to allow the captain the sole occupancy of the weather side.

"Keep an eye peeled for the lights at the Navesink," the captain mumbled through clenched teeth, tossing his voice over his shoulder with the spent match, as Gunn retreated. "Two lights, side by side. One blinks, the other's steady."

The captain glanced over his left shoulder. Gunn immediately noticed the sail on the port beam, hardly visible in the violet twilight.

Too late.

"When were you going to tell me about that sail on the port beam, Mr. Gunn?" he asked, over his shoulder, without looking back.

A small ship had appeared, hull down, perched on the horizon. She seemed to be heading into New York. The lookout on the bow had not seen her yet, either.

Well, bless Billy's bawbees.

"I'm sorry, sir. Hadn't noticed the sails until just now."

"Not acceptable, Mr. Gunn." There was a cold, metallic note in his voice, a quality that hadn't been there before, but as discernible now as that sail on the horizon. Gunn couldn't quite make it out, but he did not like what he heard.

He spotted Richmond, his relief, standing with Brent and Suttle in the waist of the ship, next to one of the guns. The three had their heads together. Suttle patted Richmond's shoulder and they shook hands. Richmond nodded as Brent handed him what seemed to be a book of some sort. They all laughed and parted, Brent going below to the wardroom while Richmond headed aft, stuffing the item into the pocket of his frock coat. His expression was even more smug than usual.

Richmond approached the captain and asked for permission to

relieve the watch. The captain returned his salute.

"Very well, Mr. Richmond. I want to rendezvous with that brigantine out there on our port beam. Hail her as soon as we're close enough to do so. My guess is, she's headed for New York, and I hope her captain is willing to provide transport to our two guests."

"Aye, aye, sir," said Richmond. "Does that mean we're not heading into New York?"

"We are not. Our orders are to deliver the prisoner to Norfolk, as expeditiously as possible. That's what we're going to do."

"So, we're keeping the prisoner on board, sir?" asked Gunn.

"Do I need to repeat myself, Mr. Gunn?"

"No, sir."

When Richmond relieved him, Gunn started for the wardroom companionway and met Prouty on the way.

"Mr. Prouty, is it—ah, did you know that Burns will remain with us, when Suttle and Brent go ashore?"

"Yes, Mr. Gunn. That is the case." Prouty seemed ill at ease. "Why do you ask?"

"I assumed he would be going ashore with Colonel Suttle. May I ask why he is remaining onboard?"

"We—the captain and I were concerned that putting him ashore north of the Mason-Dixon Line might incite further unrest. We wanted to avoid that at all costs. Our orders were to deliver him to the authorities in Norfolk. Suttle will make plans to meet us there."

"I see."

"Is there a problem?"

"Well, sir, honestly, I am a little taken aback that nobody told me until now, since I'm responsible for the prisoner."

"The captain is responsible for the prisoner."

"Yes, of course. But you had put him in my charge."

"I realize that."

"Is there any reason I shouldn't know what the plans are for him?"

"Were you to be consulted?"

"No, sir, but—"

"But, what? See here, Mr. Gunn. If you must know, the captain thinks you might seem ... a bit too zealous where Burns is concerned. He doesn't want to invite any further disturbance."

Dusk had settled in, so it was hard to read Prouty's expression.

"Were you about to say something, Mr. Gunn?"

"Uh ... "

"It's just that your mouth is open. I can't hear what you said."

"I see. I regret he's been disturbed."

"I wouldn't worry too much about it. He has a lot on his mind and doesn't care to have any more disagreements. Simple as that."

"Mr. Prouty, may I ask one more question?" Perhaps the twilight might mask his own expression of concern.

"Certainly."

"Sir, is there another reason?"

"Such as?"

"Does the captain doubt my loyalty in this matter?"

Now Prouty was quiet.

"Doubt is a strong word, Mr. Gunn. And it is not a matter of your loyalty, I assure you. I daresay he wonders whether your judgment might be in question on this particular issue. Whether you might like to see Burns go ashore. Whether you might like to see him ... freed, if he had the chance, once he reached New York, if that should happen."

"Wouldn't you like to see him go free, Mr. Prouty?"

"It does not matter what I like or do not like. My duty is to deliver the prisoner to Norfolk in one piece. That is all I need think about."

"I see."

"Do you, truly?"

"Yes."

"Then, you should think about that, Mr. Gunn. Think about something in the larger world other than what *you* might like to see or how you might feel about it."

23

An hour passed before the cutter closed within hailing distance of the inbound vessel in Ambrose Channel, about a mile out from the Lightship *Sandy Hook*. The captain spoke the master of the brigantine, who identified her as the *Somers*, five days out of Charleston. At first wary that the two passengers might be ill, the master of the *Somers* expressed reluctance to take them aboard. Whitcomb assured him nobody was ill. The master relented, finally agreeing to take them into New York.

Suttle and Brent waited on deck as Gunn oversaw the transfer of their luggage from the dinghy to the starboard longboat. Within minutes, the boat was lowered to the water, tailing along by its painter in the lee of the cutter. As soon as they were ready, Brent made his tentative climb down into the boat. Before following, Colonel Suttle turned to the captain.

"Captain, I thank you for the kind hospitality that you and your crew have shown us. I shall certainly mention it, next time I see my good friend, Senator Mason of Virginia, which I expect will be soon, very soon."

"Give the senator my very best regards, colonel."

"Oh, I shall, sir. I shall. Goodbye, then," Suttle said, tipping his panama hat to all. "And god speed. Please take good care of Tony for me, won't you? I would that nothing untoward should happen to him. He is quite dear to me, as you know."

He handed his cane to one of the men in the longboat. Then, with considerable aid from the crew, he eased his lanky body into the boat, gingerly stepping tiptoe onto the center thwart. The boat rocked and sank a few inches deeper in the water, as he lowered himself further. He steadied himself in the sternsheets, knees almost to his chin. Moriarty handed a sack of mail to one of the crew, who placed it between Suttle's feet on the bottom boards.

The oarsmen began pulling, and the longboat was away, lugging its load through the relatively calm water in the lee of the cutter. Bright starlight and a half moon shone in the charcoal sky. The dark outlines of the boat and the men in it remained discernible as they reached the *Somers*.

Gunn watched from the port rail as the two men clambered aboard the *Somers*. He had a sudden, unusual urge to spit, failing for the moment to notice he was on the windward side. The spittle flew back onto his own face and arm. Dobbins had made it look so easy.

"Stunner," he said, wiping his chin with his sleeve.

***

In a moderate breeze, the *Morris* turned south along the coast. By morning, however, the wind died down, and the fog set in once more. It was slow going again, sailing through late afternoon to reach Barnegat Light, off the coast of New Jersey. The weather did not clear until early afternoon, when a less favorable wind came up directly from the south.

Despite the slow progress, however, the mood onboard, at least among the officers, seemed to lighten with the departure of the wardroom guests, although nobody mentioned the difference. The crew hardly seemed to notice or care, for that matter, except for Cookie, who said he was always happy to have two fewer mouths to feed.

Even Butman appeared a bit more cheerful. He arrived on deck while Gunn and Moriarty, the ship's quartermaster, were taking a sunline with the sextant. Butman lit a cigar and strolled over to him.

"Well, only a few more days and you'll no longer have to put up with us, Mr. Gunn."

"I think we'll all be very glad to reach port."

"Some more than others, I would say. Anyway, come up to tell you Burns ain't feelin' so good again."

"What's wrong with him?"

"I dunno. Jest belly-achin', if you ask me. But he's been askin' for you."

"What does he want with me?"

"Won't say. Jest keeps on askin' if you'd please come and talk with 'im. Figured you'd wanna know."

"All right. I'll go."

Butman took a long draw on his cigar. "I wouldn't, 'f I was you."

"Why not?"

"No good can come of runnin' to the beck and call of a nigger."

"Guess I'll take that chance."

"Suit yersef, lieutenant." Butman walked off, smoke trailing over his shoulder.

Gunn found Burns lying on his side in the near pitch-black of the hold.

"Tony."

"Mistah Gunn, is that you?"

"What is it you wanted? Are you feeling sick?"

"Yes sir, Mistah Gunn. But it ain't too bad. I just have a touch of the scours. It'll pass, I 'spect." He sat up. "I wanted to give you something," he whispered. "Keep it safe, for me."

"What is it?" Gunn asked in a low voice. He could hear rustling, as though Burns were searching for something in his clothing.

"Four dollars." He handed Gunn a small wad of damp, soiled rag that passed for a handkerchief, inside which he could feel several coins. "It's all the money I got in the world. Reverend Grimes, he give it to me at the courthouse," Burns whispered. "Said I might need it to buy favors, if they send me to jail."

"What do you want me to do with it?"

"Keep it for me. These men, they knew I had it, and 'spect I still do. I think they must have figured out I hid it in my sock. They keep trying to get it from me, and they won't stop 'til they do. One way or the other."

"All right, Tony. I'll keep it for you." Gunn patted him on the shoulder. "Get some rest," he said aloud, so he could be heard outside. "I'll send Cookie to look after you. He'll fix you right up."

"Thank you, Mistah Gunn. You're a good man."

24

Cookie called it *chorro*, a term he had picked up during his service aboard a cutter in the Mexican War, where diarrhea had been a constant ailment. Burns had a mild case of it. However unwelcome, his illness made it easier for Gunn to convince Butman to keep the prisoner topsides as much as possible, so he could remain closer to the heads. At least one deputy marshal always stayed somewhere nearby, loosely guarding him. The others stayed on deck as often as possible too, playing poker or checkers to pass the long hours, obviously relieved to spend more of their days outside the stifling hold.

After a day or so, Burns seemed to be improving. Gunn went to check on him.

"Feeling any better, Tony?"

"Yessir, I am, thank you. Cookie's been takin' real good care of me." He sat hunched over on the foredeck, trying to hold a bowl of broth made from dried beef stock and rice cupped in his lap while he ate. It was hard to avoid noticing his almost useless claw. Burns raised up and saw his stare. Gunn looked away.

"Most folks cain't hardly look at it," he said. "Me, I hardly see it anymore."

Gunn returned his gaze. "How did it happen, Tony? If you don't mind my asking."

"Nossir, I don't mind. It happened when I was a boy, not more than about twelve, maybe thirteen years old. Mas'r Charles, he lent me out for a year to a man clear up in Culpepper. Foote was his name. Owned a sawmill. Said he needed a boy to tend his steam engine. Mas'r Charles told him I could do most anything he wanted me to. So, along I went."

"Alone?"

"Oh, yessir. But that wasn't unusual. That's how it was ever since I was a nub, old enough to cut wood, draw water, or run errands, like that. I think I was maybe seven, the first time he hired me out."

"So, you lived there, at Foote's place?"

"Yessir, sure did. Didn't like it much. He was a Yankee. Wife, too. She's meaner than he was. Used to, she didn't like what we did, she'd beat us facedown with a board had holes in it. Didn't leave any signs that way. Fed us meat you could see through, if you was to hold it up to the light. Not like Mas'r William and his wife. They's always good to me. Always."

"Who?"

"Mas'r William ... you, know. Brent, the man who came with Mas'r Charles to get me."

"*Brent?* Good to you? I find that very hard to believe."

"Well, it's true, believe it or not. Worked for him more than once. Didn't mind that so much."

Gunn leaned against the windlass, across from him. "So, is that how you hurt your hand? This woman, Mrs. Foote was it? She beat you with a board?"

"Nossir. This happened 'bout three, four months after I got there. One morning, Mas'r Richard, man owned the sawmill, run up the machin'ry, no warning. Pulley belt caught my hand, and just like that—" He flipped his hand. "It was over quicker than you can blink."

Gunn winced. "Did they take you to a doctor?"

Burns snorted. "Wasn't no such a thing. Not for miles. Mas'r Richard had his cook to fix me up. She wasn't no Cookie, though. Took three, four months just to heal like this." He held up his hand, turning it. "That's that. Been like this ever since."

"What did Colonel Suttle do?"

"Well, when I got back home, I showed him this cripple thing. He takes one look at it—says, 'I wish you'd look. What have you gone and done to your hand, Tony?' And I says to him, 'Wellsir, you bragged to Mas'r Richard that I could do most anything.'" Burns shrugged and pointed with his good hand. "And, I guess that there's what you'd call *most anything*. But he didn't much like me saying that. Told me best not be getting so uppity, especially so young, if I knew what was good for me. He says that a lot."

"What happened then? How did you work?"

"I did whatever my good hand could find to do. I finished out my year with Mas'r Richard. He found small jobs for me to do. Then Mas'r Charles lent me out to other folk, some good, some bad. I learnt what I could from everyone. Wherever I went, I tried hard to learn how to cipher, so I could do work that didn't need two hands. Some children of one mas'r give me a spelling book and taught me how to read a little. Wasn't supposed to. It was against the law to teach a slave to read and write. But I learnt. Mostly, I just tried to do the best job that I could do. Worked *hard*. And I always put in a honest day's work. Never cheated nobody, nor tried to get out o' work. Didn't always like it. But I did it."

"I believe you," said Gunn.

"Never gave nobody cause not to," said Burns. "Ask Mas'r Charles. Ask Mas'r William. Ask anybody. They'll tell you. I always tell the truth. Try to, long as I have breath."

Gunn wanted to hear more, but he had work to do. Besides, he didn't want to give anyone more cause to accuse him of being "overly zealous," as the first lieutenant had said.

"I'm glad you're feeling better, Tony. Is there anything you need?"

"Nossir. I think I would be fine if I could just get a little shuteye. I still haven't been able to sleep much."

"I'll tell Cookie. He might have something for that, too."

"I thank you, Mistah Gunn."

Gunn found Cookie and told him about Burns not being able to sleep. Cookie nodded and poked a finger in the air.

"Got just the thing, Mr. Gunn." He smacked his lips. "Fix him right up."

***

As he stood the watch later on, just after midnight, Gunn had to remind himself of the passing of days. He started a new page in the ship's log, *Wednesday, 7 June.* They had been gone only five days, but it seemed longer. It would probably take at least another three or four days to reach Norfolk, unless a storm caused the cutter to alter course.

The weather was calm, but lightning flashed somewhere in the distance, followed by low, rolling thunder. Gunn took in the gaff topsail and put reefs in the mainsail and foresail as a precaution. Progress was still slow, since what little wind there was still came from the direction in which the cutter needed to go. As the watch ended in the early morning hours, the wind stirred and backed, and there were other indications of an approaching squall, so he informed the captain, who came up on deck and ordered him to take in all sail.

When Richmond relieved him at four o'clock, the heavy rain was falling in sheets. Gunn climbed down into the main hold to check on Burns. The deputies were asleep, except for Riley, who stirred as Gunn climbed down the ladder. The low flame in the oil lantern spread only a small, dancing circle of light underneath.

He unfastened the netting and stepped inside, tripping on one of Burns' feet, but he hardly stirred. Cookie's special brew had done the trick.

On the way out, Riley lifted his hat from his eyes and snorted.

"Didya find what ya was lookin' fer, Mr. Gunn?"

"What do you mean?"

"He used ta keep it in his sock, but it ain't there no more. Musta hid it where the sun don't shine, but a man ud have ta be pretty low to go after it there."

"I don't know what you're talking about."

"Sure, ya don't. Whatever you say."

25

In his own hand, Captain Whitcomb had scrawled across the page of the rough log:

Monday, 5 June, 1854, 11:40 pm: Suttle, Brent, sent ashore at New York aboard a passing brig, due to urgent personal business.

As one of his collateral duties, it was Gunn's turn this month to keep the smooth log. He faithfully copied the notation, recording the inglorious departure of their two passengers into the smooth log with a neat, steady hand. It occurred to him that at some point, someone with the slightest bit of curiosity, perhaps even years hence, might ask how it was that Suttle would have learned of emergent business while cloistered for three days on a ship at sea. Better, though, not to ask any more unwanted questions for the moment.

During that next day, another heavy thunderstorm set upon them, and the captain again ordered all sail taken in. By late afternoon the rain stopped, the fog lifted a bit, and they were under full sail again beneath the pall of shrouded skies.

When it wasn't raining, Burns now had the liberty to spend as much time as possible above decks. He was improving by the day, and obviously feeling far better than he had the previous day. Once the evening meal concluded, Gunn took the opportunity to sit down with him for a few minutes to inquire more about his unusual life.

The youngest of thirteen children, Burns guessed that he was about twenty years old. He related that he had no memory of his father, who took ill from years of breathing quarry dust and died when Burns was a small boy. His mother had described his father as a very intelligent man who had once been a freeman from the North, arrested and pressed illegally into service on an ill-fated venture into the southland.

He had not lived with his mother or seen her much since the age of about twelve. She died three years ago and was buried in an unmarked grave somewhere near Alexandria.

"Tell me about your mother. What do you remember about her?"

"She was a fine woman. Kind and wise. A godly woman. She'd always tell me the most important thing in this life was to obey God."

"To obey God?"

"Yessir. She said everybody in this whole world does somebody's bidding. No matter slave nor free man. She'd say nobody is totally free in this world. Everybody is a slave to someone or something, but the one choice we always have is to do what God wants us to do. Every day. We ignore the Almighty at our own peril. That's what momma taught me."

"Did you believe her?"

Burns put down his soup bowl and held up his bad hand.

"Not 'til I hurt this hand, I didn't. Before that, I was a bad kid, you know. Always angry, hated everybody and everything." He rested his hand in his lap. "Thought I was going to die that awful day. All the bad things I'd ever done come back to me then, like lying, and thieving, and fighting. But after that day, I remembered what momma taught me. I started praying for God to spare me and save my soul. I promised to start living right from that day on, and I did. I was baptized in the Church of Christ, once Mas'r Charles allowed that I could. Even give me two dollars for new clothes to get baptized in. And I learnt to preach God's word. He give me the gift of preaching when I was baptized. Preached wherever anybody'd listen, colored man or white.

"So, you still believe her now?"

He shook his head. "That don't matter none anymore. Now, I believe only in what Jesus tells me. I try every day to do what he tells me to do. He tells me to pray, I pray. He tells me to sing, I sing. He tells me to preach, I preach."

"Uh-huh. Well, now, did Jesus tell you to run away up north?"

Burns turned his head away, gazing toward the bow, where some of the crew had gathered, laughing and feeding a stale biscuit to a gull hovering above them. One man straddled the mended bowsprit, lunging out, trying to capture the bird by the feet, but it teased him, staying just beyond reach.

"I'm sorry, Tony. That was out of line. Forget I said that."

Burns faced him. His eyes took on an odd expression that seemed both to seek and grant forgiveness, at once.

"I ain't nothing special, Mistah Gunn. Just a sinner saved by grace. Same as you, I expect. It was my idea to run when I did. It wasn't Jesus telling me. Nossir."

"Well, how do you know?"

"A man died 'cause of what I did. That's how I know. Ain't no way a man should die for what another man done. God's never pleased about one of his creatures dying at the hands of another one, whatever the cause might be. No good cause for that."

"Was it your fault a man was killed? You know, he was killed fighting the men who were trying to free you."

"I never wanted that, Mistah Gunn. I never wanted nobody to die to set me free. It hurts way down here to know that he did." His crippled hand covered his heart. "I will carry that burden 'til the day I die."

Burns turned to watch the gull fly away, lofting into the gray, clouded sky.

"Are you serious?"

"I am."

Gunn walked over and sat next to Burns. "Don't you think God was happy when you were free, even if only for a while? Isn't that what truly matters, Tony?"

Burns looked him in the eye. "Now, you see, a man's freedom ain't the only thing that matters, Mistah Gunn. It ain't even the thing that matters *most*. It ain't what makes a man a *man*." He pointed toward the gull, which had returned for more hardtack, bringing a companion along. Gunn turned to see where he pointed. "See that bird? That bird is free. But it ain't a man. Birds might be free, sure enough, but they ain't made in the image of God. Can I tell you something—something that I been thinking a lot about, since I been on this ship? Being in the dark makes a body think a lot, you know."

"Go ahead. By all means."

"A man is the only creature on God's earth that can know the truth, and the only one that can live by what he knows is true. That's what makes a man to be a man and not like some other animal, like some orn'ry mule, or a dog, or a bird. It ain't just knowing things. It's knowing what's true and what ain't. And the truth is, we ain't free. None of us. We're all bound to something, or somebody."

"I know a lot of people who would disagree with you, Tony. There are many people who took your side in Boston, who think freedom is the most important thing about living and being happy. In fact, they see it as a blessing from God to be cherished above all things in life. To them, there isn't anything more important than liberty. Some have even said, 'Give me liberty, or give me death.' That is the truest thing they know."

"Maybe so, but—"

"Even that young woman said it. Remember? During the march to the waterfront. She asked you why you didn't just kill yourself, rather than be a slave again."

"Killing myself wouldn't solve anything. It just means that evil won out. What I'm trying to say is, freedom ain't the most important thing in life. There's other things just as important."

Burns held his gaze, until Gunn turned away.

"Would you please look at me, Mistah Gunn?"

Gunn looked back toward him. He had never heard anyone talk this way, so direct, so simple, with such assurance, as though speaking with an absolute certainty of knowing. *Not even Thoreau, and he usually seems quite sure of himself.* He wondered what it would be like to know that kind of certainty, yet he wanted to deny it was even possible to think that way.

"That's better. I need to look in a man's eyes to know who he is, to know whether his eyes are open or not. I know one thing. You can't open another man's eyes for him. Ever tried it? You can lead a man—drag him with a chain any which way you want him to go, strong as he might be—but you can't open his eyes for him."

"Go on. I'm listening."

"God has already given us the most important freedom a man can have. Is the freedom to choose between good and evil. Is the freedom to choose the truth. Freedom don't mean much apart from that. No other man can take that kind of freedom away from you or give it to somebody else by killing, or dying, or suffering in any way."

"Sometimes … sometimes suffering, or dying, or even killing is necessary, Tony. The fathers of our country thought it was important enough to fight a war to secure freedom for all Americans. Some of them died doing it." He immediately realized the thoughtlessness and incongruity of what he had said, but it had been an impulse. It simply came out.

Burns shrugged and spat. "Maybe they's *your* fathers. Not mine." He sat up and slowly shook his head. "All due respect, Mistah Gunn, but I don't think any man ever died to set another man free, except one. Maybe they done it for money, or for land, or to get power, or some other cause. Maybe just to prove they's right, or to make their own evil look good, somehow. Nossir, you can't kill a man and expect to get freedom of any kind, if you want the truth." The fierceness in his eyes faded, changed in an instant to serenity. The lines in his furrowed brow smoothed out. "Now, someday—*some day*—mark my words, I will be set free by the hand of God himself. I do believe that. This may be not the day, but it's coming. I know it down deep. My spirit's free now, and some day this body will be, too. 'Til then, I'm bound to rejoice in obedience to him. His word says to always rejoice, no matter what. D'you know that?"

"Is that why you sing?"

"Mostly. Have you heard me sing?"

"I have. It amazes me that you can find something to sing about in that hole."

Burns grinned. "It ain't what I be singing about, Mistah Gunn. It's who I be singing *to*. That's the truth."

"You'll make quite a preacher someday, Tony."

Many of the words which Burns had spoken were not new to Gunn. He had heard them preached from the pulpit all his life, even by his own faithless father. But never had he seen them lived out in such a way, especially under such extraordinary circumstances.

He found himself wondering whether any other living man, black or white, slave or free, was any more at liberty than Anthony Burns.

26

L'il Bill Powers, the captain's steward, stood a few paces away, saluting him. "Mr. Gunn, the captain requests your presence in the cabin, sir."

"Very well, Powers. I'm on my way." Gunn got up from his seat on the foredeck. He returned the salute, and Powers proceeded on his way forward to the galley.

He left Burns with Riley on guard, nodding off at the rail. Making his way aft, he passed Sam Miller on watch in the cockpit, who queried him with a raised eyebrow. Gunn shrugged and climbed down the companionway into the cabin.

Whitcomb sat in his usual seat, the chart spread before him under the glow of the oil lamp overhead. Prouty was seated at his right hand, Richmond to his left. The three had been talking, but they ceased as Gunn removed his cap and took his place, standing at attention on the far side of the table, facing the stern.

"Good evening, Mr. Gunn. I have a couple of questions for you," said the captain. "First, Mr. Richmond has informed me of a report he received from Asa Butman, a report about some money that apparently has gone missing. Money that belonged to our prisoner. Butman claims that Burns had four dollars in coins in his possession, but it went missing last night, so he says, after you visited Burns at midnight. Do you know anything about that?"

"I—yes, sir. I do." He pulled the wadded piece of rag out of his watch pocket, and unfolded it, revealing three silver dollars and two half-dollars. "Burns gave it to me earlier for safekeeping."

"Is that so? Tell me, Mr. Gunn. Did you order Cookie to give Burns something to make him sleep last night?"

"Yes, sir. I did. He was having difficulty sleeping, so I asked Cookie to see what he could do for him."

"I see."

"Captain, surely you're not suggesting that I drugged Burns and took his money. You can't possibly believe such a ridiculous—"

"Frankly, I'm not sure what to believe these days. Credibility seems in short supply aboard this ship of late."

"Look, sir, this is simply a blatant attempt by certain people to cast aspersions on my character. It's a rotten game that needs to end."

"Of course. Obviously. I see that now." The captain's shoulders relaxed.

"I'll keep it in the ship's safe. That will end the matter," said Prouty. "Satisfied, Mr. Richmond? You can tell Butman the money has been found. He and his men can rest easy now."

Richmond could not hide the chagrin from his face.

Gunn wrapped the coins in the rag and handed the modest bundle to Prouty, who placed it in front of himself on the table. "Is that all, sir?"

"No, Mr. Gunn. I have a more serious matter to discuss with you," Whitcomb said.

"What would that be, captain?"

Richmond took an item from his lap, placed it on the table, and slid it across to Gunn. It was his book—the same book he thought had gone over the side, lost forever. Though it appeared somewhat worse for wear, there it lay, dry and in one piece.

"Does this item belong to you, Mr. Gunn?"

"Yes, Mr. Richmond. Where did you get it, may I ask?"

"Brent gave it to me, before he departed the ship."

"Where did he get it?"

"He claims to have found it in the dinghy when he placed his luggage there, before it was moved to the longboat."

"Why didn't you give it to me earlier? I thought I had lost it."

"Mr. Richmond thought it was important for us to see what he found inside the book," interjected Whitcomb.

"There was a letter inside, captain. A personal letter. One that Mr. Richmond had no right to read, I might add," said Gunn.

"There was no letter inside, Mr. Gunn. Only this." Richmond reached forward and opened the book. Tucked within the pages was a sheet of paper, doubled over twice, which he removed, unfolded, and handed to Gunn. It was a broadside advertising the meeting of the Vigilance Committee at Faneuil Hall the night before they left Boston. It called for an uprising of the people of Boston "against this present tyrannical government, with victory at all costs." How it happened to be there he could only guess, but it was not a hard guess.

"Is that yours?" asked Prouty.

"No, sir. It is not. I have no idea how that item came to be inside my book."

"A likely story. Incredible, if you ask me." said Richmond, thumbing his mustache.

Prouty turned to Richmond. "Thank you, Mr. Richmond. That will be all."

"Aye, aye, sir." Richmond pushed away from the table and rose from his seat. He replaced the chair deliberately, took his cap from a hook on the bulkhead, and gave Gunn a sideways glance. Then he left the cabin, climbing the ladder to the cockpit. He paused next to the open skylight before moving on.

Prouty sighed. "Mr. Gunn, I am going to ask you this question once. Just once. I want your answer straight. Why did you attend the meeting of the Vigilance Committee last Friday night?"

"I told you, sir. I was there with a woman. Her name is Elizabeth

Faulkner. She was my main purpose."

"So you've said. Very well," said Whitcomb. "We'll take you at your word, Mr. Gunn."

"Is that all, sir?"

"No, it is not," said the captain. "It has come to my attention that you have been spending far too much time with Burns. I understand your interest—somewhat—but it has gone too far. If you have so much time on your hands that you can sit idly and chat with someone who is no more to us than a duty to discharge, then Mr. Prouty will find more work for you to do. Something more constructive. I will not have you shirking your duties. Not on any man's account. Understood?"

"Yes, sir."

Whitcomb exhaled through pursed lips. "You may stand at ease, Mr. Gunn."

Gunn relaxed his stance but was not at ease.

"Let me ask you something. You said earlier that slavery should be abolished. Are you a free-soiler, Mr. Gunn? Are you an abolitionist? I want to know. Tell me honestly."

"I don't have—I do not belong to a particular party, captain. Let me just say that once you've actually heard one man haggle for another with your own two ears, as I have, everything changes. Nothing is the same for me after that. Slavery is wrong, period. There is no way to justify it. I defy anyone to say otherwise."

"Very well, then—"

"But I will say also that I do not believe citizens should take the law into their own hands. I've seen the direct result of that, too. I don't believe that violence will resolve the issue of slavery, or any other issue. It only breeds more violence, and very likely could lead to something worse. Maybe even war."

"Well, at least we agree on that, lieutenant. Where *are* your loyalties, then?"

"Sir?"

"I would like a clear testament as to where your loyalties lie, Mr. Gunn. I think we deserve that. You've already said you think the president is wrong in this matter. So, I will come right out and ask you. Do you support the actions of your government, of the service, in this matter? Right now, today."

"May I ask you a question, first, before I answer, captain?"

"If you are careful to mind your station. Your career depends on it."

"Captain, do you believe the government can be wrong in any given matter?"

"Of course, I do. Our whole system of checks and balances is based on that premise."

"Do you think our government could be wrong in this matter, sir?"

"I do not think that it can ever be wrong to abide by the law as it exists, and as expressed by the constitutionally represented will of the people, which we've sworn to uphold." Whitcomb spoke firmly, without hesitation.

"Do commissioned officers have no moral choice in the matter, sir, as individual citizens of this republic?"

"In such cases, we as officers do have a choice, Mr. Gunn. We certainly do. We can raise our voices to change any laws that we find offensive to matters of conscience and to exercise our right as citizens to vote accordingly. But taking the law into our own hands or choosing which laws we will or will not obey or enforce is not liberty. No, sir. It is anarchy. 'Liberty is the right to do whatever the law permits,' as a wise man once said. Wouldn't you agree?"

"I suppose so, yes. Of course."

"Then, you do have a choice to make, lieutenant, and you are free to make it. Will you carry out your sworn duty, willingly enforce the law, and thereby keep your current post? Or will you choose some other course of action, perhaps more suited to your personal taste and sensibilities?"

"I understand, sir."

"No, I don't think you do, Mr. Gunn. I want you to choose. I want your answer. *Now.* This minute."

27

Stunned as though he had been stripped naked in public view, Gunn stood on deck near the mainmast. Before he left the cabin, he told the captain he was persuaded what they were doing was wrong morally, if not legally. Nothing would change his opinion. But when all was said and done, he had sworn to uphold the law. And that's what he would do.

"I want your solemn word on that, Mr. Gunn."

"You have it, sir."

Twilight had set in. The gray sky hedged the ship on every side.

Richmond climbed up through the main hatch. He stepped over the coaming and stood before Gunn, blocking his advance.

"Mr. Butman sends his regards and thanks you for looking out for the welfare of his prisoner. He is glad to know the money is now in good hands." His half-smile was as smug as the tone in his voice.

"I'm sure he is."

"And I'm glad you recovered your book. Was it a favorite?"

"It is. Where is the letter that was inside?"

"How should I know? I received it from Brent in exactly the condition I returned it to you. There was nothing but the flyer inside the book. Was it an important letter?"

"Important enough for me to ask about it."

"I'm terribly sorry, Gunn. Brent said nothing about the letter. Perhaps it fell out of the book. How did you come to lose it, anyway?"

"I dropped it from the foremast. I thought it had gone overboard. Never mind that."

"Well, the important thing is you have it back. You should be less careless in future."

"The important thing is that you mind your own business, Mr. Richmond."

"Mr. Gunn, need I remind you that you are speaking to a superior officer?"

"I am reminded, sir, that I should put no trust in those who speak in friendly words."

"I don't know what you mean."

"I think you do."

"Look, if you are suggesting that I am somehow responsible for your present trouble, you are sadly mistaken. I am merely the messenger. Do not shoot the messenger, Mr. Gunn. You are the one who is under scrutiny here. You, sir, are solely responsible for your questionable actions."

"That flyer was planted in my book, and you know it."

"And if so, what of it? Would that make it any less true that you disobeyed a direct order? The flyer simply called you out and showed you for what you truly are."

"You know nothing of the circumstances."

"Nor do I need to."

"I've been set up. Brent was stirring up trouble. He knew I was not at that meeting for any wrongful purpose."

"Did he? And how would he know that, Mr. Gunn? How could he possibly know you aren't some wild-eyed, blood-thirsty abolitionist, who might undermine or even sabotage his efforts to get Burns back? How would anyone know?"

"I am nothing of the kind."

"You, sir, are a lily-livered seditionist, and that's a fact everyone aboard this ship knows now. Admit it to yourself, Gunn."

He took a step toward Richmond. "Say that again."

"You heard me. You are betrayed by your own actions, and they have betrayed your country. You and them high-minded ideals." His grin had turned to a thin-lipped snarl. "See here, Gunn. I don't much like you—never have."

"The feeling is mutual, I assure you."

"No doubt. I'm sure, among other things, you despise the fact that I am a southerner."

"My own mother hails from Savannah."

"Nevertheless, since I arrived on this ship, you have made it quite clear that you don't think I should be here. You think I took your job, don't you?"

"It's much simpler than that, Mr. Richmond."

"Pray, tell."

"I just don't like foppish mustaches or the men who wear them. Never have."

Richmond fumed. "I didn't take your job, you know. It wasn't yours to have. You simply aren't anywhere near ready for promotion. I saw it. Mr. Prouty saw it. Now, the captain sees it. Well, I am glad they all finally see what I see. You're a shirker, a thief, and a liar, and I will do everything in my power to make sure they don't forget it. The fact that you are a seditionist who hates his own country just clinches it."

Gunn flexed his fists. His vision narrowed.

"Go ahead, Gunn. Hit me. You know you want to. Nothing would make me happier."

At that moment, Prouty stepped down from the quarterdeck and approached them. "Is there a problem here, gentlemen?"

Richmond started to smooth his mustache, then deferred. "No, sir. None, at all."

"Mr. Gunn, you appear to need some rest," said Prouty. "Tell you what. I will stand the midwatch tonight. You can relieve me for the morning watch. Get a good night's sleep."

"No need, sir."

"I insist."

"Thank you, sir. I'll say goodnight, then." Gunn turned and slid down the companionway ladder into the wardroom. He went directly to his stateroom, undressed, and prepared for bed.

It was well past midnight before he drifted off to sleep. He slept fitfully and awoke several times, the last well before his next watch. Unable to get back to sleep, he lay in his bunk, worrying about all that had happened and what might be in store. At last, his unsettled feelings drove him from his stateroom. He climbed to the main deck to seek the solace of the open horizon.

At half-past three, he relieved Prouty on watch, glad to have something to do. He relished the quiet of the ship under the stars and hoped the sun would take its time rising. The air was clear and mild and the wind steady.

Just as the upper limb of the sun broke over the horizon, Nelson approached and stood next to him at the rail on the quarterdeck. They saluted each other without speaking. Gunn removed his cap and examined it, then replaced it on his head.

"What are you looking for, sir?" asked Nelson.

"Just looking to see if the word 'Dunce' is written there. You'd tell me if it were, wouldn't you, Boats?"

"Ha. We're in fine spirits this mornin', sir. I can see that."

"Nothing a good thumb in the eye wouldn't cure."

"I suppose it has somethin' to do with your little chat with the Old Man, then?"

"You might say so. You heard about that, eh?"

"It's a small ship, sir. And when the cap'n talks, the parrot squawks."

"No shortage of parrots in this ship."

"And why would this one be any different? Any ship is like a woman, sir. Best not expect her to keep a secret untold, unless it be her age."

"I'll remember that."

"Or how many men she's had her way with and jilted in her wake."

Gunn smiled. "My trouble is my own, Boats. Can't blame it on the ship."

"Well, then, my advice is simple. Like I said before—"

"Find the wind's eye and sheet home."

Nelson gave a curt nod. "Right, sir. If you'll excuse me, then, I come up to pipe reveille. It's nearly four bells."

"Best get to it."

"Aye, sir." Nelson went over to the mainmast, and rang the ship's bell, waking the ship to the new day. Then he sauntered forward with his rolling gait, his boatswain's pipe to his lips, trilling the familiar notes of reveille.

"Reveille, reveille, reveille!" He banged his fist on the forward hatch cover and shouted down into the forecastle. "All hands heave out and trice up. The smokin' lamp's lit in all common spaces. Now, reveille."

The boatswain's pipe also sounded a wakeup call to Gunn. In the broken stillness of the dawn, his mind formed a new resolve as clear as the brightening sky, his uncertainty fading with the dim stars in the coming light of day.

He wanted his career. He needed his promotion. But he must have a clear conscience. Perhaps Thoreau was right, after all. From now on, he would let his own conscience be a law unto itself. And he would enforce that law as well and as diligently as all others, come what may.

There was nothing else for it. He would find the wind's eye and sheet home, all right, and see where this tack would take him.

28

As would any sailor worth his salt, Gunn sensed the nearness of land, like detecting the perfume of an alluring woman in the next room. Like most of his shipmates, Gunn was anxious for landfall. Virginia beguiled them all, however, and kept them waiting just out of reach, her seductive scent borne on the light and variable breezes of late spring.

It was nearly noon on Friday that the *Morris* finally drew close enough to meet the pilot boat, by the oddest chance named *Hope*. There, just north of Cape Henry, a pilot embarked to guide the ship into Norfolk.

At two bells that afternoon the captain called the crew to quarters for an emergency conflict drill. It was as much a distraction as practice to sharpen skills.

Connelly, the ship's gunner, joined Gunn at his post near the number two cannon after distributing sidearms to the officers and carbines to all the men not serving as gun crews or otherwise occupied in handling the ship. Together, Gunn and Connelly urged the men on as they ran out all three naval guns on the port side, with powder and shot apportioned to each one, simulating full loads. Mr. Prouty stood by, timing the process from start to finish.

"Two minutes, thirty-three seconds," declared the first lieutenant.

"Let's beat the rust off, shall we, Mr. Gunn?" said the captain from his perch at the weather rail on the quarterdeck. "As the ship's gunnery officer, you must be appalled. I know I am. We can't have that, can we? Try it again. This time, under two minutes."

The captain ordered the drill again—three more times in all in quick succession, until finally Mr. Prouty announced a time of one minute, forty-eight seconds. The exhausted crews leaned on their guns, chests heaving.

"That'll do, I suppose, Mr. Gunn."

After the weapons were stowed, Gunn and Connelly took inventory of the small arms and ammunition, a tedious, but necessary part of each drill. While they worked, calling out the numbers to each other and recording them in the weapons log, Connelly was tight-lipped, as usual, until he stopped working and looked up.

"Mind if I ask you somethin', sir?"

Gunn hesitated. "Speak your mind, Connelly."

"Oh, I know better than that, sir. Been flogged three times back when I was in Her Majesty's navy. Once for drinkin' too much, once for swearin' too much, and once for speakin' me mind."

"You don't have to worry about that, Connelly. You're not in the Queen's navy and there's not been a flogging in the Revenue Marine for quite some time."

"The regulations still allow it, sir. That's what the bible says, anyway."

"Speak up. Say whatever you will."

Connelly drew his sleeve across his lips. "The men wants ta know."

"Know what?"

"Whose side you'd be on."

"What do you mean by that?"

"We don't understand, sir. Why the bloody blazes ya'd be stickin' your neck out for a, well, a person o' color ... who has no future? 'Tis whistlin' into a gale, seems like."

"I think it is necessary to stand up for any man who suffers, free or not, if we can help even a little. But Burns makes it easier to do, somehow. There's something about him ... something unlike anyone I have ever met. I think we could all learn something from him. Don't you?"

"And just what the Sam Hill would that be, lieutenant?"

"What it means to strive for freedom, I guess, even though we might suffer for it. None of us has had to experience that."

Connelly looked bemused. They continued counting.

"Some men deserve to suffer, if y'ask me," growled Connelly, after a minute or so. "They bring it on themselves."

"Maybe so, but not for being guilty of striving to be free. That's no crime. No cause to suffer. Not in my book, anyway."

"Does he not have food to eat and clothes to wear? Are they not provided for him? I've known some whites who've suffered a good deal more for far less, sir. And didn't deserve it, neither." Something like resignation and spent sorrow spread over his wizened features. "Wifey and two boys died in the famine back in Ireland while I was at sea. Starved to death. Nobody gave 'em a second thought."

"I didn't know. I'm sorry to hear that, Connelly."

"But they'd be free now, wouldn't ye say? Free from sufferin', that is. What can we learn from that, lieutenant?"

After that, Connelly grew morose and even more tight-lipped than usual toward Gunn, speaking only when directly spoken to and averting his eyes whenever their paths crossed. His attitude spread among the rest of the crew with the exception of Yarrow, Moriarty, and Nelson, whose demeanor never wavered. Cookie and Li'l Bill Powers, on the other hand, went out of their way to greet Gunn with respect and newfound admiration.

Meanwhile, the *Morris* labored on, her progress steady, but slow, standing up from the mouth of the Chesapeake Bay under the expert guidance of the pilot. Both wind and current conspired against the ship nearly the whole way, as though the entire natural world opposed her mission.

Despite setting all sail to catch the moderate breeze, it took the cutter until noon of the next day to arrive in the city of Norfolk at the mouth of the Elizabeth River. Directly across the river on its western bank, the town of Portsmouth and the federal naval shipyard dominated the landscape.

The *Morris* sailed past a hundred or so vessels of all kinds, both steam and sail, at anchor in the harbor. She at last came to rest at Colley's wharf, midway along the waterfront. The final day had seemed by far the longest of the eight.

Waiting on the wharf, feet spread wide and elbows akimbo, William Brent, Esquire, greeted the cutter upon her arrival. He appeared even more cocksure, if that were possible, now that he stood firmly on dry land in a southern state.

29

As soon as the lines were made fast to the wharf, the brow was put over, and Brent walked aboard with two other officious-looking men. Suttle was not present. They asked permission of no one.

Captain Whitcomb greeted them at the gangway, with Prouty at his side. Richmond was at the mainmast, his post for mooring. Gunn stepped forward to listen.

"Welcome aboard, Mr. Brent. I am glad to see you made the trip safely," the captain said.

"No thanks to you, Captain Whitcomb."

"None sought, I assure you. And the colonel? He is not with you, I see. How is he?"

"A little worse for wear, I'm afraid, due to our recent travails. He was fatigued and unable to make the journey, so he's retired to his home in Alexandria. He sent me to tend to his affairs. He does send his regards, along with those of his dear friend, Senator Mason."

Brent introduced his companions. One was Congressman John Millson of Norfolk, a close associate of Senator Mason. Millson's top hat accentuated a gaunt, hawkish face. He was dressed in black, except for a blue silk forget-me-not pinned to his lapel.

The other gentleman was Mr. Conway Whittle, Collector of

Customs in Norfolk. He was a man of medium stature with a dark, well-groomed horseshoe mustache and a matching fringe of balding hair, revealed as he tipped his broad-brimmed panama hat. He sweated profusely and carried a handkerchief, often dabbing his chin and forehead.

The four men filed toward the cabin in silence, and Gunn stood aside. Brent shot a malicious glance at Gunn, but the others paid him no heed.

It was not long before Powers scampered up the ladder from the cabin and hastily shut the hatch.

"The captain don't wish to be disturbed," he said, as he passed Gunn at the gangway. Powers hurried toward the galley and out of sight.

Word of the cutter's arrival had preceded them, no doubt telegraphed during the past few days by sightings along their slow inbound approach. A sizable crowd soon gathered, clamoring to get a better look at the famous fugitive slave.

A brass band assembled along the head of the wharf, playing a medley of military marches. The band leader teetered with his back to the wharf's edge, in danger of falling into the river. The spectacle, reveling in a man's return to slavery, could have rivaled a celebration of Independence Day in any medium-sized town.

A middle-aged man followed by a small entourage pressed forward through the growing crowd. He smiled broadly with open arms, shouting to be heard and asking to see the captain.

"Simon Stubbs, at your service. Mayor of this fair city. Welcome, welcome."

Stubbs waved his hand, signaling to the band master to stop playing, which the instruments eventually did, horn by horn.

Prouty walked across the brow to meet him on the wharf and was immediately engulfed in the throng. The mayor pumped Prouty's hand and slapped him on the back. Others took turns shaking his hand. A few women touched the sleeve of his tunic and turned to relay their breathless excitement to others in the crowd. Three cheers went up. The band played a popular Stephen Foster tune, "There's A Good Time Coming," The crowd struck up the chorus.

The attention was more than Prouty's Yankee sensibilities could bear. He led the mayor back to the main deck of the cutter, where they could talk unmolested.

At the same time, Butman exited the main hold with Burns, whose hands and feet were bound in shackles. The other deputies followed. When the crowd saw Burns, their cheers turned to resounding jeers. They taunted him with epithets and snide queries about how he had enjoyed his grand adventure.

Burns gave no sign of hearing them. He stood silent, wearing the rags from the lucky bag, his head and feet bare.

"What a sight, Tony," Butman said. "Here we bought you a new suit of clothes, but you won't even wear them." He spoke as though to a wayward child. Burns didn't answer, his head held high.

Stubbs snickered. "A sure waste of money, if you ask me. Why in the world would you do such a thing?"

"Who wants to know?" demanded Butman.

"This is the Honorable Simon Stubbs, Mayor of Norfolk," said Prouty. "Mayor, allow me to introduce Asa Butman, Deputy U.S. Marshal."

"Pleased to meet you, Mr. Butman." The mayor held out his hand.

Butman eyed him. "Well, your Honor, since you asked, me and the boys thought it might be fun to see if the old sayin' is true that the clothes make the man." Butman stopped to relight the stub of cigar in his mouth, spewing a great cloud of smoke as he waved out the match and tossed it over the rail. "We found out, didn't we, boys? Ain't a bit o' truth to it." He laughed a puff of smoke into the air.

"Where are you taking him?" asked the mayor.

"Hall's jail yard, is what I was told. Can you kindly direct me, sir?"

"Head on up Church Street, take a left on Freemason, then right on Brewer. Directly on the other side of town. Can't miss it. You'll smell it before you see it, I'll wager."

"Time to go, Tony. We need to get you bedded down before the day gets any more gone." Butman grunted through his teeth, clenched tightly on the end of the cigar. "We're all gonna need some rest before we make the long haul up to Richmond."

"Sir—the money." Gunn reminded Prouty of the four dollars that belonged to Burns.

Prouty reached into his vest pocket and pulled out the wadded handkerchief. "Ah, yes. Burns, I believe this belongs to you."

Burns stared at the bundle Prouty placed in his shackled hand.

Butman snatched the coins away and thrust them into his own pocket. "He won't need that where he's a-goin'."

Gunn stepped forward. "Mr. Butman, that money does not belong to you. Give it back."

"It's none of your affair, Gunn. Better let it alone. From here on out, you'll be interfering with the duties of a federal marshal, if you say or do one more thing to get in my way. Besides, the way I see it he owes us for the suit of clothes."

Butman shoved his prisoner toward the gangway.

Burns stopped short and turned toward Gunn. "Thank you for your many kindnesses, Mistah Gunn. You are a very good man. God sees all, even what nobody else sees."

Gunn nodded in reply, conscious that all eyes were on him. "I trust he'll watch over you, Tony."

"The only one who'll be watching over him is the jailer up at Hall's. Let's go, Burns." Butman shoved him again, and he stumbled forward. "Mr. Prouty, many thanks for your hospitality. First-rate accommodations," he sniggered. "Give the captain our regards. I guess Mr. Brent is still with him. Would'ja tell him for me that we got his man, and we're headed up to the jail yard?"

"I will, Mr. Butman."

"Riley, there, is gonna take care of our kits—get 'em ashore and all."

The deputies led Burns, hands shackled in front of his waist, down the precarious gangplank and off the ship. The crowd parted, allowing Burns to pass. His unceremonious departure left them subdued and disappointed. They had come to witness the spectacle of a rebellious slave being dragged from the ship, hogtied and screaming for mercy or vengeance. His quiet dignity left them hollow.

"Well, sir," said Mayor Stubbs, speaking so everyone could hear. He rubbed his hands together and beamed his lofty smile, obviously pleased that his city had been honored to host the return of the notorious runaway. "Lieutenant Prouty, the city of Norfolk is hosting a grand reception this evening, right here at the Custom House. We want to welcome you and your fine officers to our beautiful city and to take the opportunity to show our deep appreciation for your services so gallantly rendered to our glorious commonwealth. I understand that the governor himself is on his way from Richmond. Should be here shortly."

"Thank you, Mayor Stubbs. I will pass the invitation to Captain Whitcomb, who is detained at present."

"Most welcome, indeed, sir."

The band played another march as Stubbs departed the ship. They formed ranks and followed him down the wharf, over the quay to Widewater Street. The parade turned and marched down the street along the mile-long waterfront, past the long row of wharves of various sizes and in all manner of conditions that jutted into the river like a mouthful of irregular teeth.

Almost directly across the quay from Colley's wharf stood the imposing brick-and-stone edifice of the Custom House. Although the building looked shabby and in need of some paint and shingles, it had no rivals among the sheds, warehouses and ramshackle office buildings on either side.

Shortly after the mayor's departure, the captain emerged from the cabin with Brent, Millson, and Whittle. Whitcomb appeared red-faced, his brow furrowed. Brent wore his usual insolent scowl, but the other two men seemed contented. The captain walked them to the starboard side and stopped at the gangway, bidding them goodbye. Prouty stood by to see the men off.

When his guests had gone ashore, the captain turned to Prouty.

"I would like to see you in the cabin, Mr. Prouty. Now."

The captain led the way below.

Curious about what the issue was, Gunn remained on deck, directing his attention to tidying up the lines and gear. He didn't have to wait long to find out, however. Prouty returned within a few minutes. He crooked his finger to Gunn.

"Mr. Gunn, your presence, if you please."

30

Gunn followed Prouty down the companionway into the wardroom.

"Be seated," said Prouty, settling himself at the head of the table. He cleared his throat. "I'll get right to the point. Brent is claiming that you tried to sabotage the delivery of Burns to Norfolk, and that you lied about it to the captain to cover your tracks, who then forced him and Suttle off the ship."

"That's not true, sir."

"Doesn't matter. This is a huge event among the people of Virginia. Those men are convinced that you tried to stop it. Congressman Millson wanted to see you punished and dismissed from the service."

"What? I haven't—"

Prouty held up his palm.

"Fortunately for you, the captain came to your defense. He has made the case that the ship is wildly popular right now, at least among Virginians, and that bringing any such charges would shed dishonor upon the service. Obviously, Mr. Whittle is opposed to that. The congressman also doesn't wish to spoil the governor's visit. The smart play is to avoid any controversy. So, the captain has taken all the blame upon himself. He has offered a full apology and paid the travel expenses incurred by Brent and Suttle out of his own pocket. The matter is settled, at least for now. It probably didn't hurt that the captain and Congressman Millson happen to be brother Freemasons."

"I am grateful, sir. And I am more than willing to repay the captain. I'll do whatever it takes to smooth things over."

"Good. Then you may begin by taking the in-port watch. Best that you not attend the event this evening. Captain's orders."

Prouty told him to pass the word that liberty would be granted as soon as cleanups were completed. Of course, the crew was not invited to the reception. Only the officers of the ship were welcome, whose status would permit their socializing with Norfolk's finest citizens.

The off-duty watch went ashore for the night. A clutch of women, presumably from a local bordello, waited to greet them with crooked smiles. Moriarty and a few others sought comfort there, but most of the crew, Nelson among them, were content to find the nearest public house and keep to their own kind for amusement.

Two chose to remain aboard, however. Cookie allowed that he would sooner step on a double-headed rattlesnake than set foot in Virginia ever again. Li'l Bill decided it was not the place for him, either. He didn't care to find out if the tales he'd heard were true that he could be captured and sold into slavery.

At the appointed hour of seven o'clock, the captain and the other officers left the ship, dressed in their finest gold-braided uniforms, to walk the short distance to the Custom House. Whitcomb acknowledged Gunn's salute as he departed but did not offer his usual good-natured quip. Richmond told him to watch out for ghost ships, which Gunn ignored. Sam Miller gave him an apologetic look. Prouty brought up the rear and charged him to keep a sharp watch.

After he had walked the entire cutter, inspecting to make sure all was shipshape and secure, Gunn indulged himself by reclining on the seat built into the aft section of the cockpit, which he never dared to do while the captain was onboard. Nobody did. There, he passed the better part of an hour alone, listening to the orchestra music and occasional laughter coming from the open third story windows of the Custom House. The strains of a familiar waltz, "Do They Miss Me at Home," lingered on the warm and humid air.

A brilliant, multi-hued sunset filled the evening sky, reflected in the serene surface of the river. A pelican preened on a nearby piling, taking in the last of the daylight. At Gunn's elbow, on a flagstaff thrust out over the stern, the red-and-white striped ensign of the Revenue Cutter Service stirred in the dying breeze.

Clusters of anchored ships crowded the river. The ferry wended its way among them, headed to Portsmouth. Over at the naval shipyard sat the decommissioned *USS Pennsylvania,* lately placed into ignominious service as a receiving ship and naval barracks. Now stripped of her rigging and finery, the largest warship ever built by the United States had never engaged an enemy in defense of her country. She lay at anchor like a dissolute, napping dowager. It was a vignette of would-be distinction fallen to ruin due to misspent, squandered purpose. Was that to be the fate of a divided nation—not to mention his own? Not if he could help it. But what was to be done about it? What could any one man do?

He thought about what Thoreau had called him, "a fool made conspicuous by a painted coat"—as though he were some blind tin soldier. He knew Thoreau often could be blunt and prickly in his dealings with other people, so to a certain extent he could overlook the insult. However, he had no doubt that the man meant what he said. He regretted that their friendship might be the first casualty of a decision to keep his job.

He fought the rising temptation to quit the service. He loved his life at sea. He valued his profession and took pride in serving his country. He had chosen this service, and it suited him, despite his recent troubles. Yet, now he felt his career slipping away, even before he had a chance to make it count. Or maybe he just hadn't taken the chance.

As twilight descended on the harbor, there was a commotion at the gangway. Two male figures crossed the brow, both in officers' dress uniforms. One of the men was Sam Miller. Gunn got up to take a closer look as they approached him. He recognized the face of their former shipmate, Second Lieutenant Desmond Bulloch of the *Andrew Jackson*, the man with whom Richmond had exchanged places.

"Look-ee here, Andrew. I found this scallawag at the reception," said Miller.

"I don't believe my eyes."

"Hello, Andrew. Decided to sit down here to jaw with all your friends?" Bulloch's lilting southern drawl, always present, had deepened since they last had seen each other.

"It's so good to see you, Des. How are you?" He pumped Bulloch's outstretched hand.

"Finest kind, Andrew, as you Yankees say. We've been stuck here in Norfolk for the last three weeks or so. Our ship's in the yards over at Gosport." Bulloch jerked his thumb toward Portsmouth.

"How long will you be there?"

"I'd guess another two months, maybe more. It's pretty bad. She needs some major work on the hull. Leaking like an old plowman's boot. Boat hasn't been hauled in about ten years. There is never enough money, it seems. You know how that is. Finally got too bad to ignore. Strange how money always seems so scarce until the ship is actually sinking beneath us."

"Ha. What else is new? So, you came to the party?"

"It is the event of the season, gents. Not to be missed. The *Morris* has made some real friends in Virginia," said Bulloch. "Especially among the ladies of Norfolk, so it appears. Too bad I departed before the ship became famous," he chuckled.

"We'd certainly be glad to have you back. Very glad, believe me," said Miller.

"No, no. I am happy to be home in Savannah. Of course, it would be nice if we stayed there once in a while. We've been away from homeport a good deal, lately. Hey, now, I've got a great idea. Why don't both y'all request a transfer to the *Andrew Jackson*? It'd be like old times."

"You're joking, right?"

"Couldn't be more serious. Captain Dawes would be glad to have you two scoundrels. He cashiered our other officers. Claimed they were incompetent. I'm acting first lieutenant now, and he's recommended me for promotion. Still waiting to hear. If it happens, we sure could use a new second and a third. How about it?"

"Captain Whitcomb would likely approve our transfers right now, given what's happened," said Miller.

"I don't know. I don't think so, Des," said Gunn. "My roots are in New England. It would be hard to leave family. You know that."

"Suit yourself, Andrew, but think about it. An officer's pay goes a lot farther in Georgia than it does up north. I may be partial, but Savannah has a certain charm that no Yankee town can hold a candle to, not to mention some gorgeous women. Some of the prettiest in all the world. And they don't hold any crazy notions in their heads about getting the right to vote or taking on a profession."

"Sounds like a perfect idea to me," said Miller.

"Hey, Des, speaking of great ideas, I have one for you," said Gunn, ready to change the subject. "What do you have planned for tomorrow?"

Bulloch grinned. "Jee-hosaphat. Here comes trouble. I've heard that wind blow before."

31

One of the newest and grandest churches in Norfolk, Freemason Street Baptist marked the ecclesiastical heart of the city at the intersection of Bank and Freemason Streets. Its Gothic Revival buttresses fronted nearly sixty feet along Freemason Street, supporting a spire and bell tower that soared two hundred feet into the sky, high above all the surrounding structures.

Sunday service ended just after noon, following a forty-minute sermon, during which the Reverend Tiberius Gracchus Jones preached about the importance of keeping the Sabbath. Lately, the shops along Main Street had started opening on Sundays, and he was none too happy about it.

Gunn figured it likely the poor man's wife was spending too much money in those shops. Then again, not every preacher was as self-serving as his own father. Witness Anthony Burns, who truly seemed to practice what he preached. No need to become so cynical. He decided to afford this preacher the benefit of the doubt.

After the last hymn, he and Desmond Bulloch hurried down from the "free seats" in the upstairs gallery. Outside the grand double doors, Reverend Jones greeted them with a firm smile and an infirm handshake. They both assured him of taking his message to heart and descended the broad, granite steps to the street.

"So, will you go with me, or not, Des?"

"Where?

"You know where. To Hall's. To the jail yard to see Burns."

"Tell me you're not really serious."

"I'm dead serious."

"It's not exactly my idea of a pleasant Sunday afternoon diversion, Andrew."

"Well, then, I'll go by myself."

"Look, I said I'd go to church with you, but I'm starting to believe that your main reason for coming here this morning is that it's so close to the jail yard."

"Wrong. That's my second reason. The main reason is to have an alibi."

"Aha. I knew it."

"Now, I *am* joking."

"I'm not laughing. As I told you yesterday, this is nothing like a great idea."

"You must admit, we are very close. It's just a few more blocks." Gunn tugged his arm. "Come on."

A stray cow ambled down Freemason Street toward the church. Her bawling calf followed. The cow stopped in the middle of the street to relieve herself.

Bulloch pointed and laughed. "Now *that's* funny. I wish you'd look. You know, truth be told, I have about as much interest in this Burns fellow as that cow."

"At least the cow has someone who cares about her. Somewhere. Eventually, somebody most likely will come looking to make sure she's all right. She's going to be fed sometime today. We are talking about a desperate human being, here, Des. And nobody, *nobody* gives a green cow pie about him."

Bulloch pulled him aside.

"Andrew, let me warn you as a friend." His voice was low and calm, but with an edge to it, the way a doctor warns a stubborn heart patient. "This is not Boston. It will not do you well at all to associate yourself with Burns. There are some folks who would sooner watch him choke to death on a raw chicken neck than to worry the least bit over whether he got enough to eat. Slaves have been shot or hanged for less than he he's done. Show too much interest, and they might start thinking the same thing about you. Follow me?"

"Are you coming, or not?"

Bulloch sighed. "Forget Burns. Somebody needs to tend to *you*. You need a halter, Andrew, same as that dumb cow. I swear, if the shops are open, I'm going to buy you one, no matter what the preacher just said. All right. You win. I'll go with you on one condition. Promise that you won't do *anything* that would make white folks more upset than they are right now about high-minded people from up north telling them how to handle their black folks."

"Let's go." Gunn started walking toward the corner.

"Promise?" Bulloch gripped his arm.

"All right."

They crossed Bank Street and started on their way. A thunderstorm had rolled in from the sea during the early morning hours. The streets were wet and puddled in places, the air warm and humid. The fragrance of honeysuckle wafted toward them, its source topping a nearby garden wall.

"Let me ask you something, Des."

"What is it?"

"Does your family own slaves?"

Bulloch was slow to answer. "Yes, they do. My father owns a small plantation outside Savannah."

"How many?"

He shrugged. "Fifty or so. Field hands and house servants."

"Do you own any of them?"

"No. My father offered one as a gift when I graduated from Annapolis, but I refused. No need on a man-of-war. Or a Revenue Cutter."

"After the war ended, and you left active service in the navy, did you have any thoughts about going back to plantation life?"

"I did. But that's why I decided to join the Revenue Marine, instead, rather than wait for recall to the navy. Life on a cutter might be less exciting than sailing around the world on a warship, but it's a far sight better than being stuck on a cotton plantation."

"Would you ever own a slave?"

"Well, I am my father's youngest son. I will likely not inherit his land. I doubt that it would ever be necessary for me to own any slaves. Besides, I do believe it is wrong for one man to own another. Any thinking man must come to that conclusion sooner or later."

"Then, why don't you have much interest in Burns?"

"I like to mind my own business, Andrew. It's not my affair."

"Maybe it should be."

Gunn quickened his pace to keep up with his friend's stride, which was a half-step longer than his own. Bulloch was a head taller than most men. His handsome features—the gray-green eyes set in a finely carved face, dark hair and mustache, along with his height and athletic form—won him the admiration of most women and the envy of many men, as was apparent when he tipped his hat to occasional passersby. He was thoughtful and intelligent, too, and more certain of his place in the world than Gunn, which he envied most of all.

"All right, now, let me stick my nose into your business," said Bulloch.

"Fair enough. Have at it."

"How are things between you and Richmond?" Bulloch shot him a knowing glance. "He had some disturbingly unkind comments to say about you at the reception last night."

"Are you asking as a friend?"

"Should that make a difference?"

"Well, you've always taught me not to speak ill of another officer. Let's just say we are not on good terms, right now."

"Why is that?"

"He's working as hard as he can to poison my relationship with the captain, with Mr. Prouty, and anyone else in the crew that he can convince. If I stand still for it, I will be done for. I am not going to let that happen."

"What will you do?"

"Make him regret it."

Bulloch stopped short and grasped Gunn's arm.

"You'd best pocket it, Andrew. You need to stay away from that man. Don't underestimate men like him. Besides, how do you intend to make him regret anything?"

"I don't know, yet." Gunn walked on, brushing past Bulloch, who hastened to catch up. "But he deserves whatever comes his way."

32

all's Jail Yard occupied an entire corner at the far end of Brewer Street, a walk of only three or four more blocks north, just as the mayor had said. And he was right about the smell, too. As Gunn and Bullock reached the intersection of Brewer and Queen Streets, the sour stench of rot filled Gunn's mouth and nose and clung to the back of his throat.

Directly across the street on the northeast corner stood a whitewashed brick wall, about twelve feet high, extending in both directions to present a dead front to the corner. A stagecoach stop and boarding house, known as McGrady's according to the sign, occupied the opposite corner of Queen Street. And there was Riley, one of the deputies, dozing on a bench in the shade of the front porch. The others most likely were inside or somewhere nearby.

Crossing Queen Street, they continued along Brewer and walked the length of the wall until they reached a two-story brick building with an unmarked entrance, next to which was a small window, opaque with grime and dust. Near the top of the building's face appeared the name, "W. W. HALL," painted in large, faded block letters. The wall continued around the side of the building.

The two exchanged glances, then mounted three steps to the door. They entered a dim room, empty except for a long L-shaped counter, behind which rows of hardbound record books lined several shelves. Toward the right side sat a block of wood about three feet high and as wide, worn smooth, with an iron ring riveted to its center. A window and an open doorway at the rear revealed an enclosed yard out back. In the far-right corner, a set of stairs led to the second floor.

Footsteps sounded on the stairs, and a thickset, surly man in shirtsleeves descended to the main floor and approached them, obviously annoyed.

"Closed. No business today."

"My name is Andrew Gunn. This is Lieutenant Desmond Bulloch. We're both officers of the Revenue Cutter Service. We have come to see a prisoner."

"What prisoner?"

"Anthony Burns."

The man shook his mane of gray hair. "Marshals looked in on him this morning. Left word that he is not to have visitors. Nobody here right now. Git along with you."

"Look here, Mr.— "

"Brecht is the name."

"Mr. Brecht, we don't mean to cause any trouble. We will only be a minute. All we want to do is see him."

"I think you will not."

Bulloch pressed forward, his hand waving to indicate that Gunn should let him handle the matter.

"You needn't be concerned, Mr. Brecht," he drawled. "This gentleman here is the federal officer who's personally responsible for bringing the runaway back from Boston on the Cutter *Morris*. Fought off a mob in Boston to do it. That boy in there gave him a heap of trouble. He simply wants to make sure the nigger's getting what he deserves."

Brecht's eyes darted back-and-forth between them. "Well, then." He started toward the back door. "Follow me."

The jailor led the way into the adjacent backyard. A long, unpainted shed occupied the left side, and beyond that a ramshackle barn stood at the back corner. A live oak spread its gnarled branches over the right half of the yard. Under the tree, chained to its trunk, lounged a huge black hound, which raised its massive head to see who had dared to enter.

"Never you mind, Kirby," said Brecht. The dog stood and scratched himself, snapped his jowls at a passing fly, then slumped back down with a groan.

A worn path led through the patchy weeds to another whitewashed brick wall with an iron gate. Brecht took the keys dangling from his belt and unlocked the gate. They entered a small, open square partially paved with cobblestones.

At the center of the inner yard stood a whipping post, crowned with iron rings fastened around the top. It was blackened with sweat and blood, but none appeared fresh. A sparrow perched on the post. As the door groaned shut, the bird flitted to the top of one of the cells, twittered a warning, and took flight beyond the high brick wall.

"Did you whip him, Brecht?" asked Gunn.

Brecht frowned and shook his head. "He'll get his thirty-nine when he gets to the capital. Governor's orders. They're planning quite a show up in Richmond."

The wall along the left side of the yard housed six cells, each gated with solid wooden doors on heavy iron hinges. A single hole, the size of a playing card, was cut into each door at eye level, the only source of ventilation or light.

As they entered, the stench of all manner of human waste so assaulted Gunn that his lungs refused to inhale it. If it could be named, this was surely the odor of despair.

Without a spot of shade, the oppressive heat of the afternoon sun plastered the shirt to Gunn's back, underneath his wool frock coat. No sound came from any of the cells other than the buzzing of swollen flies, the only sign of life other than the departed sparrow.

Brecht led them to the third cell and stopped at the door.

"Here he be. One minute. No more."

"Thank you, Brecht. That will be all," said Gunn. Brecht shrugged and shambled outside the iron gate to wait for them. Gunn peered through the door's vent into the void of the cell. His eyes watered. Nothing stirred.

"Burns?" he called. Not a sound. He kicked at the door. "Anthony."

"That you, Mistah Gunn?"

The clank of chains drew Gunn's attention to the dark form huddled on the floor. "Yes, Tony. It's me." He turned his back toward Brecht and pressed his sweat-drenched face against the vent. The stench made him gag.

"Could I ask you to do something for me?" came the weak voice from inside.

"Yes, I'll try."

"They taking me to Richmond t'morrah. Get word to Reverend Grimes in Boston. He knows where I'll be. Do what he can to get me out." The chains shifted again.

"I will do that, Tony."

"Don't think my days will be long, there, if he cain't. They already talking like I'm good as dead."

"Not if I can help it. Hang on, Tony. Don't give up."

"Lieutenant, need to lock up, here," called Brecht, from the gate.

Gunn whirled to face him. "Open this door, Brecht."

Brecht shook his head. "Not happening."

Gunn pushed himself away from the door and walked toward the gate. Bulloch faced away, his eyes glued to the far corner of the yard, his face stone. Gunn grabbed him by the arm.

"Des, we've got to get him out of here. Help me."

"Andrew, I warned you," Bulloch muttered. "Don't be a fool. I will do nothing of the kind. You got what you came for. Now, let's get out of here, before you get us thrown in that cell with him."

Sickened by the fetid smell, Gunn pulled a handkerchief from the pocket of his frock coat and covered his face.

"My God, what an awful stench. How do you live with that, Brecht?" He spat against the bloodstained post to rid his mouth of the putrid taste.

Brecht laughed. "Like anything else, lieutenant. You get used to it. You think this is bad, it ain't nothin'. Tomorrow, he's going to Lumpkin's in Richmond. This place is paradise compared to that hellhole. They don't call it the Devil's half-acre for nothing. He'll wish he was back here, before long."

Gunn passed through the iron gate, followed by Bulloch. "We all get our just desserts, don't we?"

"You bet." The jailor smirked as he locked the gate. "You Yankees ain't ever seen such as that, 'ere ya? Ain't got the stomach for it, I reckon. Had your fill?"

"There's only one thing that I would like more to see happen."

"From your mouth to God's ears, lieutenant."

"We'll be leaving you now, Mr. Brecht. Thank you for your trouble."

A loose cobblestone underfoot nearly tripped him up. In one continuous motion, Gunn bent down, picked up the paver, and spun around.

"Hey, now." Brecht's surprised yelp woke the dog. The startled animal scrambled to a ready stance, a low growl rumbling in his throat.

Gunn aimed the rock at Brecht's head. "I swear I'll smash your ugly skull like a gourd, you mangy cur. Now, do as I say and open that door."

33

The hound leaped and strained short against the chain around his neck, barking and snarling. Strings of spittle wrapped around his muzzle.

"Andrew! Have you gone mad?" yelled Bulloch.

"Stand back, Des. Just stay out of it."

"All right, all right," rasped the jailor. "Put down the rock."

Gunn took a step forward. "Open the door, or I'll put it down right on your top knot."

Brecht fumbled for the keys on his belt. They jangled to the ground. He bent down to retrieve them. When he raised upright, his left hand held a derringer, pointed at Gunn's forehead.

"Now, git out of here, both o' you bungholes, before I pull the trigger on both barrels."

Gunn drew back and dropped the cobblestone. Brecht waved the muzzle of the derringer toward Bulloch.

"Get over there with him."

The two men stood together, facing Brecht. The dog lunged against the chain.

"Git, I said. Both of you, or I'll feed you to that blasted hound. He'd like that. Kirby don't get much white meat. It'll be his lucky day."

Gunn turned toward the office. Brecht gripped his collar with one hand and shoved the pistol deep into his back with the other. They exited through the office the way they had come.

"You. Open the door."

Bulloch opened the door and tripped down the steps. Gunn's cap fell off as Brecht kicked him into the street. Brecht stood in the doorway, straight-arming the pistol at Gunn's chest.

"Stay out."

They stood in the muddy street, chests heaving. Sweat trickled down their faces. Acrid bile surged into Gunn's throat, but he choked it back.

"What's going on, here?"

They whipped around to find the source of the familiar voice.

Butman crossed the street toward them. The other deputies followed two-by-two off McGrady's porch.

"Are these men bothering you, Brecht?" hollered Butman. He stopped in the middle of the street, the others with him.

"Not hardly anymore," Brecht growled. He tucked his pistol into his belt. "You'd better get 'em outta here, though, before I get my back up." He picked up Gunn's hat from the threshold and flung it into the mud at Butman's feet. Butman stepped on the crown, crushing it into the mud. Brecht stepped back inside and slammed the door.

Brent and Richmond jumped off the porch of the boarding house and walked across the street toward them.

"What are you doing here?" Gunn asked.

"What are *you* doing here, Gunn? Or need I ask?" Richmond chortled. "You two look like a couple of bilge rats, caught with the captain's cheese."

"We're just leaving." Bulloch took Gunn by the arm, but he pulled away.

Richmond picked up the muddy hat and held it out. "Here's your hat, Gunn. What's your hurry?"

"I'll get it," Bulloch muttered.

"Desmond Bulloch. So good to see you. Why in the world are *you* here? Let me guess. You have accompanied our good Mr. Gunn to visit his dear friend in prison. What a Christian thing to do."

"Shut up, Richmond."

"Shut me up."

Bulloch snatched the hat from Richmond's hand and stalked back toward Gunn. "Let's go."

"Hold on a second," said Gunn. "Did you follow me up here, Mr. Richmond?"

"Don't be stupid. Why would I do that?" Richmond swayed on his feet, like he'd been drinking.

"Why are you here, then? I thought you'd gone home."

"Let's just say we had some unfinished business. Mr. Brent was kind enough to offer a ride in his coach up to the state capital. From there, I can take the train home."

"What sort of business? It can't be legal, whatever it is."

Richmond laughed. "You'd be surprised. If you only knew." He chucked his chin toward the jail. "This is all for nothing, Gunn."

"What's that supposed to mean?" asked Gunn.

Richmond turned to Bulloch. "You're his friend. Tell him the world don't need another do-gooding savior. Would you tell him that?"

"Tell him yourself," said Bulloch.

"What? What's all for nothing?"

"Never mind. Forget it," sneered Richmond.

"It's of no concern to you, Gunn," said Brent. "Just mind your own business, or you'll regret it. Leave things be, and everything will be just fine. You'll see."

Gunn tried to read Brent's expression, but his rodent eyes gave nothing away.

"Come on, Des. Let's go."

"Just a minute." Butman held up his hand. "Hang on. We ain't finished here. From the looks of things, you fellas was interfering with a federal prisoner. The law don't take too kindly to that."

"Look, it was a mistake to come here," said Bulloch, "which we intend to rectify. No harm, no foul, deputy." He returned Gunn's hat. "Let's go."

"What does the law say about holding a man prisoner in his own filth?" Gunn brushed the mud from his hat and beat it against his trouser leg. "I'm sure Marshal Freeman will have something to say about it."

"I've had just about enough of you and your big mouth, you little piss-ant," said Butman. "Maybe I should have shot you while I had the chance, back in Boston."

Richmond scoffed. "He's already done for, Asa. Brent saw to that. Dead man walking. He just doesn't know it, yet."

"I just don't get it. What do you want from me, Richmond?" said Gunn.

Richmond shrugged. "Nothin'. What could I possibly want from a lily-livered seditionist who hates his own country? You're not worthy of that uniform."

The next few seconds were lost to him. Before anyone could react, Gunn charged Richmond and tackled him. The force carried them both into a nearby puddle, where they splashed in a writhing heap, Gunn on top. He straddled Richmond, fists flailing as fast as he could make them land. Richmond squealed like a wounded boar, trying to push him off, grasping Gunn's uniform, and ripping a button from his coat.

"Stop, Andrew." Bulloch yanked them apart and pinned Gunn's arms behind him. "Quit, now!"

Butman bared his teeth and pelted Gunn in the gut. Gunn grunted and doubled over, then crumpled to the ground, wheezing, unable to catch his breath.

"You had it comin', boy."

Bulloch wrestled with Butman, shoving him away. "Stand off, you stupid ape."

"Get your cotton-pickin' hands off me," Butman growled.

Riley drew his sidearm. "I'd do as the man says," he said.

"Put it away, deputy," said Bulloch. "There's no cause for that. We're leaving."

Richmond jumped up and sloshed through the puddle, mired and dripping wet. His nose and split lip trickled blood into the sanguine mud smeared across his chin. He spat blood at Gunn's feet.

"I'll see you charged with insubordination, Gunn. I swear it," he hissed. "Do you hear me? He bent down and held out his hand with the uniform button in it. "And this will be my proof."

"You'll do nothing of the kind, Richmond," said Bulloch.

"You saw what he did, Bulloch. You saw it. He struck a superior officer. I will press charges when I get back to the ship, and you must be my witness."

Bulloch shook his head. "No, you won't."

"Why wouldn't I?"

"We both know the answer to that, Willie boy. We wouldn't want the rest of the world to find out, now, would we?"

34

Gunn and Bulloch rented a room at the National Hotel on Main Street, where they stayed awhile to get cleaned up. Few words had passed between them in the meantime. Gunn slept through supper. Bulloch tried to coax him to eat some cold chicken and dumplings, leftovers from his own meal, but he wasn't hungry.

It was well after midnight when they checked out and walked back to the ship. Gunn's plan was to slip aboard the cutter somehow without either Prouty or the captain noticing his blemished uniform.

"What were you thinking, Andrew?" Bulloch said, as they picked their way in the darkness down an unlit Church Street toward the waterfront.

"I was merely following the dictates of my conscience, Des."

"Your *conscience*? Don't give me that tripe. You do realize this isn't just all about you, don't you? What about your promise to me? What about your word?"

"Some things are more important than others. Justice, for one."

"Says who? Says you. Who died of a sudden and made you the supreme arbiter of justice in the world? You know better than that. What's come over you?"

"Can't you see? They've been conspiring against me ever since ...

well, I don't know what came over me, Des. I—I lost my head, I guess."

Bulloch stopped and held out his arm, stopping Gunn in his tracks. "Yeah, well, that's the trouble, isn't it? You might have lost more than your head. Not that it was doing you any good, mind you. I saw it coming, Andrew. That's why I made you promise. And I tried to warn you about Richmond, but you wouldn't listen to reason."

"I know. Why do you think he has it in for me? I can't fathom it."

Bulloch shrugged. "Some people just hate to see others succeed. Maybe it makes him feel like he's failed, somehow. Who can explain such foolishness?"

They walked on. "What do you think will happen, Des?"

"I don't know. But if he presses charges, it likely won't go well for you."

"Will you testify?"

"I'll have to, won't I?"

"*Against* me?" Gunn again stopped short.

"You did hit him, my friend, but as far as I'm concerned, he was as much at fault as you were. He provoked the fight. It is a private matter between you two, and it was settled. That should be the end of it. Maybe he'll drop it when he cools off."

"Why do you think so?"

"Because I know something about him that he doesn't want to come out. If it ever did, he'd likely land in the brig for a very long time."

"What's that?"

"Well, now, I'm not going to say. No true gentleman would speak of such things."

"Do you have proof?"

"No, but Richmond doesn't know that. Let's hope when he sobers up, he figures out that it's in his best interest to let this whole thing drop. I don't know what made him such a miserable, spiteful, conniving little man. But he's also a very smart little man. Let's count on that."

"This thing you know about him. Is it that bad?"

"Everybody has at least one secret, something they'd rather keep anybody else from knowing. Am I right?"

"What's yours?"

Bulloch gave a crooked grin. "Wouldn't you like to know?"

Heavy, thick rain started to fall, pelting the ground. They continued in silence.

As they reached the ship, he turned to Bulloch. A stream of muddy water ran from the visor of his cap. "Do you think I should tell the captain?"

"That's really up to you. Maybe you should just let things play out when Richmond returns, given the circumstances. Cross that reef when you get to it."

"Maybe so."

***

The rain continued for the next two days. Despite the deluge, which, as always, fell alike upon the just and the unjust, the celebrated transfer of Burns to Lumpkin's jail in Richmond proceeded without delay, according to the newspapers. Gunn hated to think of the horrors awaiting him there. He was anxious to get back to Boston soon so he could deliver the message with which Burns had entrusted him, among other reasons. But the rain delayed needed repairs to the ship and their departure.

The crew of the *Morris* remained below decks making cordage from spun yarn, which would later be turned into rope and rigging. They also occupied the hours with other menial tasks and pastimes, while waiting for a new jib boom and custom-made spars for the foremast to arrive from the Gosport Naval Shipyard across the river. They arrived on Thursday morning just before the rain stopped, ferried across the river from Gosport, on a wagon driven by two slaves. The work to rig the new spars began in earnest as soon as they were unloaded.

That evening, Bulloch visited at Prouty's invitation to dine in the wardroom. Afterward, he stayed to play cribbage with Miller as his teammate. Prouty and Gunn played opposite them.

Captain Whitcomb joined the other officers after dinner, as he sometimes did when the solitude of the cabin became insufferable. This evening was the first since they had arrived that the captain had not been invited to dine ashore at parties held in his honor by the first citizens of Norfolk.

Whitcomb sat at the head of the wardroom table. He took a long pull on his pipe. Bulloch shared his newly acquired box of Cuban cigars with Miller. Gunn liked the smell of cigars because they reminded him of his uncle and his grandfather, but he had not developed a taste for them, so he declined Bulloch's generosity.

The conversation among them took an unexpected turn, as though borne on the wavering columns of smoke, curling languidly overhead to the open skylight.

"These came in on a ship that arrived yesterday from Havana." Bulloch ruminated, taking a long puff on his cigar and savoring the smoke. "That's why they draw so well. Not like our American cigars."

Miller nodded his approval. "Hand-rolled on the thighs of fair Spanish maidens, I hear."

"Is that so?" said the captain, smiling, puffing his pipe, an eyebrow raised.

Miller splayed his hands. "That's what they say."

Prouty chuckled. "Ah, you see, gentlemen. It must be so. Mr. Miller's heard it said."

"Cubans, eh?" Whitcomb seemed preoccupied. "Not smuggled, I hope."

"No, sir. These are perfectly legal," said Bulloch.

"Good. Glad to hear it. Of course, if some in Washington have their way, it won't matter much longer."

"What do you mean, sir?" said Gunn.

"There's a growing movement afoot for us to buy Cuba. Or take it by force."

"Buy it? Whatever for?" said Miller.

"There are those who want to make it another slave state. Of course, tax-free cigars and sugar would be a convenient side benefit."

"Well, that's one way to eliminate smuggling, I suppose," said Gunn.

"Good. One less thing to worry about," said Miller, puffing on his cigar while studying his cards.

"I doubt we can ever eliminate smuggling," said Prouty. "There will always be something or someone to smuggle."

"That's very true, gentlemen," said Whitcomb. "The slave trade has been a capital offense in this country since oh-eight, but even that hasn't stopped it."

"Folks around here are more worried about the Underground Railroad. Ships transporting runaways to your neck of the woods. That's illegal, too, you know." Bulloch said.

"I heard that's how Anthony Burns got to Boston," said Miller. "I wonder what ship brought him." He raised his head, grinning. "Ha! Think of it. We could be moored right next to her and not even know it."

Gunn played his cribbage hand and took the points. It was his turn to deal the cards. "I heard Colonel Suttle trying to get that information out of him before he left the ship. Burns said he couldn't recall, at least from what I could overhear."

"Brent succeeded in getting that intelligence in the end, or so he told me," said Prouty. "Well, at least in part. Burns claimed that he could not remember the exact name, or the name of the captain. But he said the ship's name was something like *Percy-ville*."

"*Percy-ville?*" The captain took a draw on his pipe and scratched his head. "Doesn't ring a bell."

"Maybe the homeport?" asked Miller. "Perhaps he confused the two. Is there a town called Percyville?"

Gunn stopped dealing the next hand. He blinked, feigning something in his eye, then sat upright, shielding his face from the others.

"Hey, you didn't deal my last card," said Miller. "Are you all right, Andrew?"

"Yes, yes, Sam. Sure. Just smoke in my eye."

It could not be. That name sounded too much like *Parsifal*, the name of one of his uncle's ships. After returning from a trip to England some years ago, Aunt May had insisted that each of his ships should bear the name of an Arthurian knight. Some of them had been rechristened to accommodate her wishes.

"Let's check the logs. Could be we've come across this *Percyville*," said Prouty.

"Good idea." Whitcomb sat up in his chair and jabbed the stem of his pipe in the air. "If there is such a ship, and she's sailed into Boston, we've probably either sighted or boarded her. I think Burns arrived in Boston in February or March of this year. Mr. Gunn, you have charge of the smooth logs this month, do you not?"

"Aye, sir, I do."

"Well then, I'll leave it to you to investigate. See if you can find such a ship called *Percyville,* or the like, among our encounters."

"Aye, aye, sir."

Most likely, he wouldn't have to look very hard.

35

The crew worked feverishly through much of the night to complete all repairs by late afternoon on Friday.

The ship made preparations to get underway. Fresh produce and dry stores were hoisted aboard and stowed for sea. Wood and water had been reprovisioned earlier. All the rigging received a final inspection. The captain went to the Custom House to pay his respects to the collector and to inquire about recent weather reports from watchers on the bay.

When the captain returned, he announced that the cutter would sail after the evening meal. He planned to head out into the harbor and anchor there overnight. All further liberty was cancelled. Gunn figured he wanted to avoid any trouble on their last night in Norfolk. So far, the only man arrested was Connelly for being drunk and disorderly the night before. Fortunately for him, the local magistrate, whose mother was from Connelly's hometown in Ireland, had been buying the whiskey all night.

That evening, Bulloch arrived to spend a last meal with his friends in the wardroom. He brought with him the captain of the *Andrew Jackson*, Robert Dawes, whom Whitcomb had invited to dine in the cabin. After dinner, as they prepared to leave, Gunn accompanied Bulloch to the gangway.

"It was good to see you again, Des."

"And you. Keep in touch. And don't forget my offer. We'd be glad to have you aboard, even though you are a knucklehead. Keep you out of trouble. Try, anyway."

"Thanks. I'll think about it."

The two captains arrived at the gangway to say their farewells. As the officer-of-the-day, Miller had arranged sideboys to attend the departure. He stood by with them, waiting to render honors.

Bulloch introduced Gunn and Miller to Captain Dawes, who offered a warm farewell.

"Mr. Bulloch has sung your praises, both of you. And I've learned to take him at his word. The *Morris* is lucky to have you. It is rare these days to find good officers who know their craft and take responsibility for their actions. I have rarely been so fortunate. The last two young lieutenants we had didn't know a sextant from a stereoscope. My compliments to your captain for his hand in training you properly. Should you ever care to come south to Savannah, I would be pleased to have you aboard my ship." He winked at them. "And you may stay as long as you like."

Whitcomb answered with a terse smile. "As Poor Richard said, 'This world is too full of compliments already.' But thank you, nonetheless, Captain Dawes." Then he turned his eye on Bulloch. "I must say that I still haven't forgiven Mr. Bulloch for being so willing to leave us. And his obvious regard for these two makes me question his judgment, yet again."

Bulloch laughed. "Sir, I make no apology for longing to return home to Savannah. But if I failed to adequately express my deepest regrets for leaving the best of shipmates, then I do beg your forgiveness."

"You will always have a home here, Mr. Bulloch. On that you can rely."

Bulloch shook his outstretched hand. "Thank you, sir."

"Fair winds, gentlemen," said Dawes. He shook hands with

Whitcomb. The others rendered sharp salutes, which he returned. Miller signaled the quartermaster to strike the ship's bell four times as Dawes went ashore.

"So long," said Bulloch, trading firm handshakes with Gunn and Miller. "Sorry to see y'all go," he added. With a salute to Whitcomb, he followed his captain ashore.

Whitcomb wasted not a moment. The smile faded from his face. He turned perfunctorily to Miller. "My respects to Mr. Prouty and inform him that I wish to shove off as soon as possible." He brushed past Gunn with barely a glance and walked aft toward the cabin.

The time for pleasantries clearly had passed. Perhaps the captain's recent displeasure with him had grown more deeply rooted than any compliment, even the most liberally strewn, could salt. Only time might eventually cause it to wither and fade.

Mr. Prouty sprang into action, calling the crew to sail stations, heartening the hands who quickly responded and spurring those who did not. Few needed encouragements, however. Most were eager to head home to Boston.

The captain took his place on the quarterdeck.

"Mr. Gunn, whenever you're ready."

Gunn gave the orders to set sails and get underway. The breeze had diminished toward evening but was strong enough to back the new topsail, setting the ship in reverse. The handlers ashore eased the mooring lines and tossed them aboard the ship. The *Morris* continued backing until she entered the ebbing current. The stern swung to port, bringing the mainsail to bear, finally catching the wind and speeding the turn of the ship into the stream.

The cutter slipped handily away from her berth and wended through the flight of mostly larger ships at anchor, finally alighting at the captain's chosen spot among them. The *Morris* came up into the wind, gradually slowing to a standstill, at which point the anchor dropped into the rippled water with a modest splash. The ship settled back on her rode, sails folded in place like wings, waiting for night to fall.

As the cutter sailed away, there was no brass band, no spirited crowd to herald her departure. Instead, a somber assembly of two dozen or so black men and several women, children clinging to their skirts, gathered on the wharf. They watched in sullen silence, their shoulders rounded and feet planted as though braced against a mighty wind.

36

Captain Whitcomb plotted a more direct route home that would take advantage of the prevailing currents and winds. The cutter sailed well offshore, heading northeast-by-east toward Cape Cod, intending to skirt Nantucket Shoals by about five miles.

For the first two days, that plan worked well, due to the confluence of the Gulf Stream and the Azores High, typical in June. The weather remained clear and warm, the breeze steady from the southwest. The cutter's advance sped with the current, making good about ten to twelve knots. The *Morris* sailed along in fine form on a broad reach, all sails spread like bright wings lifting in the wind.

Everything seemed as it should, now that their dirty mission was done, and order was restored. Nobody spoke of Burns, as though doing so might bring bad luck upon the ship.

Mackerel streaked across the wave tops, trying to escape unseen predators. Now and then, schools of flying fish broached the surface, their cobalt tails snaking through the water, translucent wings flashing in the sunlight. Once, a stray landed on the deck next to Yarrow, who sat mending a sail. The fish that fell from the sky so surprised him that he jammed the sailmaker's awl into his palm. He proudly displayed his wound to Gunn.

On the third morning, just after dawn, the weather turned foul. As the day drew on, the ocean swells grew longer from the south, and the waves started to build. Low, thick clouds rolled in, along with a series of minor squalls. The wind picked up, whistling through the rigging with the whine of a sling whirling overhead. The barometer fell precipitously through the hours.

Concern registered on the captain's face, and no wonder. Nantucket Shoals lay only ten miles to the northwest. The relentless current drove them toward shore. They needed to claw off the lee shore as far as possible, or the coming storm would run them aground, so he ordered the cutter to turn east. At around ten o'clock that morning, he called all hands to shorten sail.

By the time Gunn took the evening watch, a full gale had backed to the northeast. The sea was a churning cauldron of ridged waves streaked with foam. Spindrift, spraying into vapor, flew from the tops of the twenty-foot crests. In the troughs, green water broke over the bow and across the deck with a force capable of sweeping any careless hand into the raging sea.

The cutter fore-reached, flying a storm jib from the forestay, close-hauled to the wind, with a triple-reefed mainsail eased to lessen the driving force of the gale. Two helmsmen were needed to steer the ship at an oblique angle into the oncoming waves, to avoid broaching. They hunched against the wind, each man in turn taking a hand off the wheel just long enough to wipe the rain from his troubled eyes.

Sheets of stinging rain fell from every direction. The oilskins and sou'wester covering Gunn from head to foot did little to keep him dry, as he tucked his chin into his shoulder against the onslaught of wind and rain. The mixture of melted grease and wax smeared on his Jefferson boots failed to prevent water from sloshing in them. Water trickled down the small of his back. Even the flannel on the inside of his sou'wester, protected as it was by the broad brim of the hat, was soaked through by the time Miller relieved him.

"I don't think the rain has let up any," shouted Miller.

"If it has, I didn't notice," Gunn yelled back. "I haven't been so wet since the day I was born."

The captain paced the quarterdeck in his oilskins, seemingly impervious to the weather. His beard soaked and dripping, he faced the wind, watching for any change in the conditions. He held his unlit pipe upside down in his teeth to keep the rain out of the bowl. Miller asked him for permission to relieve the watch, which Whitcomb granted with a nod.

After being relieved, Gunn headed for the wardroom, anticipating a brief period of rest and shelter before he would have to come up again to face the weather. As he reached the companionway, one of the deck guns on the starboard side broke loose from its lashings and swung across the main deck, in danger of breaking away. It had been his responsibility to secure the guns for heavy weather. Gunn leaped toward it, calling for the men on watch to help him wrestle the gun back into place. Three came to his aid. A wave crashed over them as they fought to replace the lashing. They managed to finish before the next wave hit.

When he at last looked up, sure that the cannon was secure, his eyes met Whitcomb's glaring down from the quarterdeck. The captain's silent reproach stung more than the cold rain.

37

Gunn retreated to the comfort of his stateroom, but nowhere on the ship was completely warm and dry. After exchanging his wet clothes for some less so, pangs in his belly reminded him that he hadn't eaten since midday. He would have paid a week's wages for a steaming bowl of stew and a cup of hot tea.

The weather was too rough for the galley stove to be lit, so he had to settle for tepid potatoes and a slice of cold corned beef left over from the noon meal. The leftovers felt warm to the touch only because his hands were colder than the meat. Even so, he was grateful. It was likely better than what the crew had eaten.

The first lieutenant sat alone at the table, wedged into a chair, his feet hooked around its legs. He was writing in his journal with a pencil, rather than his usual scrimshaw-shanked nib pen.

Gunn grappled the table with one hand while balancing his plate with the other, trying to counter the heel of the ship. He asked Prouty if he might join him.

"Don't mean to disturb you, sir."

"By all means, sit."

Gunn sank into a chair at the table and ate his spare meal in silence. A dull thud and the roar of raging water sounded every time the ship's bow plunged into a heavy wave, followed by a shudder down her spine.

The lamp overhead swiveled as the ship crested each wave, splashing light against the opposite bulkhead and elongating the shadows. The damask curtains concealing the staterooms swayed as in a breeze with the roll of the ship.

"Lovely weather," muttered Prouty. He laid his pencil inside the journal and closed it.

Gunn swallowed a small bite. "Fit for neither man nor beast."

"Have we made any progress in the last four hours, do you think?"

"Not even five miles, I would guess. Mostly sideways."

"Any ground made is good, lest we end up high and dry on Nantucket."

He couldn't recall the last time they were alone, awake, and at rest in the same room. The ship's business had all but ceased, due to the weather. The time was right. He played with the scraps on his plate and cleared his throat.

"Is there something on your mind, Mr. Gunn?"

Where to begin? There was the fight with Richmond, of course. But for the past day or so, what had troubled him more than anything else was the discovery in the ship's logs that they indeed had sighted his uncle's ship, the *Parsifal,* near Minot's Ledge, enroute Boston, right around the time Burns had arrived in March.

But first, he had some ground to windward of his own to make up.

"Sir, it's only that—"

"Well?"

"I seem to find myself at odds with the captain, of late. And with you, for that matter. In fact, I am fairly at loose ends these days. I've made some missteps. I regret that, and I'd like to find a way to fix it, to make it right, if possible."

Sliding his journal aside, Prouty readjusted his position to regain a measure of comfort against the constant motion of the rollicking cutter.

"Let me tell you a story, Mr. Gunn. It is the kind of story that lends itself to a calmer surrounding, but there is no time like the present, I suppose. Perhaps it will help make my point." He took a deep breath. "Some time ago, a young officer, let's call him Smith, was entrusted by his captain to do something very important. Now, it happened that the ship had the honor of hosting some dignitaries on a special visit to Boston Light. They had not chosen just any day. It was the fourth of July.

"These were no ordinary men, I must tell you. They included notable politicians and officials. I won't name them. Let's just say, it was important not to do something regrettable under their watchful eyes. You understand."

Gunn nodded. "Of course, sir." He pushed aside his empty plate. The cutter lunged, causing the plate and utensils to skid across the table. He caught them before they could crash to the floor, clambered to the pantry, and placed them carefully in a sunken wash basin.

"Well, the captain asked our young Mr. Smith to conn the ship during this little excursion. The day began well enough, and it was a fine one. Everyone was in high spirits."

Reeling back to his place, Gunn held tight to the table's edge until he reached his chair. He sat, relieved that he had managed not to fall.

"Toward the end of the day, after they had visited the lighthouse, they started for home, hoping to make it back in time for the evening festivities. The captain decided to take a shortcut, one we had taken quite often."

"I know most of the shortcuts through the islands. My brother and I grew up sailing there on my uncle's boat. Those tides and currents can be tricky."

"Quite. I didn't know you had a brother."

"Yes. He died several years ago."

"Oh. I am sorry. Anyway, all was well. Perfect, except for one thing. Our man Smith was weary after a long day and distracted by one of the dignitaries. He miscalculated the tides and currents through the shortcut and cut the corner too close. Before he realized his mistake, the ship hit bottom. On the second bounce, she hitched up solid. Everyone topsides lost their footing and ended up sprawled on the deck, tail over teakettle. Luckily, there were no serious injuries. Except to our young man's pride, that is."

"And the ship?" asked Gunn.

"Well, the ship was a different story. She was hard aground, on the rocks, no less. Started taking on water, but none too serious. The pumps took care of that. They had to wait for the tide to come in, and once it did, they sailed her right off. But it was late that night when they finally arrived back in port."

"Was there much damage?"

"Enough. Later, when the ship went into drydock, they found they needed to replace the entire shoe along the keel and some of the copper sheathing."

"What did the captain have to say?"

"What do you think he said? We had our own fireworks that evening."

"I can imagine. What happened to the lieutenant?"

"It took him a little longer to recover than the ship. Not much he could do about that, other than own up to his mistake and try never to repeat it."

"Did the captain ever forgive him?"

"No, not that one. Until quite recently, in fact, our man had yet to be considered for another promotion."

"I see. Earlier, you said, 'we.'"

"Beg pardon?"

"You said, '*we* had our own fireworks that evening.'"

"Did I?"

"Yes, sir. I believe you did."

"Hm. Slip of the tongue, I suppose." Prouty wore a shrewd smile.

"So, what am I to take from your little parable, Mr. Prouty? Some sins can't be forgiven?"

"No need to look so perturbed. Not at all, Mr. Gunn. The story is not finished. You see, Captain Whitcomb is the most fair-minded captain I have ever known. Unlike some others, he understands that we are all fallible and deserving of a second chance. Last month, in fact, he recommended me for promotion. Keep that under your hat, for the moment."

"Yes, sir, I will."

"I guess he figures I've suffered long enough. And, I've tried hard to prove to him that I will do everything I can to avoid making the same mistake. That's the thing."

"I'm glad to hear it, sir. About the second chance, that is."

Prouty sat for a moment and studied him.

"Sometimes you can't sail a straight course to wherever you want to go, Mr. Gunn. You've got to consider the conditions. Take this storm, for instance. We must sail in the opposite direction to our desired destination, at least temporarily, so we don't end up on the rocks. We have to shorten sail and ride out the storm."

"I see what you mean, sir. That's a wise lesson."

"I can't take credit for it. Captain Whitcomb taught me that. Shorten sail and ride out the storm. Don't lose heart. You'll get where you want to go, eventually."

"Aye, sir."

Find the wind's eye. Sheet home. Shorten sail. What he wouldn't have given for a bit of standard advice.

***

The storm abated the next day. Wind, waves, and current had pushed the cutter well off its intended track, at one point less than a mile from the shoals. It had been "a close shave with a dull blade," as the captain put it.

Afterward, the skies cleared, and the air turned cooler and dry. The crew aired their wet clothes and bedding, even though it was midweek, not waiting for the usual Saturday routine. Almost every article of clothing they owned was either damp or soaking wet. With the wind again favorable, the small ship pressed on, making the most of a beam reach in a much calmer sea.

Despite the better conditions, Captain Whitcomb seemed to be in no hurry. They spent the following two days boarding ships near the approaches to Cape Cod Bay, stopping eight to ten ships each day. Gunn came to wonder if the captain had delayed their arrival on purpose. Perhaps he was reluctant to return home to a hostile public, who previously had held the ship and her captain in such high esteem.

As much as he wished to see Elizabeth and smooth things over with her, not to mention the need to deliver his urgent message from Burns, Gunn had mixed feelings about the delay in returning to homeport. He had a reason of his own to live temporarily with the delay. Most likely, Second Lieutenant Richmond would be on the pier to greet them.

38

At daybreak on the third day after the storm, the *Morris* entered Cape Cod Bay, and the captain announced his intention to inspect two nearby lighthouses, Long Point and Highland Light, both on a list of overdue inspections. The ship anchored off Provincetown in the early morning hours.

Beyond the forested masts of countless fishing boats, Provincetown spread out along the shoreline, a frieze of picturesque cracker box houses and white church spires. Among the wharves and warehouses on the waterfront stood a score of weathered windmills, mounted on stilted scaffolds. They faced the bay breezes, turning in the wind, pumping seawater into shallow, covered vats, where the brine would evaporate, leaving deposits of sea salt. Fishermen used the salt to preserve their prized catches for market.

After breakfast, Whitcomb ordered two teams ashore. As soon as they were ready, Miller took Moriarty with him in a longboat to inspect Long Point, a two-story dwelling sided with cedar shakes, its gabled roof topped by a lighted cupola. It stood a little to the northwest at the fingertips of the cape, which curved around like a hand cupped to protect the harbor against the wind and waves of Cape Cod Bay.

Gunn and Nelson headed east in the other longboat toward a

landing just north of Truro. From there, they would walk roughly two miles across the spit of land to inspect Highland Light, a tall brick tower that overlooked a bluff on the Atlantic shoreline.

The longboat crew covered the distance across the harbor in less than thirty minutes. There was no surf to speak of in these protected waters. Small wavelets lapped at the sandy shoreline. The boat landed at the mouth of a creek that emptied into the bay. Nelson and Gunn waded ashore onto the pebbled beach. Gunn told the boat crew to come back for them in six hours. Reardon, the coxswain, tossed a salute, put over the rudder, and turned the boat back toward the ship. He called for the other men to put their backs into it, and the longboat glided over the surface like a water strider.

The two men searched the beach until they found a narrow path leading through the dunes. The path wound along the stream to a pond and a little inland settlement, aptly named Pond Village. A rutted dirt road served as the main street, lined with a post office and general store, a livery, a church, and a meeting house. A dozen scattered homes, gable-roofed and unpainted, surrounded the buildings. As they walked through town, nobody seemed to be stirring, except an ancient-looking woman, rocking in a chair on the porch of the general store. The men were likely out on their boats, fishing.

Beyond the village, the dirt road became little more than two ruts separated by a ridge of poverty grass. It meandered over and through a series of swales and hillocks, heaped like waves made of sand. Everywhere the ground was covered with huckleberry bushes, bayberry, tufts of seagrass, and thickets of wild sea roses.

Most of the large trees had been cut down to build boats or houses, or to burn for heat in the frigid winter months. A few meager groves clung to the low places, mainly pitch-pines no more than ten or fifteen feet high with dwarfed scrub oaks mingled among them, gnarled and twisted into tortured shapes by the ceaseless wind.

Sand had drifted across the road, making their footing unsteady, especially where the climb steepened. As they walked along, the two men chatted casually and joked about the recent storm, the latest politics of the forecastle, and bets on how long the captain would delay their return home.

A red fox crossed the road ahead of them and darted into the undergrowth, looking back as they passed. They stopped a moment to marvel at the odd, late-morning appearance and watched the wary fox steal away, disappearing into a thicket of laurel.

In the distance, the breaking surf pounded against the bluffs like far-off thunder. The day had turned overcast and unusually cool for mid-June. Despite the vigorous two-mile hike, the damp air, chilled by a constant wind, seeped through Gunn's uniform. The lighthouse would be welcome shelter. They continued on.

As they approached the lighthouse, the sand plateaued into a heath covered with waving seagrass and occasional purple thistles, very much like the ones in Elizabeth's garden, as far as the eye could see in both directions. Not a tree stood in sight. Patches of milkwort and indigo weed crawled over the ground. Gunn smiled to himself. Elizabeth would like this view. Then again, he might never get the chance to tell her about it, unless he could somehow convince her that he wasn't the ogre she likely now thought he was.

Near the cart trail, gravestones marked a forgotten cemetery, where victims of several shipwrecks had been laid to rest. Worn smooth with time and the elements, the slates leaned at odd angles in the sand among the huckleberry shrubs. They presented a stark reminder of just how treacherous the local waters could be in a storm.

Beyond the shoreline lay the wide Atlantic. In the foreground, its violet hue matched the sky. In the distance, bands of silver and indigo lined the horizon. Several sailing ships were visible out to sea, solitary yet sharing the same vast panorama.

The lighthouse loomed before them, a tall cylinder of white brick surmounted by a black iron cap, streaked with rust. The keeper's quarters, a two-story wood frame house painted red, was connected to the north side by a short, covered passage. The roof sagged over the weather-beaten house. A small, whitewashed barn stood a short distance away.

The buildings perched together on a bank of clay and sand, only forty yards from the precipice, which dropped more than a hundred feet to the beach and roaring surf below. To get a better view of the scene, Gunn and Nelson walked beyond the lighthouse, sidling as close as they dared to the bank's semi-circular edge, worn ragged by torrents of wind-driven rain. Great chunks of loose land had fallen to the base of the cliff, where the relentless sea beat against the wild shore.

The lighthouse keeper came to the door of his dwelling in response to Gunn's first knock, which was brief, but insistent. The careworn face of the slight old man grew inquisitive, but he remained quiet while Gunn and Nelson introduced themselves and stated their purpose. He told them his name was Leroy Fisker.

As he invited them in, the keeper's fingers smoothed the wisps of white hair that sprouted from his balding head. Since it was almost noon, he offered them something to eat. They accepted gratefully, and Fisker guided them through his little house to the kitchen, filled with the savory aroma from a small pot of simmering chowder and a loaf of sourdough bread.

As they ate at the kitchen table, warming themselves by the heat of the potbellied stove, a young girl entered the kitchen. She had come silently from somewhere at the back of the house, carrying a cup and saucer in one hand, and a burning candle in the other. She stopped short at the sight of two strange men. The cup and saucer clattered to the floor, splintering on impact. She bent to pick up the shards.

"Leave it, girl," said Fisker. You'll cut yourself."

The girl, barefoot and dressed plainly, looked up at him with sad, brown eyes. Her porcelain face was smudged with dirt. She had long, untamed hair, the color of the fox they had seen earlier. Her eyes searched their faces with a peculiar, far-off look, as though she could see things others could not. She rose to her feet, and her gaze rested on Gunn. He smiled at her warmly, wanting to ask her if something was wrong, but he held back.

"Hello, lassie. What is your name?" asked Nelson.

The girl did not take her eyes away from Gunn's face.

"Dis here is my niece, Marianne. She's been living wid me for de last three years. Her modder died when she was just nine."

"Hello, Marianne," said Gunn. She didn't answer.

"Cat got your tongue, lass?" said Nelson.

"She got no manners. Nobody to teach her. My own wife died two year ago. An old lighthouse ain't no place for a little girl to come of age. But ..." He shrugged. His words were clipped, with an unusual inflection that sounded Scandinavian, perhaps by way of Montreal.

The girl stared without uttering a word. Then, she left the room as quietly as she had come. They heard the outside door open and close.

"Well, you can't blame her for bein' scared by the likes of us," said Nelson, laughing.

"Keeps to herself a lot. It does her no good 't'all to stay here by de sea. Some church folk up in Provincetown said dey might take her. I t'ink dat might be best. But dey never come."

They finished their chowder. Fisker swept the broken cup onto an empty plate with a whisk broom. Then he struck a long match and lit a briar pipe, clenched between his teeth, and used the same match to light a small oil lamp, which began smoking like a censer. He motioned for them to follow, escorting them through the cottage to a storage room, where a door led to a narrow, whitewashed passageway. At the end of the short passageway, another door opened into the lighthouse.

The interior of the lighthouse measured about five paces in diameter at the base. Just inside the door, a dozen casks of oil were stacked against the circular wall. An open, wrought-iron staircase spiraled upward into the dim light above. A small, square window was cut into the wall about two thirds of the way up. Another door on the opposite side gave access to the outside. Above that door, Gunn noticed a jagged crack in the brickwork that extended from the door jamb at least twenty feet above them. The crack was as wide as his thumb at the bottom.

"Looks like trouble," he said, pointing to the crack.

"I t'ink de foundation, she shifts," replied Fisker, nodding in agreement. "Gets worse by de year. But she's three-and-a-half feet t'ick at de base. I expect she'll stand a little longer."

Holding the lantern high, Fisker took to the stairs. He climbed slowly, with a pronounced limp.

"I am sorry to be so slow, gents. You will to forgive a frail, old man. I was a whaler when I was your age. Had a temper. Took a wild man's harpoon to de t'igh. Never been de same since."

He continued up the dark, winding staircase, which rose some forty feet above the floor. The smell of oil and lamp smoke hung in the air, which thickened as they ascended toward the lamp house. Fisker paused to open the trap door above his head. A shaft of light enveloped him, and he disappeared through the bright opening, the cloud of smoke rising with him. Gunn followed into the light, and Nelson joined them.

The stifling warmth of the sunlit room washed over them. The space was clean and orderly, nothing out of place. The light itself, standing eight feet tall in the center of the room, comprised sixteen oil lamps, all facing outward, and arrayed in two horizontal circles, one above the other.

Overhead, soot covered the ceiling of the iron dome, but the lamps themselves shone spotless. From constant polishing, the silvering had worn off the copper reflectors, some of which were warped by the heat. All around the light, the large windowpanes were clean and clear, but three of them showed full-length cracks, probably due to the settling of the tower. Gunn took notes with a pencil and notebook retrieved from the inside pocket of his frock coat.

Picking up a bell-shaped brass oil can, Fisker filled the fountain on each lamp in turn, moving counterclockwise. He talked softly as he worked, speaking of his solemn responsibility to keep mariners safe, having been one himself. That thought led to his complaint about the poor quality of the oil provided by the government. On cold days it would congeal, and he would have to heat it on the coal stove in the kitchen. When the weather turned cold, the lamps burned too dimly. He worried that on frigid wintry nights when sailors most needed the light it didn't shine bright enough for them. Sometimes the oil stopped flowing altogether, causing the light to go out. Then, he would have to reheat the oil and refill the lamps.

"But dat takes time. Who knows how many ships have been lost when de light be darkened?" He shrugged. "Dere is better oil, you know. Spermaceti oil. Costs more. Eight hundred gallons a year, at, what, a dollar a gallon, is a lot of money, sure, but spending more to save even one ship would be well worth it."

Gunn made careful notes.

"I tell odders de same t'ing," Fisker frowned.

The old man trimmed the wicks and lit the lamps, demonstrating how brightly they shone, each with the light of seven candles, made even more brilliant by the reflectors. The temperature inside the glass beacon grew uncomfortably warm, raising sweat on their brows despite the coolness outside.

At the western side of the room, facing the land, an iron door led to the open air. Its hinges bucked and groaned as Fisker opened the door and motioned them outside.

"Watch your step," he said. "Long way down."

An iron platform encompassed the light room. It was rusted through in places, revealing the ground below. Holding to the railing, Gunn edged around to the sector facing the sea. The wind blew stronger and cooler at this height. He snugged the cap on his head to keep it from being carried off, while wondering if it had ever snowed there so late in June.

The sky had grown darker. In the distance, a squall was forming. A curtain of rain streamed down from the clouds to the sea. Lightning flashed, and a low peal of thunder echoed across the water.

A young dove lay dead on the platform at his feet, one broken, bloodied wing outstretched, its feathers ruffling in the wind. The unlucky bird had probably tried to fly through the windows. Gunn nudged it over the lip of the platform with the toe of his boot, and it cartwheeled to the ground.

Nelson followed him outside. Fisker stayed inside to extinguish the lamps, since it was still daylight.

"This lighthouse has seen a better day," said Nelson, when he had settled himself with Gunn at the railing, looking out to sea.

"That's what my report will say, but you know how your Uncle Sam works, Nelson. It will likely have to fall into the sea, before he springs the money to pay for a new one."

"No doubt. He *is* a skinflint, at that," Nelson agreed. "A lot of good it does to have a rich uncle. I doubt he'll leave me anything."

Gunn eyed the coming squall. "I suppose we're done here. Better be heading back. We're already likely to get wet."

"Aye, sir."

They went back inside. Fisker had finished extinguishing all the lamps. Blue smoke hovered and swirled overhead, filling the top of the dome.

Gunn opened the trap door and led the way down the spiral staircase. Fisker retrieved his lantern, pulled the door shut behind them, and they descended together.

"Had a dog, died last winter," said Fisker. He limped one step at a time, holding the lantern high so the others could see. "Followed me up here one night. Lost his feet and fell right dere. Broke his neck, just like dat." He snapped his fingers. They reached the bottom of the steps and stopped to listen to Fisker's story. "Next day, strangest t'ing. At sunrise, I come up to darken de light, and what do I see? T'ree suns on de horizon." He held up a thumb and two gnarled fingers. "T'ree suns. You eber see dat?"

"They call them sun dogs," said Nelson. "I've seen them, too, usually the mornin' after tyin' one on." He grinned.

Fisker's expression was dead serious. "*Solhund*, in Norwegian," said Fisker. "Sun wolves. I do not drink, no more anyhow. Strangest t'ing I eber did see. T'ink what you will. I know what I see." His quiet voice lilted up at the end, as he pointed a crooked forefinger to his eye. "In Norway, *Solhund* is de sign of de twilight of de gods ... de, de end of days, you know, when de world is again a vast *ødemarker*."

"A what?" asked Nelson.

"A desert. A wasteland." Fisker limped over to open the outside door and walked through. Nelson shrugged, grinning. Gunn cocked an eyebrow and pressed on. They followed Fisker outdoors.

"You will want to be heading back, I am sure," said Fisker, eyeing the sky.

They agreed and said their goodbyes. Fisker told them he hoped their visit had been worthwhile. Gunn assured him it had and thanked him for his hospitality. Accompanying them to the door of his cottage, the keeper turned to them.

"Soon, gentlemen," he said. "Maybe bery soon. T'ings fall apart. You'll see." The old man placed a forefinger alongside his nose and nodded. Without another word, he walked inside and shut the door.

Their boots scrunched on the path of crushed seashells that led from the door as they walked away from the house. Nelson tapped Gunn's shoulder and pointed to a nearby clump of sea roses, beneath which sat Marianne, her hands clutched to her breast, guarding something. Tears streaked her dirty face. They walked over to her.

"What is it, lass?" said Nelson.

"What do you have there, Marianne?" asked Gunn.

She looked squarely in his eyes, then opened her hands and held them up for him to see. There, cradled in her palms was the dead dove.

"I'm sorry to say, I think she's gone, lass," said Nelson. "Flown to heaven, she has." His voice carried an indifferent tone common to a man who rarely showed his feelings.

She turned her eyes to the ground, dejected. Gunn took the bird gently from her hands.

"I'll tell you what, Marianne. We'll bury her in the cemetery, just off the path over there, shall we?"

She nodded, then took his outstretched hand and stood.

Nelson turned a worried eye to the coming rain clouds. "Mr. Gunn, we best be makin' tracks, don't you think?"

"If you want to go on ahead, Boats, it will be all right."

The three walked together toward the small graveyard, as rain fell in heavy droplets from the lowering, gray sky.

39

At dusk on Saturday, the captain finally gave the order to set a course for home. A little before daybreak on Sunday, June twenty-fifth, they dropped anchor in the inner harbor, near the end of Central Wharf.

Nobody seemed to notice their arrival. That was fine with Gunn, because Richmond was nowhere in sight.

It was his turn to take the in-port watch. After the lines and sails had been secured and liberty granted to the crew, he asked Miller to spell him long enough to attend worship services ashore.

Anxious to see Elizabeth, he hoped to find her in church. His doubts about her feelings for him had increased with each day that he'd been gone. The more time passed, the more he recalled the look of disdain on her face the last time he'd seen her on the corner of State Street. If only he still had her letter to reassure him. He could have kicked himself again for losing it.

Gunn put on his undress uniform, the one he had worn during his fight with Richmond. He'd sewn on a spare button himself and had it cleaned of mud in Norfolk. The laundry on Market square, kept by an elderly negro man with good reputation, had done a decent job. Most likely, his own reputation wouldn't come nearly so clean once the second lieutenant returned to the ship.

Covenant Church met in a small, rented auditorium in a five-story office building at 19 Milk Street, directly across from the Old South Meeting House. The greatest distinction of the building was that it stood on the site of Benjamin Franklin's birthplace, which had been destroyed long ago. It was the latest in a series of temporary dwellings for the small congregation, started twenty years earlier by a few staunch members of the Presbyterian Church. They had broken from a congregation that had become liberal in its theology and invited Reverend Faulkner to come to America from his home in Scotland to lead them. Though lacking sufficient funds to buy their own building, they had no interest in borrowing any.

Milk Street led away to Gunn's left, curving uphill and into the city. The streets in this land of steady habits were typically quiet on Sundays. The eight-block walk to Central Hall usually took about fifteen minutes. He did it in less. The relative lack of humidity in the air compared to what he had experienced in Norfolk made the stroll pleasant, even at a quick pace.

He stopped at the corner across from Central Hall in front of an upscale clothing store. He frowned at his image reflected in the store's large display window and straightened his cravat. The cut across the bridge of his nose had healed and was almost unnoticeable. He was glad not to have something else to explain right now. The store window exhibited men's suits and clothing in sartorial splendor that he could never hope to afford on sixty-five dollars a month.

Entering the building, he removed his cap and took the steps two at a time to the second floor. He recognized a few people outside the auditorium and nodded politely as he entered, searching all the while for Elizabeth. Her seventeen-year-old brother Robert chatted inside with a friend.

"Hello, Andrew. Good to see you. Welcome home."

"It's good to be back, Robert. Where's your sister?"

"She isn't here. I'm sorry."

"Not here? Is she sick?"

"She's gone off to pursue her passion." He rolled his eyes. "So she says. The Normal School in Framingham started their summer session last week. They had a vacancy in the dormitory and she asked my father if she could live there to finish out her schooling."

"Stop kidding. Where is she?"

"It's no joke, Andrew."

"When will she be back?"

"Well, most likely at the end of the summer. But only for a short while. Then, she's back to Framingham for at least two more semesters, I think."

"What brought that on?"

Robert shrugged and pointed to his temple. "You know women."

"Apparently not."

"Apart from that, Andrew, she was hopping mad when she found out that you had joined in the slave thing. We were all pretty upset."

"I didn't join in the slave thing, Robert."

"Sure seemed like it."

From the pulpit, the Reverend Angus Faulkner—an "Auld Light," steeped in the Calvinist doctrine of the Reformed tradition—began the service on time with the call to morning worship. Gunn started to leave, but Faulkner caught his eye, and the minister's clean-shaven jaw began to twitch. Maybe it would be best to stay and smooth things over with the old man. Gunn found a seat close to the exit.

When Faulkner spoke in his booming voice with a Scottish brogue, he seemed a head taller than his medium stature, much like Gunn's own grandfather. In fact, much about him was very similar, from the wispy steel-gray hair to his broad chin and firm mouth. Gunn found the similarities appealing.

"I feel led to observe that we are fast approaching Independence Day, the anniversary of this nation's *rebellion* ... against the unjust rule of a tyrannical government," Faulkner intoned. "Let me begin by asking a simple question for us all to consider. To what good purpose do we observe our liberties in this great nation, and what reason do we have to celebrate, if we are so willing to turn a blind eye when those very liberties have been brutally violated?"

His voice began to rise.

"I speak of a subject that I have touched already on two earlier occasions, yet if I say nothing more, the very stones in the street will cry out. That is, the recent abduction and rendition of a man from this city, and his return by force of arms to the state of slavery from which he so desperately sought his freedom. And, in response, our fair city has risen to express her corporate outrage—a public outcry, denouncing such an act of tyranny perpetrated by the federal government. Some of us have responded in righteous anger to the revulsion that is aroused within the human breast as a natural result. And, where do we find the justification of our righteous anger? That justification is written on our very hearts, is it not?"

Gunn squirmed in his seat, toying with his cravat, while those around him grumbled approval.

"Of course, it is. You might be surprised to know that it is also written elsewhere. It is recorded in scripture. God's word is quite clear, and leaves nothing to question on the matter. We can find it by turning to the Old Testament, the Book of Deuteronomy."

Faulkner opened his Bible and began turning the pages. He found his place in the book, paused, and raised his piercing eyes to the congregation.

"Deuteronomy chapter twenty-three, verses fifteen and sixteen, read thusly—and I will give you a moment to find my text."

A rustling of pages preceded a resumed quiet among the audience, except for a few muted coughs.

"It reads thusly: 'Thou shalt not deliver unto his master the servant which is escaped from his master unto thee. He shall dwell with thee, even among you, in that place which he shall choose in one of thy gates, where it liveth him best. Thou shalt not oppress him.'"

His voice trembled, rising in crescendo until the last word hung in the air. He pressed the open book with both hands.

"Here we have before us not the law of men, but the law of God handed down to us, from which the law of men must derive, if it is to be blessed by his almighty hand. It is a good law, and was calculated, I must suppose, to bring the sin of Hebrew slavery to a practical end. It is a law from above, from a just God, and thus infinitely more worthy to be obeyed than the Fugitive Slave Law of the United States or the laws of any other nation on this earth."

There was more to the sermon, of course, which Gunn presumed was aimed directly at him. He had heard enough, and it was almost unbearable to think of sitting through to the end. Leaving now would be cowardly, though. He took out his watch, opened it, and placed it on his knee, waiting for Reverend Faulkner to finish.

It would be worth staying if he could say what he came to say.

40

Gunn sat for an eight-count after the service ended, as though he had been bloodied in another fight—winded, the breath knocked from his lungs, once again. Yet, not a mark on him.

Robert Faulkner lingered at his side. "Another stemwinder. I thought he'd never stop."

Gunn agreed and tucked his watch away.

"You all right, Andrew? Everybody is leaving."

"Yes, I suppose so. Fine."

He got up and sidled out of the row of seats. The two walked up the aisle toward the exit. Gunn hesitated until he was last in the line of disciples waiting to congratulate the reverend on such a powerful sermon.

"Good luck. See you outside," Robert whispered, as he departed.

Mrs. Faulkner stood at her husband's side. Gunn surveyed her face, hoping to find a little solace there.

Beathas Faulkner, about average in stature, was just on the cusp of being beautiful. Her hair, graying slightly, was of the same chestnut brown as her daughter's. Her mouth held a ready and pleasant smile, but her eyes always spoke of a far-off disappointment in the way of a homesick child. As Gunn approached, her smile broadened.

"Good morning to you, Andrew." Her voice lilted as she spoke his name. Her Scottish accent was more pronounced than her husband's, perhaps because his had rounded off a bit with so much speaking in public.

Gunn greeted her, asking about her health, which she assured him was fine.

"I am sorry to have missed Elizabeth," he said. "I had hoped to see her this morning."

"Aye, well, she will be so very sorry to have missed you, too, I'm sure. I suppose Robert has told you the news."

"Yes, ma'am, he has."

Reverend Faulkner finished shaking hands and laid his full gaze on Gunn.

"Well, Andrew, back from the sea, once more, I see. I am truly glad to see you in church this morning." His face matched the granite of the building, giving no hint of any such gladness.

"Yes, sir. It was … good to be here."

"You look a little uncomfortable. Not ill, I hope."

"No, sir. Not exactly. I wonder if I might speak with you privately."

"Well, I must be getting Mrs. Faulkner home. We are having guests for Sunday dinner."

"A moment, sir, if I may."

"If it is about the sermon, I will not apologize for speaking the truth. But I would be happy to answer any questions you might have."

"It is, but it isn't, sir. I do have a question for you."

"Very well, then. Beathas, why don't you go along to the carriage?"

Her smile faded. She gave Gunn a sympathetic look and touched the sleeve of his uniform as she passed by.

The two were alone at the top of the stairs. Lingering voices echoed in the stairway, rising from the ground floor.

"I was wondering, reverend, why you might have chosen today to give that sermon?"

"It was merely a continuation of a series on the issue of slavery, a subject that bears repetition, especially so now. I'm sorry you missed the earlier ones, Andrew. I'd be happy to review them for you, if you like."

"Not necessary, sir. I got the gist of them, I'm sure. I would like to ask you about something else, though. Something very important to me. I'm glad to know Elizabeth has decided—"

"She is anxious to finish her schooling. It was, indeed, her decision, not ours. But I suppose this is a good situation for her to complete her studies sooner without distractions and without the inconvenience of having to take the train to and from Framingham. High time. All that travel makes for long days."

"Of course. I'm sure it will be good for her to concentrate. But I can imagine that she might enjoy some company, being away from home. I wonder—"

"I have no doubt that she will be well preoccupied. No need to worry. But thank you for your concern. I know how much you care for her welfare."

"Yes, sir. A familiar face now and then might be welcome, even so."

"Her mother and I will find time to visit now and again. And Robert has assured her that he will spend time visiting on odd weekends."

"What I am getting at is—"

"I know what you are getting at, son. I know very well what you're getting at. The answer is no, I'm afraid." His voice was firm, but not angry.

"I see. May I ask why?"

"I am her father. And as her father, it is my duty to guard her heart and keep it from harm, until such time as she finds a suitable husband, if that day should come."

"Am I not what you would call suitable?"

"You are a fine young man, I'm sure."

"But?"

"Listen, I'm well aware of your interest in my daughter, and I know she has enjoyed your company. That's been evident since you started coming to church here. We've welcomed you into our house and to our table, Andrew, happy to do so. It's so rare to have a man such as yourself show interest in the enduring truths, and I've encouraged—"

"A man such as myself? Tell me, reverend, what sort of man am I?"

"You're a man of the sea, Andrew. You have already chosen your bride. And, as a military officer, your loyalties … obviously lie elsewhere. You must know that I'm not an admirer of the federal government, most especially at this moment."

"Are men of the sea not to take wives?"

"Not Elizabeth."

"Does she feel that way?"

"I assure you, she is quite disappointed, you know, to learn of your latest adventure. You might have told us about it beforehand. We could have talked—"

"We were ordered not to tell anyone beforehand."

"Yes, well. We were disappointed, nonetheless. All of us. Dismayed is more precisely the word."

"Did Elizabeth say so?"

"In so many words."

"What words?"

"Look here, Andrew. I am not willing to stand here and quibble with you. I have spoken my mind, and I hope you can respect that."

"Yes, sir, I certainly can. Thank you for your candor. Allow me to be equally frank. I love your daughter, and I believe she still loves me. I intend to marry her, if she'll have me. If she won't, so be it. But I want to hear it from her own lips. And I hope you will respect that."

"That's not how it's done, I'm afraid. At least, not in my house. Let me be clear, Andrew. Leave my daughter alone."

Gunn looked him in the eye. "Happy Independence Day, Reverend Faulkner."

Robert waited outside for them when they emerged together from the building. Reverend Faulkner lifted himself into the waiting coach next to his wife and took up the reins. The horse started away, but he pulled back.

"Whoa, there." His jaw twitched. "Are you coming, Robert?"

"Just a moment, Father." Drawing Gunn aside, Robert spoke in a quiet voice. "You have no idea what a firestorm you've started around here, Andrew."

"I think I just doused it with coal oil, Robert. I sure hope it eventually burns itself out."

Robert shook his head. "It's too bad. We're still friends, though, eh? I sure hope so. Hey—maybe we could go fishing again sometime soon? I'd like that."

"I need to get word to Elizabeth. Would you tell her—"

"Ooooh, no. That would be fishing for trouble." He left Gunn standing at the curb and swung himself up into the carriage to join his mother and father.

"Good day to you, Andrew," said Mrs. Faulkner. She smiled again, but her eyes were full of regret. "Be well."

"Thank you, ma'am. I intend to."

The reverend tipped his hat. "Walk on." He slapped the reins on the horse's croup. The startled animal broke into a trot. The carriage careened around the next corner, and the echo of falling hooves and grinding wheels on cobblestone faded as they soon passed from view.

41

The eight-fifteen Fitchburg train left the station on time, but Gunn missed it due to his slow-running watch. He waited ninety minutes for the next train and settled in for the one-hour ride to Concord.

He had decided to go home once the captain had granted forty-eight hours leave to each watch section. Whitcomb had reasoned they all probably had some "fence-mending" to do among relatives and friends. He thought about visiting Elizabeth in Framingham, but the way things were going it would likely take more than two days to fix the breach between them. He needed time to figure out what to say to her. Besides, it had been quite a while since he'd been home.

Gunn wore the oldest suit of clothes that he owned—a black double-breasted frock coat frayed at the sleeves, a well-worn buff-colored vest, and dark brown, checked trousers. A group of unruly boys had egged his uniform on the way home from church on Sunday, to add insult to injury, so he wasn't taking any chances. A black, soft-crowned felt hat, second-hand, rested on the seat next to him, beside the window. It would all have to do. He could not afford to replace his best clothing, should it get ruined. He was saving his money for other things.

After the conductor punched his ticket, he stuffed it into his wallet, already filled with a month's pay, less a dollar and twenty cents for his round-trip fare. As usual, a third of his salary would go to help support his mother and sister, which he intended to leave with them.

The train lurched out of the station, clattering over the bridge into Charlestown, above haphazard clusters of buildings in the shipyards along the waterfront. Down in the naval yard, the wooden keel and ribs of the newest warship, the *USS Merrimack*, lay open to the sky, swarmed by workers. Though a sailing vessel, word was that she would also be powered by steam and driven by a single propeller, rather than paddlewheels. Technology seemed to be advancing at breakneck speed, faster than he cared to keep up with.

The waterfront gave way to residential streets. New construction mingled with old in the working-class, largely Irish neighborhoods that housed the shipyard workers. Farther on, toward the crest of Breed's Hill, in the shadow of the Bunker Hill Monument, townhomes and even a few mansions lined the streets, interspersed with soaring church spires.

Beyond Charlestown, the various stops along the way in Somerville, Cambridge, Waltham, and Lincoln interrupted miles of rolling hills and dense woods. As sailors do, whenever possible to get some shuteye, Gunn tried to nod off, but the jerks and tremors of the car butted his head against the window frame, jarring him awake each time the train came to the next stop.

The ride gave him time to turn over in his head some of the things that had troubled him over the past few weeks, not the least of which was the quarrel with Elizabeth and her father. He wasn't sure what to do about it, since her father had forbidden him to see her. Maybe Marguerite could be of some help. Among the more useful qualities possessed by his younger sister, she had a knack for navigating around the strictures of social norms.

He closed his eyes again, trying to wipe clean the slate in his mind, crowded with a list of problems he would rather not think about. He dozed for a while. When he awoke, the train was passing Walden

Pond, just visible in the distance.

The locomotive screeched and chugged into the station, less than a mile from the center of town. He grabbed his small valise and stepped out of his car to the platform, searching through the smoke and steam for the faces of any acquaintances. As it happened, Ralph Waldo Emerson stood on the platform, waiting to board the next train to Boston, but he did not seem to take any notice.

Gunn didn't see anyone else he knew. Rather than spending money on a cab, he shifted the grip on his valise and started a brisk walk toward town.

Sudbury Road wound into the village of Concord among the ubiquitous rambling stone walls, weathered barns, and whitewashed farmhouses, all highlighted in bright sunshine. The trees in the fields and forests caught his attention. Many of them were stripped nearly bare of the usually vibrant green foliage of early summer. Some leaves had withered and fallen to the ground, like autumn, but without the brilliant color. Such a blight astonished him.

As he reached the intersection of Main Street, a man crossed on the opposite corner, headed toward the center of town. He was not surprised to see that it was Thoreau, since the itinerant often flitted from friend to friend around town each day. Gunn hailed him as they approached each other. They stopped under a locust tree and exchanged a tentative greeting.

"I was just on my way to visit the Emersons," said Thoreau.

"I saw Mr. Emerson on the platform, waiting for the train, not twenty minutes ago."

"Ah. I see. Well, then. Thank you for that."

"I'm on my way home to visit for the day. My ship returned—"

"Yes, Andrew. I'm well aware that your ship was away. And for what purpose." Thoreau lifted his straw hat to bid a good day.

"Sir, I was merely doing my duty." Gunn touched his lanky arm.

Thoreau paused, replacing his hat. "Your duty."

"Yes, sir."

"You were once among my brightest pupils, Andrew. I should think you would know that your first duty is to your own conscience. Has my teaching had so little effect?"

"Mr. Thoreau, there was more than my conscience at stake."

"I could not agree more, Andrew. We, all of us, are at a turning point. Anyone, that is, who champions the cause of freedom in this country."

"The cause of freedom also depends on upholding our nation's laws, does it not?"

The perpetual teacher gave a heavy sigh. "My friend, the law will never make men free." He furrowed his prominent brow. "You must be your own law, if the law of others fails to render justice."

"I tried that, sir. It didn't go well. Somebody could have gotten hurt or worse."

Thoreau looked him in the eye. "Even suppose blood should flow. Is there not a sort of blood shed when the conscience is wounded?"

Gunn returned his glare. "It was not just an imagined sort of blood that was shed at the courthouse in Boston last month, sir. That blood was real, and it bled from a man who died for the sake of another man's so-called wounded conscience. And nobody answered for it, except his widow, who was left to collect the body and bury it before it began to stink."

Thoreau didn't blink. "I fear we have nothing more to say to each other, then. You somewhat remind me of a boy I once knew, a fine young man of superior sensibilities. Sadly, the resemblance is only cosmetic." He touched his hat. "Goodbye to you, sir."

"Wait a moment."

"What more have we to do with each other? Nothing, I'd say. Stand aside."

A wave of anger swept over Gunn as he stepped aside. Resentment and regret warred within him. He tried to say something, anything. A pang of loss knotted his throat, preventing him from speaking a single word more.

Thoreau passed by and proceeded on his way, shoulders braced, without looking back.

42

onument Square occupied the heart of town, surrounded by the small, though bustling, commercial center with a county courthouse, all so familiar to Gunn as he passed along the tree-lined streets. His mother and sister lived just beyond the other side of Concord, a short distance down Lexington Road.

As Gunn reached the outskirts of town, a farmer stopped his cart and offered a ride. The man was a local by the name of Ephraim Bull, who recently had reached a modest level of regional celebrity by developing a hardy variety of grapes that could better survive the severe New England winters. Gunn thanked him, tossed his valise into the cart, and climbed up on the seat beside him. The empty cart smelled faintly of new wine.

The ride down the country lane would have been unremarkable except for the barren trees. Even some of the evergreens had turned brown halfway to their tops. They passed an old orchard, where the tree boughs lacked any sign of fruit.

"Mr. Bull, I've been wondering, what's the matter with the trees around here?"

The farmer hardly turned his head. He pulled at his long gray beard. "Tent catahpillahs, don't-ya know. Worst evah, leastwise that I seen. Been aftah my prize grapevines, too." He tossed the mane of hair that poked from under his broad-brimmed hat. "Nasty, wicked things."

"Can't anything be done?"

"Too many. Fire is the best remedy, but yud have to burn down the whole county."

Bordered by the occasional farms, country estates, and cottages, the road eventually led past The Wayside, Nathaniel Hawthorne's sprawling home. The house was empty. Hawthorne was abroad in England with his family. He'd been away for the past fifteen months, assigned by President Pierce to a post as the American consul in Liverpool.

Too bad. Gunn needed somebody to talk to. Though not one to socialize much, his friend would sometimes offer a sympathetic ear, especially in the summer when he usually put down his pen for the season.

Moments later, they arrived at the modest wood-frame house he had called home since the age of eleven. It was just after midday. He retrieved his valise, hopped off the cart, and thanked Bull, who nodded and told the mule to walk on.

The saltbox colonial, painted green with black shutters, sat a few paces from the south side of the road. It held many boyhood memories, some that he'd like to forget if he could, truth be told. At the moment, however, he was glad just to have a place to call home.

He climbed the steps to the front door. The door latch stuck, as usual. He'd meant to fix it. Entering the parlor, he called out for his mother and sister. No answer. He dropped his valise next to the staircase and tossed his hat onto the nearby settee. He called again as he passed down the hallway to the kitchen at the back of the house. Familiar voices carried through the open back door. The two were seated in the garden, having lunch under the shade of the large sycamore, one of the few trees around that had not been at least partially denuded.

"There you are."

"Andrew! What a pleasant surprise." His mother arose from her chair.

"Sit down, Mother, sit down." He stepped off the back porch and walked over to kiss her cheek.

"We hardly know when to expect you anymore, son. When did you return?"

"Yesterday." He leaned over and kissed Marguerite on the cheek. She offered him a faint smile in return. "The captain gave us liberty until Wednesday morning, but I'll have to return tomorrow night."

"Always too soon. Won't you have some lunch?"

"I am not hungry just now, thanks."

"Tea? It's a little cold, I'm afraid." His mother lifted her hand toward the teapot on the small table beside her.

"No, thanks. Are you well, both of you?"

"Vexed, my dear. This whole affair of returning a runaway has made true abolitionists of almost everyone in this town overnight. As a southerner, I'm fearful and ashamed to show my face in public, even among friends. I'm so distressed that you were mixed up in it."

"It was most distasteful, I will admit. The hardest thing I've ever had to do."

"Well, I shouldn't doubt it. What a horrible business. I never would have imagined. Sit here beside me and tell us what happened. Then, tell us the latest news, perhaps something more pleasant."

He sat on the bench that encircled the sycamore. "I won't trouble you with the sordid details, which would only spoil your lunch."

"Oh, do tell," said Marguerite, flatly. "Do." Her eyes narrowed as she brushed a strand of dark hair from her face.

"I think your brother is right, my dear. Some things are better left unsaid."

"Suffice it to say that I have never seen a man in such a miserable state as Burns when we left him. And I'm sorry to say we left him."

"I think my dear brother is right about many things. And wrong about a great many others." Marguerite shaded her eyes with her hand. Her smile was that of a chess player who opened with a Queen's gambit, laying a trap. "If he thinks that women shouldn't be told unpleasant facts of the real world, he is sadly mistaken. It is only because men have shielded us women from the facts of their own unsavory doings that the world is in such a sorry state."

"Ah. Such a fine speech. Well, you'll get no argument from me on that score, Marguerite."

"Such cowardice." Her eyes teased him.

"Or discretion."

"I suppose so. It worked for Falstaff, didn't it? But then he was a buffoon. Oh, I do like the comparison. It suits you. Tell me, what part of valor was that on display at the courthouse last month, would you say?"

"I was only interested in your safety, dear sister."

"Were you there, Marguerite?" asked their mother.

"Oh, she didn't tell you?"

"If only you valued your honor as much as my safety," Marguerite interrupted.

"For shame. I value my sister's safety more than my manly pride. What a bad brother I am." He bowed his head in mock contrition. "Can you forgive me?"

"Tell me, what happened at the court— "

Marguerite laughed nonchalantly. "Oh, nothing, Mother. I just met some very nice marines. They were all what you might call stand-up fellows."

"Will someone please tell me what happened? For heaven's sake, if you two are just going to bicker—"

"I don't need the protection of you or any man," Marguerite said.

"Careful, Meg, your bloomers are showing," Gunn smirked.

"Well, that suits me just fine." Marguerite smoothed a hand over her housedress, altered in the fashion of the women's movement to remove the bottom flounce. Hemmed just below her knees, the blue gingham dress exposed a set of white bloomers, tied with matching ribbons at her ankles. "And kindly do not call me by that name. I haven't liked it since I was thirteen."

"Well, I'm sure that Margaret Fuller would approve, if she were alive to see it. I dare you, though, to wear that silly costume beyond the front door."

Marguerite emptied the contents of her teacup onto Gunn's boot. "Oh, how clumsy of me," she said. "By the way, why in heaven's name are you wearing that dowdy old suit? Not very becoming at all."

"This is why," he chuckled, wiping the spilled tea from his boot with her napkin. "Folks seem to want to throw food at me these days. Everybody's gone a bit mad, haven't they?"

"All right, now, that's quite enough, you two." Eleanor Gunn's once-sable hair had a touch more silver in it these days. "I raised you both to have the courage of your convictions. There is no need to try each other on that score. Andrew, whatever happened, I am sure you did what you thought must be done. Marguerite, nobody could ever accuse you of being afraid to express yourself. Let's leave it at that, shall we? Peace. Let's welcome our dear Andrew home."

"Very well, then," said Marguerite. "Let's start again, shall we?"

"Yes, let's." Eleanor settled a wary eye on her daughter. "Tell me, Andrew, how is Elizabeth these days?"

"I wouldn't know, Mother. I haven't seen her. She has gone to live at the teacher's school in Framingham."

"What brought that about? Did something happen?"

He shrugged. "The school had an opening in the dormitory for the summer session. She decided to take it."

"Just like that?"

"Just like that."

The two women exchanged glances.

"Well, that's a good thing," said Eleanor. "Right?"

He searched the sky for a change in subject.

"Passed by the old orchard near the Hawthorne place. So many of the apple trees are without leaves. Practically barren. The whole countryside looks like a wasteland. Mr. Bull says it's caterpillars. Terrible."

"Oh, yes, the plague of forest tent caterpillars. They are especially bad this year. The last invasion was ten years ago or more, but it wasn't nearly this bad."

"I don't remember that."

"Neither do I," said Marguerite.

"Yes, well, they don't much care for sycamore trees, thankfully," sighed Mrs. Gunn, shading her eyes as she peered into the tree above them. "At least not this one. But my poor roses ..." She waved her hand toward the rose bushes near the house, shrouded with cheesecloth. "I've tried to cover them, but even so, I have to pick the ugly critters off every morning. I've given up on most everything else. Dreadful. I don't recall anything quite so destructive while I was growing up in Savannah. Of course, I was but a girl, then. Children hardly notice those things, do they?"

"It is depressing," Gunn said. "I hope the damage is not permanent."

"We're in desperate need of rain, too. It hasn't rained in weeks, it seems."

"Apple trees. Rose bushes," scoffed Marguerite. "Oh, my word. It's nothing compared to the blight that has fallen on our nation, thanks to his most excellent highness, President Pierce, and his foolish minions," said Marguerite.

"It wasn't his minions who swarmed the courthouse like a plague of locusts," said Gunn.

"I declare, if y'all are going to keep after each other, I will leave you to your squabble. I'm sure I can find something far more productive to do in the house." Mother got up from her chair.

"Sorry, Mother," they said in unison.

"Y'all need to let off some steam. Let me know when the kettle stops whistling, won't you?"

Andrew stood while she gathered the lunch tray and carried it to the house, then seated himself again under the tree. Marguerite waited until she was out of earshot.

"How could you, Andrew?"

"You're still angry."

"Well, brother, at least you haven't suffered a complete loss of sensibility. You can bet your life I am."

43

Despite the cool shade of the sycamore it was proving to be a hot day. Gunn removed his worn frock coat.

"I sent you a letter, sis, to explain and apologize for what happened at the courthouse. Did you get it?"

"I seem to recall that it arrived." Marguerite rubbed an ink stain on her middle finger. "Ended up in the dead letter file. It will take a while to process, I'm afraid."

He shook his head, smiling. "You've always been an imp, Marguerite. You love to agitate—"

"I simply say whatever is on my mind. Few people do. You should try it sometime. You might even discover what you *really* think, not to mention how wrong you've been."

"Oh, come now. Get off your high horse. What do you know of all this, Marguerite? You're barely a woman. Still so idealistic. You have no idea, really."

"Andrew Jackson Gunn. Don't you dare patronize me." Her dark eyes flashed. "I have a brain. And I have a heart, which apparently is something you lack."

"Look at me." He drew himself closer, leaning forward and locking eyes with her. "Here is what I think and what I know. A man was killed, Marguerite. His blood cries out from the walls of the courthouse—the seat of law, mind you. And now who is responsible for that? Who? You tell me."

"Sometimes, a little blood must be shed, to—"

"To do what? To dip your pen into? Blood is dearer than ink, my dear sister, though there may be more of it."

"That's a monstrous thing to say, Andrew."

"Monstrous. Let me ask you something. What is more monstrous, Marguerite, taking a man's liberty, or taking his life? Somebody took the law into his own hands and killed another man because he felt justified by his own heart, his own conscience, his own passion to do so."

"Life without freedom and passion is not life at all." She paused, blushing, as she read his face. "Don't look at me that way."

"Passion. Listen, dear sister, you don't have to look beyond your own little world to see the results of passion played out." He lowered his voice and glanced over his shoulder toward the house. "I've had my fill of it. Remember what happened to us, to this whole family, when our own father decided to feed his passion, to follow his own foolish heart. Maybe it served him, God only knows, but it certainly didn't serve *us* well, now did it?"

"Is that what this is all about?"

He did not answer. The old hurt had returned.

"Andrew, you can't possibly equate—"

"I can, and I do equate them," he said. "Passion is passion. It can be a very destructive force, whatever form it takes. Our father's passion put this family at great risk. If not for the kindness of relatives and friends, we would have been destitute. His passion utterly destroyed our brother. If Thomas had not taken his own life at sea, he would have drunk himself to death over what happened."

"You don't know that he took his own life."

"Believe me, I do know. Without a doubt, I know how deep his pain went. I know exactly the burden of shame we had to bear together as sons of a dissolute and derelict father. We just dealt with it in different ways."

She tried to reach out and take his hand, but he drew back. She spoke hardly above a whisper. "Thomas was responsible for his own actions. Our father was not to blame."

"No?"

"Of course not."

"Not to blame, eh?" He hesitated a moment. The revived images flooded his mind and the words spilled out unchecked. "I suppose it was *our* fault that we walked in on Father in his study that day. Of course, he had instructed us never to disturb him while he was working on a sermon." Gunn cocked his head, smirking, and stabbed the air with his forefinger. "Come to think of it, we did break the commandment to honor our father, strictly speaking. Hard to keep that one, though, under the circumstances. Anyway, imagine our shock to discover our godly father in all his" —he clenched both fists— "naked glory, satisfying his ungodly passion with his so-called true heart. Another man, no less."

Marguerite gasped. "What? Why that's—"

"Yes, unspeakable, isn't it?" Gunn continued. "Now what do you think such a sight would do to a boy not yet eight years old? What would it have done to you, I wonder? Let me tell you, it's a sight my eyes can never un-see."

"Now you're just being cruel." She brushed back another wisp of sable hair from her face. Her troubled eyes moistened, and the wry smile that often graced her lips faded.

"Am I? These are the unsavory facts, as you put it, from which you claim to need no protection. Very well, then."

"I don't want to hear any more. It's all in the past and doesn't matter now. I was only four or five. I hardly remember any of what happened."

"And I wish to God I didn't."

"So, then, what about forgiveness?"

"Forgiving is one thing. Forgetting is another. And maybe I have more to forgive than you do."

"Perhaps you do." She studied her hands, quiet in her lap. A tear streamed down her cheek.

Gunn relaxed his fists and rose to his feet, feeling the tension release in his neck and shoulders. He reached for his coat, withdrew a handkerchief from the pocket and handed it to her. "I'm terribly sorry, Marguerite. I should never have said such things to you. It was cruel of me. Monstrous, really. I don't know what came over me. Forgive me, please."

"Of course, I do." She wiped her eyes. "And I understand now. At least, I'm trying to. I'm sorry for what you—I'm sorry, too."

"I think I will take a walk. Care to join me?"

"No, I'll stay. You go on."

His aimless stroll took him several miles through the surrounding fields and forests, across shallow streams and dried up creek beds. It hadn't rained here in a while and it showed. Up close, every living thing seemed to thirst for water. Thunder pealed in the distance, echoing across a dull bronze sky.

Eventually, he circled to the hill behind The Wayside, where Hawthorne's frequent solitary pacing had worn a path along the crest. He'd give a month's pay to be able to talk to Hawthorne right now. He had never been more agitated in his life, more ill-tempered. Nothing seemed right to him anymore. Everything appeared opposite to what it should have been, upside-down, inside-out. He had to find a way to make things right again, if it wasn't too late. As for Burns, it might already be too late. He hoped something could be done for Burns but had no idea what that something might be. As far as his own future was concerned, he knew that Richmond would return soon and then any desire to set things right wouldn't much matter anymore.

As he walked, he said a brief prayer, begging God to help him know what to do and for time in which to do it. Years had passed since he had prayed in earnest for anything. It came as a relief to know that he still could. His prayer came haltingly, like a timid rain after a long drought.

He stopped to rest under the trees. A soft patter sounded in the quiet of the woods, like droplets of light rain falling in the canopy and undergrowth. He felt a mist on his hair, face, and outstretched hands. Searching overhead for the source of the sound, he was shocked to find the crooks of every branch seething with knots of tent caterpillars. The voracious larvae were excreting the remains of the leaves almost as fast as they could devour them.

***

That evening, after a late supper, the family sat together in the parlor for a while, talking about nothing in particular. Marguerite offered to read an excerpt from her latest short story, which she hoped to publish soon in a new magazine. Gunn tried to accommodate her, but after she caught him yawning the second time, he apologized for being such poor company and excused himself to retire.

Marguerite stopped him.

"You know, Andrew, there's going to be a grand picnic next Tuesday to celebrate Independence Day. Music, games, contests, fireworks, the whole thing. People will be coming from all over. Why don't we go together? We all could use some amusement."

"Such a good idea. I think it would be great fun," said Mother. "You two should go. I dare not venture out."

"Oh, Mother, you do exaggerate, I'm sure," said Marguerite. "Anyway, I hear that Mr. Thoreau will be one of the main speakers. I think it would be a fine opportunity, Andrew. You two can make amends after what happened at the courthouse."

"Again, with the courthouse," said Mother. "What in the world?"

"You really should patch things up with him. Thoreau has always been kind to us, you know. He still calls on us after all these years when he walks about here in Concord." She smiled broadly at Mother. "He seems to prefer Mother's biscuits."

Eleanor blushed. "He's welcomed to them anytime."

"He may not be visiting for a while."

"Whatever do you mean?" said Marguerite.

"I saw him in town again this morning. We had words and didn't part well. In fact, he said we should have no more to do with one another."

"Oh, I see. That's terrible," said Marguerite, crestfallen. "I'm sorry to hear it. You musn't let that be the last word between you. He's such a fine man. I take great comfort from the things he has written and said. I recall hearing him say more than once, 'It takes two to speak the truth—one to speak and another to hear.' I especially like that, don't you? It is a fine sentiment."

"I've had my fill of his fine sentiments for a while."

He took a step toward the stairs, but Marguerite reached out and touched his hand.

"Come with me, Andrew. Won't you?" Her voice had a plaintive note.

"It will depend on where the ship is at the time and whether I have duty. I can't promise. Where is the picnic?"

"In Framingham." Her smiling eyes teased him. "You never know who else might be there."

"Framingham? Are you sure?"

"Of course I'm sure. It's been advertised for weeks, you ninny."

"I've been gone for weeks." He shrugged. "Guess it wouldn't hurt."

"I thought you might think so." She laughed and gave him a shove.

Picking up his valise, he climbed the stairs to his small bedroom. Although used by the occasional boarder to help make ends meet, the room remained unchanged from the years when he had shared it with his brother. It was sparsely furnished with twin beds, a writing desk, and a straight-backed chair.

He laid his valise next to the old walnut desk and sat in the chair to remove his boots. As he undressed in twilight, he placed his pocket watch on the desk. He noted that a crack had developed in the edge of the desktop, which threatened to split it in two along a seam in the wood.

He crawled into one of the beds. Soon, he drifted into restless sleep, dreaming that he was lost on a windswept coast, standing high above a wide, empty ocean. Twilight darkened the face of the fathomless water. Far in the distance, along the shoreline, a lighthouse flashed its steady warning. There were no ships out to sea, nothing else on the horizon in any direction. He was alone.

He walked to the bluff. Below him in the heavy surf tumbled a small, black-and-white form that he couldn't quite make out. He crept closer to the edge to gain a better view of what might have been a lifeless shearwater, its tangled wings broken and heavy with brine, but there was no way to tell. Perhaps it would wash up on the beach, and he would know.

Then, the ground beneath him gave way. He lost his footing and fell. Terrified, he opened his mouth to scream, but nothing came out. He had the sensation of falling for what seemed like minutes but was only a few seconds by his slow-ticking watch, which had to be wrong. It had to be. He wondered what it would feel like to hit bottom, if he ever did.

When he awoke, the dream was a vague fragment of memory.

44

Taking an earlier train than he had planned, he arrived back in Boston on Tuesday afternoon. He had decided not to wait until evening, because he wanted to visit Reverend Leonard Grimes of the Twelfth Baptist Church. He owed it to Burns to relay his desperate message.

The church was twelve blocks from the train station. The threat of rain, which he welcomed, urged him to take a cab to the seedy area along the waterfront of the Charles River, commonly referred to as the West End. The cab driver stopped at Belknap Street, refusing to go any further into that part of town. Gunn paid the driver and walked through the narrow, winding streets of the remaining four blocks. The alleys were choked with trash and crates, shelters for the homeless, among which lay the occasional vagrant or drunken sailor.

Arriving at the small church, he removed his hat and entered through double doors into the narrow sanctuary. Simply appointed, the plain interior bespoke humble service to God and man.

The sanctuary was quiet and empty, except for a lone figure sitting in the first pew, head bowed. A few seconds of silence passed before the man lifted his head and turned to watch him walk hat in hand down the aisle toward the front of the church. His steps echoed on the uncarpeted hardwood floor.

"Good afternoon, sir." The short, stout man stood to greet him. His receding hair was close-cropped, his eyes hooded and sharp, his mouth stern and downturned.

"Good afternoon, Reverend Grimes."

"Do I know you, sir? You have me at a disadvantage."

"We met briefly, once, at the courthouse several weeks ago. I was there with Marshal Freeman when you tried to purchase freedom for Anthony Burns. You ... left with Reverend Parker."

"I'm sorry. I don't remember you."

"It was a difficult time."

"Were you there to help Tony?"

"I'm afraid not. I am Third Lieutenant Andrew Gunn, of the Revenue Cutter Service. It was my duty that day to escort Tony to my ship in the harbor."

"I see." His mouth drew even further downward.

Gunn shifted his weight to the other foot. "It was not a duty that I relished."

The preacher's lips opened and then closed again tightly. His eyes examined Gunn's face.

"Reverend, I understand that Tony was one of your flock."

"Yes, that's true. He's a fine young man. How did you know?"

"He told me so. He also told me how you tried to help him."

"Is that a crime?" The defiance of the words echoed in the empty sanctuary. "Have you come to arrest me, too?" His fierce eyes blazed, and his shoulders drew back.

"Certainly not, sir. No, most assuredly not. I have come on Tony's behalf."

"How so?"

"He asked me to give you a message."

"And what message is that?"

"When I left him, he was in a jail cell in Norfolk awaiting transfer to the slave pen in Richmond. A place called Lumpkin's. It's a horrible place from what I hear."

"I know the place. I have been there."

"I can't imagine it being any worse than the jail in Norfolk."

"That is a haven, in comparison. You have not told me anything yet that I do not know."

"He asked me to tell you that he did not think he would survive it. He asks that you do whatever you can to rescue him. He doubts he will live otherwise."

Reverend Grimes bowed his head. His shoulders sagged, and his knees bent, as though he might slump to the ground. Gunn reached out to grasp his arm, but hesitated.

"Oh, Lord," Grimes whispered. His hand swiped the length of his face, and he opened his eyes, blinking, searching about for the closest pew, and pulled himself into it. "When did you last see him?"

Gunn seated himself in the next pew. "A little more than two weeks ago."

"I don't know what I can do now." Grimes sighed. "We had raised enough money to buy his freedom. At least, we thought we had. Suttle would not take the money. He feared that we were trying to trick him into breaking the law. He left word through his attorney that we should contact him again, once he returned safely to Virginia."

"Do you think it is too soon? I know for certain he has arrived there."

Grimes shook his head. "I fear it is too late. Some of the money we had raised came from the members of this church. When the law … when you sent Tony back, several of them left town as soon as they could and fled to Canada. They feared for their own safety and did not wish to take any chances. Do you understand? They needed the money for themselves."

"I'm sorry."

"Many of our people are afraid to stay very long." He looked around the sanctuary. "That's the main reason our building is in such bad shape." He stopped talking and turned his eyes toward the arched ceiling. It was stained by an obvious leak in the roof. "But you have delivered your message. Thank you, Mr. Gunn."

"I wish there was something more I could do."

"I appreciate your concern. But ... why should you care? No offense, but you are one of the men who sent him there. What difference should it make to you now?"

"I—"

"Feel guilty? This is a Baptist Church, Mr. Gunn. You cannot buy your penance here."

"That is not what I meant."

"You have a lot of nerve, coming here, young man. You have no idea what people like you have done to the hearts of all people like Anthony in this city. You have made us most miserable of all men."

Gunn dropped his gaze to the floor. He got up to leave.

"I do thank you, at least, for keeping your word," said Grimes. "Most white people, even those who call themselves Christian, would not have done as much, I'm afraid. Not for a black slave. Maybe not for any negro."

"If there is anything else I can do ..."

Grimes took a deep breath. "It's in God's hands, now. Are you a praying man, lieutenant?"

His latest experience with prayer in the woods behind The Wayside came to mind. "I was thinking of something more practical, reverend."

"There is nothing more practical than prayer, Mr. Gunn."

***

Sam Miller, cradling a spyglass in his left arm and looking rather glum, met him at the gangway as he walked aboard the ship later that afternoon.

"You're back early."

"Just couldn't stay away. I love my job."

"Well, you'd better love it, my good friend, because you're going to be doing a lot more of it. You will never guess what happened, Andrew."

"After the last few weeks, I doubt that anything could surprise me, Sam."

"Richmond sent a telegram yesterday, requesting an extension of his leave until mid-July. It seems his father has taken a turn for the worse."

Gunn's jaw dropped. He was stunned at the news, although not enough so to use his new favorite word. At least one of his prayers had been answered.

45

The next evening, Gunn walked uptown to Kilby Street, where he had seen a jewelry store that advertised watch repair. The shopkeeper had put the closed sign in the window, but Gunn convinced him to open the door. The grizzled jeweler behind the counter gave the worn watch a cursory inspection through dirty spectacles, then frowned and said he'd do what he could to repair it.

"Can you put a rush on it? I'm very dependent on a watch keeping good time. Keeps things in order, you know. I really must have it back as soon as possible."

The jeweler peered over his spectacles. "Dese things take time."

"That's very funny."

The man wasn't smiling. "Come back in a veek or so."

During the next few days, he focused diligently on his work, glad to fill the gap created by Richmond's absence. He also was grateful for the distraction from thoughts about Elizabeth. And Burns.

Between them, he and Miller boarded a dozen or so incoming vessels a day among those at anchor in the outer harbor, waiting to offload cargo. The *Morris* spent each night at anchor a short distance from the end of Central Wharf. Although the captain had made inquiries, the owners of Central Wharf would not allow the cutter dockage alongside the wharf, due to their objections to the rendition of Anthony Burns.

In the evenings, Gunn worked on completing the log abstracts for the month of June. On the second of July, he presented them to the captain, ready for his signature, to be forwarded promptly to the Secretary of the Treasury, as required by regulations.

Whitcomb raised his head from the work laid out on the table before him and regarded Gunn at length.

"Mr. Gunn, a short while ago I gave you a special task. Do you recall?"

"Of course, Captain."

"And, what did you find out?"

"Well, sir, I have scoured the logs back through the first of March, those we haven't archived yet. The only possible match I have found is a brig with a homeport of Boston, named the *Parsifal*. None others come even close."

"*Parsifal*," the captain repeated. "Yes. That's close enough to *Percyville* to be a likely match, I think. And did we board this vessel?"

"No, sir, we did not. We did speak her, though, off Provincetown on the fourteenth of March. She declared her last port of call as Norfolk, bound for Boston with a cargo of rice. We were boarding a foreign vessel at the time and let her pass."

"Well, that would be about the same time Burns escaped to Boston, according to Suttle, anyway. What else do we know about this ship?"

"Not much, sir." The truth was too much to bear. "She usually docks in South Boston, I believe, along Sea Street."

"Very well, then. Tomorrow is Monday. I want you to go ashore, first thing. Take these abstracts with you. And take these reports on the lighthouse inspections."

"You've read mine, sir?"

"Course I did."

"Highland Light's in bad shape."

"As it was the last time we inspected three years ago. We report what we see, Mr. Gunn. Head over to the Custom House and deliver these to the collector's office. Then, I want you to investigate the *Parsifal's* background and her movements. I want to know who owns her, where she trades, what she carries in cargo, and how often she comes and goes. If she is not in port right now, I want to know when she last departed and when she will likely return."

"Aye, aye, sir."

"We'll sail without you tomorrow. When we return tomorrow evening, I will expect your full report with that intelligence and more. Whatever you can find out. Is that clear?"

The next morning, the longboat ferried Gunn ashore. The wharf already bustled with activity. Dodging drays and handcarts that trundled its length, he walked to shore, where the Custom House dominated the waterfront like an Olympian temple.

He ascended the stairs of the east side of the building, which faced the harbor, and passed between the large columns into the portico. The front doors were open to the breeze, which swept past him as he entered. The interior, which never failed to impress him, matched the palatial exterior, built on a grandiose scale unlike any other in Boston.

The main hallway led to an open rotunda, faced with marble, at the center of the building. A circular skylight pierced the dome overhead, flooding the floor with light. Two grand marble staircases, lined with curved, bronze railings, led upward on either side to the second story. In all, the building was magnificent, designed to express stability and endurance, as well as commercial and civic pride.

Gunn exited the rotunda to his right, into the office of the Clerk of the Collector. At the counter inside, he dropped off the package marked for Mr. Charles Peaslee, Collector of the Port of Boston.

Crossing to the opposite corner of the building, he found the offices of the Naval Officer, Charles Greene. Contrary to his outdated title, Greene did not hold a commission in the navy. A political appointee, his main function was to act as an auditor, estimating taxes and fees on cargo and keeping a separate set of books from the collector, to mitigate the potential for fraud. In other words, his job was to keep the Customs collector honest. In addition, he administered the permits for coastal vessels on entering port, certifying they did not carry any goods from foreign ports, on which customs duties must be paid. Every arriving vessel was required to clear Customs, regardless of its last port of call. Greene was required to keep meticulous records of the comings and goings of all ships, including the *Parsifal.*

Greene was a punctilious official, far too busy to tend to the inquiries of a lowly third lieutenant. He pointed instead to a bespectacled clerk, who broke away from another task to listen, nodding impatiently, head cocked, eyes closed. When Gunn finished describing what he needed, the clerk asked Gunn to be seated while he went to find the necessary records.

When the clerk returned, he piled several bound volumes and a stack of loose paper on a nearby counter, indicating with a wave of his hand that they were Gunn's to peruse to his heart's content.

After several hours of research, he learned the *Parsifal* made regular coastwise trips from Boston to Richmond and Norfolk, returning with usual cargos of rice, tobacco, cotton, and molasses. The trips would last from three to five weeks, depending on the weather, with a layover upon return of about four days, on average. Occasionally, she would go as far south as Savannah, Georgia, and these trips lasted longer—from five to seven weeks. These were details he could have guessed, based on his working knowledge of his uncle's business as a former third mate aboard the schooner *Galahad.* However, he was looking for confirmation, wanting to have the facts straight.

The *Parsifal* had arrived in Boston on the sixteenth of March, which coincided with the approximate date Burns had landed. After that, the latest return had been on June third, a day after the *Morris* had left for Norfolk. On that instance, she had stayed in port for two weeks, which seemed odd. She set sail again on June eighteenth, bound for southern ports, which meant that she'd return sometime in mid-July, if the pattern held.

He found the clerk, who was busy tabulating a record, and asked if he knew why the *Parsifal* had stayed in port for two weeks on her last return to Boston. The clerk shook his head and shrugged, saying he had no idea, but Mr. Greene might.

Greene glanced up from the stack of paper on his desk, pen poised in mid-air. "As I recall, it might have been a collision at sea or something. Nothing too serious. But I don't know the details."

"A collision? Was there much damage?"

"Two weeks' worth, I would say. But Mr. Andros knows the captain quite well, I believe. Perhaps he knows. Do you know the Deputy Collector?"

"Oh, yes. We are well acquainted. Thank you, Mr. Greene."

The Deputy Collector's office was at the opposite end of the building. He asked the clerk outside the office to see Mr. Andros. The clerk inquired whether he had an appointment, and then shook his head and motioned toward a chair against the wall, inviting Gunn to wait there, if he chose to. Mr. Andros was busy with a visitor. He was not sure when the Deputy Collector would be free, so it might be better to make an appointment and come back later. Gunn decided to wait.

Twenty minutes later, the door to the office opened, and Andros emerged. He asked the clerk about his next appointment. The clerk uttered something Gunn could not hear and motioned toward the chair where he sat.

Richard Andros was a man of middle age and apparently nearsighted. He squinted in Gunn's direction, and then nodded.

"Mr. Gunn. How good to see you again. What do you hear of our friend, Mr. Hawthorne?"

"Not much of late, but I'm sure his schedule is very busy with his duties in Liverpool."

"Yes, I'm certain of it. I, myself, have only had one letter from him in over a year. Is there something I can help you with? How may I be of assistance?"

Gunn got up and approached Andros. "I'm here on behalf of Captain Whitcomb. I wanted to ask a brief question of you, if I may."

"Why, certainly. What is it?"

"Mr. Greene tells me you might know something about the damage sustained recently by the brig *Parsifal,* during her last trip. Is that so?"

"Well, yes, I suppose so. Apparently, she hit some heavy weather on her way home."

"Heavy weather?"

"Why, yes. At least, that's what I heard. But why ask me? Why not ask your uncle? He owns the *Parsifal,* after all. You realize that, of course?"

"Of course, but I have not seen him of late, and, well, I happened to be here on other business."

"What a coincidence. You can see him right now and ask him yourself. It so happens that Captain Mitchell is sitting in my office this minute."

46

Andros led the way into his office, a spacious, airy room with cathedral ceilings, lined on two sides with windows that looked out upon State Street. William Mitchell sat comfortably, legs crossed, his back to the door, in one of the two chairs facing an enormous oak desk.

Seating himself in the leather chair behind his desk, Andros gestured for Gunn to take the empty seat.

"Well, now, isn't this a pleasant surprise," said Andros. "I believe you two know each other." He grinned at Mitchell as he slid a thick, letter-sized envelope from the desktop into the top drawer and closed it. He bellied his chair up to the desk, while shooting a furtive half-glance toward Gunn.

Mitchell chuckled and the two exchanged warm pleasantries.

"How have you been, Andrew? I imagine it's been a difficult few weeks for you and your ship."

"It has. I can't deny it."

"When did you get in?"

"A week ago."

"Things are just getting back to a normal footing around here. Most folks were pretty upset about what happened."

"Yes, that's been quite apparent. In fact, three boys egged me in uniform last Sunday after church as I was walking down Milk Street. The rest of our crew has had much the same welcome."

"You don't say," said Andros.

"I expect it's a common sentiment," said Mitchell. "Of course, I'm appalled that it happened, Andrew, especially to you, but I'm not surprised. Nobody working for Uncle Sam is very popular around here these days."

"I'm beginning to wonder if things will ever be back to normal again," said Gunn.

"So, what brings you here, Andrew?" asked Mitchell.

"Well, Captain Whitcomb sent me here to get some information."

"Your nephew had asked whether I knew anything about the damage to your brig, the *Parsifal*. Isn't that right?"

Gunn nodded.

"It's good of you to be concerned." said Mitchell. "Nothing too serious. But I'm curious. How did you find out about the damage?"

"I—ah, we heard it about town. They said she might have had a collision at sea. Captain Whitcomb asked me to find out more about it."

"No, no. It was some heavy weather coming north, just off the Cape."

"Heavy weather?"

"That's what was reported to me."

"When was that?"

Mitchell frowned. "Oh, I don't know. Sometime around the second or third of last month. Why do you ask?"

"No reason, really. I was merely curious. No one was hurt?"

"No, thank goodness."

"Is Webber still the captain?"

"Yes, that's right."

"Well, if that's the case, then I'm sure nobody was ever actually in danger, despite the weather."

"He's a fine captain," asserted Mitchell.

"Of course."

"Risky waters around the Cape," said Andros. "Anything can happen."

"Very risky," said Mitchell.

Gunn cleared his throat and crossed his arms. "The *Morris* recently had some trouble there, too, as a matter of fact. We collided in dense fog with a ship that was sailing with no lights, and not sounding fog signals."

Andros leaned back. "Yes, yes, just a week or so ago, I received a written report from Captain Whitcomb of a collision on your transit south last month. Seems it was around the same time, too. Isn't that odd?"

"Yes, the whole incident was very odd. The other ship never even stopped to assess the damage."

"Is that so? Not very seamanlike," said Mitchell. He exchanged glances with Andros. After a second, he added, "Was it serious? Nobody was injured, I take it."

"We had some damage to our rigging, lost the foreyards and the jib boom, but nobody was hurt."

"That's good. Glad to hear it." Another brief silence. "Well, I really must be going," said Mitchell, rising to his feet. "We can finish our business at another time, Andros."

"Yes, I should let you get back to your busy schedule, Mr. Andros," Gunn said as he got up from his chair. "I'll walk you out, Uncle William."

"Well, gentlemen, it has been a pleasure to see you both. Please stop by any time."

The two exited the deputy's office and walked to the east entrance, stopping outside on the steps to talk.

"Your sister came to stay with us in town last night. She said you two are going to the Independence Day picnic in Framingham tomorrow."

"Yes, we are. It was Marguerite's idea. She thought it would be a nice time."

"Should be. And your mother?"

"Home, I guess. She's not one for picnics. Besides, she is concerned that as a southerner she would be unwelcome in public these days. Can't say as I blame her."

"That's a shame. You should bring them both to visit sometime this month. It's been far too long. Your Aunt May would like that very much. We'll be staying at Stormcrest after the Fourth. Why don't you come out and stay with us for a weekend, when you get the chance?"

"Thank you. We'd like that, Uncle William, though I can't say what the ship's schedule will be just now."

Mitchell turned to go.

"Uncle," Gunn stopped him. "Just so you know, we were out there, near the Cape, in the early morning of June third, heading south in heavy fog. There was no heavy weather. The sea state was less than two feet."

"Is that so?" Mitchell rubbed the side of his nose. "How are you so sure?"

"I just finished reviewing the abstracts for our logs, so I know. Besides, it's hard to forget an incident like that."

"How strange. I may be off on the dates. Or maybe the location. I will check with Captain Webber again."

Every instinct urged Gunn to press his uncle further about the damage to the *Parsifal*, but even more so to ask whether he knew anything about the smuggling of fugitive slaves. Yet, he respected this man more than any other on the face of the earth, due to his generosity and forbearance toward their family, especially in light of the circumstances. He had never seen William Mitchell act in a disingenuous way toward anyone, even outside their family. It was hard to imagine that his uncle would willfully break the law and conceal it. He could not even think of a way to broach the subject without giving offense. But something wasn't right.

"Was there something else, Andrew?"

"No, sir."

"Good man."

Somehow, the accolade sounded different when Anthony Burns had said it.

47

That evening, Gunn relayed to Captain Whitcomb the information he had learned about the movements and manifests of the brig *Parsifal*. Whitcomb reclined in his chair and listened, as Gunn stood before him. Prouty sat at the table beside the captain.

"Is that all you have to report, Mr. Gunn? Who is the master?"

"Ross Webber."

"Can't say I know him. And the owner?"

"Sir, his name is William Mitchell. I should point out that he's my uncle. If you remember, I mentioned his name to you when we spoke the night of the collision."

"Ah, yes. Uncle, you say?" queried the captain. "William Mitchell. That wouldn't by any chance be the same 'Billy Bones' Mitchell who used to run a privateer operation off the coast of Maine back in the day, would it? Made a fortune the easy way, until things got too hot for him. At least that's the way I heard tell."

"I don't know that name, sir. But I do believe my Uncle William to be an honest man," Gunn asserted. "A respectable man." An image flashed through his mind of the thick envelope Andros had attempted to shield from view in his desk. He tried to ignore it for now.

"Yes, of course. I'm sure he is. Why are you mentioning this connection just now? Why save it until last?"

"I hesitated because I did not want you to think I might have any partiality in this case."

Whitcomb looked at Prouty, who returned his glance, without expression. Then the captain lifted his gaze to Gunn. "Did you happen to think that your hesitation might indicate your partiality?"

"Not until just now, sir."

"Very well, Mr. Gunn. Thank you for telling me. We'll plan to intercept and board the *Parsifal* on her next trip north. When did you say that would be?"

"Sometime mid-July, sir, the way I figure it."

"Very well, then. I trust I do not have to remind you to keep our plans confidential, do I?"

"No, sir." He met the captain's gaze.

"Is that everything?"

"No, sir." He cleared his throat. "There is one more item. The fact is, I think the *Parsifal* might have been the ship that collided with us near the Cape. But I can't prove it. Not yet."

"What makes you think so, Mr. Gunn?"

"The *Parsifal* needed repairs to her sails and rigging when she last arrived in Boston. Webber claims they hit heavy weather the night before, just off the Cape."

"What date was that?"

"The third of June, the same date as our collision."

"But the weather off the Cape was calm that day."

"Yes, sir."

"I don't know this Captain Webber. If what you say is the case, then why do you suppose he's not telling the truth? Why would he lie about such a thing?"

Prouty joined the inquiry. "To cover something illicit. That's the best reason I can think of, captain."

"Precisely," said Whitcomb.

"Tell me this, Mr. Gunn," said Prouty. "Do you have any regular contact with your uncle? Might he provide some better light on this matter?"

"As it happens, sir, I ran into him this morning at the Custom House."

"This morning?" Prouty asked. "Did you by chance ask him whether he might know anything about a fugitive slave on one of his ships?"

"No, sir."

"Why not?" pressed Prouty.

"Without any real evidence, it did not seem right even to ask the question. It was my judgment—"

"I would agree that asking him a direct question about his knowledge of a crime would be inappropriate at this stage," said Whitcomb. He sat thoughtfully for a moment, tapping his forefinger on the table. "Even so, we must investigate further, it seems to me."

"Sir, I know William Mitchell well—better than I know any man alive. I can certainly vouch for his character. It is hard for me to harbor any suspicions that—"

"Come, now, Mr. Gunn. I can certainly see how you might think so." Prouty peered up at him, his eyes pleading with him to tread carefully. "But wouldn't it be fair to question whether you might be a bit prejudiced given your relationship, not to mention your apparent misgivings on the subject?" asked Prouty.

"What subject?"

"The enforcement of the Fugitive Slave Act. You have made your misgivings fairly plain, Mr. Gunn."

"But I did report my findings, sir. All of them."

"You certainly took your time, didn't you?" said the captain. "It was a bit like drawing a cable through a thimble eye to get it out of you, I must say."

"My misgivings about the law have no bearing on this case, I assure you, captain. I would ask you to keep in mind, it may very well be that my uncle knows nothing whatsoever about fugitive slaves on his ships or any other. Nothing yet says he does. He should be given the benefit of the doubt, don't you think? We do still hold to being innocent until proven guilty, I should hope."

"That may be true. But are you willing to find out whether he does or not? That is the question, Mr. Gunn. You might not like what we find."

"I hope you know the answer to that question, sir."

"I'd like to think so, lieutenant. But if I did, I wouldn't have asked it." Silence filled the cabin. "We'll find out the answer together. Very well, Mr. Gunn, thank you for your report. You are at liberty to go."

48

U p with the dawn the next morning, Gunn couldn't wait to leave the ship. He had won the coin-toss with Miller, which decided who would remain on duty for the holiday. Although he lost the deciding Liberty silver dollar to Sam in the bargain, he would have paid far more for the chance to make himself scarce for the day.

As soon as liberty was granted, he departed the ship dressed in his best uniform. He was proud of it, despite the risks.

His search for a cab proved impossible given the holiday, despite or perhaps because of his being in uniform. Instead, he took an omnibus to Tremont Street, where he and Marguerite previously had agreed to meet at Aunt May's townhouse, should he be able to attend the picnic.

When he arrived at Aunt May's, the tall, elegant woman welcomed him in the front parlor and offered coffee while they waited for Marguerite to come downstairs.

"Your sister wasn't at all sure you would come, Andrew."

"Neither was I, Aunt May. But here I am. And where is she?"

"Down presently, I expect. It is a woman's prerogative to keep men waiting, you know. It's about the only one we ladies have. Not given up easily, mind you."

Talking nonstop in her restive way, Aunt May told him all about the new bow-front brownstone she and his uncle were building further out along Tremont on Weston Street in the South End.

"They are building these gorgeous new developments out there designed around small parks, just like the town-homes in London. I just love London so. Always have."

"I'd think you would get tired of moving, Aunt May. Won't this be your third townhouse, since you sold your house on Beacon Street and built Stormcrest?"

"It is simply getting too crowded in town these days. So many new people from all over are coming into the city. Besides, who's counting? One must keep up with the changing times, Andrew. These new planned communities will be the most modern of any city in America. Out with the old, in with the new, as they say."

Marguerite came tripping downstairs, finally ready to go. Her dress looked somewhat familiar, but the white cotton skirt had been made over and shortened to just below the knee. It was trimmed in federal blue, matching her bodice. Her bloomers were tied at the ankles with blue ribbons, overtop new white kid boots. Apparently, Aunt May had taken her niece shopping for shoes the day before. The ensemble was completed with a straw bonnet tied with tricolor ribbon at her throat. She flashed a self-satisfied, defiant smile at him.

"How do you like my Syrian dress?"

"You're not wearing that, Marguerite. Not really."

"Of course, I am. You said I should."

"I did nothing of the kind."

"You certainly did. You dared me to. Remember?"

"You can't be serious."

Aunt May chuckled. "One must keep up with the times, Andrew."

"Well, don't expect me to bail you out of jail, if you're arrested for indecency."

"Don't be silly. If that happens, it will be a true injustice," said Marguerite. "In that case, you may leave me in my cell. As Mr.

Thoreau has said, 'Under a government which imprisons any unjustly, the true place for a just man is also a prison.'"

"I'm not sure he meant it to hold true for women as well."

"It certainly does. Why shouldn't it?"

"No reason at all that I can think of," said May. "You two had better go, before you set off your own fireworks. Don't forget your lunch." She handed Gunn the picnic basket that her cook, Louisa, had made up for them.

They managed to hail a cab. Gunn credited Marguerite's dress for the unexpected ease in finding one. The grinning cabbie eyed her exposed ankles as they got in. Gunn told him to mind his business and promised a large tip if they reached the South End train station without another glance.

"This is what I have to contend with all day, I suppose," Gunn said, as he paid the man upon their arrival. The cabbie took one last lingering look before he told his horse to walk on.

Marguerite laughed. "You'll go broke if you keep that up, Andrew. Ah, well, suit yourself."

They entered South End Station among a throng of people waiting to board the ten-thirty train to Framingham on the Boston and Worcester line. They found seats in the last car, which was nearly full. The train departed on time. Their casual conversation drifted along unhindered, until Marguerite touched a sore point.

"You know, Andrew, I meant to ask you about Elizabeth. You barely mentioned her last time we saw you at the house. That's not at all like you. What's going on?"

The houses and shops of Jamaica Plain drifted past the train window.

"Andrew?"

"I haven't seen or heard from her."

"Since when?"

"Last month. Since the day the ship departed. While I was gone, she decided to move into the dormitory at the teachers' school."

"Yes, of course. So you said. What you didn't say is what brought this on?"

He shrugged and turned to face her. "She's angry with me. And so is her father. He doesn't want us to see each other anymore. She won't answer my letters."

"And why is that?"

"Because of what happened. With Burns, I mean. They're upset that I had something to do with the whole mess."

"I see. Imagine that. You poor thing."

"I can do without the sarcasm."

"Have you told her that you're coming?"

"No."

"Bad idea, brother."

"Why do you say that?"

"If she is at the picnic, she won't be there because she's hoping to see you, that's for certain."

"It will be a surprise."

"And then some." She sighed, shaking her head. "You don't know anything about women, do you?"

"Enough."

"We'll see. How do you even know she'll be there?"

"She'll be there."

"Well, if not, you'll just have to be happy to spend some time with your dear little sister." She smiled and tossed her head.

"Of course."

"I think it will do us both good to spend the day trying to have a grand old time, even though we both know that's the last thing on your mind, right now."

"Not the very last thing." He half-smiled. "The last thing on my mind is what you might think about it."

She kicked his shin. "You deserved worse."

By the time the train pulled into the station at Framingham almost three-quarters of an hour later, his ears had started to ring, dulling the clang of the train's bell and its shrill whistle. Gunn grabbed the picnic basket and helped Marguerite step out of the car onto the platform. The din of the crowds and the music of the brass band filled the air in the town square nearby, drowning out everything else.

Thousands already filled the streets and Harmony Grove, the picnic grounds. The entrance was festooned with red, white, and blue bunting. Children everywhere waved tiny American flags. Uncle Sam roamed the main street on stilts, handing out lollipops and tossing hard candy. Handbills posted on nearly every vertical surface by the Massachusetts Anti-Slavery Society heralded the presence of eminent speakers for the day. William Lloyd Garrison, Sojourner Truth, and Henry David Thoreau were among those slated to speak.

With Marguerite on one arm and the basket on the other, Gunn walked to the middle of the grove, where Garrison, the renowned editor of the abolitionist newspaper, *The Liberator,* was winding up a fiery speech. Standing on the raised speakers' platform, he held up a copy of the Constitution of the United States in one hand, struck a match on the podium with the other, and set it on fire with the final words, "…a covenant with death, and an agreement with hell." A tremendous clamor from the crowd all but drowned the last of his speech. As the document burned, and the embers floated to the platform around his feet, he exclaimed, "So perish all compromises with tyranny. Down with Pierce, the ignoramus president!"

The crowd roared their approval again, despite a few distinctly angry boos. Waving hats and handkerchiefs high in the air, the audience pressed in from all sides. Garrison mopped his bald head with a handkerchief and removed his spectacles to wipe the sweat from them.

Across the platform banners proclaimed, "Down with Virginia!" and "Redeem Massachusetts!" Above Garrison's head hung an inverted American flag, draped with black crepe—a familiar sight these days, which Gunn would have been happy never to see again.

49

After the speech, the rally suspended for lunch, and the crowd began to scatter. Gunn had little appetite, however, after Garrison's rash anarchic display. It was utter folly to incite public lawlessness. The man had no idea what he was asking for, in Gunn's opinion. He had seen all he needed to of mob violence, and he feared that it would escalate out of control, given the chance.

His irritation with Garrison's words and deeds was heightened by the thought that he had no idea how they would possibly find Elizabeth among this wild throng. He glared at Marguerite, who laughed, tossing her head again, making the dark ringlets of hair dance under her straw bonnet.

"You wanted to come," she said.

Andrew searched the thousands of faces for one. Elizabeth was nowhere to be seen. He gave his arm again to his sister, conscious of critical glances at her dress from other women and catcalls from the men, all of which Marguerite gleefully ignored. As they walked to the outskirts of the thinning crowd, Gunn was surprised to see other women in similar dress. Some wore white sashes bearing the slogan, "VOTES FOR WOMEN." They were young and old, married and single in greater numbers than he would have expected. Perhaps he simply hadn't paid them any notice before.

He finally did spot Elizabeth, standing with two other women in the shade beneath one of the large, thinly leaved oaks. The tree stood on the banks of Farm Pond, where children played by the waterside catching frogs, and couples in boats rowed lazily by in the background. He started toward her, drawing Marguerite along with him.

When she noticed him, Elizabeth's face brightened, then dimmed, the way shadows drift across a placid sea. She whispered to her two friends, and they turned to watch Gunn and Marguerite approach. The rush of blood thrummed in his ears.

Elizabeth's hand flitted over her flowered muslin skirt, smoothing its violet-trimmed flounce. Her chestnut hair was pulled back over her ears into a loose bun at the nape of her neck. She wheeled to face him. Her leghorn bonnet, perfectly shaped to her delicate face, cast a shadow over her eyes, which glistened as they settled on him.

Without uttering a word in greeting, she introduced her two companions, also students at the Normal School. Mary Rice was tall and gangly, with a face that held a constant gaze of disapprobation. Alice Stemple was short and wore spectacles, through which peered a pair of fawning eyes that lingered on Gunn.

"I am very happy to make your acquaintance, Mr. Gunn," said Alice, her eyes fluttering.

Gunn bowed slightly. "Likewise, Miss Stemple."

Elizabeth greeted Marguerite with a kiss on both cheeks. Marguerite returned her greeting.

"So good to see you again, Elizabeth," said Marguerite.

"Yes, it is good to see you again at last, Elizabeth," Gunn said.

"Hello, Andrew," Elizabeth said softly, finally acknowledging him. "Such a surprise." She tried to smile.

"A pleasant one, I hope," he said.

"Of course it is. You know that." She extended her hand, which he took in his and touched it to his lips.

"I just adore your dress, Marguerite," said Elizabeth. "It's so brave, isn't it ladies?"

"Thank you. That's sweet of you to say," said Marguerite. "It was entirely Andrew's idea." She smiled at him.

"Is that so?" said Elizabeth. "I never would have guessed."

"It was nothing of the kind, I assure you," he laughed.

"Shall we eat something?" Marguerite pointed to the basket Aunt May had prepared for them. "Won't you and your friends join us, Elizabeth? Our Aunt May has outdone herself. There is more than plenty."

Mary pursed her lips. "Well, thank you, but we were just going to—"

"Of course, we will," said Alice, smiling. "We'd be happy to." She'd hardly taken her eyes from Gunn's face.

They found a shady spot by the pond to spread the blanket Alice had brought. The ladies each sat on a corner of the blanket, and Gunn lounged in the grass beside them.

As they shared the lunch of cold fried chicken, fruit, and cheese, Mary commented on Marguerite's kid boots, saying she couldn't help but admire them, all the while eyeing her bloomers with a frown.

"Why, thank you. I simply couldn't resist when I saw them in the shop window," said Marguerite, grinning. "I like them because they are lovely, yet so demure." She waggled her feet. "I hate to draw too much attention to myself. Fashion is so overdone these days. Don't you agree, Miss Rice?"

Mary averted her gaze, pretending renewed interest in the boaters on the lake.

Elizabeth wore brown leather shoes more common in design, which she discreetly allowed to peek out from beneath the hem of her full-length skirt. With a sly, playful smile, she thrust them into full view and hitched up her skirt a few inches, as she stretched sidelong on the blanket.

"I for one couldn't agree more," she said, pairing the soles of her shoes with Marguerite's. The two broke into laughter, to the ill-concealed astonishment of Elizabeth's friends.

Gunn rolled his eyes. "Corrupted by my own sister. What *is* this world coming to?"

Elizabeth pointed to her shoes, the soles of which pressed against Marguerite's. "Haven't you noticed, Andrew? We're kindred *souls*, your sister and I." They chortled again.

"You must forgive my brother," said Marguerite. "Sometimes, he can be such a goody two-shoes."

Elizabeth shot him a sideways glance. "I'm sure he means well." she teased.

"Ah, very funny," he said, chuckling. "Ha, ha. We're all amused, aren't we, ladies?" He turned to Mary and Alice, mocking affirmation. They offered simpering smiles in return.

"Oh, my, never mind," said Marguerite. "Let's discuss something truly important, shall we? My brother and I arrived too late to hear all of Mr. Garrison's speech. It sounded rather scorching. What did you think of it, Elizabeth?"

"We could not hear very much from here," Elizabeth said. "I'm afraid it was a bit too warm over there near the podium. Standing in the sun, I mean."

"I'm so very sick of hearing about slavery," interjected Mary. "It's all anyone ever talks about anymore. What ever happened to good old-fashioned patriotism on the Fourth of July?"

"It was dreadfully cataclysmic," said Alice. "From what we could hear, he made it sound as though the world is soon coming to an end in a ball of fire, and that President Pierce would fiddle a tune as it does."

Elizabeth nodded in agreement. "The apocalypse is upon us, so it would seem, according to Mr. Garrison. He's not the only one who thinks so."

"Strange you should say that," said Gunn. "You know, a few weeks ago, I heard someone else say very much the same thing, while we were inspecting Highland Light out on Cape Cod. He was the keeper of the light. The oddest old man. Fisk … or, Fisker, was his name. Leroy Fisker, as I recall. Insisted he saw three suns at once on the horizon one morning, out over the sea. 'Sun wolves,' was what he called them. *Solhund*, in Norwegian, I believe. They're supposed to be the harbingers of the end of days."

"Was he a drunkard, too?" asked Mary.

"No, he quit drinking long ago. A lonely old fellow. His only companion was a little girl who lived with him, named Marianne, about eleven or twelve years old. She's his niece. Little red-haired girl. I can't forget her. Just showed up as we sat talking in the keeper's house. Stood there, didn't speak a word, holding a candle in one hand and a cup in the other. Strange. She was wild-looking, hair all dirty and knotted. Face and hands were filthy. No shoes, her feet were bare. It was all very pathetic."

"Did this little girl have no parents?" asked Elizabeth.

He shook his head. "Both dead. She seemed so lonely. As we were leaving after the inspection, we found her crying over a dead turtledove. Poor thing had probably killed itself trying to fly against the windows of the lighthouse. I had nudged the carcass off the edge of the platform at the top of the light. I guess she must have collected it after it fell to the ground. She wanted me to help her bury it in an old graveyard nearby."

"How dreadful," said Mary.

"Did you help her?" Marguerite asked.

"Of course, I did. How could one not?" He paused.

"Of course," said Elizabeth.

He sat upright. "But now that I think about it, the question really is, did I help her enough? Isn't there something more that can be done? Something to keep the sun wolves at bay, at least for a time. You know?"

Elizabeth sat quietly, studying his face, with a quizzical look on hers.

"What a terribly romantic story," said Alice. Her wide, spectacled eyes stopped blinking.

"Oh, yes, romantic," said Marguerite, smiling suspiciously. "Very amusing. Sounds like something out of that book of yours, Andrew, the one of Hawthorne's twice-told tales," she teased.

"So, it's not a true story, then?" said Mary. "You made it up?"

"No, it's true. Every word. I swear it." He crossed his heart. "Odd, though, don't you agree?"

"One shouldn't swear," said Mary.

"It is true, nonetheless."

The conversation lagged for a moment. Gunn rotated his ankle, exercising the stiffness out of it.

This time, Elizabeth changed the subject. "How is your injury, Andrew?"

"What injury?" asked Marguerite.

"He injured his foot, while so gallantly trying to save me from being run over by the mob that stormed the courthouse in Boston last month. The night the man was killed."

"You didn't tell me about that, Andrew," said Marguerite. "You were there that night? Well, well."

"Nothing to tell. It was just my ankle. Still a little stiff. But almost good as new. In fact, I was just thinking that I might enjoy a walk. Would you care to join me, Elizabeth?" He stood and offered his hand to her.

"I—well, I suppose so." Elizabeth took his hand and he helped her to her feet.

"Won't you ladies excuse us for a little while?"

Elizabeth's two friends nodded politely with twin faux smiles. Marguerite darted a glance toward them, and then caught his eye with a glare.

"You wanted to come," he said, smiling. "Don't worry. We won't miss the fireworks."

"Oh, brother, you can count on that."

50

Elizabeth had brought a parasol, which Gunn retrieved for her. She brushed her hand lightly against his as she took it from him, then opened and raised the sunshade above her head. He offered his arm and steered her in the direction of the pond. They strolled along the pebbled path.

"Imagine my surprise," she said, after they had walked a short way.

"Imagine mine. Why did you leave without a word?"

"Why did *you*? Did it just slip your mind? You simply forgot to mention your little part in sending a man back to a life of misery?"

"Our ship's involvement was kept quiet until that day to reduce the potential for violence. It's been a difficult time, the whole Burns thing."

"It was probably hardest on him, I would think."

"Yes, of course. I didn't mean—"

"I know." She walked a few steps in silence, then turned her face up to his. "Did you have second thoughts?"

"About Burns? Yes, and then some."

"I know it must have been hard to do. I don't think I could have done it. Why did you?"

"It was my duty, Elizabeth."

"I understand that. But why did you do it?"

He could not hide the incredulity in his voice. "Didn't you receive my letter? I hoped that I wouldn't have to explain it any further to you."

"Yes, I did receive it. I understand duty, believe me, Andrew. But don't you think there are times when duty calls us to do things that we know are not right? What about obeying your conscience?"

"We obeyed the law, Elizabeth. And we enforced it. I shouldn't have to apologize for that."

"You didn't answer my question, Andrew. Are we not also called to adhere to our own conscience? And what about honor?"

"Honor." He stopped short and she with him. "Let me tell you something about honor. It is my honor to serve my country, even though I don't always agree with her. Do you understand that? I risked my own neck to stand up for Burns while he was—I did my best to—they'll probably toss me out like rubbish, you know. Aww, for the love of Pete. What's the use?"

"What are you trying to say? What happened?"

"I struck a superior officer and threatened the jailor while trying to free Burns."

"You did what?" Her eyes widened. "When? Where?"

"In Norfolk, at the slave pen where he was being held. You should have seen the sty. And it was only going to get worse for him."

"How awful. But at least you tried. What do you think will come of it?"

"I don't know. I might very well lose my commission."

"Would that be so terrible? At least you would no longer be in the business of shipping slaves to the South. I'm sure there are many other occupations you could do, instead."

"That's not fair, Elizabeth. You know better than that. Look, I did not come here to argue, especially with you."

"I don't mean to argue, Andrew." She walked on. "These are merely questions on my mind these days."

"As they are on mine, believe me." He caught up with her. "But I have another question for you."

"Do you?"

"Yes. A more important one. Come with me."

Taking her by the hand, he drew her underneath the bower of a linden tree, away from the pond. He removed his hat and dropped it to his feet. Without hesitation, he took her in his arms, his hand on the small of her back, pressed her to him, and tenderly kissed her mouth.

She returned his kiss, hesitant at first, but then earnest and passionate, her eyes shut tight. She dropped her parasol and circled her arms around his neck. He drew in the savory scent of her rapid breath, and it stirred him to prolong the kiss and press her even closer against him. Her body tensed. Then she pushed away, keeping him at arm's length.

He waited for her to say something, anticipating a tender note of renewed longing to replace the disappointment in her voice, but she was silent. She stood with her eyes closed, trying to take deep breaths. Her eyes opened, anger flashing in them. She drew her hand back from his chest and swung it toward his face, but he caught her wrist.

"How dare you, Andrew."

"What was that for?"

"Get hold of yourself. What has come over you?"

He might have asked himself the same question, but the answer was clear. It was his passion for her and hers for him.

"You shouldn't have done that," she whispered. "We shouldn't have."

"Why not? I love you. You liked it, didn't you?

"That's not—"

"Ten minutes ago you were teasing me about being a goody two-shoes."

"Ten minutes ago you hadn't taken undue liberties."

"Liberties? Tell me you're still joking."

"I've never been more serious."

"I want you to marry me, Elizabeth."

"Marry you?"

"Don't look so surprised. Will you? Marry me? Now. This week."
She hesitated.

"Well? Don't you want to get married? I thought we had an understanding."

She lowered her face. "I—I don't know, Andrew. I did once, but now I'm not so sure."

He gently cupped her chin in his hand and raised her eyes, brimming with tears, to meet his. The satin ribbon on her bonnet cast a violet reflection on her cheek. "Why? Why not?"

"I think you know." A tear ran down her face into his palm.

"It's your father, isn't it? Listen to me. What your father thinks matters far less to me than how we feel about each other. You must know that."

"My father is not the reason. Not the main reason."

"What are you saying?"

"I need time to think about it."

"What is there to think about?"

She held her eyes on his. "I think this is a good time for both of us to take a step back and find out what is truly best for us. Maybe to seek God's will in our lives."

"God's will? What about your will, Elizabeth? My will?"

Elizabeth took off her bonnet. The highlights of her rich, brown hair shone like amber in the dappled light under the tree. Her beauty made his heart ache.

"This is my will, Andrew. I need some time. I cannot say that I will marry you. I do still love you. But I despise what you are now willingly a part of. I think it's horrible. Everything is different now. We're very different people. That fact has become painfully obvious. I don't know how I could be Mrs. Andrew Gunn and hold my head up while you go off to sea in your uniform, dashing as it may be, and do whatever you're ordered to do. I'm not sure I want that. I was sure once. But not anymore."

"Now, wait a minute. Wait just one minute. Why can't we put away all this black crepe? My involvement in the Burns affair was not my will, Elizabeth. You must know that."

"Whose was it, then? You've made your choices. And now, I must make mine."

Anger welled in his chest. The resentment that had been brewing for quite some time, dissenting against all that lately seemed to be acting against him, burned in his throat and turned his voice bitter.

"What would you have me do, Elizabeth? Do you want me to quit a career that I love? Suppose I do, and then what? Let me tell you something. I am no quitter. Besides, if the power of the federal government can send a man back into slavery, then maybe someday it can free him, too. And, I'll be right there to see it happen. You can count on that. And, so can your father. He can stuff that in his pipe and puff till he darned well chokes on it."

She turned her back to him. "You've given me a lot to think about, Andrew. You wouldn't like my answer, right now, I'm afraid."

"I'm sorry, Elizabeth. Truly, very sorry. I did not mean to say anything of the kind." He tried to take her hand, but she refused.

"Just give me some time. That's all I ask."

"Take whatever time you need."

She wiped her eyes, replaced the bonnet on her head, and tied the bow under her chin. He picked up his hat, dusted the brim, and placed it firmly on his head. In silence, he retrieved her parasol and handed it to her.

They continued their walk around the pond, talking about trivial matters whenever the silence became too great. She pointed out a family of ducks that scurried from the bulrushes into the still water and swam away, single file. He remarked on the barren appearance of so many trees. She agreed and said how sad it all appeared.

Finally, they returned to the place where they had eaten lunch, but discovered their company was gone. The luncheon was over.

Another crowd had swarmed to the stage as Thoreau railed against the evils of slavery and the tyranny of the federal government. The two wended through the audience to the front, finding Marguerite and Elizabeth's friends near the stage. Thoreau was reaching mid-stride in his speech. His bearded chin trembled, as he spoke in a fierce, strident voice.

"The whole military force of the state is at the service of a Mr. Suttle, a slaveholder from Virginia, to enable him to catch a man whom he calls his property. But not a soldier is offered to save a citizen of Massachusetts from being kidnapped. No, sir." Thoreau's glance settled on Gunn, then burned right through him. "The slave was carried back by our men in uniform, by the soldier, the sailor, of whom the best you can say in this connection is that he is a fool made conspicuous by a painted coat."

Gunn had heard that drumbeat before. He whispered in his sister's ear. "Let's go back."

"We'll miss the fireworks."

"I doubt it," he muttered.

The pageantry of the day had lost its luster, and he'd lost all further interest in it.

51

Three days passed before he next went ashore. He had heard nothing from Elizabeth since the picnic, nor had he expected to. Meanwhile, his disappointment and anger at what she last said to him continued to smolder unabated. He was determined to do something about that and everything else that lately had troubled him.

Late that afternoon, he walked up to the Atlantic Bank on Kilby Street and emptied his account, save ten dollars. Of the four hundred eighty-three dollars he withdrew, he asked the teller to make out a bank draft for four hundred to the Twelfth Baptist Church of Boston. He pocketed the remainder in cash. The teller placed the check in an envelope, thanking him for his business with a shrug and a pinched, patronizing simper as if to say, *I hope you know what you're doing, young man.* Gunn nodded in return.

Next door to the bank was the jewelry shop where he had left his watch. The old shopkeeper wasn't there, but an eager young clerk retrieved the watch and presented it to him in a velvet-lined box, which made the watch appear even shabbier than he remembered. The clerk removed the watch, set it to the right time, and wound it for him, while offering to sell him a new one.

"A watch says a lot about a man," the clerk said, looking sideways at him.

"Yes, it certainly does. And I happen to like this one. It's my lucky timepiece. At least, it was."

Gunn took the watch, thanked him kindly, paid in cash, and walked out, leaving the box.

When he left the shop, he walked around the corner to the Merchant's Exchange on State Street, which housed the nearest post office. The afternoon sun caught the casements of windows and doors, facades and fluted pilasters, casting light and shadow along the great, craggy precipice that formed the south side of this street of banks, insurance companies, real estate brokers, and newspaper publishers. Rising two, three, or even as many as five stories high, the buildings lined the street on both sides, reminding Gunn of the walls of a river gorge he had once explored in the Berkshire Highlands.

He entered the post office, asked the clerk to look up the address for the Twelfth Baptist Church, addressed the envelope, and mailed the check with no return address. Before he mailed it, however, he wrote in bold, block letters at the top edge of the check, "FOR ANTHONY BURNS."

He would try to do more, once he could think of whatever that might be. For now, this check was a start. The amount of money was small by the world's standards. It was all he had for the present, and all he had saved for his future with Elizabeth. She had questioned his honor, which cut him to the quick. He considered the contribution as the cost of honor, at least in part.

He also mailed a letter addressed to The Honorable Mr. Nathaniel Hawthorne, at the American consulate in Liverpool. The letter told his friend of the past events surrounding the rendition of Anthony Burns, news of which had probably already reached him, and asked his advice regarding his future. Given Hawthorne's close relationship to President Pierce, he might lend a singularly sympathetic ear, not to mention a father's wisdom.

As Gunn left the Post Office, a group of half a dozen or so well-dressed men stood in front of the Merchants' Exchange, underneath the American flag still hanging conspicuously upside down, as it had during the march to the waterfront. The men stopped talking and turned toward him.

He could no longer hold his peace. "As an American, and as a commissioned officer in service to my country, it pains me to see her flag disgraced," he declared. "One would hope to see it displayed properly or otherwise taken down."

A short, wiry man with long, white hair flowing from under his top hat stepped from the group and approached Gunn, a wooden cane raised in his right fist.

"My name, sir, is Samuel May. I happen to own that hardware store." He gestured with the cane to the storefront across the street. "The one this flag hangs from. Let me tell you something, young man." He shook his cane. "I, too, am an American, and a native of this city." His reedy voice rose in pitch. "And I declare that my country is eternally disgraced by what happened here last month. That flag hangs there by my orders. Touch it at your peril." His red-rimmed eyes burned with fire, and his wrinkled mouth closed to a resolute firmness.

"Best go and do the bidding of your master," sneered another man from the group. He was short and squat with a red face and fleshy lips clamped around a smoldering cigar. "That buffoon, Pierce, is unfit to be president of this great country. He's a tyrant, a traitor, and a stupid fool, who is determined to destroy the union. He makes me want to retch." The man took the cigar from his mouth and flicked the ash toward Gunn's feet. The ash hit the street and rolled, disintegrating on the cobblestones in the light breeze that swept down the street. "And so does anyone who supports the man. You're a disgrace to the uniform."

"Very well. If you will excuse me, then, gentlemen."

"Not likely, son. There is no excuse. We don't take kindly to enemies of this city," said a third man.

"Gentlemen, I assure you, I am not your enemy," said Gunn. "Good day to you all."

52

As soon as Gunn arrived back at the ship, he asked to see Captain Whitcomb privately in his cabin. He presented eighty dollars in cash, his hands still trembling from his encounter in the city, as he placed it on the captain's green felt-covered table.

"Captain, I am deeply indebted to you for taking my part in Norfolk. Please allow me to repay you, at least as much as I am able, for causing such an inconvenience at your expense. Not to mention the dishonor I brought to you and to the ship, for which there is no remedy, I think, except to say again how deeply sorry I am. And I hope this will cover your loss."

Whitcomb thanked him for the gesture, but said it was unnecessary, dismissing it with a wave of the hand.

"Captain, please. I insist that you take it."

"I appreciate what you are trying to do, Mr. Gunn." The captain, seated at the table, puffed on his pipe, sending layers of smoke adrift above his head. He looked down at the cash, spread upon the table. "But I don't want your money." Leaning forward, he reached out and slid the bills across the tabletop to Gunn.

"But, sir—"

The captain removed his pipe and pointed the stem at Gunn. "The only thing I want from you, lieutenant, is to strive to become a man of true integrity. Do you know what that word means?"

"To be an honest man, yes, sir."

"No, sir. Wrong. It means that you are the same person on the inside that you appear to be on the outside. That you are whole. Undivided, integrated. Be what you represent yourself to be, or else it will eat at you from the inside out. Your friend Hawthorne wrote about that."

"Yes, sir. *The Scarlet Letter.*"

"That's right. Learned it at Bowdoin, I expect. Be a man of integrity or take that uniform off and go home. Will you strive to do that?"

"Yes, sir. I will. It's what I want, too."

"Very well. Good man." The captain nodded. "Now, go do it."

Gunn raised himself to his full height and stood at attention.

"You're dismissed."

Gunn stood stock still.

"Well?"

"Captain, I must confess—I regret to inform you that I have violated the regulations of the service by striking a superior officer."

Whitcomb placed his smoldering pipe on the table. "Which officer?"

"Mr. Richmond."

"And when did this act occur?"

"While we were in port at Norfolk, sir."

The captain sat back in his chair. "Say no more, Mr. Gunn." He sighed, shook his head, and rubbed his eyes. "We will take this up when Mr. Richmond returns to bear witness. In the meantime, you will remain confined aboard this ship."

"Aye, sir."

Miller's head appeared in the light of the companionway above.

"Captain, pardon me, sir, but there's a Mr. Charles Greene here to see you. From the Customs office."

"Ah, very well. Show him to the cabin. Oh, and send my respects to Mr. Prouty. Ask him to join us."

"Aye, aye, sir."

"Anything more, Mr. Gunn?"

"No, sir."

Whitcomb stood. "This is a very grave situation for you, lieutenant. For all of us. You've done well to come forward, though it does not bode well for you. I must say, it does not, sir."

"I understand, captain. I take full responsibility for my actions and will accept whatever punishment may come. By your leave, sir?"

Whitcomb nodded. "Very well."

Gunn climbed the ladder to the cockpit and walked forward. The evening sunlight shimmered on the water, backlighting the two figures coming toward him. The first was Prouty, to whom he offered a salute, which the first lieutenant returned. As they passed by, Greene nodded in greeting and shot him a furtive glance, which aroused Gunn's curiosity as to why the Naval Officer should be visiting so late in the day. He hesitated, watching the two men descend the ladder into the cabin, and then stood near the rail. The cabin skylight was open, through which drifted snippets of polite conversation as the captain greeted his guest.

"To what do I owe this pleasant surprise, Mr. Greene?"

"I'm not sure you'll find it so pleasant, captain. I certainly do not."

"Sounds serious. Let me order up some coffee, while we talk."

"No, sir. I shan't stay long." He lowered his voice, so Gunn could scarcely hear. "I've come to convey some information that I know will be of interest to you."

"By all means. Go on."

"A few days ago, one of your officers came into my office, inquiring about some damage to the brig *Parsifal*."

"Yes, of course. Lieutenant Gunn. I sent him."

"Well, sir, his inquiry piqued my interest. After he left my office, I did some investigating on my own. As it turns out, there are conflicting reports as to what happened to cause the damage to her rigging."

"Yes, I am aware of that."

"I thought you might be. What you might be unaware of is the fact that, for quite some time, there have been some irregularities in her manifests."

"What sorts of irregularities, Mr. Greene?"

"The sorts, captain, that are not easily explained away, although Bill Mitchell, the owner, has tried mightily to do so."

"Have you reported them to Mr. Andros, or Peaslee, the collector?" asked Prouty.

"Andros told me not to worry about it. I haven't spoken to Mr. Peaslee, yet."

"What do you think is going on, sir? Do you suspect smuggling of some kind?"

"Mr. Gunn, there you are." Gunn started as Moriarty called to him from the gangway. "Sir, can I get you to initial a change to the log from yesterday? I had to make a small correction."

"Yes, of course." At the sound of Gunn's reply and footsteps on the quarterdeck, Greene's voice died, as did those of the other two men in the cabin with him.

Whatever else was said could not have made the situation any worse. Gunn was sure of that. A few minutes later, Greene departed and went ashore unannounced, leaving the added trouble he had brought with him.

53

The following day, the *Morris* departed on a routine patrol. After waiting for a favorable tide, the ship weighed anchor mid-morning. At quarters, Mr. Prouty announced to the crew the captain's intention to sail north for several days, since they had not patrolled the coast of New Hampshire for quite some time. They sailed northeast on a broad reach with a favorable wind, making excellent speed over ground. As they rounded Cape Ann, Gunn relieved Miller and took the afternoon watch.

"Sam, where were you this morning after breakfast, before we set sail?" Gunn asked.

"Strangest thing. About an hour before we departed, the captain sent me up to the Custom House and along the wharf to spread the word that we were headed north to the Bigelow Bight. He said not to make it obvious, but to tell anyone who cared to listen that we would be away from homeport for at least three weeks. Why do you think he would do such a thing? He's never done that before. Always wants to keep our movements kind of quiet."

"That is odd."

"What do you make of it?"

Gunn shrugged. "Maybe he wanted to send a message. Give the false impression that the coast was clear for a while."

"I guess that makes sense. If that's the case, why didn't he send both of us? Two could have spread the word faster and farther."

"I'm sure he had his reasons."

Gunn was glad for the chance to see waters that bore no reminder of the last several weeks. The weather was fine, the sails were full, and the sparkling blue waves seemed to welcome their passage, parting without resistance to speed the cutter on her way.

Toward the end of his watch, the *Morris* approached the town of Newburyport. Known principally for its shipbuilding and fishing industries, the town's popularity with the cuttermen centered mainly on its rum distilleries, which converted molasses from the West Indies into "demon water." Whenever in this vicinity, the crew always hoped fervently, some even prayed, that the ship would make port and remain overnight.

The lookout spotted a vessel aground on Plum Island, near the mouth of the Merrimack River, in the approaches to the town. It was an inbound hermaphrodite brig, whose master had misjudged the swift, tricky currents around the tidal river, perhaps trying to dodge an ornery drift fisherman.

The *Morris* anchored in four fathoms of water and sent a longboat with Sam Miller in charge to assist the stranded vessel. After boarding the brig to assess the damage, Miller sent back word that it appeared the grounding had breached the hull, but not badly. The ship's bilge pumps could keep up with the leak.

Within two hours, the tide turned to flood. The cutter's two longboats together with the brig's dory pulled the ship off the shoal of sand and rock. The brig set sail and made a wide jibe to the north this time, allowing plenty of room for drift, as she headed back toward the port.

Although twilight was upon them by the end of the rescue, the captain decided not to make port, to the great disappointment of the crew. Moriarty seemed most downhearted of all.

"I was so lookin' forward to dropping the hook upriver, Mr.

Gunn. Can't you get the captain to change his mind?"

"I wouldn't even try, Moriarty. You'll live."

"Aye, but not so well, mind you. There's a young lass lives there with catheads that won't quit and follow-me-lads down to there." He cupped both hands over his chest, then pointed a thumb to his mid-back. "I sure could have used a little hogmagundy."

"I thought you have a wife, Moriarty. And she's expecting a baby soon."

"I do, and she is, though I ain't at all sure it's mine, sir." Moriarty stood at the rail and watched bleakly as the town and his hopes receded in the gathering darkness.

For the next several days, the ship ranged all throughout the Bigelow Bight, as far north as Cape Elizabeth, boarding the incoming merchant vessels, making sure her presence was well-established in those waters. The entire crew wished for something to happen to break the tedium of patrol.

On the fourth day after leaving Boston, the captain laid down a southerly course to take them to the outer reaches of Cape Cod. He chose a spot on the chart about eight miles offshore, due north of Highland Light. They spent the rest of that day and part of the next sailing to that spot.

When they arrived, the captain drew a trackline on the chart, extending about six miles in either direction, on a north-south axis. He set up a barrier patrol for the ship to sail, hoping to intercept the *Parsifal* on her next trip north.

Every four hours, with an occasional desultory glance passing between them, Gunn and Miller shared the pall of routine, punctuated by the change of watch. The odd thing was, the captain had them identify and log every vessel sighted, but they performed no boardings of any ship whatsoever, so they didn't even have that duty as a distraction. And so it went, each day hardly different than the one before, as they settled into a steady, monotonous routine.

Thoughts of Elizabeth constantly lingered, making regular visits to Gunn's conscious mind, usually during the moments of inertia, or at night before he drifted off to sleep. They rarely provided any solace.

Several days passed. The wind blew out of the southwest most of the time, varying only in speed. Facing the bow, Gunn could tell which direction the cutter sailed without looking at the compass by feeling the wind either on his right cheek, or behind his left ear, since the heading of the ship had become as consistent as the southwest wind.

Toward late afternoon on Wednesday, the nineteenth of July, the dark clouds of a cold front gathered in the northwestern sky, and Gunn could see the storm coming their way. At least it would break the monotony. He called the captain to tell him about the approaching wind and rain. Whitcomb ordered him to shorten sail.

By six o'clock, the first squall was upon them. The wind soon died, then veered to the northwest, gusting to about twenty-five or thirty knots, whistling in the rigging. Whitecaps topped the waves, and spindrift blew across the crests. They had to change direction, heading on a more oblique angle to the coast, trying to keep up the barrier. Gunn called for a second helmsman. The rain, falling in heavy sheets, started soon afterward but then eased into a steady drizzle.

Miller relieved him just before eight bells. Near twilight, the rain stopped, but the gusting wind continued. Gunn came back on deck to take some air before going to bed, using the dinghy on the leeward side to seek shelter from the wind. Head on, its briskness took his breath away.

The lookout sighted a sail on the horizon near Highland Light, claiming it to be a small brig, hull down. The vessel looked to be about six or eight miles away to the southwest, hugging the coastline.

He also reported a steamship to the west-southwest, apparently loitering, just north of Race Point. A rocket launched from the steamboat, arcing its red tail through the lowering sky, and fizzled out. Perhaps it was a distress signal, but Gunn had his doubts.

The captain ordered Miller to set a course to intercept the brig. Meanwhile, the steamship started making way south with a belch of black smoke from its single stack.

It was soon apparent the brig was outdistancing the cutter. A reefed mainsail and jib would not provide the power they needed. The captain ordered more sails on, starting with the new fore topsail. When that proved insufficient, he double-reefed the mainsail, raised the reefed foresail, and added the inner jib. At last, the cutter was gaining ground.

The *Morris* heeled over nearly to her port gunwale, slicing through the boiling water. The deck heaved under Gunn's feet. Spray crested over the bow, and the wind whisked it toward him, stinging his face.

Low clouds scudded across a darkened sky, hanging over the distant sails off the port bow.

Nelson noticed him standing there and walked to meet him with a steady, rolling gait, hardly affected by the ship's gyrations.

"Where are we bound in such a hurry? The boys want to know."

"The captain plans to speak that brig, I think."

Nelson eyed the burdened sails. "He must have heard that Jenny Lind herself is aboard, as much sail as he's carryin'."

Mr. Prouty came up on deck to take in the chase, securing himself at the rail on the weather side opposite Gunn. After a quarter hour, as twilight began to fall, the distance between the two ships began to close, and it appeared that the brig and the steamship had slowed as they came together within hailing distance of each other. Gray smoke streamed from the stack of the steamship, which looked like a small tug.

The brig shortened sail, preparing to heave to. The steamship turned to put her bow into the waves and slowed to a stop. Then her lights disappeared. The brig also ran a darkened ship.

The captain dipped under the main boom, and scuttled over to the leeward side, where he braced against the rail to get a better view, peering intently through his binoculars. Miller was right there, at his side.

"Well, frisk me a footy!" Whitcomb exclaimed. "Those two are getting ready to meet." He turned to Miller. "Get somebody up in the rigging with these binoculars. I want both ships identified."

Miller, aghast that the captain would entrust his treasured binoculars to a crew member, did not respond right away.

"*Now!*" shouted Whitcomb.

Nelson grabbed the nearest seaman by the collar—Yarrow, it so happened—and shoved him toward the foremast shrouds. Gunn ran back to the mainmast and bounded up the steps to the quarterdeck. He took the glasses from the captain, and scrambled forward to the foremast shrouds, placing the strap over the seaman's neck.

"Don't lose these, Yarrow. If you do, you'd best go over the side after them," he said. "Get up there and see if you can get the names of those two ships. Lively, now."

Yarrow scampered up the rigging like a cat into a favorite tree. The captain stood by the mainmast, peering into the foretop.

"What do you see?" asked Whitcomb, his booming voice both impatient and anxious.

"Two ships meeting, captain."

"I *know* that." Exasperation elongated the vowels.

"The steamship ... it looks like ... well, it looks like the tug *John Taylor*, sir, the one that towed us out last time."

"And the other?"

"P-A-R-S-I-F-A ... L," the seaman spelled out. "Boston, I think."

"Stunner," muttered Gunn.

"Good. Come on down."

"Captain?"

"Aye, what is it?"

"They are splitting up."

"By the great horn spoon. She's seen us." He dived back under the main boom to the weather side. "Light our navigation lamps, Mr.

Miller. And hoist the holiday ensign, so there's no mistaking us."

Sure enough, the two ships had separated, both still darkened. The steamship had turned north, and the brig tacked east, heading out to sea.

"Stay on the brig," shouted Whitcomb.

Miller ordered the helmsmen to a new heading to intercept.

"It's getting harder to see her, captain." There was enough light to see a vague outline of the brig in the distance, but they were much nearer now, and the gap was closing fast.

"She's going to make a run for it." Whitcomb spoke to the wind. "Trying to get outside three miles, I expect. A lot of good that'll do her. She can run, but she cannot hide. We'll chase her to hell and back."

54

R eady about. All hands to sail stations," Miller yelled at the top of his lungs. "Stand by your sheets and braces."

The crew rushed to their stations. Gunn took his position as captain of the foremast, Prouty at the mainmast. The brig cut across the bow of the *Morris* on the opposite tack, heading farther out to sea, straining under as much canvas as possible. A few minutes later, the cutter crossed the *Parsifal's* wake, passing her stern, about two hundred yards off.

"Helm's a-lee." The speaking trumpet hardened Miller's voice, giving it a metallic edge.

The cutter began a wide swing to the east, giving time for the fore topsail to be braced around. As soon as the wind caught the sail, and she came through on the opposite tack, the captain told Miller to fall in line with the brig, off her port quarter. By then, the *Parsifal* led them by a quarter mile, but even with that lead, and close reaching with all sail set, she was no match in speed for a cutter. Before long, the *Morris* had pulled within a ship's length of the slower brig. In another ten minutes of chase, the two ships were side by side.

"We've got her, now," said Whitcomb, the glee shining on his face. "We've got the weather gage on her. We've blanketed her wind."

He pointed the speaking trumpet at the other ship.

"Ahoy the *Parsifal*." No answer from the brig. "Ahoy the *Parsifal*. This is the Revenue Cutter *Morris*. Heave to and stand by to be boarded!"

No answer but the wind in the rigging and the ships' hulls broaching the waves. Without warning, the brig took a sharp turn into the wind toward the *Morris,* rapidly closing the divide between them.

"He's mad." Whitcomb said. He turned on Miller. "Put up the helm. *Now.*" He dashed toward the ship's wheel. "Put up your helm, I said."

Both helmsmen whipped the wheel to starboard, turning away from the wind. The *Morris* slowed immediately, but the two ships narrowly missed colliding. The brig's stern passed within a few yards of the cutter's bowsprit, and the *Parsifal* continued turning into the wind.

"Ease your sheets! Steady on a beam reach, Mr. Miller!" ordered the captain.

"Do you want to wear ship, captain?" Miller asked, wide-eyed.

"No, it'll take too long, and we'll lose too much ground. I want to come about, as soon as we're able."

When he saw what was happening, Gunn ordered his foremast crew to tend the foresail sheets and overhaul the topsail tacks, sheets, and braces. Nelson handled the three headsails with a small crew up forward. Prouty had it easier on the mainmast, with only the mainsail to worry about.

The cutter's head continued to fall off the wind, until she settled on a beam reach. Meanwhile, the *Parsifal* had come about and was heading away on the starboard tack, back toward land.

"All right, Mr. Miller. Now."

Miller gave the orders to start bringing the cutter's head up into the wind until she was close-hauled on the port tack.

"Ready about."

The crew prepared to tack through the wind.

"Helm's a-lee."

The cutter's head came through the wind and steadied on the starboard tack, close-hauled. The crew trimmed the sails and the *Morris* again leaped into action, in hot pursuit of the runaway brig. But they'd lost considerable distance to the *Parsifal*, now a good three-quarters of a mile ahead.

"Clear for action."

Whitcomb's command swept a wave of incredulity over Gunn. *Did he really say——?*

"Clear for action, I said. Bring the starboard guns to bear."

Gunn searched the faces around him for Connelly, who appeared at his elbow with a look of grim satisfaction on his grizzled face.

"You heard the man," said Gunn.

The gun crews hastened to throw open the gunports, unlashed the three starboard cannons, and put them into battery. By the time they had finished readying the guns, the cutter had already gained three ship-lengths on the brig. Gunn figured it would take another twenty minutes to catch her.

"To arms. Arm the boarding party," ordered the captain.

Nelson immediately piped the order.

Whitcomb whipped around to face Gunn. "Mr. Gunn, come here, if you please."

He bounded up the steps to the quarterdeck. "Aye, aye, captain."

"Since Miller is on watch, I'm going to give you a chance to redeem yourself. Get your boarding party together. Make no mistake, lieutenant. This is a test. It's your uncle's ship. But remember, you wear the cloth of your Uncle Sam." He punched a forefinger into Gunn's chest. "Do not foul your gear on this one, mister. And watch yourself. Be careful, I mean. This one's a tricky devil. Take the Bos'n with you."

Gunn assembled a boarding party of six and made sure they were well armed and equipped. He sent Dwyer below to get his sword from his stateroom. The seaman retrieved it without delay and helped him fasten the belt. Connelly thrust a holstered Colt into his hands, which he strapped around his waist on the right hip. He looked up to see the cutter crossing the stern of the *Parsifal*, about a hundred yards away.

"I want you to sail up alongside, this time on her lee, Mr. Miller. Keep her quarter on our beam. And watch for any sudden moves," called the captain.

It took another ten minutes to get into position.

"Fire a warning shot over her stern," ordered Whitcomb.

Connelly looked at Gunn for affirmation, and he nodded vigorously. The gunner aimed his weapon, the forward-most gun on the starboard side, and touched the punk to the fuse. A second later a brilliant flash lit the main deck, followed instantly by the thunderous roar of the number one gun, and a split-second later by a sizable splash on the far side of the brig's stern.

"That's got her attention, then," said Nelson. The brig showed no sign of compliance.

"We're not diddling around, here. Mr. Gunn, on my command, put one in her mainsail." The captain's powerful voice left no room for doubt.

Gunn approached Connelly. "Take care, now, Connelly. We're not aiming to kill anybody."

Connelly would not meet his eye. He staggered. Gunn noticed the sweet smell of rum wafting toward him.

"Have you been drinking, Connelly?"

"Maybe a dribble, sir," the gunner growled.

"Half seas over, I'd say. Where'd you get the rum? Never mind, no time for it. Let somebody else do this. Move aside." One of the gun crew, Hayman Harrington stood next to him. "Harrington, you're a qualified gunner. Stand by to fire the number five gun. Hurry, man."

"Aye, aye, sir." Harrington knelt next to the gun and sighted it.

The cutter steadied in position abreast of the brig's stern, and the captain gave the command.

"Fire!"

Harrington timed the roll of the ship at the crest of a wave and touched the glowing punk to what he assumed was the fuse, but in the dark, he missed. In the instant it took to relocate the fuse, the ship had rolled back into a deep trough. The gun discharged, and the shot glanced off the top of a wave with a splash, and caromed into the underside of the brig's hull, blasting a gaping hole below the waterline.

"Avast," yelled the captain. "Hold your fire, there. What the living blazes are you doing, Mr. Gunn? I said the mainsail, man. The *mainsail*." He threw his pipe down, and it smashed into bits, scattering across the deck.

Whitcomb watched for the brig to react. The *Parsifal* sailed on for another ten minutes. Then, slowly, she began to come up into the wind, luffing her foresails. She brailed in her spanker, and began backing her mainsail, heaving to as quickly as possible. The cutter matched her speed.

A voice whisked across the water. "Captain of the cutter."

"Aye. Captain John Whitcomb, here."

"Captain Ross Webber, master of the *Parsifal*. Send your boarding party, sir. We are in need of your assistance."

The boat crew lowered the longboat on the port side, in the lee of the cutter, and the boarding party climbed in and cast off the painter. In a few minutes, the boat was alongside the brig, between the two ships, as they ghosted along together. Gunn was the first to climb warily aboard.

The brig's master stood near the gangway. Gunn knew who he was, since they had met once before aboard another of his uncle's ships, but Webber gave no sign of recognition. In his mid-thirties, unsmiling, square-jawed with long side-whiskers, Webber would have been tall, had his short legs matched his torso. He wore a black sack coat and matching trousers, and a leather-billed cloth cap, touched jauntily to the right side of his head.

"You bastards put a hole in my ship. No cause for that."

"You tried to run, captain. What cause had you for that?"

"Now, why would I be running?"

"I think that was my question, sir."

"All due respect, lieutenant, I think the most important issue at hand is the hole in my ship. Water's filling my hold quicker than a pitcher fills a shot glass, and I cannot shore the damage."

"Why is that?"

"She's stacked to the gills with cotton, rice, and tobacco. We are trying to move cargo around, but it's making things very unstable down below."

"We'll do what we can to give you a hand. Nelson here will help your men rig a patch."

"Need a bit of canvas and some stuffing for the hole, sir," said Nelson.

The first mate produced an old, torn sail to use as a patch on the outer hull. Gunn noted that the brig's current spanker appeared whiter and cleaner than the rest of the sails, as though newly replaced. The boarding party worked frantically in the longboat with a few of the brig's crew to cover the hole, a task made even more difficult in the roiling waves and brisk wind. They nailed canvas slathered with grease from the outside as best they could, but the hole was underwater most of the time. Even worse, the shot had split a seam between planks. Water was pouring in along the length of the seam. The damage needed to be shored up from inside the hull.

Despite their best efforts, the flood of seawater already had saturated a good portion of the cargo below, making the ship more unstable by the minute. The pumps were useless, since the cargo soaked up most of the water. The added weight of the sodden bales of tobacco and cotton caused the ship to ride noticeably lower in the water, listing and lolling drunkenly in the waves. The crew tried to jettison the ruined cargo but could not keep pace. Meanwhile, the wind rose, and the weather continued to worsen.

"I'm afraid the best thing to do now is run her aground, and try salvaging what we can," urged Webber, after a half-hour had passed, and the ship had taken on a dangerous list.

"Well, if you think that is best, captain. First, I suggest we remove all but the most essential crew and any passengers and put them aboard the *Morris*."

"Agreed."

"I will stay and help you sail the ship."

When Nelson learned that Gunn would be staying aboard, he volunteered to stay, too.

"I never done that a-purpose, sailed a ship aground," he said with a broad grin. "Somethin' to tell the grandkids about."

"You don't even have children, Nelson."

"None that we know of. Well, sir, they'll miss out on a grand story then, won't they?"

55

Twenty of the *Parsifal's* crew climbed over the side into the waiting longboats, which ferried them to the cutter, along with word to Whitcomb about the plan to run the ship aground. He agreed but shouted back through the voice trumpet that Gunn should be sure to check for anyone else who might be aboard.

Gunn turned to the ship's master. "Cap'n Webber, your ship could very well go down before we get ashore. Is there anyone else aboard not needed to sail this ship?"

Webber frowned and shook his head.

"You won't mind if we check, then. Just to be sure. We don't have much time."

Webber glanced toward the darkened shore. In the distance, Highland Light blinked its warning. He called for a lantern and motioned for Gunn to come with him. Gunn told Nelson to follow.

They opened a hatch near the stern and jumped down into the lazarette, where much of the spare gear was stowed. The removal of a coil of rope and a length of chain uncovered a trapdoor, which had been cut into the floor. Webber opened the trapdoor, which led to a tiny void beneath. He thrust the lantern into the hole. A man and a woman, both black, peered up from the darkness, eyes wide with dread. They were doubled over, crammed into the hidden space with no room to move about. Between them, they sheltered a toddler, whimpering in his mother's arms. Water had begun to seep into the compartment, sloshing on the sole beneath them.

Gunn shot Webber a glance. "Were you going to let them die in here, skipper?"

"Don't be an idiot. I was trying to help them live." Webber lifted the lantern and placed it on the deck beside them.

Gunn reached down to take the child from his mother's outstretched arms. The others helped the parents to extricate themselves from the cramped void, struggling to stand upright. The woman reclaimed her child. Squatting, she held him tightly in her lap. Nelson and Gunn climbed to the main deck and reached back down into the lazarette to help the woman climb out.

"Please, sir. Don't send us back." The man peered up at them, pointing to his right foot. "They already done took one foot, and they'll sure enough take the other." Gunn winced as he noticed the crudely fashioned, blunt toed shoe.

"Have mercy, sir." The woman refused to take Gunn's hand. She stood and shifted the child to her hip, pleading with her free hand. "Please. My baby got to be free."

Webber looked up at Gunn. "We could put them in our dinghy and they could row ashore, once we get closer to the beach, Mr. Gunn. Nobody would be the wiser."

Taken aback, Gunn glanced at Nelson, poised next to him with one arm still outstretched. Nelson lowered his hand. Nobody spoke.

Webber pressed him. "Lieutenant, these people just want the chance to be free. They deserve that, as far as they've come."

Nelson glanced over his shoulder in the direction of the *Morris* and then turned back to face Gunn. "Lieutenant, we got a job to do." He held out his hand again to the woman.

"Hang on, Bos'n." Gunn studied the frightened face of the frail black man. "What is your name?"

"My name, Benjamin. This here, Nancy. And Jonah, our boy."

Gunn repeated the boy's name with a grim smile. "Jonah."

Nelson's voice was urgent. "Mr. Gunn—"

"I know, Nelson." Gunn waved him off, while eyeing Webber. "They would need help rowing."

"I'll send one of my men to help row the boat," Webber said. "I'll even go with them. Come now, Gunn. You know it's the right thing to do."

Nelson shook his head. "Mr. Gunn, this ain't right."

"Nelson, nothing, *nothing* about this is right. Is your dinghy in good condition, Webber?"

"Good enough."

"Is it seaworthy, man?" he bellowed.

Webber nodded. "Sure."

"Mr. Gunn, may I speak with you a moment, sir?" Nelson stood up. "Alone."

Gunn stood upright on the main deck. The wind shoved him sideways. He steadied himself against it.

Nelson shouted over the wind into his ear. "Sir, you know the captain won't be likin' this."

"The captain isn't here. I can't send these people back, Nelson."

"Sir, the law says they have to go back."

"I know what the law says, Boats, better than you do. I also know what my conscience tells me to do. Now, shut up and help me. Or don't." He turned and shouted down through the hatch. "Benjamin, Nancy, stay down there where it's safe, for now. Cap'n Webber, let's get this tub moving."

Webber climbed out of the lazarette, shouting orders to the remainder of his crew to man the halyards.

"Lieutenant, all due respect, I can't shut up," said Nelson. "This is going down all wrong. Besides, chances are, these poor people won't never get to shore alive. That surf ain't no place for a dinghy and folks who don't know what they're about. Our best oarsmen would have a helluva time in those breakers. They'll most likely die tryin'.

All of them. You want that on your conscience, sir?"

The rain started again, lightly at first, then turned into a downpour.

Nelson spoke again. "Thing is, if you truly care about them, the safest place right now for these people is on the *Morris*. The longer we wait, the harder it's goin' to be. Need to sheet home, sir."

Rainwater poured from the brim of Gunn's cap. "I don't know what you mean by that, Nelson."

"Sure you do, lieutenant."

Gunn leaned over the hatch, peering into the darkness. "Benjamin. Nancy. Come on up out of there," he shouted.

Nelson and Gunn helped them climb out. Webber hastened over to where Gunn stood.

"What are you doing, Gunn?" Webber yelled. "I thought we agreed."

"Changed my mind, Cap'n Webber. We need to send them over to the cutter."

"No sir. Please. No, sir," pleaded Benjamin.

"I'm sorry, Benjamin. We must."

Gunn walked to the rail and signaled for the longboat crew to get ready for more passengers. He turned back to urge the couple into the longboat, but before he could open his mouth, Benjamin had already snatched the child from Nancy's arms. Gunn reached toward him, but Benjamin lunged through the open gangway, over the side and into the stormy sea, with the boy clutched in his arms. He surfaced, flailing to keep Jonah's head above the churning waves.

Nancy screamed. "Benjamin, no. My baby! Jonah. No, no, no, *no*." She bolted after them. Nelson grabbed her arm, but she kicked him, wrenched free and leaped over the side into the water, shrieking until her gaping mouth sank beneath the waves. Her skirts billowed around her, as she bobbed up, gasping for air. Then, she went under again, dragged down by the weight of her clothes.

Gunn dropped his sword belt and dove in headfirst after them. The cold forced the breath from his lungs as he hit the water. In an instant, he was deep below the surface, and all went strangely quiet, except for the muffled thrashing above him. He opened his eyes and searched the blackened depths below, groping for Nancy's skirts, but dark water was the only thing within his grasp. He touched something, but it was only Benjamin's stunted shoe. He felt a desperate urge to breathe.

The weight of his sidearm dragged him deeper into the dark water. He slipped out of his gun belt and pumped his arms and legs upward, his lungs on the verge of bursting. His head breached the surface. A wave slapped his face. The wind howled in his ears. Benjamin struggled nearby, one arm pawing the water, the other grasping Jonah.

"Papa." The boy wailed, whenever their heads were above water.

Gunn reached out to them. Benjamin thrust the boy toward him and lunged for his neck, pulling them all underwater. Gunn held the boy against his body and kicked for the surface. Someone grabbed the back of his collar, pulling from above. His head thudded against the side of the longboat, as he reached the surface, gulping air. He lifted an arm, and someone grabbed his wrist, pulling until his arm felt like it would be wrenched out of its socket. He yelped in pain.

"Don't worry, we've got you, Mr. Gunn." He looked up into Yarrow's worried face.

The crew of the longboat pulled him and the boy to safety. He helped grapple the father, pulling him over the gunwale until he landed like a large fish, gasping for air in the bottom of the boat. The boy fell on top of him, clinging to his father and crying for his mother.

Gunn raised himself to sit on a thwart. Stunned, but unhurt except for his shoulder, he turned to the coxswain.

"Get me back to the *Parsifal*."

"But, sir—"

"You heard me."

Soon, the longboat was alongside, and Gunn climbed back aboard the doomed ship. He picked up his discarded sword from the deck and handed it to Nelson.

"Nelson."

"Aye, sir."

"Go with them." He pressed his sword into Nelson's hands. "Get them over to the *Morris*," he ordered.

"Sir, I—"

"Sheet home, Bos'n. Tell the captain what happened. I'm all right. See to it that they are."

He held his injured shoulder, looking down at the half-drowned man, who lay sobbing in the bottom of the longboat, holding his son close and stroking his head.

Gunn called to him. "I'm sorry, Benjamin." His apology went unheeded.

"You want I should tell the old man everything, sir?" asked Nelson.

Gunn nodded once. "Everything."

***

The remaining crew of six set the *Parsifal's* sails as best they could. Gunn went aloft with the other sailors to handle canvas. His shoulder ached. He was soaked, chilled, and near exhaustion. Working aloft was always the hardest labor on a ship. It was even harder in his condition. By the time they were within a quarter mile of land, it was near midnight, and he was spent, as were the others.

The *Morris* followed, sailing as close to the shoals as the captain dared. At last, however, the brig was on her own to make landfall. The rain had stopped, but the wind still whipped around them. The closer in they stood, the higher the waves mounted.

Webber sent the helmsman forward with instructions to cut the sheets with an axe when the time came. He and Gunn took the sluggish wheel themselves, as they steered for the breakers. Gunn guided them in, using the lighthouse as a mark. It shone brightly in the darkness, thanks to Roy Fisker.

He shouted into the wind. "Your boss is not going to like this one bit."

Webber shook his head. "Do you know him?"

"He's my uncle."

Sudden realization flooded Webber's face. "He won't be happy."

"Does he know about ... you know?"

"What do you think?"

He knew the answer. He understood many things in that moment. A fresh, bitter sense of disappointment, disillusionment, and betrayal flooded through him—the same sense that he'd felt since childhood whenever he thought about his father, but deeper this time, broader. Everything was true. Nothing was true.

He looked up, peering through the darkness toward the lighthouse, but he couldn't find it.

The keel hit bottom, hard. The brig lurched to a standstill, thrusting sideways. Both masts sheared off and crashed overboard, like the felling of two great trees, taking everything with them. Rigging whipped through the air. Webber cried out as a broken spar fell on top of him, pinning him to the deck. The ship's wheel spun wildly to its stops, wrenching free of Gunn's hands and tossing him aside.

He reached out to grab for a handhold, but his feet slipped out from under him. He slammed against the rail, doubling over like an old coat thrown against the back of a chair. He spun head over heels, lofted in mid-air. Then, he hit the chilled waters with a force that again knocked the wind from his lungs as he plunged into the waves.

When he surfaced, he couldn't take a full breath, the air was so heavy with sea spray. He breast-stroked with the breaking waves toward what he thought was the shoreline, but his right leg would not respond, no matter how hard he tried. A ponderous breaker caught both legs and tumbled him forward, slamming his body against the solid bottom. Sand and water filled his open mouth. He tried to call out for help but made no sound.

He had the fleeting thought that this was a fitting end. It was all for the best. He would join his brother at last. A feeling of peace came over him.

His body tumbled in the surf. Then darkness.

56

D aylight. A stark white room. High ceilings. An anguished voice cried out. It echoed, diminished, but sounding much like his own.

Darkness fell.

***

In the air, a metallic, sulfurous odor dissolved into the smell of the sea. After a time, no telling how long, his eyes opened again, and he tried to lift his head. A man in uniform stood at the foot of his bed, marking a chart.

The man, who said his name was James, welcomed him back to the land of the living and told him that for the past three days he had been under the care of the Marine Hospital in Charlestown. He was a very lucky man. Many men would not have survived his injuries. If the broken femur that pierced his right thigh had severed the nearby artery, he'd be lying in the morgue right now instead of this hospital bed.

"You'll want to stay as still as possible, since you've also broken three ribs and dislocated your right shoulder, not to mention suffering a rather nasty concussion." The orderly raised his eyebrows. "Very lucky. I'll let the doctor know that you are awake, now. It will probably be a while before he can get to you, though."

His throat felt like someone had mopped it with a dry swab. "Water."

The orderly poured water into a tin cup, helped him lift his head, and allowed him to take a sparing sip. Then, he disappeared.

He tried to focus. The plastered ceiling above his head was cracked in the shape of an elongated uppercase letter "I".

A wave of nausea. He closed his eyes again.

***

Someone called his name. A man stood above him, his gray beard topped by a long nose, bearing spectacles that magnified tired eyes, all of which came slowly into focus.

"Are we awake? How do we feel, Mr. Gunn?"

Better off dead. With a shallow breath, he uttered, "Lucky, I guess."

"That you are, lieutenant." The beard smiled. "I'm Doctor Blake. Glad to see you're still with us. You will be here for a good while, I expect."

"Pain."

"I'm not surprised. But there is not much more I can do about that, I'm afraid. Try not to talk just yet. And you will need to lie as still as you possibly can. I don't want to have to take that leg off. As it is, most surgeons already would have done, but the break was a clean one. No splintering that I could see. I'm still worried about infection, but we'll do our best. The next few days will tell."

Gunn exhaled slowly through his nose. It was all the response he could muster. He closed his eyes again and tried to ignore the pain, but it was not possible.

***

When his mother first saw him the day after he awoke in the hospital, she wept as she kissed and hugged him gently, careful of his wounds.

"God has spared my firstborn, after all. I could not have borne it to lose both sons to the sea." She uttered words through her tears, most likely shed as much for him as for his dead brother.

319

***

The days passed, and after a few the doctor seemed pleased with the rate of healing.

"You're young and strong. You'll heal nicely, I expect."

"What about my leg, Doctor Blake?"

"You mean will you keep it? Certainly. You'll even get to use it, eventually. But I must warn you that you'll likely walk with a limp for some time to come, if not for good."

"I see."

"Small price to pay, though, considering."

"How much longer will I be here?"

"At least four to six more weeks. But then, you'll be facing another month or so of recuperation after that, I'm afraid."

Time seemed to crawl. But he had nothing with which to keep it. When his watch was returned to him, along with other items that had been salvaged from his pockets, it had quit working altogether. The crystal clouded over, and salt encrusted the dented silver case.

His mother and Marguerite visited regularly from the day after he was hospitalized. They were staying in Boston at the Mitchells' townhouse on Tremont Street. On each visit, they brought baskets of fruit and vegetables that weren't available in the hospital. They read letters from well-wishers, friends and family, who said they were praying for him. Marguerite read her latest short stories to him, including the one that had recently been published in a new magazine. When he was up to it, they played at cards or chess and discussed the newest gossip around town.

After two weeks, he was well enough physically and mentally to sit up in bed as Marguerite read the various newspaper articles of the events that had put him there. Every paper in town had printed accounts of the wreck of the *Parsifal.*

Captain Webber had died instantly of a severe head wound, along with a member of his crew, who drowned. Their bodies were recovered where the sea had spewed them onto the beach. The three other sailors survived.

Much of the cargo was ruined or lost, among which inspectors found twenty thousand Cuban cigars in crates labeled as spices. Among Webber's personal possessions, the authorities found two velvet bags containing about three thousand dollars' worth of precision Swiss watch movements, presumably being smuggled ashore. So much for lucky watches.

Of course, the newspapers lamented Nancy's death. The fact that she had been fleeing to freedom from slavery steeped the story in poignancy, which was the main thrust of most of the stories. That a man of the Cutter Service had tried to save her life was enough to earn high praise, almost sufficient to wipe the slate clean of the unfortunate fact that they also had tried to prevent her escape from bondage. They also celebrated the rescue of Benjamin and his son, attributing it to the heroic bravery of Third Lieutenant Andrew Gunn.

Marguerite had to scan that account again after reading it aloud. "Well, well," she said, eyebrows arched. "Big brother to the rescue. Impressive."

"I was merely doing my duty," said Gunn.

She smiled. "There's that word again. Unless I'm mistaken, nobody else jumped into the water to save those people that night. Context is everything, isn't it?"

The story went on to depict how a longboat crew from the *Morris* had rowed through the treacherous surf to save Gunn himself. They found him on the beach unconscious and bleeding, bandaged his leg wound, and rowed him to the safety of the cutter—no easy feat in those conditions.

According to other reports, William Mitchell had salvaged what was left of the brig, including some of the gear and the portion of the legal cargo that had not been spoiled. Customs officers seized the illegal cigars, what remained of them. Mitchell disavowed any prior knowledge of Webber's participation in the Underground

Railroad or any other smuggling venture whatsoever, including cigars or watches. His four other captains vouched for him. A salvage crew pulled the damaged hull off the beach, patched it, and towed it back to Boston when the weather finally permitted.

Captain Martin S. Dobbins of the *John Taylor* claimed that his boilers had failed that day, and his tug had been in distress. The captain of the *Parsifal* had merely offered assistance as any decent, responsible, and prudent mariner would do. According to the papers, when asked what the tug had been doing out that far to sea in the first place, he had said, "It's a free country, ain't it?" The press and the public had seemed satisfied with that answer.

***

When Gunn was well enough to receive them, Aunt May and Uncle William paid a visit. They both conveyed how deeply they regretted what had taken place. They pledged to help in whatever way possible to get him back on his feet again. Mitchell considered the damage to the *Parsifal* as negligible compared to the injury sustained by his only remaining nephew. Of course, insurance would cover most of the loss. He also declined to hold Captain Whitcomb responsible for sinking his ship, agreeing with the preliminary court of inquiry convened by the Secretary of Treasury that Whitcomb had acted within his authorities under the law.

"One thing I don't regret in all of this fiasco, though," Mitchell said, pounding his palm on the foot of Gunn's bed. "In fact, I'm so very glad that the slave—what's-his-name, Daniel—and his boy were released into the care of a minister, name of Grimes, since nobody made any claims against them. He saw to it that they made it to Canada. Good thing. Don't need any more trouble in this city. Too bad, though, about the woman."

"His name was Benjamin, Uncle William, not Daniel. Her name was Nancy."

"Yes. Too bad. Risky business. But the newspapers said you tried your best to save her. They sang your praises, Andrew, for saving the man and the boy."

"We're very proud of you, Andrew," said Aunt May.

He closed his eyes to block the image of the contorted face of the woman he could not save, her mouth gaping in a silent scream, which still haunted his thoughts.

"Are you in much pain, my dear?" she asked.

He nodded. "Now and then."

He received a letter from Elizabeth, still at school, saying she'd visit as soon as she could get away. She also confided her heartbreak over his injuries, and her utter joy that he had survived. The words were tender but made no mention of a change of heart. Gunn tried to write back, but he had to dictate his letter, unable with his arm in a sling to write it himself. Consequently, the words seemed distant, remote, even to him.

A week later, she came on a Sunday, along with her father and mother. They stayed only as long as Christian charity warranted. Reverend Faulkner said that he hoped to see him in church again soon. As they departed, Mrs. Faulkner lingered. Her kind eyes, resting on his face, conveyed that familiar far-off disappointment.

"We're so proud of you for saving that man and his son from drowning. And thank God, they are now living in freedom. Be well, Andrew. Come see us when you are able, won't you?" she said quietly. Then, she followed her husband down the row of beds toward the exit. Elizabeth remained at his bedside.

"Coming Elizabeth?" her father called.

"In a moment, Father." She waited until they were out of earshot. "I'm so glad you're going to be all right, Andrew."

"So the doctor says. I should be fine, although it might be a little difficult getting around at first. It will certainly be good to get out of this bed in another week, or so. They want me to start practicing with those." He pointed with an elbow to the crutches leaning against the wall. "But my ribs are still pretty sore."

"I … well, I just wanted to say that I'm sorry that we parted so badly last time."

"I am, too." He waited for her to say more, but she didn't. "Have you thought about what I asked you?"

"Every day."

"And?"

"Things are ... different, Andrew."

"Yes, so you've said."

"I have decided I want to finish school before I do anything else. I've always wanted to be a teacher. There's nothing I'd rather do. I just love children, you know, and I want to help them learn."

He hesitated. "Don't you want your own? Wouldn't you like to start a family?"

"Someday. Yes, perhaps. Not yet. I need more time."

He nodded and swallowed hard. "As I said, take whatever time you need."

"I'll be home in early September for a little while. Come and see us when you can."

"I will."

"We might even have a little surprise for you by then."

"Oh? What would that be?"

"Well, now, it wouldn't be much of a surprise if I told you, would it? Be well. I will keep you in my prayers." She touched his hand, then turned to leave.

"Elizabeth?"

"Yes?"

"Nothing. I'll see you in September."

As she walked on, he waited for her to toss the winsome, reassuring smile that he had not seen since the night before the ship's transit south. She swept around the corner without glancing back.

57

S am Miller came to the hospital whenever possible, which was not often, since he was the only junior officer remaining aboard the *Morris*. Gunn looked forward to his visits. It was always a comfort to see his good friend and shipmate. Three weeks into his stay, Miller dropped in to spend an afternoon with him. Gunn was eager to hear the latest scuttlebutt.

"Nelson sent word that he's sorry not to come see you, but he hates hospitals as much as he hates sawbones and would never step foot in one without first being carried in on a stretcher."

"Let's hope it never comes to that. Did he say anything else?"

"'Not to worry, Mr. Gunn,' he says." Miller mimicked Nelson's faded brogue. "'I'll be whittlin' ye a fine peg-leg carved like a staff o' life, with a nob ta hobble on. We'll make a merry timber-toe out of ye yet.'" He laughed and crossed his heart. "Word for word."

"It's just as well he didn't come," said Gunn. "It still hurts too much to laugh."

"You know, my friend, it was Nelson who took the longboat in to save you. And Yarrow refused to return until they found you."

"I had no idea. Thanks for telling me, Sam."

"Say, Andrew. Can I ask you something?"

"Anything."

"Word is that you took a swing at Mr. Richmond."

"How did that get out?"

"I dunno. Is it true? Did you hit him?"

"I did. I'm not pleased with myself, mind you."

"No. I should say not. Next time, sell tickets."

***

The days dragged on and so did the tedium of recovery. Visitors were always welcome to break up the monotony. Mr. Prouty, who had been forced to take on extra duties in the absence of two lieutenants, nevertheless stopped in several times to check on him. A week after Miller's latest visit, Prouty stopped by again, this time to give him some hard news.

"I'm sorry to be the bearer of bad tidings, Andrew, but I'm afraid we've had to suspend your pay while you remain on medical leave. Regulations require it."

Gunn drew as deep a breath as he could with painful ribs. "That's all right, sir. Truth be told, I have been thinking about resigning my commission, anyway."

Prouty gaped at him. "That's a tack I wasn't expecting. Resign? Whatever for?"

Gunn searched his face for a hint of anything unsaid. "Let's just say, I'm considering my prospects, sir. To be honest, they don't look very favorable for my future career. The service and I seem to be at odds, lately. Maybe it's time for me to move on."

With a knowing squint, Prouty waited a moment before speaking. "The captain told me what happened between you and Mr. Richmond. It's a serious matter, to be sure, but I doubt it's the end of your career. Is that what's troubling you?"

"In part, yes, sir. But it's more than that. I can't—I am against the enforcement of any law that upholds slavery."

"That's just one of many laws that we are called to enforce. And through service, you were able to save the lives of two people, Andrew. That counts for something, doesn't it? The newspapers are calling you a hero, man."

Gunn looked away. "I am no hero, sir. In fact, I hold myself responsible for the woman who died trying to seek freedom for her son."

Prouty shook his head and frowned. "You're being too hard on yourself and your country, Mr. Gunn. Look here, don't do anything rash. I think your prospects are very fine. You've made some mistakes, to be sure. But what young officer hasn't? If you have one fault, it is that you keep your own counsel too much. You can't be so self-reliant that you have no use for others, Andrew. That could lead to serious error. No man's an island, you know."

"I'm coming to realize that, sir."

"Good. What else do you have in mind to do, may I ask?"

Gunn returned his gaze. "I haven't decided, sir."

Prouty's frown disappeared. "Think it over, Andrew. From my perspective, I've never known a better navigator, and your seamanship is superb. That brig might have gone down without you, and those poor people with it. I'm fairly sure of that. Besides, I have some other news that might interest you."

"What's that, sir?"

"Mr. Richmond has written to inform us that he intends to resign his commission. He plans to stay in Tennessee for good, due to the recent death of his father. As the eldest son, he has inherited the bulk of his family's farm. They also need an additional hand to fill the void left by their father's death. Anyway, he will not be returning to the ship."

"I'm sorry to hear of his loss. When did that happen?"

"We received his letter last week."

"Did he say anything else? Anything more about the ... circumstances of his decision?"

"Yes, as a matter of fact, he did. He reported the fight between you."

Gunn swallowed. "And?"

"According to his letter, he admits provoking the altercation. I must say, I'm not surprised. Between you and me, I might have hit him, too."

"He admitted it?" Gunn winced as he sat up. He thought he had Richmond figured out. Apparently not.

"Yes, he did. I understand there were other witnesses. But he also says that he has not decided whether to press charges against you for battery and insubordination, since you struck the first blow, and he was your superior. He has that prerogative, you know."

"Yes, I realize that."

"Of course, the captain could decide to prefer charges anyway."

"Do you think he will?"

"I don't know. We'll see. Best to let sleeping dogs lie, perhaps."

"Aye, sir."

"So, given Mr. Richmond's pending resignation, the captain is looking for a new second lieutenant. Can't promise anything. It's up to him, but you will have my firm recommendation."

"Thank you, sir. I'll think about it."

"I will keep what you told me under my hat. If I don't hear from you, I'll assume you've decided to stay. Meanwhile, I wish you a quick recovery. Get on your feet as fast as you can. We need the help."

***

A few days after Prouty's visit, Nelson finally paid a call. Gunn heard him bantering with other patients even before he saw him. Yarrow and Moriarty accompanied him. They arrived at Gunn's bedside, and Nelson took a seat in the chair next to it, fidgeting to get comfortable. The other two stood at the foot of the bed. For the first time since he had known Nelson, the boatswain appeared unnerved.

"Hello, Boats. Yarrow. Moriarty. Thanks for coming."

"Evenin', sir. We brought you something."

Yarrow presented a carefully crafted shillelagh, with the initials "A.J.G." carved into the handle. Each of the crew, or those who cared to, had etched their names into the curved shaft.

"It's a loaded stick," Nelson said. "And, we made it long, so's you could cut it to suit you."

Gunn thanked them. "It's beautiful, Boats. Not quite as bawdy as Mr. Miller let on."

"Well, you know. You'd best keep respectable, sir."

"I'll treasure it."

"How are we today, sir?" asked Moriarty.

"Fine, thanks. Better every day. After five weeks, I should be. It's good to see you men. I honestly thought you wouldn't come, Nelson, given your dread of hospitals and doctors."

Nelson glanced about. "Yes, well … I do hate hospitals, it's true. I'll not be staying long, sir. Somebody might see that I probably have no right to be living. I'll find myself toes up in the morgue, if I'm not careful." He grinned.

"That would be a shame."

"I wouldn't mind so much, if I hadn't just got paid."

They all laughed, Gunn holding his sore ribs. "Well, at least you still do."

"Aye, well, it's not so very much, anyway." His grin turned sheepish. "Touchy subject, I know. That reminds me. Some of the boys 've got a pool goin' on what day you'll likely be back."

"It's up to nigh twenty dollars, Mr. Gunn," said Yarrow.

"I've picked the first of next month, in case you're int'rested," said Nelson. "Split the winnings with ye."

They laughed again, and then talked about other news on the ship.

"Mr. Richmond has resigned his commission. Did you hear that, sir? He ain't ever comin' back."

"Yes, I did hear."

"Of course, nobody's sad about that," said Moriarty.

"Especially Dwyer," said Yarrow. "He danced a jig when he heard the news. But I prob'ly shouldn't 'a said that. Beg your pardon, sir."

Nelson changed the subject. "Connelly drank himself into a stupor again. Cap'n sent him up here to the hospital to dry out. He's downstairs on the main floor. We just came from visiting him."

"I hadn't heard that. Haven't even seen Connelly," said Gunn. "Didn't know he was here."

"Well, now, you wouldn't have, would you, sir? He's down in the foc'sle, as it should be."

"I've got news, sir. My wife's just had her baby," said Moriarty. "A girl, name of Hannah."

"That's great news, Moriarty. Congratulations to you both." Gunn shook hands with him.

"Aye, a six-pounder, she was."

"But she looks too pretty to be his," said Nelson.

"That's no lie," said Moriarty. "Come to think of it, she squalls like a bos'un, too." He grinned at Nelson.

"Well, don't look at me," said Nelson. "I don't even know where you live, man."

Their raucous laughter brought the orderly to tell them to be quiet.

Nelson held a finger to his lips and lowered his voice. "Oh, and you'll be happy to hear that the captain bought hisself a new pipe, Mr. Gunn. Never seen the old man madder 'n when he broke the other one to pieces on the deck," Nelson chuckled.

"Yes, well, you can laugh now. It was not so hilarious then."

"No, sir, you're spot on about that. One tragic day, it was."

They all grew quiet.

"I—well, I want to thank you, Boats—all of you—"

"Warn't nothing, sir. We're just glad you're going to be all right, sir," said Moriarty.

"Well, I guess we'd better get out of here, before they toss us out of officer country," Nelson said.

He got up and they made ready to leave.

"Nelson, thank you for what you did. Everything you did. I would not be here, if not for you. I owe you my life, twice over."

"No need to thank me, sir. You would've done the same."

"If ever I can return the favor …"

"Sure thing, sir." His face had an unfamiliar, almost tender smile. He cleared his throat. "Well, we're all hoping you'll be on your feet and back on the quarterdeck very soon, Mr. Gunn."

58

Almost six weeks had passed. By the end of August, Gunn's injuries were healing well. He felt stronger every day. The plan was for him to leave the hospital on the twenty-ninth and stay in Hull, overlooking the water at Stormcrest, during the next several weeks of convalescence. Aunt May would not hear of any alternative. His mother and Marguerite would stay with them, too, as long as necessary to help take care of him. They all wanted to see him fully recovered as soon as possible.

The day before he was due to be released from the hospital, Captain Whitcomb came to see him. Gunn was seated outside on a bench in the shade of an oak tree. Several other patients sat nearby, taking the air to escape the stifling heat of the ward on a still, late summer's day. When Gunn saw the captain arrive, he struggled with the crutches to gain his feet.

"Don't get up. Good to see you're doing so well, Mr. Gunn. It looks like you'll be good as new before long."

"Almost as good, yes, sir. But the doctor says I have a few weeks to go before I can put heavy weight on it, after they take this thing off tomorrow." He tapped his splinted leg with a crutch. "Won't you sit down, sir?"

"Well, no rush. These things take time." Whitcomb remained

standing, quiet. "I would have come sooner, but—"

"It's quite all right, captain. I know how busy you are."

"I have some news for you, though I'm not so certain you will like to hear it. I've been wrestling with just how to say it."

"What is it, captain?"

"First off, I am recommending you for promotion to second lieutenant."

"Well, that—that's great news, captain. Thank you. I won't let you down, sir."

"You won't have to worry about that, Mr. Gunn."

"What do you mean, sir?"

"Captain Dawes, of the *Andrew Jackson*, has agreed to your transfer to his ship. They are leaving the yards and going back to Savannah, soon. He still hasn't found a suitable second. He wants you. If you are willing, of course."

"I see." He studied the toes on his bare foot. "Suppose I don't want to go? Boston is my home."

"Perhaps it would be best for all if you broadened your horizons a bit."

"I'm happy here. I love the ship, the crew. They are my home, my family."

The captain hesitated. "There is no place for you here, Mr. Gunn. I'm sorry to say it. The *Morris* will not be keeping two third lieutenants. Mr. Peaslee, the Collector of the port, will not allow it. Very few cutters now have more than a single third lieutenant, you know. The service is cutting back."

"What about Sam Miller? Why not send him? He might enjoy the change of scenery."

The captain shifted his cap from one hand to the other.

"Wait a minute, sir." The sudden realization was like a beacon cutting through dense fog. "Perhaps I'm confused. I thought you said that I am being promoted to second lieutenant. Doesn't that solve the problem?"

"Not if you refuse the transfer. I have already selected a new second. He arrives next week."

Gunn pursed his lips. There was something the captain was not saying.

"It's not that I don't want you, Andrew. You're a fine officer in most respects, and you show great potential. I like your spirit. Some would call it stubbornness. I prefer perseverance. And don't let it go to your head, but you may be the best natural sailor I've ever seen."

"Thank you, sir. That means a lot coming from you."

"Furthermore, I know you're a good man at heart. You've made some mistakes, it's true. Who hasn't? But most importantly, you kept your word to me, despite any doubts. Nelson told me what happened on the *Parsifal*. I understand and respect what you did."

"It was the right thing to do at that moment, sir. Nelson helped me see that."

"Yes. On the other hand, there is the matter of your striking a superior officer, which was not the right thing to do. Now, I have had no further word from Mr. Richmond as to whether he intends to press charges. He still might, but he would have to come here to testify. Regardless, I cannot overlook it, despite the mitigating circumstances. Your action was inexcusable, and there must be consequences. It is impermissible in my ship. You understand."

"I understand, captain."

"However, I want to avoid preferring charges. So, I think Captain Dawes and I have settled on a solution. If you accept this, ah, discipline, there will be no other consequences. Unless we hear from Mr. Richmond, the matter will be dropped."

"I see, sir, but—"

"You simply have some things to learn that I can't teach you, I'm afraid. You're going to have to learn them on your own. Away from … everything and everyone here."

"My uncle."

Whitcomb gave a curt nod. "I think it's best. It's your choice, of course."

"My choice, captain?"

"Certainly. You can either take the assignment or go home to await some … future possibilities. Of course, you may choose to resign your commission. It's all up to you."

Physical pain twisted his gut. "All right then. Thank you for coming, sir." He struggled with the crutches to his feet.

"I will prepare your orders. You decide what to do with them. I truly hope you will accept them."

"Aye, sir."

The captain smiled and offered his hand. "You'll be a ship's captain yourself, one day. I'm sure of it. Then, perhaps, you'll understand. You must trust me on this."

They exchanged a firm handshake. The captain said goodbye, wished him well, and then left Gunn to contemplate what had happened.

His chest tightened the way it had that night in the water when he surfaced, gasping for air. He found it hard to imagine living in the south. It seemed so much like a foreign country to him. This news would seal it with Elizabeth, too, most likely—as though that hadn't already happened. Unless, of course, he resigned his commission.

"Stunner," he muttered.

59

Postmarked Philadelphia, the package was addressed to Mr. Andrew Gunn in care of the Marine Hospital. It had taken two weeks to find him at Stormcrest, where he had been convalescing for the past three. The wrapping bore no return address and neither did the letter inside. The hasty, left-handed scrawl on both revealed who had sent it.

He opened the letter's seal, but several minutes elapsed before he could bring himself to unfold it and begin reading.

> *My dear Son,*
>
> *I cannot describe my distress at hearing of your terrible accident. How I have received word is not important. The singular fact of the matter is that you are recuperating and soon well, as I am told. I hope—no, I pray—each day for your full recovery.*
>
> *My love for you compels me to urge your consideration of the prospect of another, wholly different profession—and why not? You would do well to seek an occupation that allows you truly to express yourself and to be your own man, relying on none other. After all, how does it become a man to bend the knee to any vain rule or oppression, especially this American government today? A true man cannot without disgrace be associated with it. One cannot for an instant recognize a*

government which is the slave's government also.

Obey none but your own conscience, my son. Follow the dictates of your heart. Live freely. You will be the better for it.

Your Loving Father,
Daniel Gunn

P.S. The enclosed is not a gift. It has always belonged to you, more than it ever did to me. I send it to its rightful owner.

Inside the package was a leather pouch, out of which slid a gold pocket watch. It was the watch that he'd seen his grandfather consult countless times, taking it from a vest pocket with gnarled, knotted hands—the hands of a seafarer. As a child sitting on his grandfather's lap, he had played with the chain and fob, now missing.

The case popped open with the touch of his thumb. The inscription inside said, *"Wha daur meddle wi' me."* Below the inscription was the etching of a stylized Scottish thistle.

The longcase clock in the hall said ten minutes past four. He set the watch, wound the stem, closed the case, and tucked it into his vest pocket. No doubt it still kept good time.

He struck a match and burned the letter, determined not to say anything about it to anyone. He had his suspicions as to how his father had come to find out about his injuries, but love for his sister and her good intentions tempered his anger. Even so, it was as though the smoldering embers of a shipboard fire had suddenly flared into a new conflagration. Despite its powerful message, the letter from his father had an effect exactly opposite to its intention.

He broke the news of his impending promotion and transfer to his family the morning after receiving the letter. He made up his mind to accept his new orders, which had come to the house along with the trunk containing his uniforms and other personal belongings, addressed to *Second Lieutenant Andrew J. Gunn, USRCS.* The orders directed him to proceed to Savannah, Georgia, on or before 15 October, 1854, and report for duty aboard the Revenue Cutter *Andrew Jackson*.

Among his belongings inside the trunk were his books, with his treasured *Twice-Told Tales* on top, inside of which was neatly tucked Elizabeth's small painting of a thistle. Next to the books on top of his uniforms gleamed two new, gold-bullioned epaulets, bearing a single silver bar, the embroidered insignia of a second lieutenant. An attached note, signed by Sam Miller, simply said, "A gift from the wardroom of the Cutter *Morris*, wishing you always fair winds and following seas."

To celebrate his new adventure, Aunt May prepared a luncheon, served on the back terrace overlooking Hingham Bay. A hint of autumn chilled the light sea breeze under an overcast sky. He sat down with his mother, sister, aunt, and uncle to a table of clam chowder, cod cakes, a lobster salad, several vegetables from May's kitchen garden, and wheat rolls that everyone vowed were better than any at the finest hotels in town.

Once over the shock of his announcement, Marguerite said she was very happy for him. She saw the opportunity to advance his career and see new places, meet new people. And maybe, just maybe, he could straighten out some of the wrong-headed thinking of the silly secessionists, at least in one state.

"Just think of it. What wonderful irony," she said. "Being assigned to a ship named for your namesake. Why, what better missionary, or emissary, could there be? I think it's a great idea. I couldn't have written it better myself. And don't worry about us. Mother and I will fare just fine on our own while you're away, won't we Mother?"

"I'm not so sure. We might not see you for ... well, for months, maybe years at a time, Andrew. What happens if—"

"Nonsense. Why, Eleanor Gryffith," May Mitchell chided, using her sister's maiden name, "Don't be a ninny. You know very well this is a good opportunity for your son. Besides, you could always travel to see him. It's not as though he's going to be living on the far side of the world. Why, some of Mother's people still live there. We haven't seen them in years, but family is family. I'm sure they would welcome a visit. Wouldn't that be so much fun?"

"Surely, everyone's either dead or gone by now."

"Certainly not. Our cousins, the twins, Josephine and Julia, twice removed on—"

Eleanor bristled. "That very well may be, *dear* sister. But not everyone has the money to travel anywhere and anytime she has a fancy to."

May changed the subject. "Why don't we retire to the parlor to play a game of Hearts. It's become all the rage among my friends. Come, I'll teach you how, if you don't know."

His mother took him aside, as the others retired to the parlor.

"Come on, you two," called May. "You'll just love it, I promise."

"Just a moment," said Eleanor, waving from the adjoining terrace, as though bidding her sister *bon voyage*. She turned back to Gunn, who stood next to her, leaning heavily on his shillelagh.

"What about Elizabeth?" she asked.

"What about her?"

"Well, what does she have to say about your decision?"

"I have no idea, Mother."

"Don't you care to find out?"

He shrugged. "She's made it quite clear. She has other plans."

Eleanor looked into his face, as though trying to reconcile a memory. "Have you heard from your father, Andrew?"

"What makes you ask such a thing?"

"Don't look so shocked. I told him what happened and asked him to write to you."

"*You* did that? I thought it was Marguerite. Whatever possessed you?"

She shook her head. "Don't be angry, son. You need to forgive him."

"Why should I?"

"Because he's your father."

"Not good enough."

"Well, then, because ..." She laid her hand on her heart. "Because, I have. Before God, I have. And you need to," she whispered. "For your sake, if not for his."

"He hasn't even asked my forgiveness. I'm not about to do that. Why even bring it up?" He started to limp away from her, but she grasped his arm and turned him back to face her.

"Look at me, Andrew. *Look* at me. You are so much like him, you know. That same wavy brown hair, and bright blue eyes. And a nose like a Grecian statue. So handsome. But it's more than just your features. You're like him in so many ways. In here." She placed her open hand on his chest. "I think you're afraid of that, and I don't want you to be."

"What rot. How can you say such a thing? I'm nothing like him. I never will be. I'm much more like *his* father. Grandpa was a real man. Honest. True. *Loyal.*"

She hesitated. "Your Grandpa Gunn was a philanderer, too, Andrew. Oh, yes. Like father, like son. Don't scowl at me. I say it because it's true. It's up to you to break that awful legacy. But you can't do that if you won't face it head on."

"I face it every waking moment, Mother. Not to mention every time I look in a mirror, which is why I don't own one."

"I think that you might fear giving your heart to someone, completely and without reserve, to feel real passion for someone whom you love with all your heart. I don't want you to miss out on that because of something your father did such a long time ago. Don't just love the idea of Elizabeth. If that's the case, you've already been unfaithful. Love *her*. And show her that you do. Win her heart. Don't let her slip away."

"Don't be silly. I do love Elizabeth. I've already asked her to marry me. She's the one who refused."

"Are you two coming?" begged May.

Eleanor waved her off again. "Why did she refuse, Andrew?"

He bit his lower lip, and then let go. "She wants to be a teacher."

"Is that what she told you? What else did she say? What was the real reason?"

"She wants me to give up my career."

"For her sake."

"That's right."

"And you refused."

"I certainly did."

She thought for a moment. "Maybe she feels that you're pushing her away. Perhaps she thinks you already have a mistress, one with which she can't possibly compete. That's why she wants you to give it up."

"That's utter nonsense. It's my profession, Mother, nothing more. She was fine with it, until the Burns thing."

"Just think about what I've said, won't you?"

"I already have. And I've made my decision. It's all up to Elizabeth to decide, now."

60

Uncle William did not have much to say about his announcement. In fact, his uncle kept his thoughts entirely to himself until one evening a week or so later. He urged Gunn to reconsider and stay, come back to his employ as a mate on one of his ships. With hard work and perseverance, God willing, he could someday become the master of his own ship and his own destiny. He could make his own fortune. It was a pitch Gunn had heard before.

They sat alone on the porch of the big house, one late September evening when the weather had turned cooler, watching the sun set over the harbor. Ships of every size and description plied the shimmering water of indigo blue, flecked with hues of gold, coral, and violet. He could even pick out the silhouette of the Cutter *Morris*, flying her distinctive ensign from the main gaff, heading out to sea without him.

This was his favorite spot in all the small world that he'd known since boyhood. From here, it looked as though the ships were toy boats on a pond, and he could reach out, pick them up, and place them at will, making them sail wherever he wished them to go.

He turned to his uncle. "I appreciate your generous offer, Uncle William. Before I answer, let me ask you a question. I have been

342

meaning to ask this question for a while, now. I can't put it off any longer."

"Certainly. What is it, Andrew? Fire away."

He leaned closer. "Tell me, honestly. Do you have any involvement in the Underground Railroad?" His voice—low, barely above a murmur—sounded to him like a conspirator's, which was not what he intended.

Mitchell had placed a cigar between his teeth and readied a match. Removing the cigar, he took a deep breath and exhaled through pursed lips in a near whistle. He struck the match and held the flame to the end of the cigar.

"That would be illegal, Andrew. I have denied it once—in public, no less. Must I do so again? Would three times suffice?" The cigar glowed in the gathering shadows as he replaced it in his mouth and began puffing smoke. The match flamed higher with each draw, until he blew it out with a single breath and tossed it away. "The thing is, I do not feel obliged to answer that question, even coming from you."

"Well, then, let me ask another question, if I may."

His uncle nodded and exhaled a great cloud of smoke.

"Would you tell me about your father, and how he made his fortune?"

Mitchell picked a shred of tobacco from his lower lip. "Can I offer you a cigar, Andrew?"

"No, thank you."

"Are you sure? They're Cubans. Delightful, truly."

"I'm sure."

"Well, now, I've told that story many times. I think you know that he built a successful shipping company in Maine from one little schooner out of Portland."

"Mitchell and Son."

"That's right. I renamed it Glastonbury Enterprises, when I took over from him."

"Yes, but you've never mentioned the name 'Billy Bones.' At least, not to me."

Mitchell flicked the shred of tobacco from his thumb. "Where have you heard that name?"

"Someone asked me if that was you."

His uncle shook his head. "Some called my father by that name."

"Was he a privateer? Is that how he started?"

He took another draw. "Nothing wrong with that. It was an honorable profession."

"Except for the smuggling."

Mitchell studied the red glow at the end of his cigar, as though the light contained wisdom of some new, unknown source. "Well, now. Smuggling is such an unkind word."

"How would you describe such attempts to circumvent the law?"

"The law is an expediency, Andrew. As you well know, it is very often expedient for some, but not for others. That's always been the case. The law works for the good of those in power."

"And how do you discern whether a law is expedient or not?"

"When it does no harm to break it, or if breaking it becomes … necessary."

"When does it become necessary to break a law?"

"What do these questions have to do with my offer, may I ask?"

"Please, indulge me."

"Very well, then. It's necessary whenever the law requires one to be the agent of injustice. Especially injustice to oneself."

"So, who decides, then, what or who is just or unjust? Doesn't the law itself determine that?"

"The law never made any man a whit more or less just. That's up to the individual man, alone, to determine for himself. Such is the nature of liberty, my boy."

The last rays of the sun gilded the violet clouds.

"Do you ever find it necessary to break the law?" asked Gunn.

"Who is asking? My wife's nephew, or Second Lieutenant Gunn?"

Gunn held his uncle's steady gaze for a few seconds before he spoke.

"I'm sorry, Uncle William. Thank you for your offer. I owe you a great debt, which I fear I can never repay. But I also feel obliged to serve my country. No other nation like this one has ever existed in the history of the world, warts and all, and I'm proud to serve it. Not just stand off and criticize, or undermine, or condemn every flaw, as so many do these days. Above all, I happen to believe that our liberty depends on the rule of law. If we forget that, this nation won't last a hundred years, and it shouldn't. I can't begin to express my disappointment in those who think otherwise."

"Wait a moment now. I'm simply saying we must abide by our own—"

"Please, let me finish, Uncle William."

"Very well. Go on."

"I've had a lot of time to think about my decision, and, believe me, I've had many reasons to quit my commission. To be honest, I was almost persuaded to your way of thinking. I've heard it before from others—from all quarters. It sounds true, but rings hollow to me, like a cracked bell. Quite frankly, it smacks of anarchy, not liberty."

His uncle's lips held an uneasy smile. "Bravo. A fine speech, lieutenant. You have always been an idealist. Probably too much of one to ever make a fortune at any occupation." He laid his hand on Gunn's shoulder. "My lad, I've misjudged you, I'm afraid. Perhaps you should have been a preacher, just like your father. I think you have it in you, after all."

It wasn't so long ago such words would have driven him to fury. "Perhaps you're right. I'm done preaching. Here's a more practical admonition for you. Keep a closer watch on your ships from now on, Uncle William. Others certainly will."

Mitchell rose from his chair. "I must be over-tired, Andrew. What I heard just now sounded strangely like a threat. Even so, my offer stands, if you should change your mind. Now, kindly excuse me. I'm off to get some much-needed rest." He turned and strode into the house, the swirls of cigar smoke streaming over his shoulder.

Gunn sat alone with his thoughts as the sun set over the harbor, just beyond the city on a hill.

61

The gated picket fence surrounding Elizabeth Faulkner's home in West Roxbury still needed paint, as it had for more than a year. The brass buttons on Gunn's uniform could have used a bit of polish, too, for that matter, but it had been a while since he had worn it. At least he had shined his boots. He tried to muster the nerve to walk up the path to the porch of the parsonage and knock on the door.

Her handwritten note, addressed to him at Stormcrest, had invited him to dinner at six o'clock on Saturday, the thirtieth of September. Nothing else gave any indication of her state of mind or heart, other than a postscript, saying that she must speak with him and hoped he would come.

In the distance, church bells tolled as though celebrating a momentous event. They continued ringing as he straightened his cap, opened the gate, and strolled up the path, touching his shillelagh on the flagstones. The gate slammed shut behind him, and the Faulkners' little black-and-tan terrier ran around the side of the house, yapping and growling at the intruder.

"*Et tu*, Wallie?" Gunn laughed, as the terrier tugged at the leg of his trousers. "Have you turned against me, too, you little scamp?"

The front door opened, and Robert called out. "Wallace. Come here, boy."

"I've got him," said Gunn. He leaned over and picked up the frantic dog, who acquiesced, cradled in his arm.

"He's happy just to be held," said Robert.

"Of course. Aren't we all?"

"Come on in, Andrew. We've been expecting you. Why're all the church bells ringing?"

"I have no idea. Maybe a wedding or something."

"You'd think it was New Year's Day."

Gunn mounted the steps to the porch, one by one. "Well, Robert, I'm celebrating just being out of the house."

"That's as good as any reason I can think of. I'm glad to see you. It's been strange not having you around lately. And the fishing has been just awful without you to help find the big ones."

"Well, thank you, Robert. That's very kind."

"Come on in. Give me your cap. Have a seat in the parlor. I think Elizabeth will be down in a minute."

Gunn handed his cap to Robert and tucked his walking stick behind the door. He placed the dog on the floor, where the terrier danced at their feet, nearly tripping them.

"See there? Wallie is glad to see you, after all," said Robert. "It's been a while. We have a lot to catch up on."

He entered the front parlor and eased himself onto the settee. The dog jumped up beside him and nuzzled his hand, begging to be petted.

Mrs. Faulkner entered the room. When Gunn attempted to stand, she objected, her outstretched hands pleading.

"Hello, Andrew. Please don't get up."

"It's good to see you, Mrs. Faulkner. Thank you for inviting me to dinner."

"It's our pleasure, Andrew. We're so glad you could come. It shouldn't be too long, now. As soon as my husband arrives home, we'll be ready to sit down. He's late. I do wonder what's keeping him." She turned and called upstairs. "Elizabeth, come on down. Andrew is here."

He heard her light tread as she descended the steps, but it sounded like two sets of syncopated footsteps. Elizabeth entered the parlor, beaming her familiar smile, as though nothing contentious had ever happened between them.

"Hello, Andrew. Don't get up. I'm so pleased you've come. I—we have a surprise for you." She sat next to him on the settee.

"A surprise. I can't wait to see what it is."

"It's not a what, but a who."

Mrs. Faulkner crossed to the doorway and beckoned to someone, standing in the shadows. "Come on, now, girl. Don't be shy."

Into the early evening sunlight streaming through the open windows stepped the little girl from Highland Light, the one he'd told Elizabeth about during the picnic in Framingham. Her shining auburn hair was smooth-plaited, no longer wild and knotted. She wore a cotton dress of pale blue flowers, pleated and made to fit, with pantalets, white stockings, and new black shoes on her feet.

"Marianne."

The girl raised her eyes to look at him. Her face brightened. Then, she rushed forward, threw her arms around his neck and hugged him.

"How did you—when did … ?" He held her by the shoulders and drew her back, so he could see her face. She hugged him again.

"I told her that she had you to thank," said Elizabeth. "You're the one who told us about her."

"But how did she get here?"

"We contacted her uncle at the lighthouse," said Mrs. Faulkner. "He agreed that she would be better off living somewhere else with people who could care for her and give her a stable home. She'll be living here, now, and can visit her uncle on occasion, if she wishes. Whenever she wishes."

He was without words, glancing from Elizabeth to Marianne and back again.

"She needed a mother and a sister to help her grow up into a young woman, which she will soon become," said Elizabeth. "Someone to teach her. And she has you to thank for that."

"I take no credit. I had nothing to do with it."

"Certainly, you did. We wouldn't have known, otherwise."

He took Marianne into his arms and placed her on his good knee. "I don't know what to say." He smiled. "You are quite a surprise, Marianne." He drew back and looked at her face again. "Let me look at you. What a change. What do you say to all this?"

She smiled and looked around the room. "Everything is new, and ever so different. It was so lonely at the lighthouse. And it scared me to be there, especially during the big storms."

"Yes, well, they can be scary places," he said, smiling. "I hope your uncle won't be too lonely and afraid without you."

"He's used to it," she said. "Besides, he got another dog. He calls him Wolf, even though he's as little as Wallie."

Gunn laughed. "Of course. Good name. Well, I must say, you are a surprise." He gave Elizabeth a sidelong glance and smiled. "A most pleasant one."

"I'm hungry, Mother." said Robert. "I'm sure Andrew is, too. Let's go ahead and eat."

"You know better. It would be rude to start without your father. He should be here any minute."

"Here he comes, now," said Elizabeth, peering through the curtained front window. "He must realize how late he is, the way he's—"

Bounding footsteps sounded on the front porch, and the door burst open. Reverend Faulkner stood in the doorway, waving a folded newspaper in his uplifted hand.

"Special edition of *The Liberator*," he huffed, red-faced. "Anthony Burns has been freed, praise God in heaven."

"Is that why all the bells in town were ringing, just now?" asked Robert.

His father nodded. "Yes, word has spread all over the city. It's true. Burns has been freed. And he's here in the city, staying with Reverend Grimes at his church."

"Come on in, dear," said Mrs. Faulkner. "Sit down and rest yourself. You're all in a fit. You'll be giving yourself palpitations."

"What good news!" Elizabeth said. "How did it happen? *The Liberator* has been crying for his release these past three months, or more. But it seemed nobody was listening. Finally, at long last."

Reverend Faulkner sat in a nearby chair and tried to catch his breath. "Well, as it turns out, Reverend Grimes somehow managed to gather enough money to buy his freedom. He's been negotiating since the rendition, secretly, to stay any uprising among Virginians who don't want to see Burns freed. Apparently, his former master— what was his name? Remind me. It's here in the paper." He unfolded the newsprint. "Sutton?"

"Suttle," Gunn said.

Faulkner glanced up. "Ah, Andrew. Hello. How are you? Suttle. Right you are. Suttle would not free him directly. Says here that he 'feared the repercussions from the people of his own state, if he allowed northerners to buy Burns' freedom.' So, he struck a deal with a tobacco farmer somewhere near Nashville, instead."

"Tennessee?" asked Gunn.

"Of course, Tennessee, yes. Now, apparently, this fellow, this farmer is a real character. He turned around and offered to free Burns for the sum of thirteen hundred dollars, which was two hundred more than their previous offer to Suttle. What a mercenary. Can you believe such a thing?"

"And they were able to raise the additional money?" asked Robert.

"Yes. The paper credits an anonymous donor."

"Thirteen hundred dollars. What a sum," said Mrs. Faulkner. "Can you imagine?"

"Indeed, quite a tidy sum," Elizabeth said, glancing at Andrew. "Thank God. We've been praying for his release. Everyone at church has been praying since the day he—"

Gunn met her second glance, then turned to Reverend Faulkner and asked, "What was his name?"

"Who?"

"The farmer from Tennessee. Did the newspaper report his name?"

"Read it yourself. His name is Shylock, if you ask me. I think it might have been Richmond, though. Something like that. What difference does it make, Andrew?"

Gunn took the newspaper from him and scanned the first few paragraphs.

Faulkner got up from his chair. "Right there." His index finger trembled against the paper as he pointed.

The article confirmed that a landowner named William Richmond had agreed to set Burns free in return for cash payment, with transport expenses to be paid by the buyers.

"Not one whit of difference, I suppose, reverend," he replied. "Well, that is good news. I'm very glad to hear it. I guess you just never know, do you?"

"I hope their guilty consciences will keep them both awake at night," said Robert.

"I doubt either Suttle or Richmond will give it a second thought," said Gunn. "Just a hunch."

Reverend Faulkner smoothed a few strands of mussed hair back from his forehead. "No matter. It is not our place to judge another man's conscience. I can't imagine a more unfaithful guide than a carnal man's conscience, anyway. Let God's spirit prick them, if he so chooses, and as he will. Now, let's gather round the table, and give thanks for this glorious day. Eh, Mother?"

"By all means, my dear."

Marianne clung to Gunn's sleeve, as they made their way to the table. He sat down at the table next to her. Elizabeth and Robert sat opposite them, with their mother and father at the foot and head.

Reverend Faulkner gave thanks for the recent events and asked for a blessing on the food.

As the dishes were being passed, Gunn leaned to his left, toward Reverend Faulkner. "Sir, let me ask you something. I'm curious. You said earlier that a person's conscience can be unreliable. I take it, then, you don't believe in letting your conscience be your guide?"

"I do not, Andrew. The conscience is no more reliable than the heart. Left to itself, it too often will condemn what is right and justify what is wrong."

"But isn't the conscience the eye of the soul, Father?" asked Elizabeth. "I've heard you say so."

"Aye, that it is, my dear. But an eye is useful only insofar as it looks outward to the light, to the highest standard, which is God himself."

"I've heard it said—Emerson has said, that 'a man is the façade of the temple wherein all wisdom and good abide.' And that we need only look inward to know what is right. Is that not so?" said Gunn.

"Tell me, Andrew, does your own experience teach you that's true?"

Gunn laughed and shook his head. "No, sir. Not really. Not in my experience, I must say."

"No, sir. Never inward. There, inside us is found a blinding darkness and the error of our lost ways. Alone and to ourselves, we are each one just as blind as the other. We must know Christ, who teaches us what we do not know. But that's enough of a sermon. Tomorrow will come soon enough."

The conversation turned to more mundane matters, but Gunn's thoughts were preoccupied with the odd answer to his question. It was an odd answer, after all, unlike anything he had ever heard in Concord.

After the dinner of roast chicken, red potatoes, turnips, and greens, Reverend Faulkner excused himself, got up from the table, and motioned to Gunn to follow him into his study.

"Elizabeth, I'm going to borrow Andrew for a moment. You don't mind, do you?"

"*I* do," said Marianne. She grasped his hand and held tightly. Everyone laughed.

"I'll be back, Marianne," he said, smiling. "Don't go anywhere, now. We have lots to talk about."

"Be careful, Andrew. Watch his left," said Robert, raising his fists. "Papa was a pretty good boxer in his day, but he's a lightweight and he has a glass jaw. I've got the winner."

Elizabeth laughed as she touched Gunn's arm. "Just don't knock each other senseless. I still need to talk with you, too. I'll wait for you in the garden."

62

Inside the book-lined study, Faulkner offered Gunn a seat on a well-cushioned sofa, took a bottle of port from the sideboard, and poured two glasses. He offered one to Gunn and eased himself into an armchair nearby.

"I'm very glad you've come, Andrew. I wanted a chance to talk with you alone."

"Yes, sir. Of course." Gunn sank into the worn sofa, his knees almost level with his chin. He would need help getting up.

Faulkner cleared his throat, then took a sip of wine, looking directly at him. "How's the limb?"

"Healing nicely, thanks. I hardly need the cane."

"You haven't been in church, of late."

"No, sir. I've been staying with my aunt and uncle in Hull.

Faulkner cleared his throat again. "I thought I should explain some comments I made when last we saw each other."

"Oh?"

"Yes, I'm sure you remember. My remark about a person such as yourself coming to worship with us."

"Ah, yes, well … I suppose I am the only person with the last name Gunn, after all."

Faulkner smiled. "That's true, true enough. Let me ask you this, though. When you first started coming to our church, what prompted you?"

Gunn tasted the wine. It was good port. Full-bodied, not too sweet. "I was ... your church was closest to the waterfront."

"Is that all?"

"I heard you were a good preacher."

"Who told you that?"

"Mr. Prouty, our first lieutenant."

"John Prouty? I haven't seen him in a good while, either. How is he?"

"Busy. Very busy, I suppose. Anyway, I was looking for some ... meaning, some structure in my life. He said your sermons might help."

"Structure. I see. Is that also why you joined the service?"

Gunn thought for a moment and took another long sip. "I suppose so. In part."

"So, why did you keep coming?"

"Mr. Prouty was right. Your sermons speak to both heart and mind. Tough to swallow, sometimes, but that's not a bad thing. It's good medicine for me. And, to be quite honest, you remind me a lot of my grandfather. Your manner of speaking. The way you put things."

"I trust that's a good thing, too."

"I think so."

"Was he a preacher?"

"No. He was just another sailor, like me."

"Ah." Faulkner got up to refill Gunn's glass, took a sip of his own, and sat back down. "You know, my grandfather was a seaman back in Scotland. A fisherman to be exact. My father, as well."

"Elizabeth has mentioned that." Gunn swirled the wine in his glass. The ruby color flashed against the lamplight.

"He was away a great deal, which was hard on us. My mother, especially. But he was a good man, a good father. I have nothing against men of the sea, mind you. I want you to know that."

"Of course."

"It was a hard life, true enough. Despite his many absences, my father taught me some very important life lessons."

"Mine, too. Some more welcome than others."

"Yes, well. One of them was that the captain sets the course and the destination, but it depends on a good helmsman whether the ship gets where she's going."

"I would certainly agree with that, sir."

"The helmsman must pay attention to the captain's orders, of course. But the wind blows where it wills. Sometimes he needs to steer a different course, allowing for the wind and current, to arrive at the intended destination."

"Yes, sir."

"Do you see where I'm going with this train of thought?"

"I'm not sure I follow, sir."

"Well, I think I can understand your predicament. And, I thought it necessary that I should ... apologize to you, Andrew. I have—"

"You've no need to apologize to me, Reverend Faulkner."

"Hear me out. I do want to say I'm sorry for misjudging your motives. It was wrong of me to do so. Elizabeth has persuaded me that you are an honorable man, caught in a very difficult situation."

"She said that?"

"Yes, and more." He paused and took a sip of port. "She loves you, so she says."

"And I love her."

"Well, then, what are your intentions, may I ask? Do you still wish to marry her? You said so, once."

Gunn studied the glass before he answered. "Sir, I do wish to marry Elizabeth, if she'd have me, which is an open question at the moment. But I regret to say that I am no longer in any position to do so."

"How's that? What do you mean?"

"I mean, I would like to, very much. But it's not possible. At least, not right now."

"Why not, may I ask?"

He sighed. "Well, first of all, I am currently without means to make any serious plans."

"Do you mean, with respect to finances?"

"Yes. Precisely."

"Have you been frivolous, Andrew? Surely you have a sound income, though I doubt it is much."

"At the moment, I am without, though my situation will soon change. Even so, I had saved enough to …"

"What happened, then?"

"I'd rather not say, sir."

"Well, I'm afraid I must insist, if you still have any desire to marry my daughter."

"Beg pardon?"

"You heard me."

Gunn sat upright and struggled to lean forward on the sofa. "If you must know, sir, I contributed most of my savings to help purchase the freedom of Anthony Burns."

Faulkner sat silent for a moment. His head tilted, as though he'd heard a distant, unfamiliar sound. "Did you, now?"

"Yes, sir." He drained his glass. "Anonymously, and I'd like to keep it that way, if you don't mind."

"Of course. Well, I'll be …" Faulkner sat back in his chair. "So, you—you're the anonymous donor? The one mentioned in the newspaper."

Gunn nodded. "There may have been others, of course."

Faulkner had hardly touched his port, but now he drained his glass. "I see. I must say, I'm very pleased to learn this about you. And very impressed."

"You needn't be, sir. It was the least I could do, considering—"

"Nevertheless, I am, and I don't mind admitting it."

They were on unfamiliar ground. Gunn had no idea how to proceed. He started as if to stand, reaching for his shillelagh. "Well, I—"

"So, now what, Andrew?"

Gunn relaxed back into his seat. "Now I have received orders to a cutter in Savannah, Georgia."

"Savannah, eh?"

Gunn nodded. "I've received a promotion to second lieutenant."

"Well, then. Does Elizabeth know?"

"I doubt it. I haven't told her."

"When do you leave?"

"Three days. I've booked passage on the *Libertas*, a steamboat that departs Tuesday afternoon."

"Three days? Why haven't you told her?"

He shrugged. "Frankly, I didn't think it would matter. I thought both of you had made up your minds that it should not."

"I see." Faulkner got up from his chair and took Gunn's empty glass. "Is your mind made up, Andrew? Is this decision final?"

"Yes, sir. I have decided. It was not an easy decision by any means, but now it's done, I won't change my mind."

Faulkner refilled the glasses, handed Gunn's back to him, and resumed his seat.

"How long will you be away?"

"I don't know. Two years, maybe more."

The reverend shifted in his chair and cleared his throat. "Elizabeth seems very happy in school."

"Yes, sir. I'm very happy for her, and I have no intention of asking her to leave. It is enough right now for me to try regaining control of the events in my own life. I came tonight intending to release her from any understanding that might have passed between us."

"Very well, then. Perhaps the timing is not so bad. But I'm sure you two eventually will work out this brief separation on your own. All in good time. I hope so."

"You do?"

"Very much. Don't look too surprised."

"I couldn't be more shocked, sir. I'm … speechless."

"I want my daughter to be happy. I think you make her happiest. Let me offer a toast to that end." He raised his glass, and Gunn did likewise.

"I appreciate the sentiment, sir." They both drank, and Gunn put down his glass. "Better not have any more to drink. I need a clear head to speak with your daughter."

"Before you go, Andrew …"

"Yes, sir?"

"Before you go, let me just say that we all like to think we're in control of our own lives. Truth is, we don't even know our own thoughts and desires, do we? I mean, truly. Ultimately, we are not in control. None of us is. There are forces at work well beyond our ken. All we can do is act in the moment, driven by what we may deem as our purest impulses. And then, let go, knowing whatever we do, our actions cannot stand on their own, and they rarely determine the final outcome. That's up to God himself. He's the supreme captain of our souls. We are but helmsmen. Wouldn't you agree?"

"I'm almost persuaded, reverend." He smiled.

Faulkner took a deep breath. "We'll miss having you here."

"I'll miss being here. Truly, I will. Thank you, sir. You've given me much to think about."

"Pray about it, as well, won't you? A fervent prayer is far more efficacious than mere thought, however earnest."

"I'll try, sir."

"May God go with you, son."

"I hope so."

63

He pushed open the garden gate with his cane. Elizabeth waited on a bench, wearing the blue satin dress he liked so much.

As he approached, she gathered her skirts around her, arranging the finely braided trim on the flounces, carefully matched to the sleeves of her bodice. They were made with her own hands, like all her clothes. Always dressed simply, yet elegantly, she appeared as natural a feature of the landscape as the garden that surrounded her, especially in the deepening twilight.

He lit a nearby lantern, then sat beside her on the bench, as she spoke.

"Some surprise, eh?" she said, smiling.

"You mean, about Marianne? Very much so."

"Yes, I'm glad you feel that way. I also meant about Anthony Burns being freed."

"That, too. Yes, it is. Long overdue. It's a tremendous relief."

"I must say, you didn't seem so very surprised at that news."

He tugged the end of his nose. "As surprised as anyone else, I suppose."

"No. I watched you when Father told us about his release. You seemed more *relieved* than anything. By any chance, did you——?"

"Burns told me he expected it would happen, somehow. I just wish it could have happened differently. Sooner."

"We all have regrets. You did what you felt you had to do I suppose."

"I don't regret what I did, Elizabeth."

"Oh?" She frowned.

"It's what I did not do that keeps me awake."

"The same thing, isn't it?"

He didn't answer. She changed the subject.

"They look sad, but still lovely." She touched one of the last rose blooms of the season, their autumnal beauty now faded. The sun had set, and the shadows had gathered. She looked at the surrounding plants. "No more thistles." Her smile returned, but not as bright as it had been. It, too, had faded. "They've all gone for the season."

"Yes. I suppose so."

They both stayed silent awhile, watching the deepening nightfall.

She shivered. "I should have brought a shawl."

Gunn removed his uniform frock coat and draped it around her shoulders.

"I see you wore your uniform tonight." She admired the new gold straps on the shoulders. "Very dashing. Are you trying to tell me something?"

He hesitated. "I thought you should know I am being transferred. I've received my orders."

"Where to?" A hint of trouble wrinkled the corners of her eyes.

"South."

"How far south?"

"Georgia. Savannah."

"I see. When would you expect to leave?"

"Tuesday."

"Tuesday. Is—is this something ... that you wish to do?"

"Not necessarily. That's why they're called orders. Not invitations."

"Rather sudden, isn't it?"

"I've known about the orders for some time, now. They came with a promotion. I have accepted them."

"And you didn't say anything?"

"I was giving you time to think. Remember? I didn't want to complicate the issue or press you unfairly into a decision."

"What about us?"

"You tell me. What about us?"

She looked away, reached up and touched the nape of her neck, then lightly smoothed the hair over her ear. It was a gesture he had come to know, a tell that she felt vulnerable. Soon, her eyes met his.

"I think you know very well how I feel, Andrew."

He searched her glistening eyes for unspoken thoughts. They expressed a longing sadness, not unlike her mother's. "That's just it. I'm not so sure anymore," he said. "The only thing I know for certain, Elizabeth, is that I love you."

She smiled tenderly. "I love you, too, Andrew. You shouldn't doubt that. Nothing, no one stands in the way of that love. Not even my father. Except one thing. You expect me to compromise my convictions. This I cannot do."

"Ho, there. Back up the buggy, miss. You told your father that I am an honorable man, caught in a difficult situation. Or so he told me. Did you mean that?"

"Yes, I did. But I also expected that you would want to do something about your situation. Especially now, after everything that's happened, since you've had time to think about things."

He got up from the bench. "I don't wish to quarrel, but you were the one who needed time to think, Elizabeth. So, apparently after all this time, you still expect me to give up my desire to serve our country in the best way I know how to do?"

She rose to meet him. "Are you asking me, or telling me what I expect?"

"Elizabeth, please listen to me. I could have refused orders and faced court-martial. I could have quit the service. That would have been hard, but I assure you not nearly as hard as what I chose to do. In fact, those would have been the easy ways out. And they wouldn't have changed a thing, except that I wouldn't have been there to see that Burns wasn't treated like a filthy animal. I was able to make a difference, however small, because I was there. I can still make a difference, but only if I stay. These are trying times. It would be cowardly and selfish to leave now. Don't you see that?"

He took his gold watch out of his vest pocket and rubbed it between his fingers, staring at the case engraved with his initials, but not seeing it.

"Do you have somewhere to be?"

"No. Just an old habit."

"That's a beautiful watch. Where did you get it?"

"It was my grandfather's. My father sent it to me."

She took his hand and drew him back to sit on the bench beside her. "You've heard from him?"

He nodded. "His letter helped me decide what I must do, although not in the way he intended. Now, I'm the one who needs a little time. Time to do what I must."

They sat in silence. He put the watch away.

"You know, I feel as though you're trying to push me away, Andrew. Almost like that stone wall stands between us, now."

"I'm not sure that I'm the one pushing."

"Maybe you're right, Andrew. But I truly don't want to push you away. I want you to stay. We could be so happy together. I don't want anything else to come between us."

She lifted her hand from the folds of her skirt, and opened it to reveal a folded letter, creased with time and use.

"What's that?"

"The first letter you sent me. Remember?" She held the letter close, to read it aloud in the dim light.

My Dearest One,

Since the hour I first read your letter, I have been thinking about you always, trying to find a way to put words to the feelings that yours aroused. I am no wordsmith or poet. Let me rely on one who certainly was, by quoting —

'A garden inclosed is my sister, my spouse; a spring shut up, a fountain sealed.'

So says the Song of Songs. Read on to the end, and you will see your beloved find his way to open the gate and enter the garden, in all good time. My promise to you is that the day is coming when I will let nothing, no one stand between us. Until that day, know you are and will remain the one whom my soul loves.

Yours devotedly,
Andrew

She looked up. "Such pretty words. Did you mean them, Andrew?"

"I did. And I still do. I will keep my promise, Elizabeth. Let me prove it to you."

He took her hands in his, but she removed one and placed it on his cheek. He kissed her palm. She hesitated, then kissed his mouth, tenderly at first, but passion flared, and they kissed each other as though sharing between them the last breath of life. Their lips lingered, then parted.

"I told myself that it wouldn't be like this," she whispered. "I didn't want to feel—You're right, Andrew, I was pushing you away. But now—"

He gave her a gentle kiss, then she buried her face in his neck.

"I don't want you to go." She pressed herself against him, and her fingers grasped the hair at the back of his neck as she kissed him again. Her touch made his heart race, and the blood pounded in his ears. Then, she put both arms around his waist and placed her head upon his chest.

"Your heart is beating so fast," she muttered. "What are we going to do?"

"I have to go, Elizabeth, but I'll be back. Maybe I can get some leave at Christmas."

"Christmas. It might as well be the next decade."

He put his arm around her shoulders and drew her to him. Her thick brown tresses, plaited at the nape of her neck, carried a light, organic scent, something like lavender. He gently touched her hair and kissed it.

"I'll miss our long talks, but at least we can't argue anymore with such distance between us. We never used to argue."

She laughed quietly and sniffed. "Shh. Be quiet, please. Please."

He caressed her hair for several minutes. The only sound was the chirp of crickets in the garden.

"Will you come see me off on Tuesday?"

She took a deep breath. "I can't. I won't be able to bear it." She lifted her head, gazing into his eyes. Hers were clear and steady. "I'm not going to cry, Andrew." Her eyes welled with tears. "I'm telling you, I won't." She touched his face and smiled the way she had the first time he said that he loved her. A tear dropped to her cheek. "Take the time you need. I'll be here when you return," she said. Fleeting laughter broke through her tears. "But you'd better hurry. That's all I can say."

The fragrance of her hair would stay with him. Imagined or not, he caught the scent for several more days, until he could conjure it no more.

Finale

*A*s to the particulars of your inquiry, my young friend, I have none but the most ineffectual advice, I fear. Furthermore, (and you know this) I hate, hate, <u>hate</u> giving advice, especially when there is a prospect of its being taken. Perhaps you will understand and forgive the tardiness of my reply.

Nevertheless, you have pressed me for counsel with respect to attending to the good of others, especially in the face of contradicting authorities. In response, I would first point out that the good of others, like our own happiness, is not to be attained by direct effort, but incidentally. Moreover, when a man opens both eyes, he generally sees about as many reasons for acting in one way as in any other.

God's ways are in nothing more mysterious than in this matter of trying to do good. None of us knows his own heart well enough to discern whether good or evil compels us to act at any given moment. It is a profound truth, if any there should be, that the impulse to do good on one hand may yet result in the most insidious evil done on the other, though we perchance remain unaware of the effects. I also have found the opposite to be a true corollary.

In any event, we should not look inward for a verdict, though we owe it to ourselves and others to remain ever circumspect; rather, we must appeal to the Final Judge to know our deepest thoughts and desires, our triumphs and failures, and to weigh them accordingly. And in the end, the two great and overarching laws of the universe are simply thus: to do unto others as we would have done to us; and to judge not, lest we be judged, by whatever measure we should mete in judging others. If either of these laws should prove false, unworthy, or unjust, then nothing else is worth a whore's oath.

It occurs to me, however late, that the pretext of our discussion is whether or how such advice, paltry as it is, applies to performing duties while in the service of Uncle Sam, for which he generously supplies us both with a little pile of glittering coin out of his pocket every month—to our delight as well as to our detriment. As in other things, we have this petty enchantment in common, do we not? As I have said before, whoever touches it should look well to himself, or he may find the bargain to go hard against him, involving, if not his soul, yet many of its better attributes; its sturdy force, its courage and constancy, its truth, its self-reliance, and all that gives the emphasis to manly character.

I now bring the lesson home to myself, as well as to you, Andrew. It being hardly in the nature of a public officer to resign, yet I confess to having accomplished nothing of note, either good or bad, in the past two years, since being restored to public office by one whom I considered a friend. Look to yourself, Andrew, if you still consider me the same to you. Regard my own example. Fair warning.

I trust you are all well and send my highest regards to your lovely mother and fair sister, my dear little Pearl.

Yours affectionately,

—Nath'l Hawthorne

Hawthorne's letter arrived at Stormcrest on Monday, the day before Gunn's departure. It came via courier from the cutter too late to have done him any good in arriving at his decision. It was sound advice, nonetheless. Better yet, it provided affirmation, enough to send him on his way without regret or doubt, as he prepared to sail to Savannah by steamship.

That same day, he said his goodbyes to his mother and Marguerite, promising to return when he could, and they departed for home in Concord. He also bid farewell to his aunt and uncle, then retired early. He no longer felt at home at Stormcrest, or anywhere else, for that matter. The relationship with his uncle had deteriorated quickly after their last conversation, although Aunt May was as pleasant as ever, always striving to be the peacemaker. Even so, the past few days of his stay had been especially awkward and uncomfortable.

Early on the morning of his passage, he caught the first Hingham ferry and took his trunk to the steamship wharf to be placed aboard his ship. The *Morris* was out to sea. He had watched her sail the night before. He regretted not being able to say farewell to his former shipmates. He would certainly miss them, especially Miller and Nelson, and hoped someday to see them again.

But he did have one more goodbye to say.

He hailed a cab and paid another visit to the Twelfth Baptist Church. He guessed Burns would be there, perhaps still fearing to walk about as a free man, in case Uncle Sam should prove fickle.

Sure enough, he was there. When Gunn entered the empty church, he found Burns sweeping the bare floor. Anthony looked up and stopped short. A broad smile lit up his face.

"Mistah Gunn. As I live and breathe."

He grinned. "Hello, Tony."

"I was hoping I'd see you again. I didn't expect you to come, but I sure am glad you did."

"I've come to welcome you home."

Burns dropped the broom and loped the few yards between them. His face was gaunt, and he was much thinner than Gunn remembered, though livelier.

"Thank you, Mistah Gunn. It's good to be home, I do declare."

"My friends call me Andrew."

Burns' smile broadened even more. "Andrew." He reached out his gnarled right hand and Gunn took it. Burns clasped both hands over his, then pulled him into a full embrace. They hugged each other.

Gunn's vision blurred. It was the first time he had embraced any man since he and his brother had said their last farewell three years earlier, when Thomas had boarded his China clipper. Something inside him gave way, like water spilling through an open sluice gate. He shut his eyes tightly and tears rolled down his cheeks. After a moment, they parted, and both men wiped their eyes.

Burns pointed to his cane. "What's happened to your leg, Andrew?"

"Hazards of the job, Tony. It's nothing that won't mend in time."

"Well, I hope it mends better than this, then." Burns held up his right hand.

"It hasn't held you back, has it? They've got you pushing broom, I see."

"I don't mind a bit. Fact is, I'm happy to be earning my keep again."

"I'm so glad to see you, Tony. It's good to know that you are at last as free in body as in spirit."

"That I am, yes, indeed. But I knew that God would set me free in his own good time. I told you so."

"You did. He certainly works in mysterious ways, I'll say that much."

Burns burst into a hearty chortle, the first time that Gunn had ever heard his staccato laughter, and it was contagious. "No mystery. He works his ways through people, Andrew. People like you and me."

"I suppose so."

"You suppose so? Why, I *know* so."

"You didn't seem quite so sure last time I saw you."

He laughed again, this time with a cough. "Well, now, I was afraid, Andrew, wasn't I? Scared to death I was. Any man would be, I expect. But I knew deep down I wasn't alone, and it was just a matter of time. And then you came to the jail, like the angel sent to free Paul from prison. And that's when I knew you were my answer to prayer. And here you are again. Glory be."

"I don't feel much like an answer to anybody's prayer, Tony. In fact, I came to ask your forgiveness for my part in what you had to suffer."

"Oh, no, Andrew. No, no." He motioned to a nearby pew. "Sit down here for a moment, will you?"

They sat together. Burns waved his good hand, as if to erase a slate. "You don't understand. You see, I believe ... I know that God sent you to me in my hour of need. I know that in my very soul. Don't you see? You gave me hope. Without you, I would have given up. I'm nigh certain of it."

"Well, maybe he sent you to me, too, Tony."

"Praise God. Yes, he did. That's how it works, ain't it?

"I suppose it is."

"You got to stop supposin' and *believe*."

Gunn smiled. "I do, Tony. I think I do."

"Mercy me. I can't tell you how happy that makes me."

"So, tell me, what's in store for you now?"

"Well, I'm going to be a preacher, just like I said. Reverend Grimes has arranged for me to attend college at Oberlin in Ohio, free of charge. You know the school?"

"I do. It's a fine school."

"You look surprised."

He shook his head and grinned. "Not a bit surprised, Tony. Not anymore. You'll make a fine preacher."

"I intend to give it everything I've got. I will have a lot of catching up to do."

"You'll do it. I have no doubt."

"What about you, Andrew? Where you be headed?"

"I have new orders."

"Where to?"

Gunn stirred in his pew. "A ship in Savannah."

Burns gave a low whistle, same as the one in the jail cell the first time they'd seen each other. "Mercy, mercy me."

"I know. It won't be easy."

"No, sir, I expect it won't. Not for a good man like you. But with God nothing is impossible. Nothing, you know. Just do yourself a favor."

"What's that?

"Better let them sleeping dogs lie." He winked.

The image of his confrontation with the jailor and the demon-dog flashed through his mind. "Ah-ha. You heard that whole terrible fracas, did you?"

"Yessir, I surely did. Heard every word. Saw you through my little window, too. Shame on you, Mistah Gunn. Somebody could have gotten hurt or worse, especially you."

"It wasn't my best day, by far. I do regret it now."

Burns pursed his lips and shook his head. "I expect so. Mmn-mm. That poor Kirby-dog, he's a mean old hound, but I'd wager you almost give him a heart attack, threatening to crush his skull like you did. Why, that mangy cur like to never stopped growling and barking the rest of that day."

Burns let a wry smile spread across his face.

"Wore himself plum out, did he?"

Their unfettered laughter echoed throughout the empty sanctuary. Burns' laughter ended in a fit of coughing.

"Are you all right, Tony? That's a bad cough."

"Oh, it's nothin'. This little cough come with me from the jail, is all." Burns slapped a knee and wiped more tears from his eyes. "Well, now, what do you know about that? Savannah, Georgia, of all places on God's green earth. When do you leave, Andrew?"

"Today. I'm headed for the steamship soon as I leave here. My bags are already aboard. In fact, I'd better be going, before I miss it."

"*Today*, is it? Well then, before you go, I have something for you. Almost forgot. Be right back."

Burns hurried off, passing through a door at the front of the sanctuary. He left Gunn alone for just a moment. Soon, he returned, looking very solemn.

"Now, I'm not sure what he meant by it. I told him he was dead wrong about you. He said, 'time will tell' or some such. Anyway, when I left to come up here, Mistah Richmond give me this and told me to give it to you, if I was to see you."

Burns extended his crippled hand, revealing a brass button, shining in the late-morning sunlight. It was a uniform button, the one that Richmond had snatched from his coat.

"Thank you, Tony." He took the button and turned it in his fingers.

"Said be sure to tell you that you still don't know everything and likely never will. Said you'd know what it meant."

"I do." He smiled. "It means I'm free."

"If that's what it means, then hallelujah. We're both free men."

"Free as a bird." Gunn placed the button in his vest pocket, and they shook hands again. "If ever I can do anything to—"

"Just go with God, Andrew. That's the best you can do."

"And you, my friend."

"Till we meet again."

"Soon. Very soon, I hope."

He left the church and walked several blocks until he could find a cabbie that would pick him up. By the time he arrived at the steamboat pier, the mate was preparing to pull in the gangplank. Gunn showed his ticket, which read, *SS Libertas—Boston to Savannah, via New York City and Charleston*. The mate welcomed him aboard.

"Best hurry, sir. She's about to leave."

Gunn took a last look around. A carriage had just pulled up behind him and it rolled to a stop. Reverend Faulkner lowered himself gingerly out of the cab, turned and offered his hand to the passenger. Elizabeth ducked her head through the door and took her father's hand, as he helped her step down. She hurried to Gunn's side.

"I was afraid that we had missed you," she said.

"Need you to get aboard, sir," said the mate.

"Can you give us a moment?"

The mate gave a curt nod, turned and shouted orders to line-handlers along the pier to prepare to cast off.

Gunn beamed a smile at Elizabeth. "I told my family not to bother, but I'm so glad you came to see me off. I thought you had decided not to."

Elizabeth turned up her face to him, braving a sad smile. "I'm sad to see you off," she said. "I'd rather not. But I needed to tell you something."

"Yes?"

"Father told me what you did. About Anthony Burns, I mean."

Gunn peered over her shoulder at Reverend Faulkner, who raised his hands and shrugged an apology.

"I had asked him not to do that."

"I'm glad he did," she said. "I'm so proud of you, and grateful to know that the man I love is someone with such a heart." She laid her right hand over his heart. "I wanted to say, thank you."

Her touch thrilled him. He felt his heart quicken and wondered whether she could feel it through his uniform. "I can't take full credit for that, Elizabeth."

Her smile turned quizzical.

"Truth is, I sent the money in part because I was angry with you. I don't regret it one bit, mind you. Now that it's done, I see what a difference it has made, both to him and to us, to all our lives, although it's not what I had planned for us. I thank God that I was able to do what I did. But I don't know that I would have done it solely for Anthony's sake. Even so, I'm glad that I, that *we*, could help him in such a way. So, you are part of it, too, whether you knew that or not."

Elizabeth reached her hand to touch his neck and drew him toward her. She stood on tiptoe and kissed him, her lips caressing his.

"Come back to me, Andrew Gunn. Do not be long," she whispered.

He took her in his arms and kissed her again with a passion that he could not hold back. She freely returned his kiss. When they parted, he turned to Elizabeth's father and shrugged an apology. Faulkner grinned and nodded his approval.

For a moment, he held Elizabeth's face in his palm and stroked her lower lip with his thumb. Then, he turned and clambered aboard.

The mate immediately gave orders to take in the brow.

Once aboard, Gunn found a place to stand by the rail. He waved to Elizabeth and her father, and they returned his farewell.

The whistle blew loud and long as the steamboat left the pier, churning out a gray-white wake. He climbed the ladders to the top deck and stood waving until he could no longer see the details of Elizabeth's face.

He pulled out his pocket watch to check the time. Inside the lid was a portrait miniature on ivory, a likeness of his father at about his age. His mother had slipped it into his pocket when they said goodbye. She'd been right about the resemblance. He snapped the watch shut, rubbed the case as was his habit, and tucked it away.

Before long, they had passed through the harbor and the outer islands. Gunn kept vigil from the upper deck, watching until the features of Boston were lost in the mid-afternoon haze. The wake, leading back to the city like a broad avenue, dissipated in the distance, illusory as a fitful dream.

Whenever he returned home, if he returned, so much would have changed, both for him and those he loved. He knew that without a doubt. He closed his eyes against the glare of the sun glistening on the waves. When he opened them and his vision cleared, he imagined seeing his entire world, his home and loved ones, as though for the first time after a lasting blindness. No, better yet, as though he had suddenly been set free from a dark, foul prison after thinking he might never see freedom again.

In the vest pocket of his new uniform, he found the brass button that Burns had given him. He drew it out, thumbing the rough face, which bore the badge of the Revenue Cutter Service.

He smiled and tossed it once in his hand.

"Stunner."

He faced the wind and found its eye. Then he turned about, and with a settled and full resolve he hurled the button far away into the depths of the open sea.

THE END

Afterword

The rendition of Anthony Burns is well-documented in history books. By all contemporaneous accounts, he was a man of good character who lived in accordance with his belief and trust in the God of scriptures. He survived the trials and tribulations of life as a slave of men to become a servant of God.

 After gaining his freedom through the generosity of his friends in Boston, he concurrently attended Oberlin College and Fairmont Theological Seminary in Ohio, where he prepared for the ministry. In 1860, amid growing turmoil between the states over the issues of states' rights and slavery, he left the United States and made his way to Ontario, Canada.

Settling in the small town of St. Catherines, populated largely by fugitive slaves, he preached the gospel to anyone who would listen, black or white. Two years later, he died before reaching the age of thirty from tuberculosis, brought on by four terrible months of confinement in Lumpkin's Jail, the Devil's Half-Acre.

Acknowledgments

I'd like to express my heartfelt appreciation to those without whom this book would not have been written and published.

First, to my wife, Gwendolyn Cheryl Bull, who has always inspired and encouraged me to pursue and do my best work, in spite of any shared sacrifice and hardship. Thank you from the core of my being.

I owe debts of gratitude to my daughter, Marisa Nance, whose diligent efforts helped shape the raw materials of this story into a rough gem, and to Steve Vanderplas, my friend and editor, whose expert critical eye refined and polished it into something of real value. Any remaining flaws are entirely my own doing.

Several first readers offered sage advice and helpful suggestions along the way, through various iterations: Tim Tilghman, Ryan Cook, Jim Moran, Eva Marie Everson, Connie White, Anna Grace Miller, Dr. Katherine Hutchinson-Hayes, Margie DeHoust, Walt DeHoust, Rear Admiral Eric Jones, USCG; and especially Bill Wells, whose historical knowledge of life in the Revenue Cutter Service is enviable.

I'm deeply grateful to Admiral Jim Loy, U. S. Coast Guard (Retired), for his kind words of encouragement and intuitive understanding of my desire to tell this story. I will always admire his ability to lead and inspire others to do their best in all things. His dictum, "Preparation Equals Performance," has become my own. Above all, his life of selfless service to this nation through times of strife and turmoil is indeed an example to all who love liberty.

Finally, my sincere thanks to all those who provided outstanding research assistance at the Library of Congress and the National Archives. Their tireless, enthusiastic service to the public is a national treasure.

—A.F.

About The Author

A retired Coast Guard officer, Alton Fletcher enjoys sailing almost as much as writing, and sometimes regrets he can't do both at once.

 He became enamored with books and the sea as a boy, upon first reading Robert Louis Stevenson's *Treasure Island*. Since then, he has found nothing as bracing and evocative as a good sea story well told.

The literature of the sea, from the Odyssey onward, expresses our greatest dreams and desires, and evokes our worst fears and faults. He humbly hopes this book has met the mark.

He and his cherished wife of forty-five years make their home in Virginia.

Find The Wind's Eye is his first novel. Look for the further adventures of Andrew Gunn to be published soon.

Visit Alton Fletcher on his website: www.altonfletcher.com
Twitter: @altonfletcher16

Made in the USA
Las Vegas, NV
20 August 2022

53681595R00225